LAND *of* GOLDEN WATTLE

Also by J.H. Fletcher

Dust of the Land
The Governor's House
A Woman of Courage

J.H. FLETCHER

LAND *of* GOLDEN WATTLE

mira

First Published 2017
First Australian Paperback Edition 2017
ISBN 978 148923328 8

LAND OF GOLDEN WATTLE
© 2017 by John Fletcher
Australian Copyright 2017
New Zealand Copyright 2017

Published by
Harlequin Mira
An imprint of Harlequin Enterprises (Australia) Pty Ltd.
Level 13, 201 Elizabeth St
SYDNEY NSW 2000
AUSTRALIA

® and TM (apart from those relating to FSC®) are trademarks of Harlequin
Enterprises Limited or its corporate affiliates. Trademarks indicated with ® are
registered in Australia, New Zealand and in other countries.

Cataloguing-in-Publication details are available from the National Library of
Australia www.librariesaustralia.nla.gov.au

Printed and bound in Australia by McPherson's Printing Group

To my parents

The glory of the wattle
Enshrines every creek with gold
                              Traditional

Society is a partnership between the living,
the dead and those who are still to be born
                              Edmund Burke

I hold past and future in my hands
                              Bec Hampton

DESCENDANTS OF EPHRAIM DARK BY 1982

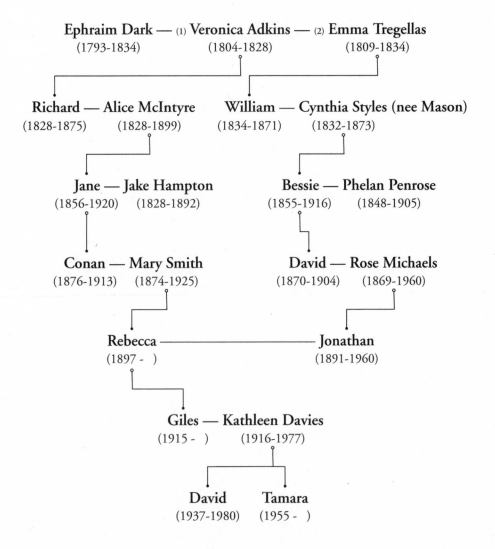

Ephraim Dark — (1) Veronica Adkins — (2) Emma Tregellas
(1793-1834)   (1804-1828)   (1809-1834)

Richard — Alice McIntyre   William — Cynthia Styles (nee Mason)
(1828-1875)   (1828-1899)   (1834-1871)   (1832-1873)

Jane — Jake Hampton   Bessie — Phelan Penrose
(1856-1920)   (1828-1892)   (1855-1916)   (1848-1905)

Conan — Mary Smith   David — Rose Michaels
(1876-1913)   (1874-1925)   (1870-1904)   (1869-1960)

Rebecca ——————————————— Jonathan
(1897 -)   (1891-1960)

Giles — Kathleen Davies
(1915 -)   (1916-1977)

David   Tamara
(1937-1980)   (1955 -)

1982

It was eleven o'clock in the morning and a kookaburra was calling from one of the stringybark trees as Rebecca, all her life known as Bec to everyone but her late grandmother-in-law Bessie Penrose, stepped on to Derwent's wooden deck. The big house, surrounded by its vast acreage, had been her home for sixty-eight years. It stood on the summit of the sharp-sided hill that for one and a half centuries had been called Emma's Lookout and from its north-facing deck you could see forever.

Granddaughter Tamara was standing with her hands on the guardrail and Bec joined her. Side by side they looked out beyond the rock-strewn hillside and the undulating paddocks flowing down the long valley to the heat-shimmered line of distant hills. All this was Derwent land, bright with golden wattle in spring but now burnt brown by the summer sun. Emma Dark had named the estate in 1831 and now Derwent was the largest property in the Tasmanian high country.

Bec could feel the sun burning holes in the top of her head. 'Looks like we got another scorcher. And me all done up like a pox doctor's clerk.'

Nothing to be done about that because today, Saturday 13 February, was a special occasion, or so everyone but Bec seemed to think. As far as she was concerned it was a load of nonsense. She wasn't slow to say so, either. She said it now.

'A lot of fuss about nothing,' said Bec.

Tamara sighed. 'It's your eighty-fifth birthday. You think that's nothing?'

'It's only important if you reckon it's the last one I'll be having,' Bec said. 'Otherwise it's a day like any other. Nothing to make a fuss about.'

It was a lot worse than a fuss. Bec thought *chaos* would have been a better word, with caterers and the florist and a regiment of women who had been brought in to set out the tables and cook the food and light the barbecue and organise the drinks and arrange the flowers and put out the birthday cards and –

'The good Lord give me strength,' Bec said.

'I guess he will,' Tamara said. 'He's done pretty well by you so far.'

Bec supposed that was true but was not about to admit it. With age she suspected she was getting to be more and more like her old nemesis Grandma Bessie: these days it seemed more fun to grouse than smile. Grousing kept the competition on its toes, and by the time people got to her age just about everyone was competition, being younger and therefore likely to outlive her if she didn't watch it.

'My hundredth might be worth a nod,' she said. 'That would be something. Isn't that what they say: not many people die above a hundred? Eighty-five is neither here nor there. You're old, even if you feel as fit as a flea, but that doesn't mean you like having it thrust down your throat. That's the only purpose I can see of having this party: to remind me I'm old. Well, I'm sorry to disappoint you but I'm not planning to keel over just yet.'

'I should hope not,' Tamara said. 'I've gone to a lot of trouble to get this blow out sorted. Don't you go dropping dead on me.'

'Spoil the mood, would it?'

'I wouldn't say that. But it would be bloody inconvenient having people tripping over your body all the time.'

Bec laughed. 'There's some would say I've been an inconvenience all my life.'

'And proud of it,' said Tamara.

That was what Bec liked about her granddaughter. Tamara had spirit. She was a fighter and Bec, who'd been a fighter all her life, valued that quality above all others. Tamara was proof that the blood was still strong. Ever since the days of Emma Tregellas, the first member of the family to set foot on the island, the women had shown them. Yet today there was something in her granddaughter's manner that seemed somehow different from usual.

'You OK?' she asked.

'Why shouldn't I be?'

'Just asking.'

There *was* something; Bec was convinced of it.

Two days before, at Bec's suggestion, Tamara had gone to the new Agfest show. It was an hour's drive away and Bec had assumed she'd be back that evening but in the event she wasn't. She hadn't said what she'd been up to and Bec hadn't asked but judging by the way she'd been since she got back it was obvious that something had happened. Bec wasn't going to push it; she'd find out soon enough if there were anything to find out. Now she looked at the cloudless sky with the sun promising to be even more of a torment by mid-afternoon.

'A birthday bash is always a good excuse for a piss-up,' Tamara said.

'This mob doesn't need an excuse,' Bec said. 'When are they arriving, anyway?'

'The first of them should be turning up in about half an hour.'

'Trotters in the trough,' Bec said. 'I can't wait.'

'Be nice,' Tamara said. 'They're only coming because they love you.'

Bec cackled like a pregnant chook. 'They're coming to feed their faces. And to try and find out whether your dad will let you go on running Derwent when he packs in being a trustee or whether he plans to appoint somebody else.'

'We'd all like to know that,' Tamara said.

'I doubt you need worry,' Bec said. 'With David gone there's nobody but you.'

She could say it now. When they'd had the news that Tamara's brother had been killed in Milan two years before, the shock of her grandson's death had left Bec so traumatised that she had been barely able to speak. She'd hauled herself out of the shadows eventually, as she had so often in her life, but talking about it would never be easy. The pain would remain but life moved on and you had to move with it and pretend all was well.

'I hope you're right,' Tamara said. 'Derwent's my life: you know that. But Dad's always been against having a woman in charge.'

'He got that idea from Bessie Penrose. Her father had set up the trust but Bessie was determined to use it to make sure I would never get my hands on it. You're running it now in any case,' Bec said.

'But I'm not a trustee.'

'Of course you're not. The man's still alive, isn't he?'

'As far as we know. When was the last time you spoke to him?'

'On his birthday. 20 June.'

Nearly eight months before.

'Anything could have happened to him in that time,' Tamara said.

'He's still cashing his cheques.'

As trustee under the family trust, Giles, Bec's only son and Tamara's father, was custodian not merely of the Derwent land but of its pride and history, but he'd never given a toss about any of that. There had been hard words about what Bec had called his selfishness but Giles couldn't have cared less what his mother thought or said. First his wife Kathleen had walked out on him then, on Tamara's eighteenth birthday, he had split too, heading to Sydney like a latter-day Paul Gauguin to play at being an artist. Unfortunately he didn't have Gauguin's talent but that hadn't affected his lifestyle. As trustee and principal beneficiary he treated Derwent as a cash cow. The pay-outs he got as beneficiary allowed him to pursue his only real talent: playing games with the succession of bimbos whom he managed, God knew how, to entice into his bed.

Bec had protested but it had done no good.

'Stop your nagging, Ma,' Giles had said. 'I could always sell it, you know.'

'It's not yours to sell. It belongs to the trust.'

'And as trustee I can realise whatever assets I like.'

To Bec that had been the ultimate sacrilege. 'You would get rid of Derwent? Sell your heritage?'

Giles had sneered. 'What's my heritage ever done for me? I'll tell you something, Ma. The only reason I *don't* sell it is because of David; I know what the place means to him. But don't keep on at me, OK, or I might change my mind.'

So Bec had said no more. She would never admit it even to herself but Giles had been a sad disappointment to her. And now David was dead.

'Is your dad coming today?' she asked.

'No idea. We sent him an invite but he didn't answer.'

'Well, ain't that a surprise,' Bec said.

'I'd better go and make sure they've got everything ready for our guests,' Tamara said.

'Mustn't keep the hogs waiting,' Bec said.

She watched Tamara walk into the house. Thank God for her, she thought. Tamara represented the future of the family and – surely? – of Derwent itself. But Bec remained uneasy, never able to forget how their lives and future were hostage to her son's whims.

A hundred and fifty years before, Emma and her husband had built the house on land granted to them by Lieutenant Governor Arthur – twenty thousand acres in the middle of what at the time had been a dangerous wilderness – and imported merino sheep from Spain. The genes of those first animals still existed in the abundant flocks that over the years had made Derwent the huge operation it now was.

Bec looked out across the upland paddocks with their grazing flocks, the watered valleys rich with canola, triticale and poppies. The initial holding had grown first to thirty thousand acres on the death of Emma's uncle Barnsley and then to fifty thousand acres after Emma's granddaughter Bessie had snared Phelan Penrose into marriage one hundred and eleven years before.

At least that was something she did, Bec thought. The old bitch.

'Laid herself out like a plate of meat,' Bec remembered telling Tamara only last week. 'You can be sure of that.'

She was the only member of the family old enough to remember Bessie and the antagonism that had inspired unremitting war between them until the moment of Bessie's death.

'He would have lived to regret it,' she said. 'You can bet your socks on that. Bessie would have made for tough chewing. Too tough for little Phelan, that's for sure.'

Below the house stringybarks towered as proud as guardsmen above the tangled scrub. Bec's husband Jonathan had had them planted in March 1914 to celebrate their marriage. In those days the roads of the high country had been gravel tracks where in winter the horses' hooves struck sparks from the frozen ground, but the road joining the house to the Midlands Highway had been sealed in the early 1970s after Bec, still fancying her grand prix chances at seventy-five, had nearly done a high dive off what she had thereafter named Nitwit Corner, the hairpin halfway up the hill, where the road skirted the edge of a hundred foot drop.

Born lucky, Bec thought. Or at least so far.

There had been tragedies along the way but on the whole the family hadn't done too badly since Emma Tregellas arrived in what then had been called Van Diemen's Land.

The living and the dead, Bec had often said, all of them both past and future.

Now, with advancing age, her thoughts turned more and more to Tamara because in Tamara Emma and the rest lived, as they did in her.

The family's history was a tale of gold, wool and a lust for land; of enmity and love, blood and fulfilment, and a scandal that Bessie at least had been determined to conceal.

She existed in their image. The past and future, both were now. She could see their faces, hear their voices, share their rain and sun and wind.

Emma, living three lifetimes in her own short life, had been the first.

1826

When Major Toby Tregellas, her belligerent father, was killed in a duel, seventeen-year-old Emma went to Norfolk to live with her bachelor guardian, the Rev Arthur Naismith.

She didn't want to go. She disliked Arthur and his pious ways. She disliked his clammy hands and his eyes, sly and pale, which undressed her when he thought she wasn't looking. She disliked the way he listed all the things a young lady was not permitted to do. She must not run. She must not sing except in church. She must not raise her voice. She must not walk unescorted. She must be obedient, quiet and respectful at all times, especially to Arthur and Arthur's patroness, the elderly and autocratic Dowager Countess of Raedwald, whose residence, Raedwald Hall, lay a mile from the Norfolk coast. Emma liked nothing about him at all.

'He wants me to be a mouse,' she told her reflection. 'I am not a mouse.'

Nor had any intention of becoming one. At Chatham Barracks, where her father had been stationed before his fatal duel, the major had treated her with more than usual indulgence, as a companion rather than a daughter.

On occasion he had even had her sit beside him at the roulette table, watching the spinning wheel, hearing the clatter of the ball seeking its slot, as he gambled and lost, gambled and lost again. He claimed her presence brought him luck. She saw little evidence of it yet somehow it never seemed to matter, the world contracted to the bright lights, the spinning wheel, the white faces of the gamblers, jewelled hands moving golden guineas on the green baize. Before the fatal shooting Emma had been a lively soul, fond of dancing and flirting, popular with the subalterns.

'That is who I am,' Emma said. 'That is life.'

She knew that life with Arthur Naismith, her long-dead mother's cousin, would not be like that at all. Life with Arthur would be like attending six funerals at once but Emma was under age, with Arthur her only relative, so to Norfolk she went, to his strait-laced and gloomy house backing on to Fairweather Broad.

The day after her arrival Lady Raedwald declared she wished to meet her.

Raedwald Hall was large with large rooms and stood in the middle of a large park, yet even Raedwald Hall was barely large enough to accommodate the dowager's over-generous flesh and the opinions she had never learnt to keep to herself.

Hooded eyes inspected Emma closely. Over-large nostrils flared; withered lips were downturned. 'Young girls these days are spoilt,' she said. She favoured Arthur with a glance. 'You agree?'

Arthur agreed.

The eyes challenged Emma, seated upright upon the uncomfortable chair to which she had been directed. 'And you, miss. Do you share my opinion?'

'No, ma'am,' said Emma. 'I do not.'

It took a brave person to say no to Lady Raedwald. Her feathered headdress quivered.

'You presume to question my views?'

'I am sure some young girls are indeed spoilt. But not all, ma'am. By no means all.'

Lady Raedwald was displeased. 'You are remarkably free with your opinions, miss.' She turned to Arthur, spearing him with her disapproval. 'One has to wonder what the world is coming to when a girl of your cousin's age should take issue with her elders in so unseemly a fashion.'

'I agree, your ladyship.'

'Discipline is what is needed. Discipline leads to right thinking and an appreciation of one's true place in society. I had thought this young woman might be a suitable companion to me but clearly she is unready. Mr Naismith, your cousin needs to learn respect.'

Emma might not have been in the room.

'I shall see to it, your ladyship,' Arthur said.

'But Mr Naismith,' Lady Raedwald said, 'that will not do at all.'

'Your ladyship?'

'A young woman living alone with an unmarried man? I cannot permit that, Mr Naismith.'

'I have a maid, your ladyship.'

Her ladyship drew herself up in her chair. 'A maid is hardly a suitable chaperone.'

Chastened, Arthur hung his head.

'I shall find work for her here. Regrettably not as my companion but rest assured we shall find something for her to do.'

'I appreciate your ladyship's concern for my welfare,' Emma said. 'May I know what you have in mind?'

Her ladyship's glare could have peeled paint. 'No, miss, you may not. The important thing, if you do not wish your good name to be irretrievably compromised, is to remove you into my care without delay.' She glared at Arthur, fidgeting unhappily on his chair. 'I take it you have no objection, Mr Naismith?'

'On the contrary,' he said. 'I am deeply indebted to your ladyship for your condescension towards my cousin.'

Emma, however, objected strongly to the old hag's interference in her affairs and on their way back to the vicarage wasted no time saying so. 'I refuse to go and live with her. She's horrible.'

She had thought Arthur and his funereal face, his funereal house, trial enough after the carefree life she had led in Chatham; now, compared with the horrors of living under the same roof as the gorgon they had just left, the vicarage seemed as desirable a residence as she could have wished. However, Arthur made it clear that her wishes were irrelevant.

There would be a four-day interlude as her ladyship had guests and did not wish to endure the inconvenience of an ungrateful and seemingly rebellious girl for that period, but after that to Raedwald Hall she would go.

The day before she was scheduled to leave the vicarage, Emma had a visitor. She had been in the upstairs sitting room when Maudie, the maid, told her a gentleman was waiting and had asked to speak to her.

'I don't know any gentlemen in these parts. Did he give a name?'

'He's Captain Dark, miss. Captain Ephraim Dark.'

'I have never heard of Captain Ephraim Dark.'

Maudie had a coy look.

Emma looked at her. 'I gather you know who he is.'

'Yes, miss.'

'Then pray enlighten me.'

'He's her ladyship's nephew, miss.'

The way Maudie coloured up made it clear there was more to the gallant captain than that.

'And?'

'He used to be here often, miss. Afore he went to Van Diemen's Land with his regiment.'

And still there was more.

'How well did you know him, Maudie?'

'Us maids was all gone on Ensign Dark, miss. 'im was a reckless devil: used to ride like the wind. We would all turn out to watch 'im, when we could. Oh yes,' she said, sighing, 'us was all gone on Ensign Dark.'

'Why does he want to see me?'

'He says he's an acquaintance of your uncle. Your uncle what lives in Van Diemen's Land, miss.'

Emma had always known Father had a brother. His name was Barnsley, Barnsley Tregellas. He lived on the other side of the world and she had never set eyes on him. All she knew about him was that there had been ill feeling between the brothers; she remembered Father getting a letter from him once and being in a black rage about it for days afterwards.

'Once Barnsley gets his hooks in you he never lets go,' Father had said. He'd given her a ferocious look. 'Be warned. He'll suck the blood out of your veins, given half a chance. Well, he's not going to suck mine.'

What he had meant by that Emma had no idea. She'd heard of bats that sucked your blood but not men. All she knew about her uncle was that he lived on an island far away where convicts were sent to get rid of them. Imogen Barnes, a girl she'd known in Chatham, had told her that in Van Diemen's Land the stars were all over the place and people walked upside down.

Emma had questioned that rumour. 'How can people walk upside down? Why should they want to, anyway?'

'It's the punishment they get for the bad things they've done.'

Emma didn't believe a word of it but since she had no plans to go there it hardly mattered. She found it difficult to imagine what her uncle could be doing in such a place. Sucking convicts' blood? That seemed even less likely than people walking upside down.

Imogen had also introduced her to the mirror of love.

Emma had been fifteen when Imogen had guided her to a pool like a shining mirror set about by stunted trees. The waters of the pool were black and still.

'Come here at night and alone,' Imogen said. 'Look into the pool and people say you'll see the face of your true love.'

Emma was determined to try it out for herself so the next night her father was busy with one of his ladies she sneaked out. She was conscious of an aura of magic. A fox barked. She came to the pool shining beneath a sky bright with stars. She looked at her reflection and waited. She saw what might be a shadow in the water. A face? A man's face? No way to know. Were those eyes watching from the pool's depths? And was there a black figure with a spear behind the first man? Impossible to be sure. She waited but saw no more.

Eventually, chilled by the night air, she returned home. Had she seen anything? She didn't know. Yet the feeling of magic lingered.

When I see him I will know, she thought.

Now, out of the blue, someone called Captain Dark from Van Diemen's Land was asking to see her. Perhaps he would be able to tell her whether the stories of people walking upside down were true or not.

Luckily, Cousin Arthur was from home; Lady Raedwald had summoned him to the hall an hour earlier.

No doubt Arthur would disapprove of her behaviour – *receiving a strange man unchaperoned?* – but Emma cared nothing for Arthur's opinion.

'Ask Captain Dark to come up,' she told Maudie.

It would be the first time Emma had acted as hostess since her arrival in Norfolk but in Chatham she had done so regularly in the intervals between her father's mistresses, so she remembered to tell Maudie to bring tea. While she waited she had a few moments to practise her hostess smile before Captain Dark stepped into the room and her heart stopped. Only for an instant but between one instant and the next a life could change.

Emma's cheeks creaked as she gave her visitor the full benefit of her smile while her heart, restored to life, smashed so loudly against her ribs she found it hard to believe he did not hear it.

The captain was tall and sturdily built, with the darkest of dark hair and brilliant blue eyes: Emma was not at all surprised that Maudie and the other maids had been gone on him.

He bowed over her hand and talked in a friendly way but he had a nasty limp that made Emma wince to watch him.

And still her heart pounded while she sat with what she feared was a foolish smile clamped to her face.

Over tea he explained that the limp was the reason for his being in England.

'Had a problem with the natives. They were making a nuisance of themselves so the governor ordered us in to sort them out.

Unfortunately some of them didn't want to be sorted. There was a skirmish and I ended up with a spear through my foot.'

A black man with a spear?

The captain laughed, although what was amusing about a spear through the foot Emma could not see.

'I suppose I must count myself lucky it wasn't my neck,' he said. 'Didn't look like much to begin with but the confounded thing festered. Local treatment wasn't doing much good so the colonel decided I should come to London to get it sorted out.'

Emma didn't know what to say to a man who on first acquaintance talked about a festering foot. Despite his fine manners it did not seem a genteel thing to do yet she found she did not care what he had to say or how he said it.

She grappled with the challenge of speech. 'I understand you know my uncle, Captain?'

'Indeed. He asked me to deliver a letter to your father. He said it was important so as soon as we docked I went to Chatham, only to find that Major Tregellas, alas, was with us no more. Then I discovered you had come to Norfolk and were living not far from my aunt's place. Couldn't have been more convenient. As I'm staying with her I thought I'd take the liberty of calling on you. I hope that is in order?'

'Perfectly in order,' Emma said.

'Aunt suggested it would be the proper form to hand the letter to your guardian but I thought I'd do it this way.'

'Lady Raedwald knows about the letter?'

'I mentioned it to her, but not what it says. Could hardly tell her that, could I, since I don't know myself?' He laughed, then winced as he eased his troublesome foot. 'I was tempted, mind.'

Emma's coolness of speech concealed the tumult of her heart. 'Give it to me and you won't be tempted any more, will you?'

The seal on the envelope was intact. She put the letter to one side and gave her visitor another of her special hostess smiles.

'More tea, Captain?'

'Mr Tregellas said the letter was important,' he said. 'Aren't you going to open it?'

Emma's smile remained undented. 'All in good time, Captain Dark. May I offer you more tea?'

'No, thank you. I must go. Since we shall be neighbours for a time maybe we shall see more of each other,' he said.

She gave him a modified smile, the one that said maybe yes, maybe no. When he was gone she sat for a while, stunned and unable to move. The dark water of the pool gleamed. The shadow floated amid a reflection of stars. Imogen's voice: *You'll see the face of your true love.*

Eventually she recovered enough to open the letter. After the trouble Captain Dark had taken to get it to her its bleak contents came as a disappointment.

Sir

I note that despite numerous undertakings to the contrary you have so far failed to repay the sum of one thousand guineas I loaned you eighteen months ago.

You will recall that this loan was for a period of six months only and is therefore considerably overdue.

I am reluctant to approach the colonel of your regiment in this regard but in the absence of appropriate action on your part I shall have no alternative. I shall therefore be grateful if you will place this matter in hand without further delay.

I shall also be grateful if you will convey my compliments to my niece.

I have the honour to be, sir, your servant
BARNSLEY TREGELLAS

Emma eased her breath as she put the letter down. She remembered a time about two years before when her father had been suddenly in funds. She had thought he must have made a killing at the tables but now it looked as though it had been a loan from his brother. That would explain Father's unkind remarks about Barnsley putting his claws into him; no doubt her uncle had simply wanted his money back.

Oh Father, Emma thought. She had loved him dearly and still did but had there ever been a more irresponsible man? Wine, women and cards had been his life, and singularly unsuccessful he had been at all of them. Drinking more than was good for him, taking up with brazen women who fleeced him and left him, he'd rarely picked up a pack of cards without losing every penny he had on him. Charm he had possessed in buckets but even charm could not keep a man afloat forever and at the time of his death Father's debts had been close to drowning him.

Of course she'd been foolish to think his windfall could have come from cards yet that had been the one time when her father had acted sensibly, handing her a hundred guineas to hold on his behalf for the time, as he put it, when Lady Luck ceased to smile.

She still had it.

No one else knew about it but there it was, in a sealed packet at the bottom of her case. How it had happened was that her father had, yet again, been drunk when he gave it to her. Later he had forgotten all about it and Emma had not enlightened him, holding it as a precaution against the day when Father's dissolute ways might land them in serious trouble.

Now Father was dead and Emma thought she had every right to treat the hundred guineas as her own. Her uncle might have had another view but what he didn't know couldn't hurt him and the money might well come in handy one day, containing the promise of a freedom that otherwise would remain forever beyond her reach.

Arthur Naismith had neither the agility nor physique to be a dancer but when he came home from Raedwald Hall he was closer to dancing than Emma had ever seen him.

Emma eyed him suspiciously. 'You look as though you've had good news, Cousin. Has the bishop decided to make you archdeacon after all?'

That was cruel because a week before Arthur had heard that the position he had craved so long had been awarded to a rival. Ever since he'd been in a foul mood, lashing both Maudie and her with a spiteful tongue until the moment he'd been summoned to Lady Raedwald's presence. The change in him now was extraordinary. Had his rival been struck by lightning? It seemed unlikely, yet there had to be a reason and Emma could not imagine what else it might be.

'Good news for me, yes, I think so,' he said. 'But even more so for you.'

The way Arthur spoke he obviously expected her to join him in his joy. Instead she continued to eye him with a caution that was beginning to edge into uneasiness.

Arthur said: 'I can say with confidence that you will find it hard to credit your good fortune when you hear my news. Pray sit down, Cousin.'

Emma wasn't sure she wanted to sit down but could think of no polite way to say so. She sat.

'This morning, as you are aware, I had the honour of attending the Dowager Countess.'

His expression invited her to share his delight at Lady Raedwald's magnanimity. Emma thought her ladyship's summons had been yet more evidence of her domineering nature but knew Arthur would not welcome such an opinion so gave a noncommittal smile and said nothing.

'Lady Raedwald explained that the reason Rupert Arkbit, that fraud, was preferred for the post of archdeacon was not in any way a reflection on my skills or character, for which her ladyship expressed her highest regard. No, indeed! It was a lack, to which – as she most justly pointed out – she had alluded before. It is something very simple and I flatter myself quickly remedied. She believes that a clergyman, especially one whose especial abilities qualify him for preferment, should be a married man.' Arthur gave her his most complacent smile. 'Lady Raedwald has assured me I am such a man and therefore – to put it plainly – am in need of a wife to provide the amiability and support that a man, seeking advancement in his chosen career, has the right to expect.'

Emma felt increasing alarm at the trend of Arthur's thoughts. She tried to speak but he raised an imperious hand and continued in the same self-congratulatory tone as before.

'I took the first opportunity to assure her ladyship that I would follow her advice. In fact, dear Cousin, I went further and confessed that in my mind and heart – my heart, dear Emma! – I had already settled on making *you* my wife. I shall not conceal from you that her ladyship's initial response was less than enthusiastic.

'"A clergyman cannot afford a wife who is too outspoken," she said, and I agreed. However, I am happy to tell you I persuaded Lady Raedwald that you had seen the error of your ways and would make an ideal helpmate for a man of the cloth. I informed her ladyship that your lack of funds could only assist you in coming to accept and indeed welcome your place in society.'

Emma did not know how she was supposed to respond to this. Never in a million years would she have chosen to marry Arthur Naismith, even before meeting Captain Dark. Mouse-like subservience to a creature like this? It was unthinkable! Nevertheless she saw it would be foolish to tell him so before giving herself the chance to consider what her alternatives might be.

Her situation was not good. She was seventeen years old and in terms of her father's will legally under Arthur's control. She was not quite as destitute as he imagined but the money would be nowhere near enough to provide her with a long-term future. Her education, to put it simply, had not been of the best; her experience outside the shuttered world of the military was nil. She was unqualified for any respectable position a lady of her years might consider. She didn't have one friend to whom she might turn for help.

On the face of it her case was hopeless. Yet one good thing had come from having such a reckless father: she had grown up more self-reliant than any other woman she had met. She would do everything possible to avoid giving in to Arthur and the abominable Lady Raedwald. She wanted more than anything to take life by the throat, although how that might be possible she had no idea.

The first step was to buy time while she planned her next move. For a moment she was at a loss; then an idea came to her.

She rounded her eyes as she looked at him. 'Mr Naismith –'

'Do not distress yourself,' he said kindly. 'I understand how overwhelmed you must be to contemplate a future so far above anything you might have dreamt possible...'

Emma sighed. 'Indeed it would be very different from anything I might have dared to contemplate.' She flew him the coyest of smiles. 'But Cousin, you have not as yet asked me.'

Arthur's expression changed.

'I hope I have not offended you,' Emma said in a little voice.

'As to that,' the vicar said, 'I had assumed that since her ladyship had given the matter her blessing a formal declaration would hardly be necessary. But I had forgotten what store ladies set by such ceremonies. Therefore –'

Hurriedly Emma cut him off. 'Wait, Cousin, wait...'

How offended he was now! '*Wait?*'

'Indeed, Cousin, I am overwhelmed by the unexpected honour you do me. I am deeply moved. But pray consider, sir, I am still in mourning for my late father. I cannot possibly contemplate taking such a step until that period has expired.'

'Oh.' Arthur looked displeased but had the sense to see he could not easily override her wishes. 'I am prepared – reluctantly, my dear Emma! – to make allowances, but her ladyship will no doubt wish to know how long you intend to keep me waiting.'

'The shortest possible time, I assure you, Cousin. Shall we say... three months?'

Arthur was horrified. 'Her ladyship will not countenance so long a delay.'

'Our domestic arrangements are none of her business. Whether we wish to get married or not is our own affair. Either way it has nothing to do with her.'

Arthur's face darkened in what in a less flabby man would have been outrage. 'You will not speak of her ladyship in such a manner.'

Emma had heard more than enough. 'Tell her to keep her nose out of our affairs and I won't. Or would you sooner I spoke to her?'

Now Arthur's fury was overwhelmed by horror. 'I forbid it. As your fiancé I must insist –'

'You are not my fiancé,' Emma said. 'You have not asked me to marry you nor have I consented. Ask me in three months, if you wish, and I shall give you my answer. In the meantime you will recall her ladyship has decreed that in the interests of propriety I shall move to Raedwald Hall tomorrow. For once we agree: I had better get my things together.'

Arthur was easily tamed. 'You will take care how you speak to her?'

'That will depend on how her ladyship speaks to me.'

Such a spineless man, she thought as she called Maudie to give her a hand. She couldn't tell whether she despised him more than she disliked him; either way she knew that neither in three months nor three hundred years would she agree to marry him. Always assuming she had a choice.

'He makes me sick every time I look at him,' she informed the furniture as she went into her bedroom.

All the same it was a problem knowing what to do about it.

'I am a prisoner,' she said, forgetting Maudie was in the room with her.

'Ain't we all?' said Maudie. 'You movin' to the big house, then?'

'In the interests of propriety,' Emma said.

'In the interests of the master,' Maudie said bitterly.

Emma looked at her. 'What do you mean?'

'I mean he's behaved himself since you been here. Quite good, it's been. But with you gone there won't be much sleep for me tonight.'

'You are surely not suggesting –'

'He's a man, inn'e? What you think maids are for? He'll have me in his bed soon as you're out the door is what I'm saying.'

'But...' Emma was appalled. 'What if you have a child?'

'Me gran give me herbs. It's still a worry but what am I s'posed to do?'

Emma saw she had more to learn about the ways of the world than she had thought. 'That is intolerable!'

'It's life,' Maudie said. 'People like me, we don' expect no bed of roses.'

That was right, Emma thought as later that afternoon she walked the short distance to Raedwald Hall, Arthur's gardener carrying her trunk on his shoulder. Not too many beds of roses in her life either. But she, unlike Maudie, was unwilling to put up with it. She would think of something. She had to; the alternative was unspeakable.

'Miss Tregellas will be marrying the vicar,' Lady Raedwald said. 'I have arranged it. It will be an excellent match for her.'

It was a small dinner party: a Mr Peter Walford and his wife, members of the lesser local gentry who were both clearly overawed by their invitation; Captain Dark; and Emma, hidden away behind a vast silver-gilt cruet set. Arthur was not present and Emma was thinking of Maudie, no doubt hard at work.

'For reasons I am at a loss to understand,' her ladyship continued, giving Emma a stern look, 'she wishes to delay proceedings, I believe for a month. I confess I find it inexplicable.'

'I have explained already, your ladyship. I am in mourning for my late father.'

'Hmm,' said sour-lipped Lady Raedwald.

'Filial devotion is surely to be admired,' said Captain Dark.

'You may admire it if you wish,' Lady Raedwald said. 'Others may have a different opinion.'

'Always assuming it is their business to have an opinion at all,' the captain said.

Lady Raedwald gave her nephew a glare but it seemed Captain Dark was impervious to glares.

'Her ladyship does not like even death to disrupt her plans,' Emma said.

'I do not like impertinence either,' said Lady Raedwald, puffing like a dozen bullfrogs.

'No impertinence intended, your ladyship,' Emma said. 'But I know you will understand that I must respect my father's memory.'

Captain Dark seemed amused but the Walfords did not know where to hide their faces.

After dinner they went together into the drawing room, Lady Raedwald no believer in leaving the gentlemen to their cigars and port. The room was richly furnished with a splendid chandelier and a piano in one corner.

'Emma, you may be excused,' Lady Raedwald said.

'Oh no, Aunt, if you please,' said Captain Dark. 'I was hoping Miss Tregellas might entertain us with a song. I am sure she has a most delightful voice.'

Lady Raedwald looked as cross as two sticks but clearly did not wish to fall out with her nephew in the presence of her guests.

'Very well. I take it you do sing, Miss Tregellas?'

'A little,' Emma said.

'Then perhaps you will oblige us, as my nephew has suggested. But I warn you, miss, my ear for music is widely admired and I can be a formidable critic.'

Emma nodded. 'Then I shall have to be on my best behaviour, shall I not?'

Captain Dark said, 'May I have the pleasure of accompanying you?'

'In my day it was normal for a singer to accompany herself,' said Lady Raedwald to Mr Walford. 'Either on the harp or spinet. But today, alas, old standards have fallen away.'

'Fashions have changed, Aunt,' Captain Dark said. 'We must move with the times.'

'Humpf,' said his aunt.

'What shall you sing?' the captain asked Emma.

'There is a song by Mr Schubert,' her ladyship said. 'Something about a boat and time passing.'

Captain Dark smiled at Emma. 'I was thinking of something more lively. Do you know *John Peel*?'

'I believe I have heard it. If you play the tune the words may come back to me.'

Obediently the captain picked out the tune on the piano and the words did indeed come back. Captain Dark joined in, they found they sang well together and ended with the rousing chorus:

For the sound of his horn brought me from my bed
And the cry of his hounds that he oft times led
Peel's view-halloo would waken the dead
Or the fox from his lair in the morning.

By the time they had finished the dowager's downturned mouth was still mourning Schubert but Emma was flushed and happy. Afterwards she sang *No place like home* unaccompanied after the captain had given her the key. Mrs Walford even clapped her hands briefly until quenched by her husband's warning elbow and her ladyship's grim lips.

All in all it was a far more comfortable evening than Emma had expected but the following day was a different story, with Lady Raedwald's fat fist pounding the arm of her chair and her fat face a picture of disapproval.

'How do you account for your behaviour last evening, miss?'

Emma had no idea what the old bat was on about. 'I beg your pardon, your ladyship?'

The dowager's face darkened to purple. 'Do not pretend to be innocent. Simpering and making eyes at my nephew! I will not have it, miss. Do you hear me?'

Lady Raedwald might or might not be a great lady but Emma Tregellas was a lady, too, daughter of a major in the 33rd Foot, and unwilling to be bullied. 'I was invited to sing, your ladyship. I sang. Captain Dark chose to favour me by accompanying me. Certainly on my part there was no simpering.'

On my part... Because Emma's evening gown, which she had brought with her from Chatham, was cut fashionably low and last night she had observed – as no doubt Lady Raedwald had also – the direction of the captain's appreciative gaze.

'Dressed to catch my nephew's eye… Or should I say undressed? I will not have it, miss. Do you hear me?'

'I hear your ladyship very clearly,' Emma said. 'But that does not justify the misplaced suspicions your ladyship seems to hold.'

The silence that followed lasted only a moment but was as menacing as an earthquake.

'Never in all my days have I been spoken to in such a way,' declared Lady Raedwald. 'And by whom, I ask myself? By whom?'

It might be impossible for Emma to win the war but she would not give ground in what was no more than a skirmish. 'By a lady like yourself,' she said.

'By a young woman of no background, an orphan without a penny to her name. And she dares defy me? It is not to be borne, miss! Not to be borne.'

'My mother was second cousin to the Earl of Leominster; your background and mine are therefore comparable, your ladyship,' Emma said.

Lady Raedwald grew calm; ice could not have been calmer. 'You will leave me now,' she whispered. 'I shall discuss with Mrs Hadgwick, my housekeeper, the duties you will be required to perform while you remain in this house. Now: get out!'

Emma inclined her head. 'As your ladyship pleases.' She gave a composed curtsey. 'I hope you will feel better as the day progresses.'

She turned and walked slowly from the room. The door was barely shut behind her when she heard a scream of fury followed by the sound of a bell being rung by an angry hand. A footman came running.

'Best straighten your wig before you go in,' Emma warned him.

'Thank you, miss.'

He did so before opening the door and walking straight-backed into the furnace, while Emma took her parasol and went out into the rose garden, where she considered what she must do to escape what was becoming an intolerable situation.

Mrs Hadgwick would have been another Lady Raedwald had she been able to carry it off.

'You have displeased her ladyship.'

'I regret that,' Emma said.

'I have seldom seen her so angry.'

'I regret that,' Emma said.

'She believes you abused her kindness in permitting you to sit at table with her guests last night.'

'I regret that,' Emma said.

The housekeeper's eyes were spikes in her sour face. 'Is that all you have to say?'

'Yes. And who are you, Mrs Hadgwick, to question me in this manner?'

'I am following her ladyship's instructions –'

'In that case it would perhaps be best if you confined yourself to doing so, Mrs Hadgwick. I would not want you to forget your place.'

A daughter of the 33rd could also wield a blade when needed.

'I am sure I never intended to cause offence,' said the house-keeper in a careful voice.

Emma's smile was the picture of condescension. 'In that case you may proceed,' she said.

'In the library there is a compendium of documents relating to the family's history. Some papers go back over two hundred years. Her ladyship thinks that sorting them is a task you might usefully perform.'

'Thank you, Mrs Hadgwick. I shall examine the papers and let you know if I can assist in this matter.'

Mrs Hadgwick's lips set in a disagreeable line. 'I shall take you to the library and you may judge for yourself.'

'Thank you, Mrs Hadgwick.'

The library was a scene of chaos with ancient documents spilling in dusty piles about the floor. Even the books in the shelves looked tired, as though they had been neglected for so long they had grown weary of life. It was clear no one had used the room for a long time. It was also clear that if Emma agreed to undertake the work the task would keep her occupied for many weeks.

I can always make a start, she told herself. As to what the future might hold, who could say?

'I shall be happy to assist her ladyship if that is her wish,' she said. Her smile – so sweet! – was calculated to set the housekeeper's teeth on edge. 'Perhaps you could arrange for luncheon to be brought me on a tray?'

'Her impertinence knows no bounds,' Lady Raedwald said when Mrs Hadgwick made her report. 'She instructed you to have her luncheon served in the library? On a tray? Are we sure she did not ask to be attended by Mr Wallace at the same time? With a flagon of claret, perhaps?'

Mr Wallace was the butler.

'Miss Tregellas did not mention claret,' Mrs Hadgwick said.

'I should hope not!'

But Lady Raedwald was in a bit of a fix. By banishing the Tregellas girl to the library and giving her a nightmarish task, she had thought she would get her out of the way and punish her at the same time. Of course she had intended to send her food on a tray, but now the wretched creature had *suggested* being served in this manner. By allowing her to have her way her ladyship would in effect be giving in to her. That would never do.

'Miss Tregellas will eat in the dining room,' Lady Raedwald said. 'We shall have no picnics in Raedwald Hall. Kindly advise Miss Tregellas accordingly.'

'Certainly, my lady. Will you be joining her?'

'I shall eat in my room,' the dowager said. A picnic wasn't a picnic where Lady Raedwald was concerned.

By midday Emma had made barely a dent in the mass of papers. She was tired, dusty and beginning to feel hungry when the door opened behind her.

'Put the tray down over there,' she said without turning her head.

'No tray,' a voice said. A man's voice.

Startled, she looked up. 'Captain Dark!'

'I thought you should know that luncheon will shortly be served in the dining room.'

His voice was full of smiles and she smiled in return. 'And her ladyship?'

'Is otherwise engaged. So we can relax and have a pleasant meal in peace.'

'That sounds an attractive option,' she said.

'I think so too,' he said.

Emma placed the documents on the table with the others she had examined and they went down to the dining room together.

There was no fire in the large fireplace. Captain Dark stared at Mr Wallace and his voice was as cold as the room. 'Why is there no fire?'

Mr Wallace coughed. 'Her ladyship gave orders that a table should be set up for you in the small study, sir. This we have done. There is a fire there.'

'Why in the small study?'

'I believe she thought you would be eating alone, sir.'

'The table in the study… Is it set for one or for two?'

'For one, sir.'

'Perhaps you can instruct the maids to change that?'

'The table is very small, sir.'

'You are saying there is no room for two?'

'It would be cramped, sir.'

'I see. What do you have for us, Mr Wallace? Something hot, I hope.'

'A cold collation, sir. Some beef, a ham –'

'It is a brisk day, Mr Wallace. I believe we would prefer something warm.'

'But it is a Tuesday, sir.'

'As you say. What of it?'

'Her ladyship's instructions are that we should always serve a cold collation on Tuesdays, sir.'

'And if it happened to be a Wednesday?'

'It would be baked ham and a guinea fowl, sir.'

The captain pushed back his chair and stared at the butler. His voice remained calm but Emma thought that in Mr Wallace's place she'd be running for cover.

'Pray explain,' the captain said.

'They are her ladyship's standing instructions, sir. For every week.'

'Winter and summer?'

'Yes sir.'

'Then we shall change it.'

'But sir –'

'We shall change it, Mr Wallace. I shall discuss it with my aunt later but in the meantime, Mr Wallace, we require something hot on this cold day. Do I make myself clear, Mr Wallace?' The tone was soft but with a bayonet in every word.

'But the kitchen range… There is nothing prepared, sir.' Mr Wallace, exposed so unexpectedly to the fire of this suddenly ferocious infantryman, looked close to tears.

'You are saying there is no hot food?'

'Perhaps the kitchen could heat up some soup, sir…'

'Then we shall have soup.' Dark turned to Emma. 'Soup and some cheese. And bread to go with it, I think. How will that suit you?'

'It will suit me very well,' Emma said.

'And we shall have it in the study, Mr Wallace. Where you say there is a fire.'

'A good fire, sir.'

'Excellent. You say it is a small room. Well, we shall cram in somehow.' He gave Emma a brilliant smile. 'And I think a bottle of the Constantia to go with the cheese. I understand Napoleon Bonaparte was partial to Constantia. What was good enough for a fallen emperor should be good enough for us, wouldn't you say?'

Emma found herself looking at Captain Dark with appreciative eyes. What had she been saying to herself only the other day? *I shall take life by the throat.*

Mr Wallace led them to the study. He wore a woeful expression, no doubt troubled how he would explain his part in what the dowager would no doubt consider an outrageous challenge to her authority, but the room was cosy and the fire warm – altogether a much better bet than the cold and empty dining room.

Captain Dark slapped Mr Wallace on the shoulder. 'Cheer up, man. We'll all be dead in a hundred years.'

By his expression the butler was fearful that death might descend on him a good deal earlier than that. Emma choked back a smile. Poor Mr Wallace…

They managed to squeeze around the little table. The captain's eyes sparkled and once again Emma could have laughed out loud; they were like naughty children outsmarting the grown-ups.

The soup came and a splendid mound of cheese. The soup was hot and satisfying. There was bread and some pickles. There was the opened bottle of Constantia wine. The fire crackled in the hearth. As picnics went, Emma thought, this was close to being a banquet.

They finished and Emma said she should get back to work.

'No rush,' Captain Dark said. He gave her a lazy smile and she felt a tingle flow through her. 'Those papers have been there for years. They aren't going to run away, are they?'

'I wouldn't think so.'

'So stay and talk.'

Emma was more than happy to do so.

'You have served in Van Diemen's Land?' she said.

'That's where I picked up this foot. I told you when we first met.'

'When you gave me my uncle's letter.'

'I hope it contained good news.'

'It explained some things I hadn't known before.'

He topped up their glasses. 'Capital wine,' he said. 'Bonaparte was right.'

'Tell me about Van Diemen's Land.'

He played with his glass. 'It's an island. Very beautiful, thickly forested. Many lakes, many mountains.'

'And savages.'

'Plenty of savages but most of them are white.'

Emma was surprised.

'Convicts and ex-convicts, bushrangers… There are black savages too, of course. They know how to fight – my foot is proof of that – but they have no chance against us.'

'Why?'

'Spears against guns? There aren't many of them, either. Can't help feeling sorry for them. It was their place, now we're pushing them out.'

'And my uncle?'

'Some people are making a lot of money over there. Whaling, building, forestry: a lot of money. Your uncle's one of them.'

'Does my uncle have a family?'

'My understanding is he's a bachelor. Got a grand house, though, on the high ground overlooking the river. Why do you ask?'

'Just interested,' Emma said. 'What are your plans when you are well again?'

'To rejoin my regiment.'

'In Van Diemen's Land?'

'If it's still there.'

They drank the last of the wine.

'Tell me, Miss Tregellas,' Captain Dark said. 'What are *your* plans?'

'Last night your aunt said she had arranged a marriage for me with Mr Naismith.'

'It's none of my aunt's business.'

'Except that Mr Naismith agrees with her.'

'I didn't ask his opinion either,' Captain Dark said. 'I'm interested in what you think about it.'

Emma's eyes met his. 'I am under age, Captain Dark. Mr Naismith is my guardian. I am not permitted to have thoughts.'

'I doubt that stops you having them, though.'

'Perhaps not. But I have learnt one thing in life, Captain.'

'Which is?'

'To keep my thoughts to myself.'

'Even if it means marrying Mr Naismith?'

A teasing smile. 'Would that be such a terrible fate?'

'For you, I think so.'

'That is a most improper thing to say, Captain Dark.'

'I do not believe a woman of your spirit would ever be content as the wife of a man who would crawl through mud if my aunt told him to.'

'Then what would you have me do?'

'I would have you be true to yourself. If you believe Mr Naismith is the man for you then I apologise for my remarks. But I do not think a woman of your courage and strength *could* believe that.'

Emma stretched her eyes very wide at the captain's words. 'Courage and strength? Come now, Captain Dark.'

'I do not withdraw a syllable. It took both strength and courage to stand up to my aunt.'

'She didn't thank me for it.'

'She is a woman who has had her own way all her life and has forgotten what it is to have anyone, especially another woman, stand up to her. She is a bully, Miss Tregellas, and will make your life unbearable if you put down roots in this district. And I am sure you are under no delusions that Mr Naismith will raise a finger to help you. Your life will be a war, constant and unending.'

'Perhaps I would win the war? If I have the courage and strength you attribute to me?'

'It would be impossible for you to win. My aunt holds all the cards. And do not imagine she would not use them.' He took her hands in his. 'I cannot believe you could contemplate such an existence.'

Emma looked at him. Her inclination was to trust this man but for the moment she remained cautious. She freed her hands. She said, 'A shortage of funds can limit one's choices.'

'How well I know it,' he said.

'But you are a man. For a woman, Captain Dark, the choices are few. If I do not marry what options are available to me?'

'You can live.'

It was aggravating that he was so slow to understand. A man could be a soldier or even turn highwayman, if he were sufficiently desperate. There were a hundred things a man could do. For a woman there was nothing.

'To live, you say? Pray explain how I am supposed to do that,' she said. 'Give myself to a protector? Someone like you, perhaps?' She saw that she had shocked him by mentioning the unmentionable and that stoked her anger. 'Should I perhaps become a harlot and sell myself on the streets?'

'Have you considered becoming a teacher?'

Emma's shoulders slumped. She saw he really was concerned for her and was ashamed of the way she had spoken. 'I have no training, no experience with children and I suspect no aptitude. But I thank you for the suggestion.'

'Vicar's wife or not, my aunt will eat you up if you stay here. She will not tolerate a rival.'

Despite herself Emma had to smile. 'In what way could I possibly be a rival to Lady Raedwald?'

'You are young. You are beautiful, if you will pardon my saying so. She would not tolerate youth or beauty in another woman. She would regard you as a deadly rival, I assure you. She does so already.'

'Why then does she wish me to marry Arthur Naismith?'

'Because then you will be in her power. Also she believes it unseemly that the vicar should remain a bachelor.'

'But why me?'

'Perhaps you are the only candidate for Mr Naismith's hand?'

'And if I decide to leave how can she prevent me?'

'Believe me when I say she would do whatever was necessary to stop you.'

'She could hardly kidnap me.'

'I would not put that past her for a moment.'

She saw he was serious. 'That would be monstrous!'

'In defence of what she considers her own interests my aunt is a monster. I am surprised you did not know that. If you plan to leave here, Miss Tregellas, I would counsel you to get as far away as you can as quickly as possible, for she will surely send men after you to bring you back.'

'I find that incredible.'

'Might is right, Miss Tregellas. It is a doctrine my aunt has pursued all her life. She would not hesitate.'

That night Emma sat in her room and considered her situation. It was clear that Lady Raedwald was determined she should marry Arthur Naismith. If she did so she would have a respectable if modest position in life. There would be few financial worries. She would have a measure of respect within the community. She would no doubt have children whom she would be expected to bring up in accordance with her husband's wishes. She would live a worthy non-life until the day of her death.

She would be a nothing at her husband's side, a creature of duty and obedience with no voice of her own. She would be patronised by the lesser gentry and humiliated by Lady Raedwald, who would be satisfied with nothing less than the utter negation of her personality and will. Forever.

What about her feelings for Captain Dark? She knew it was futile to feel anything for a man who in local opinion was so far beyond her reach but the feelings existed and were not to be denied.

Marriage to Arthur would be to reject the life force that ran in her veins, but how could she avoid the fate that had been planned for her?

When she went to bed she was as low as she had ever been, but in the night she woke upon a thought so outlandish she knew she must put it out of her mind at once. She did not; when she rose to face the day it was still there, as potent as ever.

Captain Dark had told her she was a woman of courage but was she courageous enough to risk the humiliation of failure? Was she up to handling the unknown challenges she would face?

She had no answers. She knew nothing about the real world. She told herself to settle for her lot in life and be thankful, as the Bible enjoined. She would stay where she was and accept the limitations of a life that would be its own reward.

She bent her head over the dusty papers and got on with her work.

After an hour she took a break. The sun shining through the window cast rectangles of golden light across the floor. She went to the window and looked out. Beyond the slope of the roof she could see the wooded park where fallow deer were grazing and the drive running between ancient elms to the high wall that marked the property's perimeter. The Yarmouth road lay on the far side of the ornate drive gates with the gatekeeper's cottage beside them and beyond the road the waters of Betty's Mere shone golden in the sun.

She stood by the window, staring and thinking. Freedom… She had told herself the matter was settled, that she'd made up her mind to accept her situation, but now she listened to the staccato beating of her heart and knew that nothing had been settled at all.

The days passed, with Emma still having no idea what she could do to secure a future better than the bleak one her cousin and his patron had mapped out for her. To begin with she did not venture beyond the park gates. After a couple of weeks she decided she would explore further but when she tried a pugnacious man emerged from the gatekeeper's lodge and told her his instructions were that she was not to be let out alone.

'Why is that?'

'Wouldn't want you gettin' lost, now, would we?'

She went back to the house and complained, not to her ladyship – who was unavailable – but to the housekeeper.

'Am I to believe I am a prisoner?'

Mrs Hadgwick had not forgotten their earlier conversation. Now her smile would have put the sourest lemon to shame.

'You must believe what you wish,' she said.

'What I wish,' Emma said, 'is to be able to go for a walk outside the park. If you will not authorise it I shall ask her ladyship's nephew to speak to her about it.'

'Captain Dark is away in London,' said Mrs Hadgwick.

'But will return,' Emma said. 'I wonder what he will have to say when he discovers his aunt's housekeeper has taken it upon herself to imprison a guest of this house?'

Mrs Hadgwick's mean eyes flashed red but two days later she told Emma Lady Raedwald had approved her request to walk outside the park in the company of a sub-keeper.

'Her ladyship is too considerate of your safety to allow you to roam the countryside unescorted.'

'A walk is hardly roaming the countryside,' Emma said. But saw that was the limit of the concession she would be granted.

Every day when the weather permitted she walked, with one or other of the two sub-keepers strolling behind her. One of the men was friendly, the other not. Occasionally she talked to the friendly one, asking him about the birds whose bubbling cries echoed across the marshland.

'They's curlews, them,' he said.

'And the others?'

'All sorts. Some stays all year round. T'others they's what you might call birds of passage, them.'

Like me, Emma thought. She liked the wild birds of the empty places, the curlews' lonely cries, the honking of the geese. In time she might have come to think of this as home but as things were that was impossible. Her spirit was oppressed by the dowager's unseen presence and by the image of Arthur Naismith waiting in his narrow house. Then the freedom of the marshlands seemed more like a prison.

The second keeper was a skinny creature with red hair, a cast in one eye and a permanent scowl. Only once did they converse – if you could call it conversation.

A track led off the road, flanking Betty's Mere and heading towards the sea.

'What's down there?'

'Mud.'

'It must go somewhere.'

'Nay.'

'I have a fancy to explore it,' Emma said.

But he stood between her and the path. He might not be big but was determined and did not give way. 'Best keep to path,' he said. 'Spoil tha fancy clothes down there. 'Ell to pay, I let thee do that. Like I say, there's nowt down there but mud.'

Perhaps he was right. She did not make an issue of it but noted the track's existence and locked it away in her mind. Another day, perhaps...

She did not like the thought of asking anyone for help, even Captain Dark – do that and she'd be a hostage to betrayal – but she had no choice. Even with help it would be hard; alone it would be impossible. Once or twice she considered giving up the idea; then she visualised what it would mean to be married to Arthur Naismith and knew she must at least try to escape. If she failed she could console herself with the thought she had done her best; give up without trying and she would deserve every moment of the dismal future that would then face her.

She took a deep breath and went looking for Captain Dark.

'He's gone riding,' a maid called Polly told her. She didn't quite say *What's it to you?* but it was close; the servants knew everything and were well aware of Emma's lowly status at Raedwald Hall.

'When will he be back?'

'Didn't say.'

A toss of the head – *Don' you go puttin' on no airs wi' me!* – and Polly took off, duster in hand.

Emma walked on to the terrace. The air was warm; beyond the road the sun shone on the rippling waters of Betty's Mere; a clamour of rooks circled above one of the elms; water from the fountain in the ornamental lake blew like silver mist in the breeze. She felt a pang at the thought of turning her back on all this and the security it offered, but she knew that at best it would be the security of the grave; at worst a loveless marriage with a man in thrall to an autocratic woman of whom nothing good could be said.

A rider on a chestnut horse turned in at the park gates. Her heart jumped as he came trotting down the drive. Careful not to run, Emma walked down the flight of steps from the terrace and crossed the grass to meet him.

Captain Dark reined in and raised his hat, smiling down at her. 'If I had known you were about I would have suggested you come with me.'

Knees weakened by that smile, Emma looked back at him. 'I have just come from the library. How do you manage to ride with that foot?'

'With difficulty.'

'Then why do it?'

'Because I won't have many more opportunities. I leave for London on Monday. Sir Edmund Wilkes is examining my wretched foot the following day.'

'And then?'

'Cut it off, perhaps.'

She disliked flippant talk about such an important matter; it might bring bad luck.

'I trust not,' she said.

He laughed. 'So do I. I'd like to get back to my regiment as soon as possible and I doubt a one-legged officer would have much future in a foot regiment. So Monday it is. My aunt's carriage will take me to Yarmouth where I'll board the London Flyer. All being well I should be in London about eight in the evening.'

She had not expected to have to act on her decision so soon. She took a deep breath but still could not utter the words.

He looked at her strangely. 'Miss Tregellas, are you quite well?'

Finally she managed to speak. 'I need your help.'

She had done it. With those four words she was committed. Once again her heart was pounding with nervous tension. She was spinning the wheel of fortune, placing her future in this man's hands.

He had remained on horseback; now he dismounted. 'I'll walk with you.'

'What about your foot?'

'I'll manage.'

They walked along the drive towards the stables that lay at the back of the big house.

'You say you need my help,' Ephraim Dark said. 'I shall certainly help you if I can. But how?'

'I have decided to follow your advice. I am going away.'

'Going where?'

'Far away.'

He touched her arm. 'I would give you money if I could but my aunt is the rich one. How will you manage without?'

They reached the stables, the horse's hooves clattering on the cobbles, and he handed the reins to a groom. They walked towards the house.

'It is not money I want but advice,' Emma said. 'I am a prisoner here. I want you to advise me how I can get away.'

'You have definitely made up your mind to go?'

'Definitely,' Emma said.

'Then you mustn't delay or it may be too late. Last night I over-heard my aunt talking to Mr Naismith in the drawing room.'

They were standing in the lobby that led from the back door into the main part of the kitchen.

'My aunt finds it unacceptable that you should keep the vicar waiting so long before marrying him.'

'I told them why. It is out of respect for my father.'

'They don't believe you. They intend to apply for a special licence.'

'What does that mean?'

'A special marriage licence means they don't have to wait for the banns to be read. It means you can get married straight away.'

'Not if I don't agree.'

'Theoretically that's true. But my aunt is a determined woman.'

'You think I would not be able to resist her for long?'

'I think she will make life very unpleasant for you if you try.'

'Does Mr Naismith have no say in this?'

'Quite apart from your other... attractions? Apparently there's been some problem over the Reverend Arkbit's appointment so the archdeacon's position may still be open. But the bishop is insisting it can only go to a married man.'

'Then Arthur would certainly agree,' Emma said. 'What do you suggest I do?'

'I am saying you must clear out while you can. Where are you planning to go?'

She drew a deep breath and spoke the words that had been fermenting in her mind since she'd read the letter Barnsley Tregellas had written to her father. 'To my uncle in Van Diemen's Land.'

He looked at her strangely. 'And you trust me with this?'

She heard her voice stripping her naked. 'With this and everything.'

On Saturday night Emma and Ephraim Dark were upstairs in the library.

'I said I would help you and I shall,' Ephraim said. 'But I hope you will forgive me if I try to protect my own interests at the same time.'

'Meaning?'

'Meaning I don't want to fall out with my aunt if I can avoid it. I doubt that will be possible if she suspects me of helping you escape. I am leaving the day after tomorrow. If you wait a few days before you go there may be a chance Aunt can be persuaded I had nothing to do with your departure. Not very heroic, I am afraid.'

'It is only sensible,' Emma said. 'But how shall I manage if you're not here?'

'I have already arranged it. Go to Raedwald hamlet. I've spoken to a fisherman who lives there. Josiah Yarm will take you to Yarmouth in his fishing smack. You can take the London Flyer from the Bugle Inn.'

'How do I get to the hamlet?'

'The track around Betty's Mere will take you to the beach. Walk along the beach with the sea to your left and the hamlet's about half a mile.'

'Why should this man help me?'

'Because I asked him. Josh Yarm and I go back a long way. He'll be happy to take you.'

'It'll have to be at night,' Emma said. 'They don't let me walk out by myself during the day.'

'He knows that. I told him to put out a storm lantern so you know where to go. He'll be waiting.'

The light was almost gone. Inside the room it was hard to see each other, which made it easier to speak their thoughts.

'Why are you doing this for me?' Emma asked.

'Damsel in distress?' She could just make out his expression, part smile, part serious. 'Because I care for you? Care deeply?'

She felt the blood rush to her face. 'You do?'

He took her hand. 'Since I first set eyes on you.'

'I never suspected it.'

'Why would you?'

Again Emma spun fortune's wheel. 'Because I feel the same.'

They looked into each other's eyes as though for the first time. Then Ephraim Dark gave a sharp, bitter laugh. 'It makes no odds; after Monday we'll likely never see each other again.'

'I don't believe that,' she said.

I have come to care for you… She had not asked him to say it but he had and she was not prepared to give him up without a fight.

He smiled ruefully. 'Nothing to be done about it, my dear.'

Later that evening he spoke again when they were alone in the drawing room.

'I've been looking at boat sailings in *The Times*. The *Admiral Cockburn* sails for Hobart Town on Friday. Leave here on the Wednesday night and you should be there in nice time.'

'Good.' But she spoke dolefully, thinking only of the prospect of losing what for a moment she had dared hope might be hers.

His eyes met hers. 'I don't like it either.'

Enough.

It was not a lady's place to be forward but she could still remember the curl of Lady Raedwald's lip as she told her she was a woman of no background. Very well. She would pretend the hag had been right. She would take her future in her hands, careless of the rules. She fixed her eyes on Ephraim's face.

'You believe Sir Edmund Wilkes will be able to mend your foot?'

'He's the acknowledged authority. I expect him to do his job.'

'What will you do after he's fixed it?'

'Rejoin my regiment.'

'When?'

'As soon as I can. When I come back I'll write to the colonel –'

'That will take months. Why come back here at all?'

Ephraim stared at her. 'But my aunt –'

'You said it yourself,' Emma said. 'The *Admiral Cockburn* sails on Friday. All being well, I shall be aboard.' Her eyes were steady on his. 'Choose.'

He opened his mouth to reply when Lady Raedwald swept into the room. On her heels came Mr Wallace, announcing that dinner was served.

It was Monday morning, a warm day with clouds high up and the wheat ripening in the fields, with Lady Raedwald's carriage standing before the open door of Raedwald Hall. The household had gathered on the steps down to the drive, and Lady Raedwald had held her nephew's arm down to the carriage, where he kissed her cheek and climbed in.

'The captain will be back in a few days, Emma,' Lady Raedwald had said to her the previous night. 'There is no need for you to see him off,' but Emma did not intend to be left out. She stood in front of Mrs Hadgwick and smiled – Ephraim nodded, and waved gaily to them all. 'See you soon.'

For a moment only his eyes sent Emma a different message. *You will be in my thoughts.*

She heard the words as clearly as though he had spoken them. *And you in mine.*

He nodded. His eyes smiled. She wondered how it was possible for them to communicate without words, but emotions, like the stars, moved in mysterious ways.

She went back into the house. *Three more days and I too shall be gone.*

Midnight Wednesday night: not even three days since Ephraim had left and already Emma was missing him more than she could have imagined.

She had packed a small case, which was the most she could hope to carry with her. What she could not carry she would have to leave.

She had decided to wait until one o'clock. By then – surely? – everyone would be asleep. Waiting wasn't easy; every few minutes she found herself checking the Josiah Emery watch that had belonged to her father.

At one o'clock she eased open the bedroom door and tiptoed down the stairs, nerves jumping at every shadow. She did not attempt the front door, which she knew Mr Wallace would have double-locked as he did every night. Instead she walked down the corridor to the kitchen. The damper was closed on the stove; she saw the red glow and heard the soft whisper of logs turning to ash. A cat blinked from a wooden chair's padded seat. No other movement; no other sound. She went through the lobby, turned the massive key in the lock and opened the door. Cool air came in, and the smell of rain-wet grass. She went out, shadow-soft, and closed the door behind her. There was no moon but overhead was a multitude of stars. She heard the muted call of an owl. Keeping to the drive's grassy verge she made her way towards the side gate that opened on to the road.

She was ten yards from the gate when a shadow moved. It solidified into the shape of a man who straightened beneath the tree where he had been sheltering and spoke in a harsh Norfolk voice.

'Stay where y'are, you! Stay still!'

For an instant shock stunned her. Breath would not come and her legs turned to ice. Feeling came back in a rush and she recognised the man as the redheaded sub-keeper. She also saw he had made a mistake. Earlier the rain had been heavy and he had taken shelter beneath the tree. Now she was closer to the gate than he was. Before she knew it she had wedged her case under one arm and flung herself forwards, outstretched hand reaching for the handle of the lock.

'Ah said stay!'

The voice was too close for comfort but her hand grasped the handle and turned it, the gate opened and she was through it and slamming it in the face of the man who had almost caught her but not quite. There was no way to lock the gate from this side and she was not strong enough to hold it shut against him; it would take him no more than a moment to force it open. She turned and ran, her case bumping against her leg. The case was a nuisance but she could not abandon it; her money was inside it and without that escape would be impossible.

On the far side of the road a line of trees separated her from the marsh while beyond it the waters of Betty's Mere shone in the starlight. She had to find somewhere to hide but there was nowhere and she could not hope to outrun the keeper.

Panic was a sickness. Lightning clawed the sky beyond the mere; thunder rumbled while clouds advancing on an east wind rapidly quenched the stars. She saw the familiar shape of the derelict jetty she passed regularly on her morning walks and hesitated but that was the first place her pursuer would look and she dared not stop. This whole area was tidal; at the peak of spring tides salt water lapped the base of the park wall. It was a land of shadows and the calling of water birds, with patches of reeds edging the mud flats and tidal pools and crooked waterways leading eastwards to the restless sea.

The keeper had lost ground after he came through the gate, unsure which way she had gone, and she thought the increasing cloud cover would make it hard for him to see her.

There were hundreds of reed beds, big and small; it would be impossible for him to search them all. The narrow track she had noted before led off to the left. Without thought she turned onto it. The keeper had been right about the mud. It sucked at her feet but she made her way as quickly as she could along it until she reached a vastness of reeds bowing and whistling in the wind. She thrust her way into the reeds as deeply as she could and crouched down. The stems rattled, in the distance were the sleepless calling of birds and the hollow booming of the sea, otherwise all was still. The keeper could not see her there; provided she remained still he had little hope of finding her.

She would have to wait him out.

It was a slow business. Where the keeper was she did not know; he might be twenty feet away or half a mile. She was up to her ankles in mud and her feet were bitterly cold. The wind from the sea was cold too. Before long her body was shaking; she tried to control it but could not.

The tide was out but eventually the water would return. She had to move before then. Thank God it was only September; she could not imagine how it would feel in winter.

It started to rain. She tried to read her father's watch but could not. She guessed she had been there about an hour, which meant soon she would have something else to worry about. In another hour it would be getting light.

She had to be well away before then.

Gingerly she parted the reeds. Nothing moved. She inched her way back on to the track and headed towards the sea. The eastern sky was showing the first hint of grey as she came to a wide beach. Drenched by the rain that continued to fall, she followed the beach until she reached the ancient Saxon hamlet of Raedwald. She looked back several times but saw no one. No one followed her; she was sure of it.

The salt-grimed shacks were hunched at the bottom of a hollow. In one of them an oil lamp guttered in the breeze. As Emma approached a man looked out. He was burly in the shoulders and she could not see his face.

'Josiah Yarm?'

'You the leddy wants get to Yarmouth?'

'Yes.'

'Come wi' me.'

He led the way over the dunes behind the hamlet. She followed and soon they arrived at an inlet where fishing boats were moored. Josiah Yarm gave a shrill whistle.

A moment later a figure appeared on the deck of one of the boats. Yarm shouted to him across the water. 'C'mon, Lob, look lively, lad. Let's get they anchor in.'

Lob raised his hand in acknowledgement, made his way to the vessel's stern and began to heave on a chain. A minute later an anchor rose dripping into the air. It was massive, yet the way Lob dumped it on the deck it might have been a feather. Josiah Yarm hauled on the mooring line and within a minute the bow of the fishing boat was nudging the wharf.

''op aboard, your leddyship,' Yarm said.

Emma did so. The smell of fish was very strong. Within minutes Yarm and Lob had worked the boat down the channel to the sea. The rain had stopped, the cloud gone. With sail hoisted, they headed south while the rising sun set sky and water ablaze with red and golden fire.

Emma was not looking forward to Yarmouth. Lady Raedwald would know by now that she'd run away. She might well believe Emma was trying to get back to Chatham, which would mean going via London. To do that she would have to take the flyer from Yarmouth, and the dowager could easily have sent one of her bully boys to intercept Emma there and drag her back to Raedwald Hall. A determined horseman would have no trouble covering the distance in the time.

Yarmouth meant danger.

The harbour was crowded with ships but Josiah Yarm managed to weave his way between them to the wharf.

'How much do I owe you?'

'That be all taken care of,' Yarm said. 'Captain Dark already settled up.'

At that moment, frightened of what might be waiting for her and lonelier than ever before in her life, Emma could have wept at this latest evidence of Ephraim Dark's kindness. No matter: all being well she would be able to thank him aboard the *Admiral Cockburn* the next night.

The idea that she might soon be sailing into the unknown with Ephraim at her side, the warmth of his hand on hers, made her breathless, but now was not the time for daydreaming.

Yarm told Lob to escort her to the Bugle Inn but on the way Emma said she wanted to stop somewhere else. The coach was not leaving for an hour and she needed to eat before that; after they left there would be no chance of getting a meal until they changed horses halfway to London.

'They serve meals at the Bugle,' Lob said.

'Not there. Take me somewhere else.'

If Lady Raedwald had sent someone after her the first place he would look was the Bugle. The less time she spent there the better.

Lob did not argue but took her to the Chain and Anchor in Alderson Road. It was only a short distance from the Bugle but when she went in the landlord looked askance at her. Not surprising – her dress had dried during the journey but was badly crumpled and her hair was a mess – but when he heard her educated voice his manner changed. Of course they would be delighted to provide her with a meal and a private room upstairs to eat and freshen herself too, if that was the young lady's pleasure. It was very much the young lady's pleasure. She was escorted up a steep flight of stairs to a room under the thatch, where she did what she could to repair the damage of the night's adventures.

The meal was excellent and afterwards she felt like a new woman as she came downstairs. She gave Lob a guinea and told him to go and buy her a ticket for the London coach.

'And see if you can find out if anyone's been asking for me.'

When he came back with her change he said that a man had indeed been asking for her.

'What did he look like?'

'Red-'aired an' with a squiffy eye. I knows 'im. Works up Raedwald 'all, him.'

She had been right, then. The old battleaxe had sent one of her keepers after her. 'Is he a friend of yours?'

Lob spat. 'Nasty bit o' work. No one in the village can stand un.'

'He mustn't catch me. If he does he'll make me go back with him.'

Lob looked at her and grinned: big teeth in a hard and weather-beaten face. 'Cain't be 'avin' that, can us?'

They walked up the road until they reached the entrance to the Bugle's yard. Inside Emma could see the flyer waiting, horses already in the shafts. There was no sign of Lady Raedwald's keeper. 'I don't see him,' she said.

''E'll be 'avin' a sup of porter inside. Likes his drink, that one.'

She looked at her father's watch. 'We have only ten minutes,' she said.

''Twill be enough,' Lob said. 'You stay yur and keep your eyes peeled. When the coast's clear you nip aboard the flyer. You'll be fine, miss. I got plenty o' friends in this town. We'll take care of 'im for you.'

'What will you do?'

He grinned, teeth like a graveyard. 'Don' you worry nothin' 'bout that.'

She gave him sixpence. 'Take this,' she said. 'And thank you very much. I shall always be grateful.'

''Tes nothin',' Lob said. 'I always wanted to punish that bully. Now you've give me the chance, you.'

He strode away across the yard, heavy shoulders working beneath his sweater. Emma saw him speak to one man and then a second. The three men laughed. With a businesslike air they went into the inn.

Emma waited.

The coachman came out. He was wiping his mouth and wore a heavy topcoat and tricorn hat. He walked over to the flyer, his boots crunching on the yard's stone flags.

A chorus of yells erupted behind the bottle-glass panes of the inn's bay window. Passers-by turned to watch as a parcel of men, punching and flailing, came tumbling out of the inn door. Emma, watching, saw Lob and his friends attempting to beat the living daylights out of the red-haired man, who was doing his frantic best to escape.

He succeeded and fled, with Lob close behind him and yelling.

'That'll learn 'ee to fool wi' another man's wife!'

Lob and his two friends stopped at the yard entrance, laughing and slapping each other on the back before going back into the inn. Emma, with two minutes to spare, ran to the coach, handed her case to the coachman and clambered aboard.

She remained uneasy, looking repeatedly out of the window, but the keeper had obviously had enough for one day and she saw no sign of him.

Promptly at noon the horn blew and the coach pulled out. Emma continued to stare unseeingly through the window as they clattered swaying through the cobbled streets. She felt as though an albatross had been lifted from her neck but knew, as the last buildings gave way to the flat East Anglian countryside, that her journey had barely begun. London would present her with still more challenges but a light shone on her thoughts.

Tomorrow, God willing, they would be together. Tomorrow all would be well.

After a long and trying journey on the flea-infested Flyer from Yarmouth and a scarcely more comfortable night in lodgings off the Haymarket, a uniformed Captain Ephraim Dark arrived on Sir Edmund's doorstep on the morning of 26 September. He was nervous; the foot was paining him immoderately and that morning he had observed a foul-smelling discharge from the wound that seemed to indicate things were getting worse rather than better. He knew if his foot could not be mended his military career would be over and had therefore persuaded himself Sir Edmund Wilkes would be able to put things to rights.

Alas.

Sir Edmund examined the foot and pronounced judgement. 'You have been walking on this foot.'

'I was wounded several months ago. Walking on it in the meantime was unavoidable,' Ephraim said.

'All things are avoidable,' Sir Edmund said. 'As it is you have done the foot irreparable harm. And, I may say, with no one to blame but yourself.'

'So what happens now?' Ephraim said.

'Infection, like all disease, is curable. Bleeding the patient is a necessary first step. After bleeding I shall open the wound and scrape it clean –' the way his tongue rasped resolutely on the word *scr-r-rape*! '– in order to rid it of foreign matter. I shall then dress the wound with a tincture of my own devising that will burn away any lingering pockets of infection. It is a heroic treatment, painful but efficacious.'

'And will cure me?' Ephraim said.

'Certainly it will cure the infection. But that will not resolve the major problem.'

Ephraim was reluctant to believe that a physician as highly regarded as Sir Edmund Wilkes could not resolve any medical problem, major or not.

'So what other action will you take?'

'My dear sir,' Sir Edmund said in a lofty tone, 'the practice of medicine requires the co-operation of the patient. Without that the most talented practitioner is rendered helpless. Helpless, sir! As, most regrettably, is the case here.'

A cold hand gripped Ephraim's heart. 'What are you saying?'

'I am saying, sir, that the spear point damaged tendons in the foot. The injury might have responded to treatment but has been exacerbated by neglect. By being walked upon, sir! By being subjected to use when absolute rest for wounds of this type is a prerequisite. What you have done has resulted in serious and I regret to inform you irremediable damage to the foot. Ruptured tendons cannot be repaired. Once severed, no surgeon can restore them to health.'

'Which means?'

'Which means, Captain, that I can and shall cure the infection from which you are presently suffering.'

'But?'

'But the tendons cannot be repaired. You will limp until you die.'

'I was given to understand that you are a pre-eminent authority in the treatment of war wounds.'

'That is true,' the physician said.

'Yet you can do nothing to help me.'

'I have already explained –'

'A reputation without performance is of limited value.'

Sir Edmund was indignant. 'I shall rid you of the infection,' he said. 'No one in the world can do more. And if you wish to blame somebody, blame yourself.'

'Very haughty he was,' Ephraim said. 'And I'll guarantee his bill will reflect it. But unfortunately that doesn't help me. He says he will clear the infection tomorrow but for the limp it seems nothing can be done.'

He was sharing a dish of roast beef with his friend the stockbroker Peterfield Adkins in Esau's Chop House in the Strand. He was also, bitterly and deliberately, getting drunk. He was trying to put a cheery face on it but the truth was his world had come crashing down. The army had been his life; he had never contemplated anything else. Now, brutally and unexpectedly, that avenue had been closed to him. An hour in Sir Edmund's consulting rooms and he had become a nothing man, without money or prospects, and his self-esteem was destroyed. He had thought to marry Emma Tregellas but how could he now, when he could offer her nothing but penury? It would mean her destruction. He knew she would accept it for him but was he prepared to accept it for her? What was the honourable course?

Beyond the leaded lights of the bow window coaches, cabs and pedestrians fought a chill wind that lifted skirts and sent hats bowling down the crowded street: London was the biggest city in England and the Strand one of its busiest thoroughfares.

'Perhaps another opinion?' Peterfield suggested.

'I doubt it. I have the feeling he's right.'

'Won't that mean resigning your commission?' Peterfield asked.

A grim smile. 'A regiment of foot is no place for cripples. So the answer to your question, my dear, is yes. No more army for me.'

'What do you plan to do? Become a gentleman of leisure?'

'I had planned to return to the Antipodes but that is now out of the question.' He stared morosely into his wine glass. 'I fear my damnable foot will mean many changes apart from the army.'

'But there is nothing to stop you going anyway, is there?'

'Nothing at all,' Ephraim said. 'Apart from a complete lack of non-military skills and an equal lack of money.'

'But surely your aunt –'

'My aunt has always been of the opinion that the money and the title should be reunited. My cousin is a dissolute buffoon who prefers London to Norfolk and has rarely visited the estate. But he has a son who in course of time will become the eighth earl. She will leave everything to young Percival.' He gave a broken smile. 'Damn the lucky lad's eyes.'

'So what are your plans?'

'At the moment? None.'

He could take her to America or accompany her to Australia. And do what? Without money or skills, he might end as a clerk in a counting house, which would drive him mad, or even as a labourer. Dear God! Could he subject her to that humiliation? Could he subject himself?

'Then I have a suggestion,' Peterfield said. 'Come in with me.'

'Become a stockbroker?'

'Why not? There's good money to be made.'

'But I know nothing about stocks.'

'Neither did I when I began. You'll soon learn the ropes. There is one condition, mind.'

'What's that?'

'Our clients expect their brokers to be married men.'

Emma had bought two dresses after her arrival in London, lighter and brighter than the mourning grey she had been wearing. She had visited the shipping agents' offices and booked passage to Hobart Town in faraway Van Diemen's Land. She had taken a coach through the brawling London streets to the docks. With her case and what remained of her precious money safely stowed in her cabin she now stood on the deck of the *Admiral Cockburn* while the crew readied the vessel, which the master, Captain Cooling, had told her would head downriver as soon as the ebb cut in.

'Wind and tide in our favour, we should be out of the river before dark.'

Emma waited.

Ephraim had touched her hand; he had smiled, speaking soft words; he had left her with her heart once again smashing against her chest.

Now she waited.

He had been confident the doctor would cure his wounded foot. He had told her he would be travelling with her.

'We shall celebrate our escape together,' he had said the evening before his departure from Raedwald Hall. She had believed him. Now she stood on *Admiral Cockburn*'s deck, fragments of ice from the windblown sleet matting her hair, and waited for him to come, the man to whom she had given her heart. Every face of every man along the wharf was his until each turned and became a stranger.

The crew bustled; the longshoremen stood by the warps; the captain was by the helm watching the first flowering of the sails along the yards. The visitors had gone ashore; the gangway was empty. Still she looked. Still she waited. He had said he would come. She willed him to come.

He did not.

The gangway was hoisted in. The warps fell splashing into the water. The vessel edged clear of the wharf. Men like monkeys scaled the rigging. The long voyage had begun. One final beseeching look at the vanishing berth; Emma went below with darkness in her soul.

You spin the wheel. You win; you lose.

'*Marriage?*' Ephraim said. 'Are you serious?'

A sudden hope. Perhaps that might be the solution? Marriage to Emma, become a London stockbroker. There was still time to fetch her off the boat...

'Never more so,' Peterfield said. 'Clients think a man with a family is less likely to take off in the night.'

'There is one woman whom I would dearly love to marry,' Ephraim said.

But within seconds his hopes, so cruelly raised, came crashing down

'No, no, that won't do,' Peterfield said. 'I am thinking of a specific woman, you see. My sister Veronica would be part of the deal. I am suggesting you marry her. Quite frankly you'd be doing me the most enormous favour if you did.'

'Why is that?'

'Veronica's driven away every suitor she's laid eyes on,' Peterfield said. 'She had her chance with Mackenzie. Owns half the Highlands, a castle that Macbeth might have envied, and she treated him like a footman! He wouldn't put up with her nonsense and I for one don't blame him. Now she'll do it my way. She's twenty-two, damn it! Before we know it she'll be too old to make a match at all and I don't plan to support her all my life. It's time she settled down.'

'Why do you think she'll say yes to me?'

'As I have just said, I don't plan to support her all my life. I've a wife and seven children. I don't have the groats or inclination to keep a sister as well. She might hanker for a duke but between having nothing and having money she'll choose money every time. She'll take you, I've no doubt of that.'

'Is she a looker?'

'She looks like a sackful of spiders. But I daresay she has all the tackle a man needs in a woman. And later, handsome fellow like you, I doubt you'll have any problem finding other women if that's what you want.'

That night Ephraim lay awake and watched Emma's face in the darkness.

His heart ached but it was no use; without funds or prospects he had nothing to offer her. To abandon his dream, to marry some-one he did not even know, would be like tearing out his heart, but the brutal truth was that he could do nothing else. He saw he had been a fool to think his damaged foot could be so easily mended. He blamed himself for treating the wound too lightly. For treating Emma, dear Emma, too lightly also. It was clear now their love had been doomed from the first.

He held her tight in his arms. Every part of his body ached for her. Tears in his eyes, he made love to his love in the darkness. He felt her soft breath.

It was no use, no use. That chapter of his life was closed. And he had to earn his living somehow.

The next day he went to Peterfield's office and told him he agreed to his terms.

1982

It was the eyes Tamara remembered. There had been other things, of course, on what had so far been her only trip to Europe – to revisit the graves of the ancestors, as Bec had put it – but the impression of the eyes lingered, soiling her skin. She'd been twenty-three then and a bit of a nervous Nelly at first but that had soon changed; she had never been one to live in terror of the unknown.

Greece, first. The islands. There, in the stark bones of marble temples, she discovered the mystery and magic of the past. She also discovered ouzo and the sensation of reeling off the walls of the corridor leading to her bedroom overlooking the fishing harbour, the boats with their multi-coloured sails, the lemon trees growing in the garden. She made much of her discovery, believing that ever more she would be able to taste the essence of the islands in the aniseed-flavoured liquor. A false hope; she discovered the ouzo magic had deep roots and could not be transplanted.

After Greece Italy, where from Genoa to Palermo she was pinched so often her bottom was covered in blue exclamation marks when she showered of an evening.

They never troubled her. They were all part of the joy of living that overflowed so exuberantly in the Italian spirit. As long as you took them the right way you could think of them as compliments.

As fun. She was young, alive, some would have said beautiful, and being pinched was part of it, telling her that others thought so too. They were harmless.

She went on to Paris, Berlin and London. Things were different there. It was in those northern cities she first encountered the eyes, hard and speculative, signalling not laughter but danger. Even on the main streets they stripped her bare as she passed. Initially she ventured no further but found she could grow used to anything in time. It wasn't long before she was exploring the shadowed alleyways piled with rubbish. From overflowing bins a hundred eyes watched as she passed, rats jealous of their citadels.

Was she looking for something? Someone? She could not have said. Late one London evening, the first darkness pressing down, she turned into a lane leading between the blank walls of warehouses to the moon-glint water of the Thames. There she found the answer in the rainbow lights of a bar, its face to the river with its wail of passing barges, riding lights shining like jewels in the darkness.

She pushed open the door and went in.

A bar room dimly lit. A handful of drinkers. At one end of the counter she met a man about her own age. He was wearing a feathered hat and told her he was an artist.

'Got a name?'

'Aladdin. Aladdin Warboys. But I lost my lamp,' he said.

They talked or mostly she did; Aladdin was not much of a talker, more a man of action. Was he ever. Afterwards, she never knew how it happened, she went back with him to his place, a garret with a skylight. She lay on the bed and looked over his shoulder at the pacing clouds. She floated. She flew.

They became an item. He came with her when she paid a visit to the Scilly Isles off Lands End. One warm night they intended to go for a drink at the Island Hotel but when they got there his hand drew her on. Instead of drinking beer or gin they made love in the heather, the loom of the Bishop light flowering in the west. She listened to the crying of gulls and knew it was time to go home.

Aladdin came with her. She discovered that, like ouzo, he was not transplantable. He didn't take to Tasmania and Tasmania didn't take to him. He soured the relationship with endless complaints, while the locals looked askance at his feathered hats. It wasn't long before they were sick of each other. He left. She stayed.

She thought she might miss him and for a few days did, but the loneliness passed. She asked herself whether their weeks together had been a waste of time. She decided that on the contrary they had been a valuable experience. Through her relationship with Aladdin she had discovered two things that stood her in good stead.

Her roots were here, in this land. She had seen as much of the world as interested her; now she was home.

The second thing was she'd found she had the courage to accept adventure. She had survived the watching eyes, the rats and alleyways; she had survived Aladdin Warboys. She saw that the family estate must be modernised to achieve its potential in a modern and competitive world. She would face opposition: from the farm managers, from Grandma Bec, perhaps even from her brother, but after Europe and Aladdin Warboys she knew she had the will to take on the lot of them.

The estate named for Hobart's river became her lover and her love.

1826–7

Ephraim Dark married Veronica Adkins, his business partner's sister, in St Michael's church Holborn on Saturday 17 December 1826, the Reverend Carmichael Strutt presiding.

Afterwards they celebrated at the Cheshire Cheese in Fleet Street. His mother-in-law disapproved, pointing out that the upper rooms had at one time been used as a brothel. On this occasion no money changed hands but Ephraim thought there were obvious similarities between the happenings of those days and what was planned for the wedding night. He also thought it would be wise not to point this out.

Later Ephraim left his wife to make ready. He walked out into the street. It was dark and cold with a threat of snow. He thought about Emma Tregellas far away. Emma, who had gone and taken much of his heart with her. Emma, whom fate had sent to a land beyond the seas, whom he was destined never to see again. Yet she was with him still and would be, he knew, both that night and far into the future. No help for it; the die was cast. Yet the thought of her was an ache in the soul.

There were moments when he thought it would have been better had he never met Emma at all.

On board ship Emma struck up a friendship with a Mrs Stephen, travelling with her husband and four children, who airily confessed that *dear Mr Stephen*, as brother to the solicitor general, had the *closest connection* with men of influence in the colony. This lady apart, Emma got to know no one on the five-month voyage.

She did one thing, however. She sent her uncle a letter by fast packet from Cape Town, announcing her impending arrival in the colony and saying how much she looked forward to meeting him.

It seemed the courteous thing to do.

'I suppose there's no hope the damned girl fell overboard during the crossing,' Barnsley Tregellas said. 'The Indian Ocean can be rough, after all.'

It was an hour after dawn, Wednesday 14 February 1827. It was a clear day but there was a slight chill in the air; the southern summer was dying and the poplar trees bordering Barnsley's land were already showing the first hint of yellow. Any day now the first storm of autumn would strip the poplars' branches in a tempest of spinning leaves.

A stocky man of fifty-three with iron grey hair and an unforgiving mouth, Barnsley stood in the drawing room of his stone-built house and stared through the window at the Derwent River shining golden at the bottom of the slope. He spoke without turning his head.

'What are we going to do with her, Mullett? Tell me that.'

'A thought did occur to me, sir,' said Mullett, his convict manservant.

Barnsley turned and stared at Mullett with hard banker's eyes. 'Enlighten me.'

'This lady what is seeking to impose herself upon us, sir. Am I right in thinking she is your brother's daughter?'

'My late brother, yes. As I told you, the damn fool got himself killed in a duel. Owing me a thousand guineas, what's more. I suppose I can forget any notion of recovering it. Unless you think she's coming to pay me back. I doubt that, Mullett. I doubt it very much.'

'I was wondering, sir, whether there might be another way to recoup your investment.'

Barnsley watched Mullett closely. The man had been convicted of embezzlement but there was nothing wrong with his brain. 'What are you getting at?'

'Did you not tell me your late brother was wedded to a lady connected with royalty?'

'Not royalty. Aristocracy, yes. My sister-in-law was second cousin to the Earl of Leominster. God knows how he managed to catch her.'

'Which would make the young lady herself quite a catch, would it not, sir? A relative of the Earl of Leominster?'

'A distant relative.'

'Begging your pardon, sir, I would say distance is of no consequence. Seeing as the colony is short of what you might call genuine aristocrats. Might be quite a catch, sir. For the right gentleman.'

'Marry her off to the highest bidder?' Barnsley paced and thought. He stopped in mid-stride, staring at the convict with a cold smile. 'By God, Mullett, I think you may be on to something.'

He returned to the window and stared down at the *Admiral Cockburn*, the immigrant ship that had arrived the previous night and would soon be discharging her passengers. Among them, presumably, his niece.

'You'd better get down to the wharf,' he told Mullett. 'Make sure you make her feel welcome. Quick as you can. Take the carriage.'

Emma came ashore at ten o'clock of the forenoon. An early gale threatened to spill the wherry and its passengers into the waters of the Derwent River but she cared nothing about that. While other ladies squealed around her she sat in the stern of the wildly rocking boat, holding the strings of her hat beneath her chin to keep it safe, and her heart was a paean of praise that she was there, free at last of Arthur Naismith and her arch enemy Lady Raedwald.

I would have ended up drowning myself in Betty's Mere, she thought as she looked up at the mountain, but here, at last, I shall be free.

The wherry reached the wharf. Emma accepted a sailor's hand, hard and rough, to help her ashore. She stood, solid ground under her feet at last, feeling it sway as though she were still at sea.

'Strange but exciting,' Emma announced to the air.

If only she were not doing it alone. But that was past. You will not think of him any more, she instructed herself. Instead she concentrated on what she saw in front of her.

The scene was remarkably familiar, which was the most surprising thing of all. The thatched cottages along the waterfront, the passers-by with their English-looking faces, a troop of soldiers marching under the command of a sharp-voiced corporal, made it seem as though the months at sea had never been and the miles that now separated her from her past life existed only in her imagination. Certainly the mountain behind the town was new, as was the exotic scent of what Captain Cooling had told her were eucalyptus trees, yet the town itself and the people wearing their familiar clothes provided the oddest echo of what until five months before had been all she had known of life.

Now she stared about her, feeling the wind pressing her skirts closely against her legs, and smiled as a ferrety little man in a blue cap and jacket came up to her.

'Miss Tregellas?' Touching the brim of his cap.

'Yes?'

'Name of Mullett, miss. Your uncle sent me to meet you.'

'That was very good of him. What about my luggage?'

'I'll arrange for it to be sent on. If you'd like to step this way I've got Mr Tregellas's carriage waiting.'

They walked along the wharf together.

'Good voyage, miss?'

'Very good. This town gives me the strangest feeling, though. There is so much that is familiar it feels almost as though I've never left England.'

'I think you'll find quite a lot of differences, miss. When you gets to know the place better.'

At that moment, as though to confirm Mullett's words, she heard an astonishing cacophony.

'What on earth is that noise?'

'A bird, miss.'

She stopped to look around. 'I never heard anything like it. It sounds as though it's laughing at us.'

'So it does, miss.' Mullett pointed. 'That's your culprit, miss.'

A big bird with a knowing look was clinging to the branch of a tree on the other side of the narrow roadway. As she watched it threw its head back, opened its powerful bill and gave the same extraordinary cry as before.

'It's called a kookaburra, miss. It's the name the natives give it.'

An extraordinary name for an extraordinary bird.

'It's welcoming me to Van Diemen's Land,' Emma said. She liked the idea of the raucous bird, so different from anything in her old life.

They reached the carriage and Mullett opened the door and pulled down the folding step. 'If you'd like to hop in, miss, we'll be on our way.'

Barnsley heard the door close as the manservant left the room and resumed his watch of the river. Nothing much was happening down there but watchfulness was a habit he had acquired over the years. Barnsley Tregellas was rich and had every intention of becoming richer before he was through. His banker's mind – shrewd, cautious and endlessly acquisitive – was always at work: watching, assessing, plotting. Information secretly acquired and swiftly acted upon was the key to his success.

Since his arrival in Van Diemen's Land, Barnsley's affairs had prospered mightily. Ventures into whaling, initially in the Derwent River and later deep in the Southern Ocean, had been his first venture. To begin with he had chartered vessels and crew; later, the voyages proving profitable, he acquired his own fleet. He had invested in merino sheep imported from Spain and pastured on the ten thousand acres he had acquired free of cost through the governor's office. He had taken on ex-convicts as shepherds, whom he armed, giving them carte blanche to deal as they chose with any who interfered in the operation of the runs. The fact that some of them later decamped, intent on robbery or worse, was no concern of his. Foreseeing Hobart Town's importance as a port and trading centre, he had speculated in property development that had also proved highly profitable.

Two years earlier he had gone into banking and banking had made him. Envious rivals dubbed him Foreclosure Tregellas: it was not kindly meant. He cared nothing for them or their foolish name-calling. Within those two years he had doubled his fortune and was confident of doubling it again in the years ahead.

His health was good; he was becoming richer and more powerful by the day; he had one of the finest houses in Hobart Town. A bachelor, he had arranged for a succession of young women to be delivered by private conveyance to his house, always after dark, either singly or in pairs, and who later, after he was sleeping, departed in the same way. The ladies and their owner, a Mrs Rice, who ran what was euphemistically called a hotel on the waterfront, were under strict instructions that all traces of their presence be removed before Mr Tregellas awoke; the rays of the rising sun discovered a house and owner washed clean in the early morning light.

Only in one area had he failed.

He could buy and sell half the gentry on the island but was aware that the arrogant sons of Satan never thought of him as their equal. He was meticulous in his dealings; he paid his bills on time; he treated even the most foolish with a respect he was far from feeling yet they had never regarded him as one of their own. They never would. The one time he had applied for membership of the town's most fashionable gaming club he had been refused. He was a rich man, a businessman who was feared rather than admired, which meant that by the standards of Hobart society he was not regarded as a gentleman and never would be. He hated that.

He would have married any woman of good family who might present herself but women of good family would never be in the market for Barnsley Tregellas.

He thought Mullett had been right; his niece's arrival might change that. The relative of an earl backed by Barnsley's money… Not many would turn up their noses at that. A good marriage for the niece and an entrée into the highest ranks of society for the uncle. He rubbed his hands.

He had sent the carriage to meet his niece. No matter; he would walk to the colonnaded building in Macquarie Street that housed the Tregellas Bank. The walk would do him good.

He told his housekeeper he would be home that evening and set off down the hill to the bank. On the way he paid a visit to a workshop where a young woman named Miss Jillibel Atkins had recently set up business and was making a name as the foremost dressmaker in the colony. It was rumoured that Miss Jillibel had even received commissions from Lady Arthur herself, and what was acceptable to the lieutenant governor's wife would surely be good enough for Miss Emma Tregellas.

Having informed the dressmaker of his requirements he crossed the road and went into the bank, where he gave a curt nod to his fawning clerk.

'I do not wish to be disturbed.'

He went into his private office, closed the door behind him and sat at his massive desk. He unlocked the desk drawer and drew out his confidential ledger. Dipping his pen into the inkwell set in the desk he began to prepare a list of the sons of men of wealth and status in the colony who might be beguiled by the thought of an heiress who was also, more or less, a member of the English aristocracy.

Blood and guineas, Barnsley thought. Nothing to beat them.

The carriage climbed a sharp hill and was soon bowling down a lane flanked on its left by a wall that Mullett explained bordered the Tregellas land. After several minutes the carriage turned through a pair of open gates into Uncle Barnsley's drive.

Emma studied the imposing building as they approached. 'It looks very grand,' she said.

Not to compare with Raedwald Hall, of course, but much grander that Arthur Naismith's squint-eyed dwelling.

'One of the best homes in Hobart Town,' Mullett said. He spoke so proudly it might have been his own.

'Will my uncle be there?'

'He'll be at his office in town, miss, but will be back this evening. In the meantime he said you was to make yourself at home. Anything you want, speak to the housekeeper about it. Mrs Alsop will see you right.'

He hopped down from the carriage, pulled out the step and opened the door with a flourish. As Emma got down he winked. She liked that: the first sign of friendship in her new land. That was how she saw it, and would make of it and herself what she could.

Mrs Alsop looked to be in her fifties with a rounded face and rounded body. She was polite enough though with a certain reserve. Not surprising, Emma thought – she was probably wondering whether Emma had come to take charge. Maybe she would, in time, but it was too soon for that.

Mrs Alsop conducted her to her room. Emma looked about her. 'It is truly delightful!'

'It has a fine view,' Mrs Alsop said.

The view down the slope to the river and the countryside beyond was indeed very fine.

'It is splendid,' Emma said. 'I shall be comfortable here.'

'The master asked me to inform you that the dressmaker will be here at four o'clock this afternoon,' Mrs Alsop said. 'He will be obliged if you will make yourself available to her.'

'The dressmaker?'

'Mr Tregellas has arranged a small dinner party for tomorrow evening to welcome you to the colony and wishes to present you with a gown suitable for the occasion.'

Emma had a horror of obligations. 'I do not believe that will be necessary.'

'That is not for me to say, miss, but those were his instructions.'
Which Mrs Alsop clearly expected Emma to obey.

Hmmm…

The housekeeper left her while Emma thought some more about this business of the dressmaker. It was a generous gesture, but Uncle Barnsley's letter to her father had not been that of a generous man. She suspected an ulterior motive. She was his guest, which created certain obligations, but he did not own her. She would go along with his plans if she wished; she would ignore them if she wished.

Of course she would meet the dressmaker. Afterwards she would see how things worked out.

'Will Miss Tregellas be requiring luncheon?' Mrs Alsop said.

'A cut of beef, perhaps?'

'Or some cold mutton?'

'Cold mutton will be fine.'

Lunch was served at twelve.

'Delicious,' Emma said. 'Please tell me when Miss Jillibel arrives.'

Punctual to the minute, Miss Jillibel Atkins arrived at four o'clock. She was as sharp as a dozen knives; also little and assertive and not about to take any nonsense from anybody, Emma included. She knew what Mr Barnsley wanted and that he would get. She had no intention of listening to objections from Mr Barnsley's niece or anyone else.

She demanded a private room and got it, Mrs Alsop leading them to a bedroom at the rear of the house with an ornate bed, a fireplace and a large mirror.

'We shall need heat,' Miss Jillibel said.

They waited until a kitchen maid came scurrying with a stack of cut wood. Within minutes a fire was blazing, the flames eating the room's chill.

Miss Jillibel snapped imperious fingers and the assistants fled, returning within minutes, staggering beneath the weight of bolts of silks, satins and taffeta, which they spread on the bed in a rainbow of varied colours.

Miss Jillibel inspected Emma, instructing her to raise her arms and lower them again, turn this way and that, until Emma began to frown with exasperation, yet the little woman exuded an air of such authority that for the moment she said nothing.

'Please remove your dress.' The imperious fingers snapped; a tape measure appeared like magic. 'Do me the favour of standing still,' Miss Jillibel said.

She measured Emma's height, ran the tape over waist, hips and bust, announcing the figures as one of the assistants noted them down. She paid particular attention to Emma's bust.

'Good,' she said. 'Good.'

Another signal and the assistants gathered up the bolts of material.

'A fitting at nine o'clock in the forenoon tomorrow,' Miss Jillibel said.

She had not asked whether the hour was convenient, nor had there been any discussion of the material or its colour. The colonel's wife and Lady Raedwald apart, Emma had never known such a high-handed woman.

'Should we not discuss the colour?'

'Tomorrow, Miss Tregellas. At nine. We shall discuss everything then.'

And left without another word.

Emma's preference was for red; red was the most striking colour as well as the colour of rebellion. She felt red best suited her temperament but suspected it was not a colour that would be favoured by Miss Jillibel Atkins. No matter, she thought. It was very simple. If she didn't like the new dress she wouldn't wear it.

That evening Emma's uncle sent a messenger to say he had been delayed and that she was to eat without him.

This she did, a solitary presence in a big and empty room at a big and empty dining table heavy with silver candelabra.

It gave her time to think. To remember.

'We shall celebrate our escape together,' Ephraim had said on the evening before his departure from Raedwald Hall. She had believed him and he had not come.

Probably he had decided she would not make a suitable wife for the nephew of a countess. He had helped her escape but had that been to help her or see the back of her?

Once again she instructed herself to stop thinking about him. Ephraim was gone; it was time to move on.

She had finished her meal and was in the withdrawing room staring into the fire's bright flames when she heard a man's voice in the hallway. The door opened.

Emma saw at once that Barnsley Tregellas was a formidable man. His large head was set on a strong neck. With his pale, unblinking eyes he had the air of a person both patient and remorseless, some-one who would always get his way in the end.

'I was surprised to get your letter,' he said. 'But I have no doubt we shall get on very well.'

'I trust so.'

'Mrs Alsop has been looking after you?'

'Mrs Alsop has been most helpful,' Emma said.

'Good, good.'

Emma saw that he was speaking for the form of the thing and not because he had any interest in her answers.

'Miss Atkins came?'

'She did. She is coming back tomorrow morning.'

He nodded. 'I explained to her the urgency.'

'She would not tell me what sort of dress she had in mind,' Emma said.

'Miss Atkins dresses the most important ladies in the colony. You may safely leave it her to decide what is most suitable for you.'

Emma sparked. 'Do I have no say in what I wear?'

Uncle Barnsley looked through her. 'You must excuse me,' he said.

He was gone.

Emma felt less a person than a thing, and an inconvenient thing at that. She had been relieved and delighted to reach journey's end. Now she looked around her and wondered what she was doing there.

In bed that night the darkness was full of questions. Had Ephraim really abandoned her? He had seemed so sure... Why else had he not joined her? Had the injury been more serious than they had thought? Would he ever return to Van Diemen's Land?

No answers; no hope. Later she slept.

The following morning Miss Jillibel Atkins arrived, once again punctual to the minute. She brought with her a team of other ladies whose purpose, Emma discovered, was to change her from the person she was into someone she barely recognised. There was a hairdresser; a footwear specialist; a lady whose interest was limited to the undergarments Emma would be expected to wear.

'What is wrong with the undergarments I am wearing at the moment?'

'I am sure there is nothing wrong with them,' said tart Miss Jillibel. 'But you must understand, Miss Tregellas, that the well-dressed lady obtains the best from her gowns by accompanying them with undergarments tailored specifically to her needs.' A hanging judge could have been no more implacable. 'If you will permit us to demonstrate...'

Outrage. 'You cannot expect me to disrobe entirely.'

Miss Jillibel sighed. 'The corset fastens down the back. You cannot secure it unaided.'

Emma also sighed. 'If I must... But you only, Miss Jillibel. Let the other ladies wait outside.'

'Miss Fawcett is the expert –'

'Out!'

Beyond the window a heavy squall was hurling rain against the glass. At least there was a fire in the room.

'I shall not remove my drawers,' Emma said.

'There will be no need to remove them,' said Miss Jillibel.

Emma undressed. She detested doing so in the presence of a woman she hardly knew and was grateful the dressmaker wasted no time in fitting the corset and securing its fastenings.

'Is it supposed to be as tight as this?' Emma said.

'Oh yes,' Miss Jillibel said.

The way it was designed, the garment constricted her diaphragm, cupping the underside of her breasts and pushing them higher than nature had ever intended.

'I can barely breathe,' Emma said.

Apparently this was of no concern. The latest fashions had never caught up with her at Chatham Barracks; now they had and fashion, it seemed, ruled all; breathing could wait.

'This is ridiculous,' Emma said.

The dressmaker ignored the comment. 'I shall ask Miss Fawcett to join us now.'

Miss Fawcett came and her hands were everywhere, pushing and probing. Emma endured, cheeks like fire.

'A little tighter I think,' Miss Fawcett said.

'Tighter?' Emma said. 'A little tighter?'

Miss Fawcett hauled on the laces and refastened them.

'Better,' she said.

'They'll be up to my chin at this rate,' Emma said.

No one was listening.

Next came a shift, long and straight, in some diaphanous material, followed by – count them! – five starched petticoats.

'Why so many?'

'To shape the skirt of the dress.'

Whose moment, at last, had come.

A heavy brocade, peacock blue with puffed elbow-length sleeves, an excruciatingly tight waist above bell-like skirts and a bust line dipping low over her pushed-up breasts.

'There…' Miss Jillibel said with the heartfelt pride of a true artist.

Emma stared at her reflection in the mirror. 'I had expected something simpler.'

'The empire line?' Miss Jillibel permitted herself a scornful smile. 'That is quite out of fashion, I assure you.'

'I don't know why I was embarrassed over the corset,' Emma said. 'With this dress I shall be naked even when I am dressed.'

'And delightful you will look,' said composed Miss Jillibel. Who Emma saw had no intention of changing one stitch of her masterpiece.

There remained only the shoe specialist, who recommended satin slippers in peacock blue to match the dress, and the hairdresser, who examined Emma thoughtfully and said she would return that evening to carry out her magic.

'When does the dinner start?'

'I have no idea,' Emma said. *I have not been consulted about the dinner or the time it is to commence.* This she did not say, but the resentment remained.

'Seven of the clock would be the usual time for the guests to assemble,' said Miss Jillibel, who knew these things.

'Then I shall come at five,' the hairdresser said.

'We need two hours?' Emma said.

'To fashion the hair in the current style needs time. One and a half hours to dress the hair, half an hour for contingencies.'

The hairdresser spoke kindly, as to a child. Emma could have screamed but saw there was no point arguing. She was in their hands and at least for that day would remain so. What happened afterwards would be another story.

The hairdresser came; the hair was done. With Miss Jillibel once again in attendance the corset was fitted, the dress with its attendant petticoats followed, the satin slippers. Emma stared at the reflection of someone as unlike her real self as it was possible to be, with her hair in tight corkscrews over each ear and braided with ribbons, her breasts exposed almost but mercifully not quite to the nipples.

'I look like a trollop,' she said.

'You look as a young lady of fashion should look,' Miss Jillibel said. 'Not only fashionable but beautiful.'

'Quite beautiful,' the hairdresser agreed.

'The ankle-length skirts show the slippers to advantage,' said the shoe specialist.

Everyone was delighted with the results of their labours. Only Emma had doubts but her opinion, it seemed, was unimportant.

'Now the gloves,' Miss Jillibel said. 'And the belt to accentuate the slender waist.'

'So charming!' the slipper lady said.

There were moments when Emma felt that as a living person she was not there at all.

She was ready, a peacock stuffed and displayed on a platter for the delectation of the guests. Or of one guest in particular, whom Uncle Barnsley had clearly selected to dance attendance on her.

Philip Snipe had a chubby body and a receding chin but did not allow his physical failings to detract from his high opinion of himself. Over dinner he told her he had recently returned from Oxford, where he had gone through the motions of studying law.

'Too deuced tedious to do more,' he told her with what he obviously thought was a disarming frankness. 'Wouldn't have done that, given the choice, but the old boy made an issue of it and there you are. He's the one with the shekels, don't you know.'

'So you don't intend to practise law?' Emma could not have been less interested but it was something to say.

'Heaven forbid,' he said, looking at her exposed bosom and not at all abashed that she should see him doing so. 'For the moment I have no choice, don't you see, but not for a minute longer than I must.'

He explained he was now working (or perhaps not working, she thought) in his father's chambers, for Sir Henry Snipe was chief justice of the colony and widely regarded as the terror of the bench. Late of Chipping Norton in the county of Oxfordshire, Sir Henry and therefore his son were connected by blood or marriage to half the coronets in England, which was no doubt why he was seated next to her tonight.

'I'm cut out for the life of a gentleman,' he said. 'Not a down at heels attorney.'

Although it seemed that *being* a gentleman did not necessarily mean *acting* like one. She'd disliked Arthur Naismith but in comparison with Mr Snipe, Arthur had been the epitome of gentility.

'So what do you plan to do with yourself now you are here?' he asked. As though he took it for granted he had a right to know.

Her father's daughter, Emma had learnt from childhood how an appearance of arrogance could repel those who wished to intrude into her life. She stared at him down her upward-tilted nose.

'I have no idea,' she said. *Nor would I tell you if I had.*

His affronted expression showed he understood very well what she had not said.

'Planning on getting married as soon as you can, I suppose,' he said. 'That seems what you ladies want most in life: a husband.'

'No doubt some do,' she said. 'Others do not. Speaking personally, I have not so far met anyone who might entice me into changing my present status.'

That for you.

After that Mr Snipe's interest in his dinner companion's life and prospects cooled considerably; Emma saw he was not a man to waste time pretending an interest in ladies who had no interest in him. He was also not a man to waste time on courtesies that promised no advantage; he turned his shoulder and began to talk to the lady seated on his other side.

Uncle Barnsley, watching from the head of the table, seethed inwardly behind his banker's smile. It was plain that Philip Snipe was out of the running. A pity, given his impressive connections, but Barnsley was a long way from giving up; Emma was an investment he was determined would pay handsome dividends if he could put her in contact with the right man. Emma needed to be careful, though; his acute hearing had picked up the tone of her remarks and he had not been pleased. He would have to caution her about that. A reputation for arrogance would do her prospects no good at all.

1827–30

The first week of November had been a time of constant rain.

Even at midday it was dark, the London streets shining in the wet, the gutters torrents of water beneath a grey and unrelenting sky. Lights shone from the buildings on both sides of Cheap Lane and in the offices of Adkins and Partners the air was as dank as a funeral.

Ephraim Dark stared out of the rain-splattered window. Behind him the quills of the clerks squeaked as they bent over the ledgers.

'If this keeps up the Thames will be coming to join us,' Ephraim said to no one in particular.

At least that might inject some excitement into the day. He felt suffocated by the rain, the monotony of a daily life in which every hour had become a day, every day a week.

He had never imagined the making of money could be so tedious, or so difficult.

His brother-in-law's assurances had proved wrong. The effects of the stock exchange crash of 1825 had not worn off when Ephraim joined Peterfield's firm. People said the number of street beggars had doubled over the last twelve months. Many banks had collapsed; money was tight, investment opportunities few. The firm got by, thanks to the contacts Peterfield and his father had established over the years, but as the most junior member of the firm Ephraim received the smallest share: cheese parings in comparison with what he had been led to expect.

It irked him. Being bored out of his mind while making a fortune was one thing; being bored while making a pittance was a different matter altogether.

'A fine kettle of fish,' he told his wife.

But there was no point taking his troubles home; Veronica, so sharp-edged that even in her wedding gown she had looked like a torment of vipers, had bricked up her mind against the dangers of the world and the wickedness of the men who inhabited it. She liked the financial security of marriage but resented the obligations that came with it; she had never resisted her husband's advances but a poker would have been more animated. Now six months pregnant Veronica was more unsympathetic than ever to troubles other than her own.

Ephraim, the soldier home from the wars and regretting the opportunities for adventure that now seemed lost for ever, found no refuge at work; not much at home, either. They hadn't been married a year; how was it possible that every evening he should return to his narrow wife in his narrow house and a domesticity as dull as the London weather?

If every hour was a day and every day a week, Ephraim was coming rapidly to believe that a lifetime with Veronica would be a century at least. I am in a coffin, he thought. The lid is closing and I cannot breathe.

Walter Cartwright came to see him. Walter's grandfather had pioneered one of the first steam mills but Walter himself had a military background. Peterfield had thought this would give him something in common with Ephraim so put the two men together in a private room in front of a blazing fire and left them to get on with it.

Walter Cartwright was unusual. At a time when most people were trying to raise cash by liquidating their investments, Walter was keen to invest more, preferably outside rainy England, and wanted Ephraim to tell him where to do it.

'Somewhere the sun shines. The sun makes people optimistic and where there's optimism there is wealth. Not Spanish-America though.' Foolish investment in Spanish-America had been what had started the crash of '25. 'Maybe in the colonies?'

Ephraim stared at him thoughtfully. It was the first chink of light he had seen since joining the firm. 'Have you considered Van Diemen's Land?'

That was the start of it. He found others who were interested; others who might be interested; still others whom he judged might be persuaded to be interested.

Like all investors, they wanted maximum returns for minimal risk. At first many were dubious; they had heard Van Diemen's Land was an island of demon-infested forests, with one foot in the darkness of the unknown and inhabited by criminals, savages and other undesirables.

Using his knowledge of the colony to his advantage, Ephraim was able to convince them that Van Diemen's Land offered huge opportunities.

'Partly because of its bad reputation,' he said. 'Timing is all-important in these cases. The men who reap the greatest rewards are always those who get in ahead of the mob.'

He had been in the City long enough to know the key phrases needed to fire the imagination of those with itchy fingers and money to burn: phrases like *twenty per cent returns* and *minimal risk*.

Ephraim believed his own stories, convinced that he, too, was destined to make his fortune in the distant colony.

I will make it my kingdom, he told himself, *mine!*

It was an intoxicating thought; perhaps the days of adventure were not past, after all.

He used his aunt's name to engineer a meeting with William Huskisson, secretary of state for war and the colonies in Viscount Goderich's government.

He spoke to him at length about the *unparalleled opportunities* that Van Diemen's Land offered to men of spirit. Men like himself, familiar with the island and its challenges. He pointed out that development of the island's economy would relieve the colonial office of the burden of paying for the colony's administration; the secretary liked the sound of that but was sceptical because scepticism was expected of him.

'And how, pray, will it do that?'

'Sheep and land. A fleet of schooners for trade with the mainland and the islands, provided land for suitable ports can be made available. And timber, of course.'

'Timber?'

'The island is thickly forested.'

'I have heard that whales may also supply a useful source of revenue,' the minister said.

Ephraim pounced on the word. 'Whales indeed,' he said. 'It would be a grave mistake to ignore them. But I put it to you, sir, that land and sheep are key. Vast acreages of well-watered grazing.' It might have been a poem, the way he spoke. 'A million sheep! More! No limit to the number the land can sustain!'

'I understand there may be problems with the natives,' the secretary said. But Ephraim saw he would welcome the idea, if it could be made to work.

Ephraim swept aside the problem. 'Former convicts as shepherds. Worthwhile work that will restore them to an honest way of life. Armed guards to protect them, if necessary. If there aren't enough of them we'll bring in South Seas islanders. We can always pack them off home later.'

Simplicity in the universe of Ephraim Dark.

The minister had been too wary to commit himself but by the end of the meeting had agreed to send a dispatch to Sir George Arthur, lieutenant governor of Van Diemen's Land, recommending he assess Ephraim's proposals.

Ephraim was halfway to the door when the minister pointed his fastidious nostrils in his direction. 'And who is to administer this project?'

'I shall, sir.'

'From afar?'

'No, sir. On the ground.'

'I see you have a limp. Will that inhibit you?'

'Not in the least.'

Ephraim made his way to Bennett's Coffee House to consider what he had just said.

Before the meeting he had not considered going back to Van Diemen's Land but now the logic of his words struck him at once. Of course on the ground. And who but himself?

The almost forgotten taste of freedom.

Veronica wouldn't like it but in a different environment she might become a different person. Someone whom he might come, however improbably, to love. Or perhaps she would refuse to go with him at all? Ephraim found himself considering that possibility with something close to equanimity.

Ephraim had another concern that had to be resolved before he could set sail into what he was confident would be an illustrious future. He needed money; without adequate funds none of his dreams could come to pass.

He formed a limited company with himself the only shareholder. With the help of a lawyer friend and a brochure packed with largely fictional information, he sold two hundred thousand pounds' worth of debentures to investors who thought they knew a good thing when they saw one.

The lawyer was uneasy but Ephraim was unapologetic, convinced the debenture holders would reap a rich reward. What did it matter if the brochure was a trifle romantic? He was doing them all a favour! He brushed aside his friend's doubts as easily as he had dismissed the minister's question about marauding Aborigines.

'They'll thank me for it,' he said. 'I shall make them rich.'

'I hope you're right,' the lawyer said.

'I *am* right.'

Ephraim Dark, man of faith.

The government moved slowly, as governments do, and it was the end of 1829 before the concept was approved and Ephraim was in a position to finalise his plans.

These differed substantially from how he had originally envisaged them. On 14 February 1828 Veronica Dark had given birth to a son, a healthy boy whom they named Richard. Two days later, affronted by the agonies and indignities of giving birth, Veronica Dark had died.

On 17 February 1830, accompanied by his two-year-old son and a consignment of boots, which he had been told were in short supply in the colony, Ephraim Dark departed from London aboard the barque *Dunblane*.

His limp made getting about the boat tricky, especially in a seaway, but determination and a good sense of balance saw him through.

On 29 June 1830, 133 days after leaving London, Ephraim Dark and his son stepped ashore in Hobart Town.

'I declare I am not prepared to put up with my niece's nonsense any longer,' snarled Barnsley Tregellas.

It was early morning. The sky was clear with the morning star hanging in the eastern sky but the ground was white and he knew that beyond the warmth of the house the air would be sharp with frost.

'Three years I've put up with her fads and fancies and a pretty penny it's cost me. I'll take no more of it, by God! Yesterday evening was the last straw.'

Mullett stood at his shoulder. He said nothing; with the pepper-tempered Tregellas that was often the wisest course.

Like his master, he stared down at the cove below the house, the small boats crossing and criss-crossing the harbour, others clustering around *Dunblane*, the barque that had come upriver on the flood tide two hours before. As he watched a wherry put out from the barque's side, bringing the first of the passengers ashore.

'More immigrants,' Barnsley Dark said. 'Just what a new colony needs, Mullett. Men to build, women to breed. Ain't that right?'

'So it is, sir,' Mullett said.

Poor sods, he thought. Most of them won't have a bean. Those that have won't have it for long with the likes of Barnsley Tregellas waiting to fleece them.

Barnsley's thoughts had returned to his niece.

'You can't say I haven't done my best for her. I've taken her to functions; I've hosted dinner parties so she could meet eligible bachelors. Quite a few seemed keen enough but she turned up her nose at the lot of them. You'd think she was an heiress, the way she's carried on! Well, she's had her last chance. I'll take no more of it, by God!'

The previous evening had indeed been the last straw.

Patrick Wishpole was a recent arrival from England: a graduate of Oxford University, no less, like Philip Snipe before him. With a rich father and a mother related to the Earl of Wight, Patrick was without doubt the most eligible bachelor in the colony. In normal circumstances it might have been hard to win such a man but Barnsley's spies had told him that because of some trifling scandal over a servant girl Patrick's parents were anxious to see him settled as quickly as possible. It had been a golden opportunity and a sensible girl would have leapt at it.

Barnsley had gone to a lot of trouble and expense to arrange things, with a string quartet and imported orchids on the table. He had spoken to Emma before the dinner, making it clear that he was running out of patience and pointing out the benefits she would obtain from such a marriage. And what had happened? More arrogant than the empress of Austria, she had looked down her nose at young Patrick from the moment he walked in and had ended by shouting at him during dinner, claiming he had tried to touch her under the table.

Well, of course he had, Barnsley thought. Every good-looking girl expected to put up with that sort of thing. It was pretty much taken for granted; he'd touched more than a few himself, over the years, and no one had complained. But there it was; she had made a fuss, Patrick's parents had been affronted and the expensive party had been a fiasco.

Fortunately he still had one more string to his bow. Not the ideal choice – the Warburtons had no significant status in the community – but the way he was feeling he would have settled for the *ferryman* if there'd been no one else.

Thaddeus Warburton was the twenty-year-old son of one of the bank's customers. Elegant as a lily, Thaddeus was still a better bet than the ferryman, for his father owned substantial tracts of land and was also a gambler. In Barnsley's experience a gambler who owned land represented opportunity so he had long thought a closer connection with the Warburton family might be worth cultivating.

Thaddeus was at least presentable. In addition, Barnsley thought he was not in the least likely to try and touch Emma under the table; he doubted he had ever touched a girl in his life. With Barnsley in the position to offer Charles Warburton certain benefits by way of low interest loans he thought he might persuade him to see that marrying his son to the banker's niece was a course worth pursuing.

She'll marry him if I have to drag her to the altar myself, he thought.

Rather than the elaborate and expensive parties he had favoured in the past, Barnsley entertained Mr and Mrs Warburton and their son to dinner at his house with Emma the only other guest.

There were no imported orchids on this occasion but it was important to make a favourable impression so the food was both good and plentiful, the wine the best in the colony.

'I had a dozen hogsheads imported from the Cape,' Barnsley said as he urged his guest to a second and then a third glass. 'I find it quite excellent.'

'Indeed,' Mr Warburton said. 'Truly excellent.'

After the meal Barnsley got rid of the two ladies and the boy on the excuse that he and Mr Warburton had business to discuss.

Over the port they got down to it.

Barnsley had excellent sources of information and knew more about his guest's affairs than Mr Warburton might have wished. He knew that his guest owned ten thousand acres of prime land in the midlands, as well as several properties on the Derwent River waterfront. He knew too that Warburton had run up gaming debts of over a thousand guineas, debts that had been taken up secretly by Barnsley's own Tregellas Bank. He knew the boy Thaddeus was a feckless fool whom his father would willingly marry off to any woman rash or desperate enough to have him.

Mr Warburton did not know – did not know *yet* – that his host now owned him body and soul. Barnsley Tregellas was not a man who believed in the forgiveness of debts but that was a matter for another day.

He poured Charles Warburton a glass of port.

'I understand you are thinking of going into whaling?'

'Who told you that?'

Barnsley shrugged. 'One hears these things.'

'What is your opinion?'

'As you may know, I have a small whaling fleet of my own. It's profitable enough, provided you own your own vessels.'

'You recommend ownership rather than leasing?'

'Absolutely. As it happens I may be able to help you. The bank has a sturdy little whaler on its books right now.'

'But at what price?'

A shark's grin as Barnsley topped up his guest's glass. 'I am sure we can sort something out.' He sat back in his chair. 'Now… What are we going to do about my niece and your son?'

The following morning Emma was sitting in a rattan armchair staring out at the creek when her uncle informed her of the arrangement he had made with Mr Warburton. For a moment she was too amazed to say anything but then horror unlocked her tongue.

'You've done what?'

Barnsley had faced bushrangers without flinching; Emma was likely to prove a more formidable opponent but nothing he could not handle. Calmly he repeated what he had just told her.

'Mr Warburton has asked for your hand in marriage to his son and I have given my consent.'

'Without speaking to me first?'

'I am convinced he will make you an excellent husband, my dear.'

'This is 1830, Uncle, not the Middle Ages. Are you seriously telling me I have no say in deciding my future life?'

Barnsley walked to the window and stood looking down at the river flowing beneath the trees at the bottom of the slope. The window was open and from the scrubland beyond Emma could hear the inane whooping of a kookaburra bird. Her uncle's back was turned but his squared shoulders offered no hope of compromise. Finally he turned to face her again.

'In law you are in fact still a child. But of course I would never compel you to do anything against your wishes.'

Emma eyed him suspiciously. 'You mean that?'

His smile was warm. 'Am I such an ogre? I would never dream of such a thing. But I do have two questions.'

'Which are?'

'I was wondering where you were planning to live when you leave this house? And on what?'

Warm smile; cold eyes. Emma had ignored her uncle's wishes for so long that for a minute she couldn't believe that he would throw her out if she denied him now. She protested; when that didn't work she tried to cajole him with sweet words. They didn't work either.

'Do not waste your breath,' he said. 'I have been patient too long. The matter is settled.'

It was so like the melodramas they had enjoyed in what passed for the cultural scene in Hobart Town that Emma might have laughed but this was no laughing matter; she saw that her uncle meant exactly what he had said.

Yet still she protested. 'I shall be twenty-one in October. An adult. I shall be able to make up my own mind.'

'By October you will be a married woman.'

Blood congealed in her cheeks. Without funds she was helpless. Fighting tears she went to her room. She looked despairingly out of the window as though hoping that there salvation might be found, but saw only nightmare.

I waited so long, knowing there was no hope, hoping all the same. He promised but did not come, but I told myself he had been delayed, that he would find his way after all. Find his way to the island. Find his way to my arms.

Even after hope was used up I continued to wait, out of habit. Continued to hope, out of despair.

But now?

She fled to Lady Arthur, wife of the lieutenant governor. They had been acquaintances, then friends, ever since their introduction by Mrs Stephen, the lady Emma had met on the *Admiral Cockburn* back in 1826.

'You must help me,' Emma said.

But Lady Arthur, belly petulant with her ninth, could not.

'My dear, you are under age. Your uncle was appointed your legal guardian when you first arrived in the colony. The law says you must obey him.'

'My guardian is Mr Naismith in Norfolk.'

'The governor felt that Mr Naismith was too far away to be of practical assistance. Whereas Mr Tregellas is rich and influential and on the spot. You must see it makes sense for him to have taken Mr Naismith's place.'

'Even though he wishes me to marry a man I despise?'

'There is nothing I or anyone else can do about that. That is the law.'

She would run away.

But run where?

It cannot be legal. Underage or not, I will not believe I can be forced to marry someone I do not wish to marry.

But Uncle Barnsley had other ideas. 'Your wedding has been arranged, the banns read. The announcement will be appearing in the Hobart Town Courier next Friday. Invitations have already been dispatched. You will marry Thaddeus Warburton next Saturday at eleven o'clock of the forenoon. The reception will be held in the Assembly Rooms. If you refuse to go ahead with the wedding you will shame the Warburtons, you will shame me and you will shame yourself. Do that and you will leave me no alternative but to wash my hands of you. You will leave this house and never receive another penny from me. Choose.'

What can I do? In bitter hard reality, what can I do?

Emma woke to the pealing of bells. Wedding bells. Her wedding bells.

Mind and body fought the sound, arms and legs lashing the bedding in frenzy, until she realised it existed only in her imagination, that the ceremony was scheduled not for that day but for seven days' time.

Panting, she lay still. Until that moment she had never known how cold the body could become when the heart stopped beating. The hiatus between one beat and the next lasted no more than a second but that second encompassed all the terrors of the world.

The wedding... Mrs Thaddeus Warburton...

She could not tie herself – for life! – to such a man. She had been indifferent to him initially – how could you have feelings about a man as charismatic as a pair of old socks? – but Barnsley's insistence on the marriage had changed her feelings from indifference to hatred.

She wondered if she would have the courage to kill Thaddeus Warburton on her wedding night. She wondered how it would feel to hang.

She beat her head against the passing hours.

Ephraim was in a good mood. He had spent an hour with Sir George Arthur, explaining his ideas about how the colony might be developed, and found a receptive audience. The prospects were good with every promise of becoming better.

Below the house a point of land jutted into the river. Later that night he walked to the end of the point and stood with the water lapping at his feet. The moon was bright and he stood tall in the night's chequerboard of darkness and silver and breathed deeply, drawing into his lungs the scent and mystery of the invisible land flowing away to the north. He could taste the unknown, the promises that were too huge to comprehend.

In the time since they'd arrived he'd made good progress: he'd sold his consignment of boots at a good profit; he'd had several lengthy discussions with Governor Arthur about the parcels of land that he would need both for his own estate and for the ports that would be required to service the fleet of trading vessels he planned to acquire; he'd met many influential people.

With the moon-bright river in front of him he spoke to the night and to the mysterious land beyond. 'You and I will do great things together,' he said.

He would build an empire and a dynasty. Excitement prickled his skin as he remembered the skirmish that had left him with a permanent limp. At the time it had seemed a catastrophe yet now he saw that it had opened the door to the future that beckoned so seductively.

One thing he lacked. Ambition might demand a dynasty but a dynasty needed a woman, a wife, a mother. Ambition might demand fulfilment but fulfilment, how well he knew it, demanded love. Without love he suspected fulfilment was impossible. Marriage to Veronica had proved that. He would never regret having married her because of the son they had made together but Veronica had not been happy. She had not been fulfilled. Neither had he.

Emma still commanded his heart but Emma was lost. She would have married long ago and by now would have a family of her own. He had been careful not to enquire after her for fear of what he might learn. Married; dead; moved away; indifferent. He feared indifference most of all. As long as he didn't know what had happened to her, dreams remained possible. In his dreams he would find her. They would be happy. In his dreams. Reality was different. Reality was as cold as the ice on Mount Wellington in winter.

Now he stood on the riverbank. His breast swelled as he thought of the vast acreages that would be his – *his!* – of sheep in their thousands, of fleeces waiting to be converted into gold.

He turned and limped back up the hill. Something small sprinted across his path, making him jump. He kicked out at it with his good foot, wanting to remind the whatever-it-was of its place in the scheme of things, but missed. The creature bustled on as though it owned the hill and everything on it. Amused by its confidence Ephraim took off his hat as though to a property owner and went on up the hill to the house.

Back in London Secretary Huskisson had spoken of whaling so at their next meeting Ephraim mentioned it to Sir George Arthur.

'You should speak to an expert if you are planning to get into that game,' Sir George said. 'I would suggest Barnsley Tregellas of the Tregellas Bank. He'll put you in the picture.'

Ephraim supposed it made sense. He had avoided Barnsley Tregellas for fear of learning something he would rather not know but perhaps it was time to reconsider.

'I shall follow your advice,' he said.

Sunday. Disturbed sleep. *By this time next week I shall be married.* Nightmares tore the breath from Emma's body.

Monday. No nightmares but no sleep either.

Tuesday. A voice crying. No, no… Fleeing panic-stricken down dark avenues, seeking escape.

Wednesday. Emma woke during the night, her body a lather of sweat. She spoke aloud to the silent room. 'I cannot do it. God knows what will become of me but I cannot, will not do it.' To go ahead with her uncle's plans would be to surrender everything she held dear, her life and hopes… She remembered Arthur Naismith and how courage had helped her defeat him and the countess.

Let courage aid me now, she thought. I will not do it.

Thursday. The bells of all the clocks were chiming as she walked purposefully down the hill into the town.

Ephraim had sent his housekeeper to the bank to make an appointment on his behalf and the following morning at eleven o'clock he was ushered into Barnsley's private office.

Pleasantries ensued. A glass of Madeira was offered and accepted. Eventually they got around to the reason for Ephraim's visit.

'Whaling,' Ephraim said.

'Indeed.' Barnsley joined his fingertips judiciously. 'And what about it?'

'I understand there is good money to be made, so I thought it might be a worthwhile investment. But would welcome advice from an expert.'

'I am a banker. Why should you imagine I am an expert in whaling?'

'Because Sir George Arthur recommended I speak to you.'

There was a noise in the outside office. Barnsley looked up sharply. 'Perhaps you will excuse me a moment —'

Too late. The office door was flung open and a young woman, shaking off the protesting hands of one of Barnsley's clerks, came bursting into the room. And stopped. And stared.

Ephraim had turned to seek the source of the interruption. He too stopped. He, too, stared.

'Emma?'

'Ephraim?'

After three years.

'Emma,' Barnsley said, angry but trying to hide it, 'I am with a customer.' He slipped on a smile like a frayed coat as he turned to Ephraim. 'You must forgive my niece. She is getting married in two days' time so is easily distracted.'

Their eyes were eating each other but Barnsley's words pierced Ephraim's understanding.

'You are getting married?' he said.

Emma with the bold expression he remembered so well, bringing a pang to his heart. 'That was the plan,' she said.

'Plans can be changed,' Ephraim said.

'And bridegrooms.'

'Now wait a minute,' Barnsley said. 'The banns have been read.'

'But a special licence can be obtained,' Emma said.

Bells, sunlight.

'Do you, Ephraim?'

'Do you, Emma?'

The yielding folds of her flesh; the imperiousness of his. Now all was summer, in their faces and their hearts. Mount Wellington's ice menaced no longer.

'Thank you for you.'

Fulfilment, joy and love.

1982

'Was that really how it happened?' Tamara said.

'It was what people said at the time,' Bec said.

'How do we know that?'

'Lady Arthur was Emma's friend and mentioned it in her journal. There's a copy of the journal in the State Library.'

'Was she shocked?'

'She was happy for her. *Today my dear Emma was united with Mr Dark, a newcomer to the colony. She made a radiant bride.* That was what she said.'

'How did Emma and Lady Arthur get to know each other?' Tamara wondered. 'My impression is that Sir George was as starchy as a boiled shirt. And who was Emma, after all? Miss Nobody from Nowhere.'

'Apparently they were introduced by a Mrs Stephen. She was the sister-in-law of the solicitor general and met Emma on the way out. Lady Arthur took to her and they remained friends.'

'Until the catastrophe.'

'Exactly. Even the warmest friendship could not survive that.'

'You're saying that despite the last-minute change of bridegroom there was no scandal at all?'

'No doubt there'd have been talk but Emma and Ephraim were living in their own private universe by then so I doubt they cared about that. In any case, with Sir George and Lady Arthur attending the wedding it can't have amounted to much. This family has always been good at hiding the bodies.'

'Plenty of practice,' Tamara said.

'You've got that right.'

'Must have been embarrassing for the bridegroom, though. Surely he would have been furious?'

'He may have been relieved. Nobody ever talked about such things. Then as now it was a criminal offence but I've always suspected he was more attracted to men than women.'

'Which wouldn't have suited Emma.'

'Only one man ever suited her. She helped him in good times and bad. She was the lodestar that drew him on from the day she met him until the end. In a very real sense she made him the legend their son William made sure he became. For his own benefit but that was William, after all. Nevertheless he did it.'

'How romantic!' Tamara said. 'Pity nobody thinks like that any more.'

'Of course they do. There's romance everywhere, if you dig deep enough. It's just a question of finding it.'

'Or of wanting it,' Tamara said. 'I've got Derwent to run. I don't have time for romance.'

'Running Derwent, for you, is one of the most romantic things you could do. Talking of which, there's a new agricultural show opening tomorrow. They're calling it Agfest.'

'How did you hear about it?'

'There was a write-up in *The Examiner*. Might be worth a look, if you've got the time.'

'Where is it?'

'Symmons Plains, just outside Launceston. Give you a chance to see what's going on in the industry. Never hurts to keep an eye on the competition.'

'You going?'

'These things are about the future. I'm the past.' A glint of wick-edness in Bec's smile. 'I'm a stay-at-home babe these days. Why not, when I've got you to run around for me?'

'Perhaps I should have a look, at that. Never know your luck. Maybe I'll fall in love with a prize ram.'

Grant saw her first.

She was in the auction tent, watching the rams coming under the hammer and wondering whether to put in a bid, when he spoke. Eleven years since they'd seen each other yet she knew his voice at once. She turned, smile like a cresting wave, and it was yesterday revisited with her standing outside Derwent's door and watching the battered ute driving away down the twisting road and out of her life.

Next thing they were hugging, she feeling the hard length of his body against hers.

'Where have you been all this time?'

'Around.'

The same laugh lines around the eyes, the same generous smile.

I'd have picked him out in a crowd, she thought.

She checked him out again and saw that in one respect he had indeed changed, or seemingly so, and she thanked God for it. The eyes she remembered as clouded by the residue of horror were clear now.

Grant Venables had never described his experiences in Vietnam, yet his silence had spoken for him. Looking at him now she thought he had found a measure of peace. It would never be absolute. Some experiences were beyond the power of human will to erase, but at least it looked as though he had worked out a way of living with his past.

She was glad for him and for herself; they went back such a long way and there had been teenage days when she had believed herself in love with him.

It was the briefest of conversations; he had to meet a stock agent and was already late but they agreed they would catch up with each other in an hour's time at the refreshments tent.

She watched him walk away through the crowd, a tall man with strong shoulders squared, trademark Akubra on the back of his head, and was at once back in the days when she had been adrift in the dangerous seas separating the child and the adult. Then Grant Venables had been a beacon to guide her through the storm.

There was a ram she fancied; she outbid the opposition, arranged delivery with the stock agent and headed for the refreshments tent through the dawdling crowd.

Grant hadn't arrived so she grabbed one of the outside tables and sat enjoying the sunshine, letting her mind travel back over the years.

Grant's father had worked as a carpenter at Derwent all his life and Tamara had seen Grant around the place as long as she could remember. He had seemed remote, a citizen of the foreign country called adulthood. He had been a presence, like his father and the sheep and the spreading acres that she had accepted without understanding were the family's kingdom.

She'd had an only child's life. Brother David was seventeen years older than she was, almost another generation, and she had grown up solitary but self-sufficient. Loneliness – if that was what it was – had not been a problem but a feature of her life that she accepted without query or resentment.

She wandered far in that childhood world, exploring the nooks and crannies of her developing life. Early on she knew she was in tune with the land, its mystery and the singing that underlay the silence.

Her mother had left home when Tamara was six. *Gone off with a man*, the servants said.

She couldn't understand that. Dad was a man, wasn't he? What did she need another one for?

It was a question that remained unanswered, like most of her questions. Father and brother left her to her own devices; only Grandma Bec encouraged her developing excitement in life and her world. Bec had shared her joy over the tiny fossils she discovered in the weathered limestone crags that stood like sentinels about Derwent's higher ground, and from the first had given her enough rope to hang a dozen inquisitive children.

By the time she was twelve Tamara had begun using her school holidays to explore the complications of many of the creek beds and billabongs spread across Derwent's vast acreage. She lay in her sleeping bag at night, listening to the water and the calling of owls. She walked through a land whose deceptive emptiness was crowded with the shadows and beings of the past. She examined the shell middens along the shores of lakes; in harmony with its ancient inhabitants breathed the air of the Kutikina Cave, unpicked the intricacies of gum nut and leaf. She walked with the Parlevar people who had known that high country before the latest Ice Age, thousands of years before outsiders came to breathe the air and disrupt the stillness of the land that some said had been dreamt into being at the creation of the world. She sensed the footprints of Moinee, child of the sun and moon, who in Aboriginal myth had created the first man; she knew herself one with all this ancient land whose emptiness and silence unfettered her spirit from the day-by-day dealings of her life.

She also knew that if she went back far enough her roots lay in the soil of England, the faraway country her ancestor had left one hundred and fifty-two years before.

'We are the living and the past,' she told Bec and herself.

'The living and the dead, more like,' Bec said. 'Quite a feat.'

But Tamara was serious. 'Not the dead. They are still alive because they are in us. I feel their presence; I hear their voices. All of us are one.'

'And with the future?' Grandma Bec teased her.

Tamara was certain. 'With the future also. That is what eternity means.'

'Have you told your father how you feel?'

'Dad wouldn't understand.' And was certain of that also.

Grant pitched up in a burst of watery sunshine. They went into the refreshments tent and came back with a couple of hamburgers, coffee in cardboard containers. They sat at the same outside table. They munched and slurped coffee.

'Cardboard flavoured but least it's hot,' Grant said.

His face was more lined than she remembered. Unsurprising; it was eleven years, after all, and given Grant's background some at least would have been problem years.

'The burgers are a bit like cardboard too,' Tamara said.

'Enlivened by the saving grace of tomato sauce,' Grant said.

'What have you been doing with yourself?' she said.

'I've got a sheep run up on the plateau.'

'Whereabouts?'

'Past Quamby Bluff, about an hour's drive from here. Why don't you drive over and take a look while you're in the district?'

'You say that to all the girls?'

He grinned, crumpling the burger wrapper in his big hand. 'As many as will listen.'

She felt the tiniest quiver. 'I might drop by. If I've got time.'

'I look forward to it.' He nodded and stood up. 'I must get moving.'

'What's its name?'

'Ringarooma,' he said.

'Isn't that a place in the north?'

'I knew someone from there,' he said.

Again she watched him walk away through the crowd.

If, she had said, but already she knew she would go. Eleven years of nothing; even before that there had been nothing between them that mattered. She'd fancied him, no doubt about that, sixteen years old with her body a seething swamp of hormones, but nothing had come of it. He could have taken advantage of her any time he liked – she had wanted him to – but he never had and his temper, after he came back from Vietnam, had made him as prickly as a bramble bush.

When his father died she had watched him drive down the hill and had believed that was the end of it but now, out of the blue, he was back, and she had no doubt there had been a measure of reconnection.

Oh yes, she would go.

She had intended to drive back to Derwent that evening but now she checked into the hotel.

'One night,' she told the receptionist.

That would be enough. A quick look at Ringarooma and Grant's mob of sheep and she'd be on her way. With Grandma Bec's birthday bash two days away she had no choice anyway.

That night she lay in bed and told herself it was just as well.

Grant didn't drive straight home but stopped at the Carrick Inn for a couple of beers while he tried to work things out.

Bumping into Tamara Penrose had been a shock and he needed time to think how he felt. He sat at the bar, savouring the wet of the beer warming his throat as it went down, following it up with a shot of Johnny Walker, and remembered her as she had been after he came home from Vietnam.

That had been a dark time.

He had been there with the battalion for twelve months. A year and a lifetime: a book with horror inscribed on every page. And not just for the time he'd been there; it was a nightmare that still had the power to paint his nights with blood and his days with a paralysing disbelief in his own worth and that of all humanity.

Images that would not die.

American soldiers stripped and strung up in trees, their skins ripped off, prey to flies and the fires of hell.

The endless fear of the metallic *crick* as a bouncing betty, triggered by one misstep, flung itself out of the earth to rip the bellies from men in an explosion that continued to resonate weeks and months afterwards.

Haunted jungle paths where every shadow was an enemy.

Peasant women reduced to carbon, their children roasted by napalm, their screams lost in the roar of flames.

Day by day; night by night.

Only one person had offered him the promise of peace, of knowing that despite the evidence of his eyes not all the peoples of the earth were devil-spawned.

Annie Phuong was a Vietnamese nurse, young, devoted to her work. She was brave and beautiful and Grant Venables was in love with her from the moment he first saw her. She had been laughing, raven hair shining, drawing his eyes after her as she wove her scooter through the hot sunlight of a Saigon street.

He saw her, loved her but did not yet know her or speak to her. That came later, by chance, at a party on the roof of the Continental Hotel, the booze flowing, the laughter as brittle as sticks, while the distant flashes of artillery patterned the night sky above the delta.

They talked, they clicked, they shared a meal of prawns and spring rolls at a roadside stall in a side street off Tu-Do Street. Whenever he was in Saigon he saw her. They became lovers.

She was a nurse dedicated to helping the sick, caring nothing for their politics.

'People are people,' she said. 'Some nice, some not so nice. Just people. When they need help, I help.'

She was a light shining in his darkness.

The light was snuffed out when some of the people to whom she had dedicated her life intercepted her on a side road outside Saigon and burnt her to death. She was twenty-three.

He went berserk when he heard.

When he arrived back in Tassie he planned to put it all behind him but from the first that had been a vain hope. Life had become a dark valley between high cliffs shutting out the light.

Once again he had met up with Tamara Penrose. She was fourteen by then, an almost-but-not-quite woman who had not learnt to hide her feelings. Her eyes were unveiled when she watched him. She was a child; he took no notice. Two years later, after his father's death, she was sixteen. Still young but no longer a child, her eyes still watching him. She was a looker too. He was tempted; for the first time since Annie there was someone who interested him, but he did nothing about it, knowing with a resigned despair that he was soiled beyond redemption.

It was Tamara and his feelings for Tamara that made him see he could not go on as he was. Ever since the trauma of returning home to abuse from a brainless mob that had waited long hours to ambush them – he had knocked the daylights out of a couple of them, whom he'd later heard boasting about it in a pub – he had been unable to settle back into civilian life.

His feelings for Tamara Penrose, tentative though they were, had somehow made his situation seem even more hopeless than it had been before. He had felt himself being shredded by his past and had known if he didn't move on he would destroy himself. Others too, perhaps.

So he had gone, not knowing where, down a hundred roads and across a hundred paddocks and through towns he knew and others he didn't, taking work where he could find it, staying a while before moving on, sleeping rough as often as not, drinking a lot, looking for what he did not know and not finding it.

He tried the mainland for a spell but that was no good either. The island drew him back yet going away had steadied him in a way he had not expected and did not understand. He stayed longer in places and eventually built enough cash and self-confidence to lease an acreage up in the mountains where he ran sheep.

Physically he had steadied but emotionally he was still a mess. He'd had a number of short-term relationships but the anguish of Annie's terrible death continued to haunt him. The women were frightened of him; he could see it in their eyes. He was frightened of himself, and it was never long before they walked out or were told to go.

For a year he had lived alone but now the shock of seeing Tamara again had unbalanced him; that must have been the reason he had invited the woman he had fled from eleven years before to step across the barrier he had erected to shelter him from the past.

He went out, got into his ute and drove up the winding road to the plateau. He went into the old cottage he'd renovated as a condition of obtaining the lease. He lit the lamp in the small parlour and poured himself a final drink.

He was no nearer an answer than when he'd left Carrick.

Maybe she won't come, he thought. That would solve the problem very easily.

He slept. In the morning he shrugged on a singlet and shirt and went out to check his sheep.

Tamara had told herself it would be madness to take up with Grant, a complication in her life she didn't need. She stood under the shower, the hot water hammering down, and told herself she would drive back down the highway to Derwent and put Grant Venables out of her mind once and for all.

She was determined about it yet when she pulled out of the car park she turned right and not left, heading north and then west to Quamby Bluff and whatever might lie beyond.

A social visit: where was the harm in that? Yet: 'You are a fool,' she told herself.

The road was steep, winding, with towering eucalypts on either side, but when she got there the property wasn't hard to find, lying a short way off the road with the name Ringarooma on the gate. She drove in and parked beside the little house. She waited but no one came. It was high up here. She opened the car door and went to look at the view.

Five minutes later Grant came. He climbed out of the cab of his ute, face glowing in the fresh air, and came over to her. 'Glad you made it,' he said. 'Fancy some breakfast?'

'And coffee?' she said.

'Of course.'

'Sounds great.'

They went into the cottage together.

While she looked around he rustled up ham steaks, eggs and mushrooms, a loaf of bread on the side, and in no time they were sitting down at the little wooden table, the coffee pot convenient between them, and tucking in.

Tamara was pleased to find Grant did not believe in conversation while they were eating but later, when they sat back after clearing their plates, they were soon making up for lost time.

Talking about what they had done since they had last met. Something of her travels abroad and his before he came to settle – if settle

he had – on the plateau. The excitement and beauty and knowledge
of other lands but never a word of Aladdin Warboys or of Annie
Phuong, so the stories they told each other were full of holes. It
didn't matter; what had never really started eleven years before had
never really ended, either.

Tamara had read it somewhere: how you travelled far in search of
something that you eventually found at home.

'Stay a while longer,' Grant said. 'There's some pretty impressive
country around here. I could show you round.'

'I would like that but I can't,' Tamara said. 'It's my grandmother's birthday the day after tomorrow. Her eighty-fifth. I have to be
there. You could come, if you like. I know she'd be glad to see you.'

He shook his head. 'I'm not much for going back.'

Then what had they been doing for the last hour? But she said
nothing of that.

'See you later,' she said and drove down the hill and home, knowing her world had changed.

Cars and utes were parked everywhere; the booze was flowing like
Niagara Falls. So far no one had fallen down but there was plenty
of time and Bec suspected there'd be some interesting driving when
the guests began to head back down the hill.

Let's hope nobody kills themselves, she thought. Or anyone else.
Life was complicated enough without that.

It had been a massive turn out, which she supposed was a com-
pliment of sorts; despite what she'd told Tamara she knew most
people hadn't come just for the grub. All those she'd expected had
made it plus a number she hadn't: even the premier had rocked up
in a car half a mile long. That had been a surprise: they'd been at
daggers drawn for years and he was up to his ears in trouble over
the proposed damming of the Franklin. No doubt he'd expect to
make a speech; pollies always did. Well, let him. It would do no
harm and most wouldn't listen anyway. He had a driver, which was
as well, the way he was tipping it down.

There were some absentees too; she and Wilmot Gladstone had
known each other for ever and she'd been looking forward to

shooting the breeze with him but Wilmot had carked it a couple of weeks back. Soon there'd be none of her old mates left, the only ones who knew what she was on about when she started reminiscing about the old days. Giles hadn't pitched either. Bec had expected nothing else but felt it, all the same. A real disappointment he'd turned out to be, but he was still her son. Secretly she'd been hoping he would make the effort but you couldn't have everything and there was no end of others there to wish her well.

Tables had been set up on the lawn at the back of the house. They were piled high with food: a dozen types of salad plus cold chicken, cold lobsters, cold ham, some fancy fish mayonnaise, scallops in a sweet and sour sauce. That was a sign of the times, Bec thought; in her young days no one would have been game to eat anything as *foreign* as sweet and sour sauce. Most wouldn't have heard of it.

The traditionalists were catered for too. On the far side of the lawn a chef in a white hat was barbecuing steaks, chops, prawns, whatever took people's fancy, the smoke and smell greasing the air most enticingly. There was a cheese table: cheeses of every type you could think of, which was as it should be, seeing the family had a controlling interest in the biggest cheese factory on the island. As for the booze... they could have started a bottle shop with the booze.

I'll be interested to see how much this lot has set us back, Bec thought. Lucky the price of wool was holding up.

Back in the house the din was building. Rupe Gillespie had Doug Harness in a corner and was getting stuck in, something about genetic crops, but Rupe would argue with a stump, given the chance.

'It's the way of the future,' Rupe was saying.

Yeah, right.

There'd been a time when Bec would have drunk one for one with the boys and thought nothing of it but those days were past. Feeling a need for air she went out on to the deck. She stood at the rail and looked over in time to see a car turn off the highway and begin the winding climb up to the house. A few minutes later she heard sounds from the living room – a shifting of chairs and clearing of throats – that told her the speech-making was about to start. She thought she'd better go back inside; that way she could at least pretend she was listening to all the nonsense.

No doubt the premier had thought to start the ball rolling but Tamara beat him to it. She sat on the edge of the table, everyone crowding in to listen.

'This family of mine,' she said, 'goes back over one and a half centuries. When Emma Tregellas arrived Sir George Arthur was lieutenant governor and there were corpses hanging from the gallows on Hunter's Island. Later generations helped build the family fortune –'

She'd do better to keep off that subject, Bec thought. Not everyone loves us for being rich.

'We are here today to celebrate Bec Hampton's eighty-fifth birthday,' Tamara was saying. 'My grandmother was born in the closing years of the nineteenth century, in a world very different from today –'

Bec accepted that she had to stay and smile modestly but it was harder than she'd expected. With increasing exasperation she thought how everyone talked of the old as though the fact of survival made them objects of reverence. It was foolish; surviving did not make people especially wise or brave or anything much. All they had done was not die. Nothing to make a fuss about.

There was applause; Bec realised she had missed most of what Tamara had said. No matter; all well meaning, no doubt, but embarrassing, too. Better not to have heard.

There was a movement at the back of the crowd as three latecomers edged their way into the room. Bec glanced casually across at them, then looked again. The woman she didn't know or the youth with her; the man she did. Giles had turned up for his mother's birthday party after all.

Their eyes met across the mob and her heart sank. She knew that look. Instinct warned that the woman's presence did not auger well. Giles had come not to celebrate her birthday but to make trouble.

The premier said his piece, mercifully short, pretending a friendship with Bec they'd never had.

Tamara was at Bec's shoulder. 'Who is she?'

'No idea.'

'I don't like the look of it,' Tamara said.

No more did Bec but it was foolish to prejudge. 'Let's wait and see what your dad has to say for himself.'

Bec had been against holding the party at all but had to admit it had gone well, despite her concerns about Giles. The food looked like wolves had been at it; the liquor the guests had put away could have floated a battleship; there'd been a couple of punch-ups, nothing serious; one of the teenagers had apparently been planning a striptease until her dad took her in his horny hand; by the time they were through even the chooks were drunk. A really great time. But even as the last guests weaved their unsteady way down the hill it was clear that Giles and his companions had taken root.

He and Bec had exchanged nods; they had said how you going but that had been the limit of their conversation. No doubt that was about to change.

Tamara was supervising the clearing up. Her expression showed nothing but Bec knew her granddaughter too well to be fooled. Even across the room she could sense the nerve ends vibrating under Tamara's skin.

To take her mind off her own unanswered questions Bec decided to lend a hand in the clearing up. It was more a gesture than anything else; there were clear physical limits to what you could do when you were eighty-five. At least it gave her the chance to check out the woman Giles had brought with him.

She was youngish, probably no more than forty. Giles was nearly sixty-seven. She was tall and thin, with dark hair and eyes. A pricey black dress and spike heels. Quite striking in a take-no-prisoners kind of way. The way she was looking around, Bec had the feeling she was putting a price on everything.

Later, when the wreckage had been cleared, Giles introduced his companions.

'Raine Armitage and her son Jaeger Lardner.'

So Raine Armitage had been married before.

Smiles and inclined heads; they were most gracious to one another but might have been in the trenches of World War I; the machine guns were muzzled for now but Bec took note of Giles's know-all smile and knew it was only a reprieve.

Whatever it was, they weren't going to hear anything that night. He yawned elaborately and said it had been a long day and they were exhausted. There were important things they had to discuss but they could wait for the morning.

Bec had never been prepared to play his mind games and was not about to start now.

'The bed's made up in your room,' she said. 'I've asked Kate to get things ready in two of the spare rooms.'

'Too kind,' Raine said.

Bec bowed her head. Lady Muck on the hoof, she thought. 'My pleasure,' she said.

'What does Dad want?' Tamara said after the others had gone.

'We'll find out tomorrow,' Bec said.

'Why couldn't he tell us now?'

'Because he's trying to wind us up.'

Tamara looked at Bec admiringly. 'Doesn't seem to have worked with you.'

'I'm too old to be wound up,' Bec said.

Yet half an hour later she saw something that might have exasperated her had she permitted it. She was crossing the darkened hall on her way to bed when she saw Raine slip silently across the landing and into Giles's bedroom.

She listened. At first all was quiet, then she heard laughter. Later she heard other sounds, at first barely audible, then louder.

The sounds told her nothing she hadn't already assumed, that Giles and this Raine Armitage were an item and that Raine's presence represented a complication in what she had already guessed would be a difficult situation. She had never been an eavesdropper yet found herself unable to move. She heard the creaking of bedsprings, sounds like pain becoming steadily more urgent. A crescendo of sounds, like a horse galloping. A split-second's silence broken by a woman's triumphant cry.

So that was Raine Armitage, Bec thought as she closed her bedroom door on the world. She and her son Jaeger Lardner. Giles had always insisted that only a man was capable of running Derwent. It was foolish; he'd never tried to run the place himself while Tamara had been doing it for years but, foolish or not, that had always been his opinion and as trustee and principal beneficiary of the family trust he could do more or less what he wanted with it.

Bec's clenched fingers were carving deep crescents in her palms' soft flesh. Surely he could not intend to do that, she thought. But the facts were stark. Jaeger was Raine Armitage's son and Raine was in Giles Penrose's bed.

Dear God.

One thing on top of another. Tamara lay in bed, eyes watching the images that came and went in the darkness, and knew there would not be much sleep tonight.

The people who had turned up with Tamara's father, their presence unexplained: who were they and what were they doing? The arrogant way the woman had looked around – at the house and furniture, at Tamara herself – you'd have thought she owned the place and everyone in it. So yes, Raine Armitage and her son were part of the problem but only a part. Not even the most important part, either.

When Bec had suggested she should go to the new Agfest show she'd had no inkling the sky was about to fall on her head. Now – meeting Grant after all these years – it had. The future was still cloudy but with willpower and good fortune it would be hers.

1831

'I declare our luck has turned at last,' Ephraim said.

'It will be interesting to inspect the land Sir George has given us,' Emma said.

The carriage, bellows top closed against the dust, drew to a stop at the top of the rise. To its right a hill thick with scrub rose steeply to a ridge sharp cut against a sky that was sapphire blue, hard and bright. The horses rested, mouthing their silver bits.

Emma opened the door and stepped out into the sunlight. The soles of her boots crunched upon the surface of the gravel road that ran all the way north to Launceston. Behind them lay Oatlands, where they had stayed overnight, and fifty miles beyond that Hobart Town, which they had left two days before and where they had left Richard in the care of a nurse. Emma had grown fond of the little boy but had decided a trip like this would be too tiring for him.

She used her parasol to fend off the sun's ferocious rays and stared about her. Her up-tilted chin challenged the future as she examined the view: the road shimmering with heat as it wound down into the valley, the lush pastures broken by isolated stands of timber extending northwards to distant hills now shading blue in the early afternoon light.

Ephraim, favouring his lame foot, had followed her more slowly out of the carriage and now stood at her side, sharing the moment. 'I swear we have entered into glory,' he said. 'When Sir George dug in his heels I wondered if it would ever happen.'

Emma smiled. 'I am so pleased you managed to persuade him,' she said.

After eight months of marriage she had learnt what she could safely say to him and what she could not. The truth was that Ephraim's discussions with Sir George Arthur had nothing to do with it because Sir George, stubborn as a post and mindful that the system of free land grants was coming to an end, would have rejected their application out of hand had not his wife, loyal to her friend, managed somehow to talk him round.

It was possible their grant was the last one that would ever be issued under the old system, and knowing how close they'd come to missing out made Emma's pleasure all the greater. It had also made her the more determined to see the land for herself.

Ephraim had been against her making the trip – she was five months pregnant – but she would have none of it.

'I am as strong as a horse,' she said. 'Surely you will not deprive me of the joy of seeing for myself the land that my dear husband has obtained for us?'

For Ephraim Dark was the lord and master, at least in his own estimation, and she had no plans to correct the notion. So, having persuaded Ephraim it was his idea, she had succeeded in what she had been determined to do. And now there it was, all twenty thousand acres of it. Or approximately; the precise area would be known only when the land was surveyed and the deeds issued.

'How considerate of you to let me see it with you for the first time together,' she said. 'I am delighted by the idea that we shall be landed gentry in our new land.'

She knew Ephraim was delighted too. She had learnt to read his thoughts, not as an intrusion or because she didn't trust him but as the first step towards the happy and fulfilling marriage she was determined they would have. She also knew Ephraim's world was peopled by visions that gave him no rest; he held their future – the future of the dynasty they would create, of the land itself – in his heart and soul. She was as romantic as he but allowed herself to believe she was more aware of the practicalities than her husband, his mind constantly enflamed by his dreams.

No matter, Emma thought. We shall work together. He will lead, I shall guide him and we shall be one.

'Dark land,' Ephraim said. 'All of it ours, as far as the eye can see.' He would have danced, had he been a dancing man.

'Have you thought where the house should be?' she asked.

One of the stipulations of the grant system was that the owners of the land should live on it, to extend settlement into the wild places.

'By the creek?' he suggested, pointing to the valley bottom where a meandering waterway shone olive green between trees whose names Emma did not know.

So much to learn, she thought happily. That too was a source of joy because knowledge was power. Power over the land, power over the future. So much to cram into one lifetime. She too might have danced, had the growing child not prevented her.

'That would be a good place and handy to the water too. But I wonder...'

He looked at her; he was coming to know her too, as it was right he should. 'Wonder what?'

'Let us climb to the top of the hill. We shall be able to see more clearly up there.'

He looked dubiously at the ridge sailing high above them in a sea of blinding blue. 'Perhaps you shouldn't.'

Stuff and nonsense, Emma thought but did not say. 'I shall be careful.' She returned to the carriage and took out the hatchet she had brought with her from Hobart Town. 'Perhaps you will carry it for me,' she said.

'Why do we need this?'

Emma smiled.

It was hard going. The scrub was brittle, as dry as tinder, and the heat was ferocious; by the time she reached the summit Emma was dripping with sweat and bleeding from a scratch on the forehead that had been inflicted by a stubborn branch. But she stood at her husband's side and looked at the land below, green and gold and russet-brown, with the grey of rock showing through the grass on the steeper slopes.

Triumph flooded. Here at last was fulfilment of the dream that had sustained her on the night of her escape from Raedwald Hall and during the interminable-seeming voyage when all had felt lost. Here was triumph after the three years when courage alone had sustained her. Her life; her future; her husband; her child.

'What is the exact acreage we own?' Emma asked.

Ephraim was not to be tied to prosaic numbers. 'The future,' he said. 'That's what we own. I see the hillsides thick with our flocks, our warehouses full of bales of the finest merino wool to be shipped to England. In our ships, Emma! From our own ports!'

'To develop our own ports where at the moment there is nothing but bush and forest,' Emma said. 'Will that not be vastly expensive?'

'We have the money,' he said.

'But not unlimited money.'

'We have the money. Do not concern yourself about that. I see vast forests, our own sawmills. I see cattle and horses. I see our sheltered valleys planted to apples… I see cider presses, wheat, potatoes… We shall be self-sufficient! You and I and our children will be kings and queens of all we survey –'

'We shall need guns,' she said.

'Of course.'

Guns would give them game for the pot. Guns would also protect them against bushrangers or other marauders. They would defend what was theirs. To the death, if needs be.

The land was the fulfilment she had brought into being by the exercise of her will. Now they would build their big house up here on the ridge overlooking the vastness that was theirs. A house for them and for the generations to come. If only there was water. Water would confirm the rightness of her vision.

She began to walk this way and that, head down and searching.

'What are you doing?'

Seeking the realisation of the dream.

'Looking for water,' she said.

There was a gully and in the gully…

'Come and see.'

A strong flow of water.

She crouched, cupping her hands, and drank. The water was cold and clear.

'And sweet,' Emma said.

It was summer yet the flow was strong. In winter it would be a torrent.

'This is the place,' she said.

She did not ask; the imperative was too strong for that. He was still holding the hatchet. She took hold of his arm and shook it gently.

'Let us mark the spot,' she said.

They looked at one another, knowing this was a mystical moment. Ephraim raised the hatchet and struck one of the trees. And the sound rang out. Several times he struck it, white chips falling, the white scar in the tree's trunk, like the sound, a statement of their intent.

This is ours.

And would be forever: for them and their children and on down the generations. Here it would begin.

The thought was so holy that Emma bowed her head in homage to her vision.

Covered in dust and glowing with the ardour of the visionary landscape with which they had fallen in love, Emma and her husband made their way back down the hill together.

Into the future.

1982

Tamara tossed and turned until beyond the bedroom window the stars grew pale. She gave up trying to sleep. She got out of bed and went to the window, feeling the breeze cool on her naked body, and watched as the first flush of the dawn fires appeared in the eastern sky.

On cue came the harsh cackle of a kookaburra from the stringy-bark trees down the slope and she remembered the legend an old Aboriginal stockman had told her when she was a child, how the bird had been created by the sky spirit to waken the sleeping world to the wonders of the dawn.

'Too late, bird. I beat you to it today.'

She slung on a robe, grabbed a towel and went out of the house and across to the pool that Grandma Bessie had had made a hundred years before by diverting the spring. Bessie's Mere she had named it, but Bec would have none of that and had changed the name as soon as the old lady had died.

'She-devil's Water,' she declared. 'Credit where credit's due. That's what she was and that's what we'll call it.'

She-devil's Water it had become, if only to the family.

The pool by whatever name was overhung by trees and the water was cold enough to make you jump. Tamara got in the only way she dared, leaping straight in and no messing about. The cold stole her breath and her body was a forest of goose bumps. She flailed about gasping and was out again within the minute, rubbing herself until her skin was red and glowing. She put on her robe and turned towards the house in time to see Jaeger, binoculars around his neck, slipping around the side of the house.

A battle column of tanks had nothing on Tamara as she marched up the slope and into the house where she found Jaeger, not a care in the world, smiling gently to himself as he went through the motions of scanning a newspaper.

'I ever catch you doing that again I'll ram those binoculars up your arse!'

Such a lady when she got going, but that was nothing for a woman who two years earlier had threatened her then boyfriend with a branding iron when he raised his fist to her.

Jaeger put down the paper, taking his time about it. 'I have no idea what you're talking about.'

'I saw you!'

'Getting our knickers in a knot, are we? No need. I can assure you the view was nothing special.'

Tamara slapped him so hard she almost took his head off his shoulders. 'Then you won't want to look at it again, will you?'

And stormed out, leaving him staring after her, hand to his flaming cheek.

'I shouldn't have done that,' Tamara said when she told Bec about it later.

'At least it wasn't a branding iron,' Bec said.

'The nerve of the man! Surely Dad can't really be thinking of getting him involved with Derwent?'

'I've given up trying to out-guess your father,' Bec said. 'Quite frankly I would put nothing past him. What I do know is we have to make sure he doesn't get away with it.'

'How do we do that?'

But Bec, as was so often the case where Derwent was concerned, was away with the fairies.

'I have been part of this property ever since the day Emma and her husband first climbed this hill and named it Emma's Lookout.'

'You weren't even born,' Tamara said.

'Of course not. But I know it just the same, as surely as if I'd been in the carriage with them.' She stared challengingly at her granddaughter: old woman's face, young woman's eyes. 'You said yourself the dead are not dead but with us always, that they have as much a claim on us as the living. That is true. And I'll tell you something else. I shall not sit idly by while my son throws away your heritage on someone outside the family. I'm not sure he can, anyway. It's a family trust and they aren't family.'

'They will be if he marries her.'

'Somehow we must prevent that. If we don't we shall be betraying them all: Emma and Ephraim and Richard and my own dear Jonathan, all down the generations. Even Grandma Bessie Penrose.' She laughed. 'I could have murdered her willingly but Derwent is as much hers as the rest of them. They created it, nurtured it and passed it down to us. Never think of us as Derwent's owners but rather its custodians. We hold it for the future: your children and your grandchildren. I am not going to let them down.'

'How do you plan to stop him? If Dad has made up his mind –'

'We shall change it back for him.' Bec gave Tamara a slow smile: Miss Crafty herself. 'I think as hospitable hosts it is our duty to make our guests as welcome as we can.'

'Find out what they're up to, you mean?'

'I extend the open hand of friendship and you suggest I could have an ulterior motive?' Bec said. 'I am shocked you should think such a thing. Shocked, I tell you.'

'You mean it's war,' Tamara said.

'You'd better believe it.'

Coffee on the deck, smiling like two friends, while a kookaburra blew its bugle from a tree down the hill.

'Tell me about yourself,' Bec said.

'What do you want to know?' Raine wondered.

'Anything you care to tell me.'

Open-hearted smile; opaque and cautious eyes. 'There's nothing to tell.'

'I am sure you underestimate yourself.'

'I am a very ordinary woman.'

'Maybe you should let me be the judge of that.'

'I hate talking about myself.'

Bec changed tack. 'Good-looking boy, your son.'

'Thank you.'

'Takes after his mother.'

'Thank you.'

'Jaeger Lardner. I take it Lardner is his father's name?'

'Yes.'

Breaking rocks would have been easier.

'And his father? Your husband?'

'My ex-husband, you mean? That was a painful period in my life. So painful…' An apologetic smile as she fought the sorrow of a bitter past. 'Forgive me, but I really don't like talking about it.' Raine drained her cup. 'Beautiful place you've got here.'

And the bitch is planning to get her hands on it, Bec thought. And reluctant to talk about her past. She's hiding something, I can smell it a mile away. Something shameful, if she doesn't want us to know about it.

How do I find out what it is?

1938–1981

Raine Armitage was brought up rough, knowing survival was what mattered: only that.

She was fifteen when one of her mum's mates put the word on her: a fat man with brown hair greased back and wet lips.

'How much you gunna give me?' she said.

'A quid?'

'Make it five.'

It was messy and painful, no fun at all, but he seemed to like it, groaning and sweating, like a deflated paper bag afterwards.

Raine reckoned she should have charged him double. He came back twice more, the third time said he'd only give her a quid.

'Used goods,' he said. 'That's all you're worth.'

'All right,' she said, mild as you like.

She checked out his wallet when he was in the dunny and helped herself to twenty quid. She also found some business cards. He'd told her his name was Alf White. It wasn't. It was Andrew Black. There were two Andrew Blacks in the phone book. The first one turned out to be a widower, old as Methuselah by the sound of him. The other was a woman, said her husband was at work.

'I'm having his baby,' said Raine untruthfully. 'Ask him what he's gunna do about it.'

And hung up. That would fix the bastard.

The episode made her see that her present course was leading her to Nowhereville. She went to night classes to improve her English. She studied tarted-up women in the street, observing how they dressed and walked and held themselves.

By the time Raine was eighteen she wore the best gear she could afford and spoke like she'd just strolled out of Kirribilli House. Her tutor helped her find a job at a legal firm in the city. Nothing supercharged – office girl and part-time telephonist – but it was a start.

She decided she needed a rich man.

Steve Lucas owned three fishing boats working out of Wollongong's Belmore Basin. A bloke with barnacles on his chest and fists the size of crayfish pots, he had dough coming out of his ears. He was also a man who took what he wanted from life, which Raine reckoned made two of them.

Felix Lardner was different. For a kick-off he was Swiss. His family owned a furniture-making business with factories in Hamburg and Milan as well as Zurich. The company was listed on the European bourses and he was in Australia to check out business opportunities. That was how she'd met him, through the law firm where she was working.

Felix told her he had a married sister and younger brother, news that did not interest Raine at all. He also said his family owned a chateau overlooking Lake Zurich, which was interesting, and that they were not just well off but rich. That interested her a lot.

Steve or Felix? Play her cards right, Raine thought, she could have either of them.

Felix took her to classy restaurants which Steve did not. He sent her flowers which did wonders for her ego. Steve didn't do that either but his hands rang bells she hadn't known she had. Felix treated her like a vase too precious to be touched. Raine wasn't a vase; she was a woman with blood in her veins and as itchy as hell.

Perhaps that was what led to her lowering her guard when Steve Lucas came on to her. She let him drive her to a place he knew, a quiet place with trees and no people. What a fool. A nail-biting three weeks while she waited and then catastrophe.

She ran to Steve in a hurry but the bastard didn't want to know. Baby or no baby, Raine was on her own.

She could get rid of it, of course, but Raine had another idea. Play her cards right and she might end up owning a chateau.

She managed to get Felix into bed with her. Several repeat performances later Raine gave him the sad news.

He stared at her, confused. 'Up the spout?'

'Pregnant,' she said.

His reaction, unlike his lovemaking, was all she could have wished.

'We shall get married,' he said.

'That would be best.'

'I shall write to my mother –'

'No time for that,' Raine said.

It was a church wedding; he told her his family, mother in particular, was staunchly Catholic. Raine didn't care one way or the other. The ceremony was supposed to open the gateway to lifelong bliss, to say nothing of lifelong riches, but two weeks later a firestorm arrived in the form of Felix's mother. Grey hair scragged back, grim mouth and determined body, she would learn later there were those in Zurich who called Ilse Lardner the Creature from the Black Lagoon. Ilse was furious the wedding had taken place behind her back. She was furious it had taken place at all.

Raine hoped his mother's ranting would stir Felix to put the woman in her place, but found there was no chance of that. Felix had never stood up to his mother in his life. It was not a wife Felix wanted but a second mother. It was a grisly thought. A crybaby had never been on her shopping list but that was what she'd got.

When Ilse put her wise to the financial situation she realised things were even worse than she'd feared.

'My son does not control the family finances; nor do I. Everything is owned by a series of family trusts. I am sorry if that disappoints you.'

It certainly did. But Raine worked for a firm of lawyers, which gave her some idea what her mother-in-law was on about.

'Who are the trustees?'

'Doctor Heinzmann, the family advocate, is one. I am another. If you need money you have only to ask me.'

Her smile was as sweet as a gallows and Raine imagined a future in which she would have to plead with Ilse Lardner for money, with no doubt a dusty answer for her pains.

No way will I do that, Raine thought, but what she was going to do about it she didn't know.

They flew to Switzerland first class. Raine was delighted. She knew that given the choice Ilse would have pitched her into the hold with the rest of the baggage but the family's reputation was at stake and that was all-important to Ilse Lardner.

It was a lesson Raine would not forget.

She had a son. At Ilse Lardner's urgings she named him Jaeger, after the founder of the business. Ilse monopolised the child but Raine remained Miss Unpopularity 1959.

The family was big on the church, as Felix had said. There was a picture of the pope in the dining room and another of the Sacred Heart. Raine attended mass every week, as dutiful as a nun, while she tried to hide her boredom.

For many tedious months she did what she could to win her mother-in-law over but had no luck; Ilse was steel plate all through.

Jaeger was five when Raine decided she could take no more of it.

A small thing triggered it.

Ilse was away for a couple of days and Raine talked Felix into taking her to a new club, the Blue Domino, which had opened in the Rosengasse. That by itself was a miracle: Felix was the original scaredy-cat where his mother was concerned and was fussed that Ilse wouldn't have approved.

How right he was. The club was packed with students and the air was thick with marijuana fumes. People were dancing on the tables while a black pianist, sweat pouring from his face, pounded the keys with be-ringed fingers and screamed what he presumably thought was a song.

To make matters worse Raine was dressed for the occasion. A shiny gold tunic revealed far more than it covered, with the neckline halfway to her navel and the skirt so short it was barely there at all. Gold and red glass spangles reflected the light in a hundred glittering points. Raine was lit up like a Christmas tree and at five foot eight stood out in the crowd like the towers of the Grossmünster Church.

'I would like the world to see more of me,' she had told Felix once.

Now was its chance. No, Ilse would certainly not have approved. Thank the good Lord she would never know about it.

Felix had thought things could get no worse but they did. The next thing he knew, Raine had clambered on to a tabletop, one maniac among a hundred others, twisting and shaking with the best of them. Her hair had come down; her revealing tunic more revealing still.

Dear God, Felix thought. Now he had seen everything. The trouble was, so had everyone else.

Even now he had not plumbed the depths of horror because at that moment came the flare and crackle of a flashgun as a camera gulped down every detail of the display.

It was too much. Surely the Lardner name stood for something in this town? He fought his way through the mob and put his hand on the photographer's arm.

'What are you doing?'

'What does it look like?'

The flashgun crackled as he took another shot.

'I tell you, there are times this job can be an absolute pleasure. Just look at the knockers on that one.'

Again the flashgun blazed.

'You're talking about my wife.'

'Well, aren't you the lucky one.' He was a young man with brawny arms and a know-all face. 'And who might you be?'

'My name is Felix Lardner and –'

'Hang about,' the young man said. 'Did you say Felix Lardner? Ilse Lardner's boy?'

Felix nodded significantly. 'Exactly.'

It was understandable the man should be alarmed. The problem was he didn't seem alarmed at all.

'You telling me that doll is daughter-in-law to the Creature from the Black Lagoon?'

He slanted another look at Raine still spinning away, hair flying and –

Never mind the rest of it.

Before Felix could move he had raised his camera and taken another shot.

'That one's going to be doll of the day on page one,' he said appreciatively. 'Tits and all.'

'What do you mean, page one?' Felix said, horror creaking in his voice.

'I'm with *Der Anblick*,' the photographer said. 'Mind you, they'll probably sell the shots overseas as well.'

Ilse Lardner came storming into the chateau, brandishing a copy of *Der Anblick* like a battleaxe about her head. The pics were indeed on page one and revealed enough to raise the most tolerant eyebrows. To make matters worse, the paper had attached a name to them. These were not candid camera shots of an anonymous young woman at an unnamed location but of the daughter-in-law of tycoon Ilse Lardner partying at the Blue Domino in Rosengasse, in the Old Town district of the city.

The paper's masthead proclaimed *The Truth Will Be Revealed*.

Now it had. Small wonder Ilse confronted Raine in executioner mode.

'You did this deliberately.'

The funny thing was she hadn't. She smiled but said nothing.

'You have brought shame on this family,' Ilse said.

'It is terrible,' Raine agreed. 'Quite terrible.'

'It will take years to regain our reputation.'

'You can repair the damage very quickly,' Raine said. 'Provided you act straightaway.'

'You do not know what you are talking about.'

'Make sure everyone knows you have disowned me,' Raine said. 'Then people will blame me for what happened and not you.'

'And how do we do that?'

'Let Felix divorce me. I shan't fight it. When I am back in Australia people will soon forget.'

'Unthinkable,' Ilse said. 'There has never been a divorce in this family.'

'Might be the time to start,' Raine said.

'You are deranged,' Ilse said. 'I shall arrange for Herr Doktor Stockli to examine you. No doubt he will recommend a mental institution.'

'Suits me. It will give me the chance to take up a certain matter with him when he arrives.'

Ilse's knuckles were white. 'What matter is that?'

'Blood typing was developed in the 1920s. It matches the blood of a parent and a child and gives a clear indication whether they are related.'

'I am familiar with the technique.'

Mention the chemical composition of Saturn and Ilse would have claimed to have it at her fingertips.

'You were saying this family has never had a divorce,' Raine said. 'What about an annulment? Someone with your influence, I am sure that could be arranged easily enough.'

'And have the world know? Which it soon would. No, there will be neither divorce nor annulment in my lifetime.'

'No scandals either?'

Teeth. 'Not until your disgraceful exhibition two days ago.'

Raine smiled. 'I am talking about a major scandal that could damage your family, perhaps forever.'

Ilse's hands clenched into fists. 'What are you saying?'

Raine fired her barb, knowing it would draw blood. 'What makes you think Jaeger is Felix's child?'

Ilse's face was purple.

'Of course Jaeger is Felix's child.'

'Then you won't object to his having the tests. Felix will have to take them too, of course. I'll mention it to Doctor Stockli, shall I?'

A major scandal, as Raine had said.

'You never wanted me as your daughter-in-law,' Raine said. 'Now I am offering you the chance to get rid of me. Do that and people will soon forget. Whereas if I stay...'

'My son believes the child is his. Jaeger will remain here.'

Raine had considered that but had decided, despite the inconvenience, that Jaeger might prove useful to her down the track. 'No chance of that.'

'If you take him Felix will have to know the truth. It will break his heart.'

'That is where you and I have the advantage over him,' Raine said. 'Neither of us has a heart to break.'

She had one more matter to discuss before she was willing to relieve Ilse of her presence.

'Let us talk money,' she said.

Three months later Raine Lardner was back in Australia, her son with her. She had managed to twist Ilse's arm into giving her a modest nest egg. It was less than she'd hoped but she was philosophical about it, knowing she was lucky to have got anything at all. Now she set out to turn it into a fortune.

It took years, and highly chequered years they were, with good jobs and bad jobs, numerous disappointments and dodgy deals along the way, but in 1981 she met Giles Penrose. She'd been looking for someone like Giles, a rich sucker many years older than herself. Now she'd found one and knew her luck had turned at last.

1982

'It's my experience people who won't tell you about themselves are hiding something,' Bec said.

'If Raine won't talk –' Tamara said.

'We find another way.'

'And if there's nothing?'

'There's always something,' Bec said.

'You could be imagining things,' Tamara said.

'I could be but I'm not. Listen, I know what it's like. When my husband and I first met just about everyone was against us. Grandma Bessie would have slit my gizzard if she'd dared. But I never doubted we would win.'

'How could you have been so sure?'

'There was a steady look he used to give me. His way of saying I was his. It rang in me like a bell and I knew we weren't going to let anyone beat us. Grandma Bessie was a tough one but when he looked at me I knew even she would never be able to stop us. "We are one being." He said that to me once, and so we were. The war messed him up psychologically. In some ways he never got over it, but I never stopped loving him. God, how I loved that man!'

'You still love him,' Tamara said.

'He was my life. I can't wait to catch up with him, when my time comes, but how will I face him if I let your father throw away everything he fought for? The war memorials we see in every town: they fought for this land. Now it's our turn.'

'To fight?'

'To hold on to what is rightfully ours. Otherwise we are saying their sacrifice was meaningless. I will not do it.'

'That look you say Grandpa gave you: you've seen nothing like that between Dad and Raine?'

'Not a hint. She's not in it for him but for what she can get out of him.'

'And he doesn't know?'

'Men are great at fooling themselves and your dad is no exception.'

'Have you spoken to him about it?'

'I have not. The one certain way of pushing him into her arms will be if he thinks I'm trying to interfere in his affairs.'

'They're our affairs too.'

'Which is precisely why I intend to go on poking about until I find out something I can hang on her.'

'Looking for skeletons?'

'I can hear them jangling from here.'

'And if she tells him you're sticking your beak in?'

'I shall have to practise my innocent look,' Bec said.

'I've an idea,' Tamara said. 'Why don't I have a go at Jaeger? At her son?'

'After your run-in with him this morning?'

'They say women say no when they really mean yes, don't they?'

'Is he really such a fool?'

'I'd say there's no limit to his stupidity.'

'Will you be able to get anything out of him?'

'It's worth a try. He's bound to know something, isn't he? And right now we know nothing at all.'

'How would you go about it?'

'Shouldn't be hard. He's as cocky as Randy the rooster. The way he looked me over last night and then perving on me this morning?'

'You never know…' Bec said.

'What?'

'It would solve all your problems if you fell in love with him.'

'With *Jaeger*? Are you out of your mind?'

'It wouldn't be the first unsuitable union we've had in this family.'

Tamara didn't go looking for Jaeger but drifted around, making herself conspicuous, and it didn't take him long to home in on her.

'Hi!'

Smirking as though he'd said something clever.

'Sorry about this morning,' she said.

'Take more than that to put me off.'

'I like a man who knows his mind.'

'That right?' He looked her over and again Tamara felt his eyes peeling the clothes from her body.

They strolled, Tamara saying little and Jaeger a lot. How he'd outsmarted this opponent and that; how he'd loved and left a whole regiment of women.

'I never let anyone pin me down,' he said. 'I'm too smart for that. It gives me an edge.'

What a show-off. Tamara was delighted. Jaeger was not the sort to resist boasting to someone he thought his inferior.

'Is your mother going to marry my dad?' she said.

'He's on his last legs anyway, but maybe she will. Act of kindness, you know? Either way it makes no odds.'

'Why is that?'

'He controls the trust, right? Mother's twisting his arm to bring us both into it. Make her a trustee and me a beneficiary.'

'Will he agree?'

'What Mother wants, Mother gets. I'm not the only smart one in our family. But you needn't worry. I'll make sure there's always a place for you here. If you want it.'

Images of blood filled Tamara's mind.

'As long as I hang around, anyway,' Jaeger said.

'What else would you do?' she asked him.

'I got plans,' Jaeger said.

'I'll bet you have,' Tamara said. 'You're a thinker. I've always respected that in a man.'

He smirked.

'You've got a degree,' he told her, making it sound an offence. 'Doesn't mean you're bright in practical things.'

'You are right,' said Tamara humbly.

'If you were you'd have seen the opportunities for yourself.'

'Which is why I'm hoping to learn from you, if you'll give me the chance.'

Now there was more smirk than man.

'What plans have you got, anyway?' Tamara said.

'That's for me to know and you to wonder about,' Jaeger said, flashing bold eyes.

She saw he wasn't going to spill the beans immediately; he liked to think of himself as the smart one, teasing her with thoughts of his brilliance, but Tamara knew he was too vain to keep his lips buttoned for long.

It took a week, by easy stages. Softly, softly, catchee Jaeger...

When she saw he was ready she made it clear she was giving up this nonsense of asking, asking and getting nowhere.

'I don't think you've got plans at all.'

That did it.

He spelt them out, gloating, watching her face.

'Won't happen until your old man pops off, of course. But what do you think of those ideas, eh?'

Tamara thought she'd like to smash Jaeger's teeth down his throat. What she said was different.

'A golf course? How wonderful!'

'And maybe a wind farm.'

'Wouldn't you need to get state government approval for that?'

'Shouldn't be a problem. We know people.'

Lord Jaeger, master of the universe.

'And what would you do afterwards?'

'After I started getting the trust income? I reckon I'd take off. No way I'm gunna waste my life on a mob of sheep. With the bright lights calling? I'd be crazy.'

'Take off where?'

'I might go back to Switzerland. Good place, Switzerland, as long as you've got money.'

'Go back, you say? You've been there before?'

'I was born there. In a chateau overlooking a lake.'

'Your father must have been rich.'

'Rich and influential.'

'Is that right?'

Tamara collared Bec as soon as she could get away.

'The cheese factory,' she said.

'What about it?'

'What's the name of the production manager?'

'Ernst Gerber.'

'From Switzerland?'

'From Bern, yes. Why do you ask?'

Tamara explained.

When Bec had taken in what Tamara had told her she went into her private office and made a phone call.

'Mr Gerber...' Bec would have preferred to call him Ernst but Ernst Gerber's European soul had always craved formality. 'How is everything with you?'

'Everything is fine, Mrs Penrose. I think we may be looking at a substantial increase in our production in the coming year.'

'I look forward to that,' Bec said. 'Now: there is something you may be able to help me with. Does the name Lardner mean anything to you?'

'It is a name not uncommon in Switzerland,' Gerber said.

'They are said to be rich and influential. A Zurich family.'

'There is a Zurich family of that name. I do not know them personally but they have a considerable reputation. I understand they own factories in many places in Europe. Could they be the people you mean?'

'Sounds like they might be,' Bec said.

Bec spoke to Mr Gardiner of Elphinstone and Partners, the solicitors who had represented Derwent after Maurice Miller died towards the end of World War II. They were a big firm with correspondents in New York and London. Also in Zurich. She explained what she wanted.

'I'll get on to it right away,' Mr Gardiner said.

Bec put down the phone and went to look for her granddaughter.

'I think we may be making progress,' she said.

'That's a relief,' Tamara said. 'On more than one front, too.'

'Oh?'

'Hopefully it means I won't have to play games with Jaeger much longer.'

Bec looked. 'Games?'

'Nothing like that,' Tamara said. 'Even pretending is bad enough. Can you imagine what it would be like in reality?'

'Yuck,' Bec said.

'You've got it.'

1834

'I think I can say we are making progress,' Emma said in response to Lady Arthur's enquiry.

Emma had been hoping to get back to the Derwent estate before this but the birth of her son William and Ephraim's increasingly fraught business interests had kept them anchored in Hobart Town.

Now, in response to a message from Lady Arthur, William's godmother, Emma and her son, plus a nursemaid to take care of the baby as soon as Lady Arthur had cooed over him enough, were paying a visit to the lieutenant governor's house.

With baby and maid safely out of the way the two ladies were drinking chocolate on the porch.

'The house is nearing completion. We are having a small church built also. I thought to name it St Madern, after a Cornish saint, provided the bishop agrees.'

'A church on Derwent land?' Lady Arthur said. 'An admirable plan!'

'And Mr Dark has arranged for our first shipment of merino sheep to be brought down from New South Wales. He plans to use discharged convicts as shepherds. I believe he has already spoken to Sir George about that.'

Lady Arthur's instincts were more maternal than agricultural. 'It was your new family I had in mind,' she said. 'They are well, I hope.'

'I sometimes think Richard is a lonely child. I am very fond of him but he seems to prefer his own company.'

'That is a pity. But I am glad my godson is thriving.'

Lady Arthur's comment gave Emma the chance to display the servility that a woman in Lady Arthur's position would naturally expect from someone of junior status.

'How could he not, with your ladyship as his godmother?'

Which gratified Lady Arthur, as aware as Emma of the favour she had bestowed on her friend's child.

'At his christening I saw what a strong boy he was going to be,' Lady Arthur said complacently. 'Your first-born son.'

Which as far as Emma was concerned he was. Lady Arthur had never known Richard's mother, which made her of no consequence and Richard almost invisible.

'The wet nurse I recommended... She has proved satisfactory?'

'Highly satisfactory, your ladyship.'

'Children can be a great consolation,' Lady Arthur said.

With nine of her own and the first warnings of a tenth, Emma reflected that Lady Arthur certainly ought to know. With her life hedged about with so many children it was remarkable that her ladyship took any interest in another woman's offspring, but it seemed she did.

'I had rather hoped to see more of my godchild than I have,' Lady Arthur said in what might have been reproof.

'I did not wish to trouble your ladyship when I know you have so many commitments.'

So that Lady Arthur was placated.

'When do you intend to take up residence on your new estate?' she said.

'Mr Dark feels that it would be best to maintain our town house for the present. It is still wild country up there and he is concerned for the safety of the children. He intends to appoint a manager to look after Derwent for the time being. And of course he has his business interests to attend to in Hobart Town.'

'I think you are wise to stay in town,' Lady Arthur said. 'For the time being, as you say. Our precious children must always be our first concern, must they not? After all, they represent the future. On the other hand I know my dear husband is eager to see the outlying areas settled as soon as possible. How else is civilisation to spread across the land, Mrs Dark? And that, surely, must be a consideration, too.'

Hmm.

'I think we should visit the estate,' Emma told her husband. 'If you are agreeable.'

Ephraim scratched his beard. 'It is not a convenient time. There are problems with *Tancred*.'

'There are always problems with *Tancred*,' Emma said.

The whaling ship which Ephraim had bought from Uncle Barnsley had been a source of endless trouble, ranging from sprung rigging and worm-infested and rotting timbers to a tendency to yaw in the heavy seas that were such a common feature of the Southern Ocean.

'Somen wrong with the keel,' the shipwright had told Ephraim. 'Tain't surprising: always bin a mongrel, that boat.'

About which it seemed nothing could be done. It had led to high words between Ephraim and Emma's uncle, who made it plain he had no interest in Ephraim's problem, while the problem itself remained.

'Surely repairs are possible?' said Ephraim, mindful of the debenture holders in London to whom no interest had so far been paid.

'Your best bet would be to scuttle her and buy another one,' said the shipwright.

With funds growing tighter by the day, that was hardly a practical proposition. Nor was *Tancred* the major difficulty. His other plans – especially construction of the new port on the north coast – were proving as difficult to realise and consuming capital at an alarming rate.

'I do not think I can get away at the present time,' Ephraim said.

'My dear,' Emma said, 'what can you achieve by staying here? I think Lady Arthur was giving us a warning. I do not believe anyone is expecting us to live there permanently – not at the moment – but it might be prudent to visit the property from time to time. To demonstrate our commitment, as it were? Not to do so might endanger our title, if Sir George Arthur chose to revoke it.'

'He surely would not do that,' Ephraim said.

'Remember, my dear, he is answerable to Governor Darling in Sydney and we know he is not in favour of the old system.'

'The word is Darling is soon to be recalled.'

'Why should we assume his replacement will think any differently?'

'You think we should?'

'It might be for the best. If in your opinion it is the wiser course.'

'But the children must stay,' Ephraim said in a strong voice.

'Of course they must stay,' Emma said.

They examined every inch of the new road leading to the area of level ground where the house was nearing completion. They inspected the house itself. The outer walls were done as was the roof although most of the interior remained to be fitted out.

'It will certainly be big enough,' Ephraim said.

'So it should, to match our position in society,' Emma said.

Ephraim laughed. 'The only society we'll be likely to see are bushrangers.'

'Or Aborigines,' Emma said.

With spears and no kindness towards those who were occupying their land.

Dangers or not, Emma, who had made sure Lady Arthur was informed of their expedition, was delighted with what she had seen. All the same, this talk of marauders made her think. Bowling back down the road to Oatlands, she asked Ephraim when he thought they would be taking possession of their estate

'Certainly not before the house is finished.'

'Of course. But afterwards?'

'At some stage, I suppose. I doubt there is any urgency.'

'Is it not one of the conditions of the grant that we should live on the property?'

'I don't think we need to take that too seriously. Not for a while, anyway.'

'Nevertheless, should we not prepare for that time?'

He stared at her while the carriage sped lurching down the uneven road with dust spilling in amber clouds behind the spinning wheels.

'What do you have in mind?'

'I should like to be on hand to ensure that the interior of the house is completed as we wish. With your permission, of course.'

Ephraim frowned. 'I do not think I shall be able to spare the time.'

'Perhaps, with a man to assist and a maidservant to observe decorum, I could base myself at Oatlands? To represent our interests? And you would obviously come up here whenever you could get away, to give guidance.'

'I suppose something of the sort might be possible.'

'There is one more thing,' Emma said. 'You mentioned bushrangers. I believe I would feel more comfortable if I had some means of defending myself, should the need arise.'

'My dear, you need have no concerns on that score. As you said, you would have servants.'

'Nevertheless…'

By his expression Ephraim had a problem coming to terms with the notion that any woman, least of all his wife, should think in terms of providing her own defence,

'What do you have in mind?' he joked. 'A sabre?'

'A pistol might be more appropriate.'

'But equally ridiculous!'

Emma challenged him at once. One of the less satisfactory developments in Ephraim's personality since his return to Van Diemen's

Land had been the acquisition of a masculine arrogance he had never shown in England. 'In what way would it be ridiculous?'

'A pistol would be too heavy. This monster of mine I can hardly lift myself. And the strength needed to pull the trigger... It makes no sense, my dear.'

'I was not thinking of a pistol like yours. Surely there must be lighter ones better suited to a lady?'

'I would have said that was most unlikely.'

She saw it was the idea of his wife having a weapon that discomfited him rather the practical difficulties of using one.

'Lady Arthur tells me that such a weapon is widely used by the ladies of New South Wales.'

Not for the first time, Ephraim found himself wishing that the relationship between Emma and Lady Arthur was less intimate than it was. Nevertheless he managed a laugh. 'A lady marksman? Or should we say markswoman? No disrespect to her ladyship, but I question whether that can possibly be true.'

The carriage was slowing as they approached the inn where they would be staying overnight. Emma looked around her with a pleased expression. 'I understand it is called a derringer,' she said.

It was not the practicality of the idea but its foolishness that made Ephraim decide to humour her, if only to put the notion to rest. His old regiment had moved on but Ephraim had a word with the armourer of the Royal Scots Fusiliers, which had replaced it.

'A derringer?' the sergeant said, stroking his chin. 'Aye, I've heard of such a weapon. I canna say I've ever handled one but there's a gunsmith in Sydney who might be able to advise.'

'I doubt that will be necessary.'

Ephraim was privately pleased that a pistol of this type was unavailable. He informed Emma that she would just have to forget the idea but the woman who had triumphed over Lady Raedwald was not so easily put off. She spoke to Lady Arthur, who was kind enough to contact the wife of the newly appointed Governor Bourke, who undertook to mention the matter to her husband.

The upshot was that within two months of raising the subject with Ephraim Emma was the proud possessor of a one-shot Derringer pistol with a three and a half inch barrel which could easily be concealed in her cloak.

'With a barrel that size you'll be lucky to hit anything,' Ephraim said.

'Then I shall just have to throw it at him,' said Emma.

'Him?'

'Whoever is threatening me.'

'And if there is more than one?'

'I shall hope to have terrified them into running away.'

Ephraim looked stern. 'In that case I shall ask the fusiliers sergeant to provide you with lessons.'

'Whatever Mr Dark thinks is best,' said Emma, so demure now she had won her way.

Armed with her derringer, an ample supply of rounds and accompanied by the maid Enid and by Monk, a sailor who had fallen out of love with the sea and been instructed by Ephraim to protect her with his life, Emma took temporary root at Oatlands in order to supervise the final stages of the construction of the house she was determined would adequately reflect the status of a family that was one of the most substantial landowners in Van Diemen's Land.

It was a big job and vastly more expensive than she would have thought possible, but a year after the first brick had been laid it was finished, down to the last Venetian chandelier and the elaborately crafted cornices in the main rooms.

Emma took delight in escorting her husband around the large house and showing him the exquisite furniture she had obtained from the leading importer of quality furniture from Paris and London.

'And what do you plan to call this palace in the middle of nowhere?' Ephraim asked.

'In the middle of our estate for which we both have such hopes and expectations,' she corrected him. 'I would like to call it

Derwent House. If that is agreeable to you.' She took his hands in
hers, holding them tight and willing him to see the visions he had
once seemed to share. 'Do you not remember the dreams we had
when we first came here? How we foresaw the time when we would
be self-sufficient in our own kingdom?'

'If we had built where I first suggested we would have saved half
our eventual costs,' Ephraim said.

'But surely it is money well spent. See how grand the present
situation is,' Emma said. 'How it overlooks all our land. We have to
remember, my dear, that we are building not just for us but for the
future. For Richard and William and any other children we may
be blessed with.'

That was how Emma saw it.

Unhappily for Ephraim the question of finance had become a concern overriding all others.

Construction of the port at Emu Bay on the island's undeveloped
north coast was still incomplete, and had consumed vast quantities
of capital without tangible reward. Lacking an operational port in
the north meant that his plan to develop trade with the mainland
was stillborn, but the half-dozen trading schooners he had ordered
still had to be paid for. He had considered abandoning Emu Bay
and basing the fleet in Hobart Town. It was possible to trade with
the Pacific islands or the mainland from there, but the stormy seas
of the Southern Ocean needed skilled crews, and skilled crews were
hard to find in Hobart Town, where demand for their services was
high.

He had also paid for large numbers of merino sheep he had
purchased from Spain but had discovered, too late, that he could
not accept delivery because shepherds were unwilling to work in
a district where so many of their predecessors had been murdered
by bushrangers or Aborigines. In London he had spoken airily of
bringing in South Sea islanders but Sir George Arthur would not
countenance it, which meant that was not a feasible idea either.

Now he was having to pay station owners in New South Wales to agist the flocks he had seen as their golden path to riches.

Even *Tancred* was not earning her keep. Despite the large sums he had spent on her the whale ship remained insufficiently seaworthy to venture deep enough into the Southern Ocean to catch the whales taken by sturdier craft. This had led to trouble with the crew, many of whom had left to pursue betters prospects with more successful vessels.

He had received letters from the London debenture holders – initially courteous, latterly less so – asking when they might expect to see a return on their investment. He had replied, painting a rosy picture and forecasting early and lavish returns well in excess of what he had originally promised, but in reality the situation was not rosy at all.

There were days when Ephraim asked himself whether he was capable of producing anything but endless disaster.

'We must be more frugal in our living,' he said.

'I shall exercise every economy,' Emma said, but he saw she did not take the matter seriously.

It was at this point in the family's fortunes that, four days after returning to Hobart Town, he received a message from Emma's uncle requesting him to call on the banker at his earliest convenience.

1913

Jonathan Penrose had been back in Tasmania less than a month when he met Judith Hargreaves at a party thrown by her parents, people he did not know, at their house on the outskirts of Hobart. The large room was crowded with guests celebrating Judith's nineteenth birthday, which made her three years younger than he was.

Judith was tall, handsome rather than pretty, with black hair and dark eyes in a pale face. She had an arrogant look and the private smile of someone who knew more than she was saying. She told him her father was Julius Hargreaves, personal assistant to the governor.

'You have heard of him, of course.'

Jonathan had not.

'You must live under a rock. Everybody knows Daddy.'

'I've only been back in the country a month,' he said.

'Where have you been?'

'To school in England and then Oxford.'

'Lucky you.'

'What's lucky about it?'

'Boys get to see the world. If you're a girl you're stuck at home.'

Jonathan would not have come to the party at all had Grandma Bessie not insisted; he had already re-discovered what he had previously forgotten, that Bessie had a remarkable talent for getting her own way.

'Of course you must go. We are all going. The Hargreaves are one of the richest and most influential families in Tasmania. It would be the height of discourtesy to refuse their invitation.'

Now she was seated at one of the side tables, Jonathan's mouse-like mother folded neatly at her side, with her basilisk eyes watching his every move.

'What does your father do?' Judith said. Her expression showed she did not care but one must say something.

'My father is dead,' Jonathan said. 'He was wounded in the Boer War and died later, after they'd brought him home.'

'And where is home?'

'Derwent.'

Her indifference vanished at once. Derwent was a name to conjure with, being one of the biggest properties in Tasmania.

'Who owns Derwent now?'

'My grandmother.'

Judith's eyes measured him thoughtfully. 'And you are her heir?'

'For the moment.'

Because you could never be sure with Grandma, an autocrat who could have taught Catherine the Great a trick or two.

'Once again, lucky you.'

'You've obviously never met my grandmother if you think that.'

'Is it true people call her The Terror that Walks by Night?'

'And by day.'

Judith's eyes invited him. 'I am sure you are man enough to handle her,' she said.

'Time will tell,' Jonathan said.

The carpets had been rolled back from the wood strip floor and there was a band, which now struck up a tune.

'The Chicken Reel,' Judith said. 'Do you dance the two-step?'

'After a fashion.'

'Let's give it a whirl,' Judith said.

'I see he's tracked her down,' Grandma Bessie said. 'I was hoping he would.'

At her side Rose squeaked. 'But isn't she the one who was involved with that terrible adventurer fellow?'

Grandma waved away the implied criticism. 'An adolescent indiscretion.'

'Should we not warn Jonathan?' Rose said. 'He's probably unaware of her reputation.'

Grandma did not condescend to look at her daughter-in-law. She was a great believer in the power of names. Ideally she would have wished her son to choose a bride called Boadicea; instead he had ended up with Rose Michaels. Rose... What else could she have expected?

'We will do no such thing,' she said.

'But –'

'The Hargreaves are rich,' Grandma said. 'Rich and influential. Wealth has a way of obliterating all transgressions. Besides, it is important to keep in with the government. I do not intend to fall out with the Hargreaves because of a trivial misstep by their daughter. Which in any case is in the past.'

Judith, Grandma thought. Judith the Hittite, wife of Esau. A strong name and by the look of her a strong woman. We need another strong woman in this family.

Father had been strong; his wife so much less so that Bessie had always found it hard to credit that the world had accepted her as Cynthia's child.

'Takes after her dad,' people said, and so she had.

People had called William Dark a ruffian, and that was true. As, it seemed, Grandfather Ephraim had been also. In his own interests William had built up the legend of Ephraim Dark, the pioneering hero who had pursued his dream in the face of endless obstacles, but Bessie's great-uncle Barnsley, no saint himself, had described him in less flattering terms. Barnsley had claimed Ephraim had stolen a lot of money from him, although others said that anyone smart enough to steal anything from Barnsley Tregellas must have got up very early in the morning to do it.

Whatever the merits of that, Bessie had inherited a substantial fortune, which over the years she had increased considerably. That would be her epitaph and the knowledge contented her: wealth, power and the family were all that mattered in life.

Acquiring Judith Hargreaves and Judith Hargreaves's money would put the seal on Derwent's status as the largest and most important property in the state. Having a question mark over the girl's background would be useful, too; it would make Mr Hargreaves eager to have his daughter satisfactorily settled; it would also make it easier to control a strong-willed granddaughter-in-law.

As for the girl's past antics... Knowledge was power and Bessie had made it her business to find out all there was to know about them.

Jonathan had never been one to dream about girls and Judith was no exception. She was amusing company for an evening but no more than that. Grandma, her eyes on the Hargreaves's wealth and influence, would not be pleased when he failed to pursue her, but there were limits beyond which he would not go, even for Grandma. Then he heard a snippet of news that delighted him.

Dropped by the girl he'd abandoned her for, Judith's former lover had crooked his finger and Judith had gone back to him as fast as she could run; Jonathan, to his relief, was off the hook.

He gave Grandma the sad news over breakfast.

When he had said his piece she flicked her finger at the maid who poured more coffee into her cup, its aroma filling the room. 'Very distressing, I have no doubt, but that is no reason to break off the relationship.'

'I don't agree. What she did before we met was her business but rushing back to Walter English the moment he called is inexcusable.'

'Stuff and nonsense,' Grandma said.

'You are saying I should excuse it?'

'Don't be pompous. What you have to do is ignore it. Marry her and the benefits will be huge to the family and therefore to you. That is what matters. Once Judith has your ring on her finger she will settle down. Give her a baby; that's a certain way to bring her to heel.'

Jonathan shook his head.

Grandma's eyes were like twin howitzers. 'You have a privileged life. Privilege entails responsibility to the family and yourself. There are times when it can be a burden but that is the price we are obliged to pay. Each of us has a duty to each other and to Derwent. As you know, neither your father nor grandfather had any interest in the estate so I have run things ever since my own father died. There were times when I might have wished things were different but I never allowed myself to be distracted. I expect no more from you than I have given myself. We have expanded the property considerably from what it was originally. Twenty thousand acres more land, complete with new sheds and managers' houses, and stocked with merinos. We have also bought – at a favourable price, I should say – land along the Murrumbidgee River at Yanco in New South Wales. It's dry country now but they are planning to irrigate it. How did we finance it? Through the bank. That is why it is imperative that the marriage goes ahead – because the bank holds this family's paper for the expansion and we need the settlement that Mr Hargreaves is prepared to make the day you marry his daughter. Judith's peccadilloes mean nothing in the context of the greater good.' She drained her cup. 'The greater good,' she repeated. 'Let that be your guide. The family's future prosperity, perhaps even its survival, depends on you.'

'I shall have to think about it,' he said.

'Don't think too long. You are my heir but if you will not accept the responsibilities you cannot expect the benefits.'

'I shall have to think about it,' he repeated.

'Very well. In the meantime we have an estate to run. The annual Campbell Town show is next week. You shall represent us there,' she said.

It made sense, he supposed. A champion merino ram was coming up for auction at the show; he'd had a word with the station agent and might put in a bid if the price looked right. To Campbell Town he would go. Judith Hargreaves was a problem for another day.

1834

It was a day of bitter wind and driving rain.

Barnsley Tregellas stood with his back to his office window and stared at Ephraim with an expression as cold and unrelenting as the icy waters of the Southern Ocean.

Through the window Ephraim could see the seething activity of the wharf. One of Barnsley's whalers had arrived on the tide and a gang of wharf lumpers was bringing ashore the tubs of whale oil, the drays rumbling over the cobbles as they departed one by one with their loads of the liquid gold.

On the far side of the river Ephraim could see through the rain the green land stretching away to the north, offering what he had once thought would be a future of promise and fulfilment. A future that now seemed as bleak as the weather.

'Believe me when I say I get no pleasure from this situation,' Barnsley said. 'I had my London agent plead for you to be given more time,' said this man who had never pleaded for anything in his life. 'I instructed him to tell your creditors I had every confidence you would redeem your promises. In time.' Slowly he shook his massive head; his sigh would have fluttered the sails of every vessel in the river. 'I regret to say they cared nothing for the promises we made on your behalf. They wanted one of two things: the immediate payment of the returns on their investment that it appears you promised them before leaving London, or a refund of their capital. Immediately, Captain Dark, and in full. They were talking law courts, Captain. They were talking debtors' prison. Or worse, Captain Dark. There was even a whisper of fraud.'

Barnsley crossed to his desk, a weighty man burdened by the sad news it was his unsought duty to deliver. He picked up his glass containing a special Madeira wine, dry and vastly flavoursome, vastly expensive. He had offered none to his visitor. He savoured the wine with every sign of enjoyment, sipping it slowly, taking his time, while his eyes observed Ephraim's ashen face.

He had been in this situation many times yet it never failed to give him exquisite pleasure: the awareness of his power and its ful-filment, the accumulation of the wealth that was the purpose of his life.

'Things would have come good. In time.' Ephraim spoke through dry lips. 'They would have received the returns I promised them.'

No more than the London venturers was Barnsley interested in Ephraim's promises. He put down his glass and sat behind his desk. He spoke briskly.

'I have responsibilities: to my niece, you understand, and to my nephew William. I am unwilling to see them put out into the street because of your business failures.'

Ephraim tried to defend himself. 'The whaling ship you sold me was unsound. Had it been in better shape –'

Barnsley was also uninterested in Ephraim's excuses. 'You bought the ship, did you not? She became your responsibility. That is clear, I think. In any case that represents a relatively minor part of what you have lost. To set out to develop a new port and infrastruc-ture...' He shook his head. 'Insanity, Captain. Utter insanity. To protect my niece I have bought your creditors' paper. Now your debts in London are settled.'

'You mean I now owe you,' Ephraim said.

'No, Captain, you owe the bank.'

'Isn't that the same thing?'

'Not at all the same thing. The bank has its own venturers. They have invested their money in the business and naturally look to enjoy a satisfactory return. We businessmen,' he said with a heavy humour that left his eyes as hard and cold as ever, 'are slaves to our investors, are we not?'

'If you have the faith in me that you say you told the London investors –'

'You owe the bank two hundred thousand pounds,' Barnsley said. 'My investors need to know how you intend to repay them. Not in five or ten years' time. Now. I am sure you understand that if you are unable to meet their just demands your assets will be seized. I have – most regrettably, Captain! – already arranged to have your trading fleet impounded.'

The hair was prickling on the back of Ephraim's neck. 'You plan to take Derwent as well?'

'Indeed. And the extravagant house I am informed you have had built there. It grieves me to be the bearer of such bad news,' Barnsley said, 'but I have always found it best to face facts, however unpalatable they may be.'

Ephraim rode slowly home, barely conscious of the rain soaking through his clothes. Inwardly he was raging over the banker's barely concealed contempt. *Settle up now – in full – or face ruin.* Dear sweet Christ, he thought, I am bankrupt. What do I do now?

There are fortunes to be made in Van Diemen's Land.

London's eager investors, thirsty for profit, had believed him; he had believed himself. He refused to accept he had been foolish or even reckless; he had been confident that his prophecies would come true.

As he remained convinced that, with time, they would have done.

It was a bitter thought because Barnsley Tregellas had made it clear it was too late. For the moment Ephraim might still own Derwent, the sheep and a whale ship, a small fleet of trading vessels, a large area of forest and a partially developed port at Emu Bay on the north coast, even a half-constructed sawmill – all of them assets that in other circumstances would have enabled him to build up the great fortune that was his heart's desire – but his debts had swallowed him up. The one essential commodity that he lacked was time and that had destroyed him.

He looked at the house as he came over the rise. The rain had stopped and the sun's rays were warm on the grey walls standing amid the trees with the river flowing beyond. Their home.

For how much longer?

He trotted down the slope, the bay lengthening her stride as she neared the stable block behind the house and the oats she sensed would be awaiting her. The groom Abraham was waiting to take the mare as Ephraim dismounted. His horse; his groom.

For how much longer?

Emma had heard the sound of the hooves and had come to the door to greet him as she always did. Baby William was in her arms with shy Richard hanging back behind her. He greeted the baby and shook Richard's hand as though he were a man and not a six-year-old boy.

Emma was wearing a day gown that was one of his favourites, her hair loose and shining in the sun. She smiled at him with lively eyes, greeting him with the warmth that never failed to move his heart. Yet her happiness at seeing him was not mindless; she leant back in his arms and looked at him questioningly.

'Something has happened,' she said. 'What is it?'

'Let us go indoors,' he said.

It was a bad business having to tell Emma that after all his big talk their hopes and dreams had come to nothing and that he could see no way out of their predicament. It was even worse having to suggest she might intercede with her uncle on their behalf.

'If he is not prepared to be merciful I fear there is no hope for us.'

Her expression had not changed as she listened to him. He had been watching her as he spoke, fearing to see contempt in her face but observing only a form of beauty he had never previously known:

a strength and resolution to ride out whatever darkness might be lying ahead of them.

'We both know him,' she said. 'I do not believe mercy is in his nature. On the contrary; I suspect he planned this deliberately. Two hundred thousand pounds? He knows we have no hope of repaying such a sum. We have known for a long time that the whale ship he sold you was no good.'

'That is only a small part of the problem. I confess I should have been more careful but I never thought he would turn on us like this: I trusted him, you see.'

'And he cheated you. As I hear from Lady Arthur he has cheated many others. It seems he has a name for it. It is he who should be ashamed, not you.'

'I do not know whether he cheated us or simply outsmarted us. What is certain is that we are at his mercy.'

'And my uncle is not a merciful man.'

'You see no point in speaking to him?'

'Certainly I would like to speak to him. In a practical sense there is no point; he will still take the land and house and everything we possess. I believe that has always been his objective and there is nothing we can do to stop him. But it would do me a deal of pleasure to give him a piece of my mind.'

She laughed: angry, defiant and – yes! – joyous.

Ephraim stared. He had feared anger, contempt, tears... Never this. Yet this was the woman who had challenged Lady Raedwald and won. Now, to see her laugh in the face of adversity...

He thought he had never truly appreciated his wife before.

She saw his expression and laughed even more. 'I love challenge,' she said.

'But what shall we do? After you've told your uncle what you think of him?'

'You still have *Ocean Rider*?'

Ocean Rider was one of his fleet, a forty-foot sloop Ephraim had bought when he planned to bring Kanaka labour from the islands to work as shepherds on their land. Barnsley might have impounded his other vessels but *Ocean Rider* had not been with them and with any luck would for the moment have escaped the banker's attention. That at least was something he might be able to sell.

'Yes, we still have her. I know a man who might be willing to give us a good price for her –'

'Don't sell her,' Emma said. 'Not for any price. Where is she?'

'In an inlet off the harbour.'

'Is there anyone aboard?'

'There's Bailey. A good man. Very experienced. I took him on when I bought the boat. He knows *Ocean Rider* and the sea.'

'Can we trust him?'

'With our lives, I believe,' Ephraim said.

'Will the two of you be enough to sail her?'

'I could manage her alone if I had to but it's easier with two. But what –?'

She did not let him finish his question. 'We must move her before Uncle can get his hands on her. Move her tonight as soon as it's dark. Find somewhere to leave her and then come back.'

'What are you planning to do?' he said.

'I'll tell you.'

Emma believed she had been touched by holiness.

This was the reason providence had brought her across the sea to this island and reunited her with the man she loved: that when the need arose the power within her would guide her in the direction she must go, do what must be done.

'We have talked so much about the unknown lands that lie in the tropics far away to the north of the settled areas,' she said.

Ephraim stared. 'What about them?'

'What better time could we have to seek out the unknown?' Emma said.

Ephraim's heart leapt at his wife's audacity, then fell back. 'Impossible.'

'Why?'

'I cannot take you and the children on such a dangerous mission but I would not feel right leaving you behind.'

'I have no intention of being left behind,' Emma said. 'Or of leaving the children.'

'But –'

'We are one family, Ephraim. You, me and our two sons. We go or stay together and we obviously cannot stay. We shall explore the north side by side.'

'It will not be safe,' Ephraim said.

'Life is not safe. We both know that. Life is for living. We shall live it together.'

'Or perhaps die together?'

'If God so wills.'

He had been afraid Barnsley might move on them straightaway but by the time he left the house that evening they had seen nothing of him or his men.

He decided it would be best to go by foot so he followed the riverbank. It was dark but the water shone in the starlight and there was no danger of losing his footing. Now he no longer felt so help-less his old injury was troubling him less than it had, so he made good time.

Ocean Rider was moored well away from the harbour's main traf-fic, in a deepwater inlet overhung by trees that grew close to the bank. It was dark, the sloop barely visible in the shadows, and the air was still.

Ephraim stood at the edge of the water and gave a soft whistle: three notes rising and then descending. He waited. There was no light from *Ocean Rider*, no sign of movement, but a few seconds later Ephraim heard an answering whistle in the same cadence.

'Coming aboard,' Ephraim said in a soft voice – sounds travelled far across water.

He drew in the mooring line. The water rippled about the bow as the sloop glided towards the land.

Ephraim stepped aboard.

Bailey was a short man with massive shoulders and arms and a large head. Ephraim had found him wandering the waterfront after his vessel had been lost in a storm, cast upon the rocks at the southern end of the D'Entrecasteaux Channel. He had been looking for a captain's berth and would take nothing less. He'd had no luck until Ephraim had seen him, liked the look of him and taken him on. To be master of a forty-foot sloop was a comedown after a two-masted brig but as he said to Ephraim it was a ship and a neat one at that and he was in charge. And maybe one day they would go adventuring.

A man with a mysterious past, he must have had a first name but Ephraim did not know it. Bailey he was and Bailey he would remain. Like the man himself, it would serve. Now he stared at Ephraim in the darkness.

'Something up, Captain?'

'You always said you wanted to go adventuring,' Ephraim said. 'Now you may get your wish.'

'Visiting Poseidon at last?' The seaman rubbed exultant hands. 'Good news, Captain. Excellent news.'

'Let's hope it's not Davey Jones,' Ephraim said.

'Up to us to make sure it isn't. No, Captain, there'll be no drowning this trip. It's Poseidon we'll be seeing. God of the sea, Captain! He saved me before and I owe him a visit. We've kept him waiting long enough. Where are we headed? Into the Pacific?'

'We're going north. See what the country up there has to offer.'

'Into the unknown? Even better! Makes my blood run hot, Captain. Maybe build ourselves an empire up there?'

'Maybe we shall.'

They went below into the cabin. Bailey lit the gimballed lantern. Ephraim looked about him in the smoky light. A tidy bunk was inset into the port side of the cabin; the wooden bulkheads glowed with polish; a chart table had navigation instruments secured neatly in a cabinet mounted behind it.

'When shall we be leaving?' Bailey asked.

'Soon as we can get away.'

'And you come a-calling after dark? My nose tells me something's up, Captain. Want to tell me what it is?'

Ephraim explained about Barnsley Tregellas and the money he was claiming.

Bailey nodded. 'Sounds a good reason to be moving on,' he said. 'I say let the bastard stew for his money, isn't that right?'

He opened a locker, took out a bottle of rum and two mugs and poured a generous tot into each. He lifted his mug.

'Here's to a prosperous voyage and damnation to all bankers,' he said.

They drank.

'So what's the plan, Captain?'

'The tide's nearly full. When the ebb starts we'll make our way downriver, find a place to lie up for a couple of days while we stock her with provisions, then head north.'

'Just you and me, Captain?'

'Plus Mrs Dark and the two boys.'

Bailey's heavy fingers played with his mug. 'Some think a woman aboard is bad luck, Captain. And people say it's wild country up there.'

Their eyes met.

'No choice,' Ephraim said.

'Whatever you say.' Bailey laughed and refreshed their mugs. 'What I've read, Poseidon was powerfully attracted to the ladies so I daresay it'll be all right.'

The hull of the sloop stirred beneath them.

'There's the ebb,' Bailey said. 'Best get under way.'

It took no time to hoist sail and cast off. Within minutes they were heading out into the main channel. The wind was from the north; with sails boomed out and the ebb strong beneath their keel they were soon making good time.

'Wind and tide with us,' Bailey exulted, his whisper like the rumble of chain in the anchor locker. 'We'll soon be clear of this lot.'

The channel ran close to the ships in the harbour. *Ocean Rider* ghosted silently past the anchored vessels, the only sound the chuckle of water around the forefoot. This was the dangerous time; some of these ships were owned by Barnsley Tregellas and Ephraim knew if they were going to be challenged it would be here, but there was no challenge and soon the scattered lights of Hobart Town had faded into the distance astern.

An hour downriver they found a narrow waterway overhung with trees on the river's western bank. They lowered the mainsail as Bailey changed course. Under foresail alone they entered the inlet, the mast brushing leaves from the trees as they passed. Ephraim plumbed the depths continuously as Bailey conned the sloop further into the narrowing inlet. Soon they were deep enough for the trees to hide them from any traffic passing along the river. Bailey eased the jib.

'Best go no further,' he said. 'We'll be running out of water directly.'

They drew into the bank and Ephraim went ashore.

'I'll be back with supplies tomorrow,' he said. 'Or maybe the day after.'

'How will you get them here?'

'Mules should do it,' Ephraim said.

'And the family?'

'Mules should do it,' Ephraim said.

'Looks like those children will be brought up hard,' Bailey said.

'No choice,' Ephraim said.

'You got a long walk, Captain. How's your foot?'

'My foot is fine,' Ephraim said.

All the same it was heavy going through the bush and his foot was indeed aching like the devil by the time he finally got back to the house, with the dawn breaking in the sky beyond the river.

Emma said she had not slept.

'Have we heard from your uncle?'

'A note was hand-delivered last night.'

'A letter of demand?'

'Yes. But not for the two hundred thousand.'

'What then?'

'He sent it to me personally, demanding payment of a thousand pounds he claims he lent my father back in 1824. The note says as Father's beneficiary I am responsible for his debts.'

'Surely your father was insolvent? Does that not nullify the claim?'

'We cannot prove it, can we? And with my uncle's influence the lawyers here will surely support his claim.' She gave a sharp laugh. 'He also wants interest: eighteen per cent per annum compounded over ten years. Seven thousand pounds, or so he claims.'

The scorn in her voice snared Ephraim's attention. 'You checked his figures?'

'At eighteen per cent for ten years the total comes to a little over five thousand pounds,' she said. 'He lied, even about that.'

'I suspect he's an expert liar,' Ephraim said. 'But it's not important. You're not going to be paying him anyway.'

'That's right,' Emma said. 'All being well we'll be long gone by the time he finds out.'

'I still think you should reconsider that,' he said. 'For the sake of the boys if not your own. It is so unwise –'

She framed his face with her hands and pressed a finger to his lips. 'No, Ephraim! We decided.'

'You mean you decided,' he said.

'Let us say we decided,' she said. 'We are one family and will go together.' She gave him a gay smile. 'Don't forget, if I stay here Uncle Barnsley will be after me for the money he says I owe him.'

'But –'

'So let us rather think what we have to do to get ready for our voyage north. Though it pains me that after all the effort I've put into it we've lost our lovely house,' she said.

'We'll get it back one of these days.'

'When we've made our fortune?'

'Exactly.'

It was time to sit down and make lists of all the things they would need to take with them.

'There is something I want us to do first,' said Emma.

He looked questioningly at her.

'Not much privacy on a small boat.'

'That's true.'

'So maybe we should do something about it while we can.'

'What do you have in mind?'

She took his hand and led him into their bedroom. She turned to him, Ephraim smiling now.

'This,' she said.

A hurried shedding of clothes. A radiant smile as she drew him down.

'It'll be weeks,' she said afterwards as they got dressed again. 'Maybe months. Do you think we'll forget how?'

'I don't think it's something you forget,' he said.

'Thank the dear Lord for that,' she said.

They sat down to prepare lists of the things they would need.

'It's hard when we don't know how long we'll be away.'

'Could be years,' Ephraim said. 'Could be forever.'

'And if your foot needs treatment?'

'We'll take an axe,' he said.

Flour, meat, fruit; axe, spade and tools of various kinds.

'We'll have to build a shelter of some sort,' Ephraim said.

'Children's books,' Emma said. 'I'll not have them growing up unable to read and write. Clothes and medical supplies too.'

'Water,' Ephraim said. 'Maybe a little whisky.'

'Guns and ammunition,' Emma said. 'We mustn't forget those.'

He looked at her admiringly: so young, so strong, so brave. 'Feeling warlike, are we?'

'Like an Amazon,' Emma said.

'You intend to go bare breasted, do you? Like I've read the Amazons did?'

'In front of Mr Bailey? I don't think so.'

The rest of the day was a whirlwind but by the end of it Ephraim had obtained the services of a muleteer and three mules and the stores were piled in wooden crates, so many that it was hard to squeeze through the door of the house.

All day they had been afraid Emma's uncle would descend on them; they had learnt to detest him because of his mean ways but neither had any doubt about his uncanny ability to know everyone else's business.

'If he comes maybe we can shoot him,' Emma said.

'And hang for it? In any case he's more likely to send his men than come himself.'

'Will I have time to say goodbye to Lady Arthur?'

'I know she's your friend,' Ephraim said. 'But she won't want anything to do with you once she hears we've lost our money. Her husband would never allow it.'

'You're right,' Emma said. 'Such a wretched business this is.'

'I am sorry I let you down,' Ephraim said.

'You didn't. Uncle Barnsley cheated you, that's what happened. I have every faith in you, Captain Dark. I know we shall be rich and famous after we've opened up the north.'

It was a declaration of faith that brought a lump to his throat.

Baby William was screaming murder when they left the following morning. It was still dark, the only other sounds the soft sighing of the mules, the coaxing voice of the muleteer as he urged them along, the creaking of the wagon carrying the stores.

It was slow going through the bush but by mid-afternoon they had reached the inlet where *Ocean Rider* lay concealed.

Ephraim paid the muleteer. 'And you've never set eyes on us, is that clear?'

'I'll not breathe a word,' the man said. 'Barnsley Tregellas would have my hide if he knew I'd helped you, the bastard.'

They off-loaded the wagon and within minutes the muleteer, his animals and the wagon had vanished into the bush.

It took the three of them a long time to get the stores on board; it took longer still to find places for everything.

'I doubt we'll be able to fit it all in,' Emma said.

But they managed in the end.

'Now we wait for the tide,' Bailey said. 'Once the ebb starts we'll be on our way.'

'Where shall we sleep?'

'There are two bunks in the forepeak,' Bailey said.

The ebb arrived on schedule. By midnight they were a mile off shore and heading north under a stars-bright sky.

Afterwards Emma had no idea how long the voyage had taken.

The wind had been cold as they headed up the east coast of Van Diemen's Land, the seas grey and at times rough with spray arching high over the bows.

A westerly gale came howling as they crossed the waterway that Governor Hunter had named Bass Strait back in 1800. The force of the wind blew them almost flat. Even with sails heavily reefed the wind and tumultuous seas combined to sweep them miles to the east, but once they had fought their way into the shelter of the mainland the seas moderated, the wind lost its edge; the days grew warm, then hot.

Emma had her hands full with the two boys. Richard, into every-thing and always wanting to explore, was more trouble than baby William, although even he caused more problems than she would have expected. She experimented, taking him out of his basket and putting him on a towel on the deck, but after he had twice come close to rolling into the sea she abandoned that idea and back into the basket he went. That infuriated him and he screamed louder than the gulls that had followed them all the way up the coast, but Emma did not relent.

'Better angry than drowned,' she told him.

For days on end she watched the coastline. Often it was barely visible over the horizon yet she still sensed the mystery and challenge of the unknown. What was there? What dangers? What treasures?

She saw water creatures, sleek and shining, that accompanied the sloop for miles.

'Dolphins,' Mr Bailey said.

'I wondered whether they might be mermaids,' she said.

She asked if he had ever seen a mermaid but he laughed and did not answer.

Even without the mermaids it was a world of wonder. She leant with hands on the rail, breathing in the salt air. She had wondered whether she would be afraid of what lay ahead of them but instead found herself falling in love with what she was coming to think was the most wonderful adventure.

A new life, she thought. After the disappointments of Hobart Town it was a thrilling prospect.

'*We were the first who ever burst into that silent sea*,' she declaimed, remembering a poem that she had read years before.

Except these seas were not silent but alive with the silver glint of sunlight, the hiss and song of the waves, the creaking of the rigging as day by day they made their way towards the unknown lands far to the north.

She asked if the men knew where they were going and what they planned to do when they got there.

'There are islands,' Bailey said. 'Captain James Cook named them the Whitsundays but I never met anyone who's been there. The only thing I do know is there's gold there.'

He told them it was a fact well known among mariners.

'Lying on the surface of the ground,' he said. 'Nuggets of pure gold.'

'If no one's been there how do they know? And why has no one collected it before?' Emma said.

Shortage of food, Bailey thought. Shortage of water. Sickness might have played a hand. There could be any number of reasons. The one thing he was sure about was that the gold was there. Many sailors had told him so. He would stake his life on it.

But hadn't they talked about building a house, establishing a settlement?

Yes, Ephraim agreed, they had. 'But surely you can see that the gold has changed everything?' he said.

It was plain that to her husband, as well as to Mr Bailey, the existence of the gold had become a matter of faith.

Four days later a succession of islands appeared over the northern horizon, a chain of green extending out into the ocean from the mainland.

Emma clung to the bowsprit with Ephraim beside her as *Ocean Rider* crested the waves. 'Are they the islands Mr Bailey was talking about?' she asked.

'I reckon.'

'So what do we do now?'

'Find a secure anchorage first of all. Then we'll go ashore.'

'On one of the islands?'

'Or the mainland.'

'And start picking up the gold,' said Emma, who had no faith in the story.

'Why not? If it's as plentiful as Bailey seems to think.'

An hour later they dropped anchor in the calm waters of a bay on the lee side of an island a quarter mile from the mainland. The anchorage was sheltered on three sides by high green hills. They watched the land but saw no sign of human activity. Richard was vocal in his demands to go ashore and turned sulky when he was told he would have to wait.

'He's been cooped up so long,' Emma said. 'Can't we let him have a run before it gets dark?'

Ephraim pointed at an object lying on the muddy bank that fringed the water.

'What's that?' Emma said.

'A crocodile,' he said. 'Bailey says there are lots of them in these waters.'

'Crocodiles?' Emma's voice went up an octave: nobody had mentioned crocodiles before. 'How do we get ashore if there are crocodiles?'

'We shoot them.'

That night they stayed aboard but shortly after first light the following morning Ephraim and Bailey rowed over to the mainland. Emma stood at the rail and watched them. She saw no sign of crocodiles but that didn't mean they weren't there. With the dinghy drawn up on the sand, the two men climbed the tree-covered slope that rose behind the beach. They crested the summit and disappeared.

Now she was alone.

1913

A kookaburra was calling from the trees that lined the dusty road as Bec Hampton walked through the early morning sunshine to the show.

She was dolled up in her smartest clothes: white blouse, the one with the bit of lace at the neck, full-length navy skirt and black boots smeared with dust, broad-brimmed summer hat of yellow straw with the blue ribbon. Bec Hampton, sixteen years old and full of the joys and juices of youth, was heading to the annual Campbell Town show to make the most of whatever excitement she might find when she got there. She would have liked to wear the little jacket she'd had from Mrs Painter of Waldren's Corner, for whom she'd done some chores, but the summer day was going to be too hot for a jacket.

She regretted that, but only for a moment; Bec Hampton was not given to regretting much in her life. What was the use? Dad and Mum were as they were, which was fair to middling at best and often a lot worse, especially Dad when he'd had a skinful, and there was no one else who mattered in her life. Cyril Stubbs would have taken an interest if she'd given him the wink but she wouldn't have touched Cyril with a ten-foot pole; his dad might own a small farm but everyone knew Cyril was a brick short of a load.

Bec was not alone; Frances Tickell had agreed to come with her but Frances had no more bounce than a rubber ball with a hole in it so Frances didn't really count except as a companion to join in whatever fun might be waiting for them.

It was Saturday 15 February and by ten o'clock it was already as hot as fire, as the Tasmanian midlands usually were at that time of year.

'It'll be fair sizzling later,' said Frances. 'You mark my words.'

'It's doing a good job already,' said Bec, feeling a trickle of sweat worming its way down her front. It tickled but it would be impolite to scratch, especially there, so she let it be.

'It's gunna be a hot one,' Frances said.

Frances was the sort who'd be married long before she'd met her husband. Because she *would* be married – you knew that as soon as you looked at her – knew too that the identity of the victim wouldn't matter.

Whereas Bec... Bec was different.

The way things worked out, that was lucky.

Campbell Town's agricultural show was an annual event, the biggest of its kind in the midlands – some said in the whole of Tasmania – and there were people everywhere. Not only people: there were mobs of sheep and cattle, produce stalls, flags and bunting, sideshows, places to eat, places to drink, a steady surge of farming folk on the hunt for bargains.

Bec and Frances picked their way across the dusty ground past the judging tents where competition was fierce for the best wether in show, the best ram, the best poddy calf, the best colt, the best bull. There was a hurdy-gurdy, steam engine pumping. There was a fat lady stall and a boxing booth. A shearing competition with five quid for the winner drew a crowd, as did the axeman competition, wood chips flying in a frenzy of blows from blokes wider than any barn door.

The dust was awesome as was the noise: the squawk and cackle of poultry almost lost behind the bellowing of livestock, the rhythmic patter of auctioneers from the auction ring.

'Ten bob I'm bid. Ten bob, eleven, fourteen. And sixpence. Fourteen bob and a tanner I'm bid. Any more? All done?' A crack, sharp as a gunshot, as the hammer came down. 'Sold!'

The girls poked their noses into this stall and that; they inspected the homemade cakes, the woolly jumpers for kiddies; the Empire mugs at the china and glass stall. They each wasted a halfpenny at the hoopla, drank a lemonade at the refreshments tent, watched sweaty men arguing prices over sudsy beers. They walked on. Along the edges of the track the grass was already wilting under the hot sun.

'So many people,' Frances said.

'There always are.'

'Even some from Hobart, I wouldn't wonder.'

Hobart was another universe to Frances Tickell.

'There always are.'

Two hours after they arrived the frenzied barking of dogs alerted Bec to trouble. First it was one dog, followed a moment later by a second. Then came a sudden cacophony of barks, a frenzied racket in the sunlight. Frances would have walked on but Bec had an instinct for dogs and cocked an ear. 'Something's up.'

'They're only dogs,' said Frances.

'It's more than that. Something's wrong.'

They walked around the corner of a big marquee and there it was.

It was a paddock where the livestock were readied for showing or for the auction ring. In the middle of the paddock was a small boy, maybe five or six years old. He was alone and a few paces from him was a bull that had somehow escaped its handlers and now stood staring at the child, head down, front hooves raking the dusty ground. No sign of the boy's parents or the bull's minders; only the dogs performing but not game to get too close.

'Ohmygod.'

While clouds of dust billowed behind the raking hooves.

Bec looked around but there was no sign of anybody.

'Maybe we should go for help,' Frances whispered.

'By the time anyone comes that bull will have had him,' Bec said.

'If we shout at it?'

Frances didn't know bulls from armchairs.

'That'll just annoy it. There's only one way to deal with this.'

The child was less than twenty feet from the bull, well inside the animal's comfort zone. If she could get him to back away…

The boy was looking about him, sensing his danger, on the edge of running.

She had to stop him doing that.

Bec walked out slowly into the paddock. The bull's head was lowered, its shoulders hunched. As she watched it curved its neck towards the boy.

One false move and it would charge. If the boy ran…

The bull would come after him.

The child was thirty yards away now. Bec's every instinct was to run to him but that would be dangerous. It might even be fatal.

Somehow she had to ignore her screaming nerves. Slow and steady was the only way.

Twenty yards.

Now she could see the child trembling, on the edge of panic. On the edge of flight.

She began to talk to him, speaking in a quiet voice, hoping to calm him. 'It'll be all right. Don't move. Whatever you do, don't move.'

Ten yards.

The bull's head was still down, its right front hoof raking the ground.

Bec stopped.

'Now back towards me. Slowly. You'll be quite safe. That's the way. That's right. That's lovely.' She sharpened her voice. 'Don't turn round. Keep your eyes on him.'

Bec too was watching the bull. She was conscious that other people had arrived and were now watching from the edge of the paddock. A woman screamed but none of that mattered; for the moment there was nothing anyone else could do. Out there she and the boy were alone. Alone with the bull.

She was calm now, her veins like ice.

'Come on now,' she said to the slowly moving boy. 'That's right. Everything's jake. Come on now.'

She had one eye on the boy, the other on the bull. Which still – thank God! – had not moved. She reached out her hands and at last took the boy by his frail-seeming shoulders. This precious child. How he was trembling!

He wasn't the only one.

She spoke soothingly. 'We're all right now. We're fine.'

They were edging backwards, moving steadily away from danger. Ten yards from the bull; twenty yards. Now – surely? – they were outside the animal's comfort zone. Now – surely? – they were safe.

They backed into the waiting crowd. The boy's mother snatched him up, weeping. Arms held Bec too. She was unsure whether her legs would go on supporting her or whether she was about to collapse in a heap on the dusty ground. The mother, sobbing, was saying something to her but the words did not register. She did not know what to do with her hands, her body. Tears pricked her eyes as she surrendered herself to the arms that held her.

Frances was fussing, her face wet with the tears of remembered terror, but Bec was too weary to pay her any attention now.

In the middle of the paddock the bull was grazing, innocence personified, while those from whom it had escaped approached it cautiously.

That blessed creature might have killed me, Bec thought with mounting outrage. Killed me and the boy. How could they have been so careless? But her weakness was such that she could not sustain even outrage for long.

'You orright, miss?'

She had no idea who the man was.

'I'll be fine in a minute,' she said.

A la-di-da man's voice said, 'I'll look after her now.'

Looking at the newcomer, Bec saw and for a moment was unsure. Then memory brought back the past.

'Jonathan?' Her voice sounded as weak as she felt, yet inside her suddenly leaping heart she was not weak at all. Inside she was all smiles. 'When did you get back?'

Jonathan had missed out on the ram, the final bid far above what the agent had thought the beast was worth. He had considered heading home again but then decided that as he was there he might as well look around the show.

He had been strolling about for ten minutes when he came across the drama of the bull, the child and the brave girl who had brought the little boy to safety. It was only after she was back in the crowd that he realised who the girl was.

Bec Hampton. It was three years since he had seen her. She had grown up a lot in that time; grown up and developed too. She had been an attractive child. Now she was no longer a child, there was no doubt about that. No longer merely attractive, either; now she was beautiful.

Oh God she was beautiful. And brave. He had seen her do something not one person in a thousand could have done. He was not sure he would have had the guts to do it himself.

So many things people did not know. About themselves. About others.

He knew this much. He saw she was trembling. Shock, no doubt, knowing how close to death she had come. How she had faced it down.

Faced it down and won.

Jonathan was trembling too. Trembling at feeling something in him that he had never expected.

This beautiful woman.

It was ridiculous to feel such a thing. She was not for him, not in a thousand years. They lived on different planets, Derwent House and... He didn't even know where she lived nowadays. He knew only that her father had looked after the Derwent horses before he'd decided to move on.

Grandma Bessie said it proved he could not be relied upon but Jonathan knew he had saved his father's life in the Boer War. He never knew the details; only knew that much because his father had told him.

He remembered Rebecca's father was called Conan. Conan Hampton. An Irish name and an Irish temper to go with it, or so Grandma had said.

At his father's funeral he'd asked Conan about the Boer War business.

'What business would that be?'

'Father told me you saved his life.'

'Did he now? I wouldn't have put it like that meself but who am I to argue with the likes of your dad?'

'He said you helped him escape after the Boers shot him.'

'I've only the haziest memory of them days. So I couldn't say what happened, one way or the other.'

And went off whistling.

Grandma had seen him talking to Conan and ticked him off for it. 'It doesn't do to get too familiar with the staff. They only take advantage.'

'He saved Father's life.'

'Is that what he told you? Bragging, no doubt.'

'It was Father said it, not Conan. He told me nothing.'

Her smile might have been dipped in acid. 'No doubt because there was nothing to tell.'

'Why are you so unfair?'

Her laugh brushed his question away. 'He works for the estate. Provided he does his job I have no feelings about him, one way or the other.'

She was lying; Jonathan sensed it but had only found out the reason years later. Derwent was like a monastery in some ways, a closed community where the inhabitants knew everything about each other's business but little of what went on in the outside world.

Ethel, one of the housemaids, told him about it.

'Put Mary Smith in the family way 'e did. Probably the only reason 'e married 'er.'

'Bec's dad?'

At that age Jonathan hadn't been sure exactly what Ethel was talking about, only that she had made it sound somehow shameful and therefore exciting, but it was another reason to think of Bec Hampton as special.

There were other reasons. The six years between them had ruled out playing together but he had seen her about the place all her life. Also Bec had been the only other child on the property, which made them allies even though they didn't speak much.

'Don't let 'er know I told you, mind,' Ethel said.

The day at the Campbell Town show brought all those thoughts and memories together. He was looking at a woman, no longer a child, whose actions had proved how special she was. The heroine daughter of a hero father.

One more thing. She was a woman who lived in a world as different from his as it was possible to be yet who between one moment and the next had driven a needle into his heart.

She had a friend with her. He remembered nothing about her. She was with them but it was as though she didn't exist.

They found a café. Jonathan forgot what they ate. Later he found he had forgotten almost everything about that meeting, the first between them as adults, yet one thing he did remember. Sitting at the little table and eating whatever it was they had chosen, it felt not like a first meeting or first anything but a continuation of everything he had ever known, as though the simple fact of their meeting had made her a party to even those episodes about which she could know nothing: his education in England for instance. By being with him now she had become part of everything he had known and done.

How that could be he didn't know. What it implied for the present he didn't know either; even less what it might imply for the future.

He had no thoughts at all yet was more aware than he had ever been in his life.

He was; she was. That was all. It was enough.

She told him she lived with her parents at her father's forge near Waldren's Corner, where she occasionally helped out Mrs Painter, the constable's wife. Jonathan asked after her parents; she said they were well. She asked after his mother and grandmother; he said they were well.

He asked if she was married; she laughed and said of course not. She asked him the same; he told her no.

They walked around the show for a while then went their separate ways. He took it for granted they would be seeing each other again, and soon. Anything else was unthinkable.

1834

The island and the sloop anchored in its protective bay were out of sight now. Ahead of them the forested ground ran steeply downhill to where at the bottom of the slope Ephraim could see the silvery glint of water.

Eyes and ears alert, the two men eased their way cautiously between the trees. They saw neither animal nor human but the weight of the silence was heavy upon them. A clatter of wings as a bird flew, then silence returned.

Ephraim's hand was never far from his gun as he remembered the skirmish that had left one trooper and five Aborigines dead and he with the spear wound that had ended his military career. He had thought it a disaster at the time but had long since changed his opinion. Without the injury he would never have met Emma and that good fortune he would treasure all his days.

It was Emma and her determination and lust for life that had lifted him from despair, bringing him and the children to this place so far from civilisation, days beyond even the most remote outpost of British power. Here they would restore their fortunes and his lost pride, and it was thanks to Emma that it was so.

The question now was how they were going to do it – and a hard question it was.

So little was known of these islands or the mainland vastness on the edge of which they now stood. People said this north country was inhabited only by wild beasts and savages but no one knew even that for sure. Bailey was still insisting there was gold there. Perhaps he was right, but it was timber, not gold, from which Ephraim hoped to make his fortune. Perhaps from fisheries and cattle, too, if adequate grazing could be found. From all three, perhaps, and even from gold if the fates were kind.

There were questions that would have to be answered before anything could be done. He did not think the heat would be right for sheep but would cattle flourish in a climate like this? Assuming they could, would they be able to ship them to the southern markets or would the costs be too great? Remembering the problems he'd had in Van Diemen's Land, would he be able to recruit enough men to take care of them? In this unfamiliar country might there not be unknown diseases that would affect both cattle and humans?

One thing was sure: there were vast numbers of mosquitoes that plagued them every step of the way. Mosquitoes did you no lasting harm, but was it not possible that other more deadly creatures might live in these uncharted woods?

There would certainly be snakes and probably savages as well. How would they take the arrival of white men in their territory?

At a distance, making a fortune in the unnamed country of the far north had sounded simple; it looked a lot less straightforward now they were there.

They reached the bank of the creek flowing along the valley floor. Sunlight kindled silver sparks upon the surface of the water and its noise was loud in the silence. Beyond the creek the land, heavily timbered, rose to another ridge.

They filled their water bottles, waded the creek, the mosquitoes worse than ever here, and pressed on up the slope. Even under the trees the air was hot and humid, with a whiff of decay from the rotting vegetation. Climbing the slope was hard work but eventually they came out on the crest and inspected the country that lay ahead. The charred stumps of trees showed where fires had burnt the forest, with the emerald shoots of new growth bright amid the ash: grass and what might be the beginnings of new trees. Pasture and timber?

Ephraim fingered the soil beneath the ash. 'Feels pretty good,' he said. 'Reckon this will be good grazing land.'

'Looks to me these fires were lit deliberately,' Bailey said.

Ephraim agreed. 'Too neat and tidy for a wild fire,' he said.

They looked at each other.

'In which case there's got to be people about,' Bailey said.

'We haven't seen any,' Ephraim said.

'But maybe they've seen us.'

It was an uneasy thought. They stared across the scorched land but saw only birds circling in the distance, the occasional plume where ash was lifted by the light breeze. No animals; no people.

'No gold either,' Ephraim said.

'It's here,' Bailey said. 'It's just a question of finding it.'

They walked on.

They found what remained of an animal that had been caught by the fire. The flesh that remained was black with bones protruding; it was this that had attracted the birds.

Still no sign of the people who had lit the fire.

'Maybe they've moved on,' Bailey said.

And maybe they hadn't.

They reached the forest fringe and stopped. The trees here were tall and strong.

Good timber; good pasture. And they had already found from the lines they had trailed behind the sloop during the last days of the voyage that the seas were full of fish.

'I've seen enough,' Ephraim said. 'Let's get back.'

Aboard *Ocean Rider* Ephraim told Emma what they had discovered.

'There is good water. Good pasturage and plenty of timber. I would say all this land has huge potential.'

'And the islands?'

'We'll explore them later but it's the mainland that interests me.'

'We came across an area cleared by fire,' Bailey said.

'But we didn't see anybody,' Ephraim said.

Emma looked at the two men. 'Are you saying the fire was deliberately lit?'

'Looks like it,' Bailey said.

'I was thinking if we could make contact with the local people, we might be able to persuade some of them to work for us,' Ephraim said.

'Why would they do that?' Emma said.

From her expression it was obvious she didn't much like the idea of having savages in the area.

Ephraim avoided answering the question. 'It won't hurt to ask.'

'Speak their language, do you?'

Ephraim was irritated by such practical considerations. 'We shall manage somehow.'

And if they're hostile?

But this Emma did not say. 'I would like to see the country for myself,' she said.

They were talking about making their home there, after all. She thought she could handle the distance and solitude, for a while anyway, but the prospect of becoming involved in a war with the locals was not something she was prepared to contemplate.

'The natives trouble me,' Emma said.

It was night. She and Ephraim lay in their bunks in *Ocean Rider*'s forepeak, whispering to each other so that Bailey could not hear them. A lantern hanging from an overhead beam cast shifting light on the lockers and bulkheads.

'When we came north we knew we'd meet up with them.'

He was right but it didn't stop Emma feeling uneasy now the notion had become reality. Yet she had been the one who had insisted they travel there as a family.

'What's the country like?'

Would it be suitable for making the fortune they wanted? Suitable for making a life so far away from everything and everyone they knew?

'We didn't go very far but from what I saw I'd say it's ideal.'

'Enough to attract other settlers to come here?'

Otherwise they would be doomed to endless solitude.

'Why not?'

Provided the natives were welcoming. But how could they find out whether they were or not?

Emma saw it would be dangerous whatever they did but that was life, was it not? She loved this man, had loved him from the moment she first saw him; that was the one certainty in her life. Both their lives, together and apart, had been subject to danger. The danger of her being forced into what would have been a cata-strophic marriage; she had avoided that. After she had been obliged to sail without him it had meant the near certainty they would never find each other again, yet find each other they had. Uncle Barnsley had set out deliberately to destroy their future, yet there they still were. Danger every step of the way, yet always they had survived. There would be danger now, if they pursued their dream of settling in this unknown land, yet they had stood by each other from the first. Would she abandon the dream now because of what might be only imaginary dangers?

Warmth filled her, a combination of love and desire that made the breath catch in her throat. She stretched out an arm to him.

'Come,' she said. 'Come.'

She was consumed by impatience. He smiled and joined her. Later, loins melting, she came to the place of certainty she had sought.

They would face the future, as they had the past, side by side.

1982

Grant Venables had said he was not much of a one for going back but two weeks after Bec's birthday, on a day when Giles, Raine and Jaeger had fortuitously decided to pay a visit to Ross, there he was, driving up the road to the big house.

Tamara was a tangle of words and hands, not knowing what to do with either.

Bec had seen him arrive but kept out of the way, for which Tamara was grateful.

Grant seemed as short of words as she, which was also a comfort. She took him for a walk, giving him the opportunity to revisit the place he had once called home. Back at the house she offered him tea, which he refused, saying he had to be on his way.

'I'm going to Hobart,' he said. 'Thought I would drop in as I was passing.'

Yet he could have followed the more direct route via Bothwell.

'I'm glad you did,' Tamara said. 'When are you coming back?'

'Reckon I'll head up the back road past Great Lake,' he said.

'Chance to do some fishing,' she said.

'Why not? If you ever feel like it,' Grant said, 'you could come by and we could maybe drop a line in the water together.'

'Sounds good.'

'Give me a hoy if you're ever up my way.'

Bec might be old but she didn't miss much.

'When are you seeing him again?'

'Who says I am?'

'It's written all over your face.'

'A sign of your age when you start imagining things,' Tamara said.

'No doubt it will be. When I do,' Bec said. 'Besides, you'd be a fool not to, wouldn't you?'

'Meaning what?'

'Meaning Derwent. If your dad is stupid enough to stick to this nonsense about wanting a man in charge...'

Tamara stared. 'You think he'd put Grant in charge of Derwent?'

'Why not?'

'Grant has a place of his own. Anyway, where would that leave me?'

'Give you a good reason to marry him, wouldn't it?'

Tamara was affronted. 'You're saying I should *use* him? I would never do that.'

'I'm not saying that,' Bec said. 'But if – by pure chance – you happened to fall in love with each other it would make things a lot easier, wouldn't it?'

A week later she said: 'For heaven's sake get up there and see him. Get it over with. You're that jumpy you're making me nervous too.'

'What if it doesn't work out?'

'If it doesn't, it doesn't. At least that way you'll know.'

'Got a spare rod to lend me?'

'Reckon I have. When are you coming?'

'Diary pretty full, is it?'

'You better believe it. I'm fair clagged out.'

'Maybe I should let you rest.'

'Maybe you shouldn't.'

It was such a lovely feeling, warm and jokey together.

'When?' he said.

'Tomorrow?'
'Beauty!'

She drove up to the plateau, trying to outrace her racing heart. He was waiting, careful not to be too obvious about it, with a tinny hitched to the back of the ute. They drove to a launching spot Grant knew and motored out, heading along the shore.

'Reckon we could give it a go here,' Grant said.

They chucked in a couple of wobblies. Tamara reeled in, taking her time, and on the third cast hooked into something that fought her with a vengeance, bowing the rod halfway to the water until she brought the tip up again, the gear shaking as she kept the hooked fish from getting under the boat.

Grant had brought in his lure as soon as Tamara had set her hook and now stood behind her, landing net ready in his hand.

The trout fought a good fight but eventually its battle was done. Its belly showed pale through the dun-coloured water as she brought it in. Grant slipped the net beneath the fish and hoicked it into the boat.

It was a rainbow, a beautiful fish. He smacked it on the head and slung it into the Esky, which was half full of ice.

'My turn,' he said.

By the time they headed back the light was fading, the temperature dropping and they had enough fish to give them a good feed that night with more over for breakfast. If she decided to stay for breakfast.

Back at the cottage he looked at her.

'I was thinking,' she said.

Still he looked.

'I don't want to impose...'

'I would hate that,' he said.

Heat stirred in her belly.

'It would be such a fag to drive all the way to Derwent tonight just to come back again in the morning.'

'Hardly seems sensible, does it?'

'Maybe I could stay over?'

'Maybe you could.'

Grant made a fire, building the logs high in the grate to keep the gathering cold at bay. They ate two of the trout with peas and sliced potatoes, with a bottle of chardonnay to help the food down. Later they sat companionably on the rug in front of the fire, drinking scotch with the flamelight shifting red and orange on their faces, until eventually Grant put his arm around her and she thought yes.

Tamara woke in the night. She sensed the cold air of the plateau beyond the window but beneath the bed coverings she was warm.

So it had happened. It had happened and she was at peace. It had been a good time, a beautiful time, with joy the factor surpassing all else. She was there and would have chosen to be nowhere else on earth.

She turned and slid back down the slope into renewed sleep.

In the morning she woke to the smell of grilling bacon and a deeply troubling thought. What did she intend to tell Grant about her father's attitude to the management of Derwent and would he believe her when she told him she wasn't trying to make use of him? She would have to think about that. But in the meantime...

She called to him. He came.

1834

Early on the morning after their arrival Emma stood on *Ocean Rider*'s deck and watched the sky as it was slowly swallowed by cloud. Even at this hour the sultry heat was suffocating and the water in the anchorage had the sheen of polished brass. A stealthy wind caused the sloop to sway uneasily to its anchor. At least it kept the mosquitoes away.

'Barometer's down and falling,' Bailey said. 'Reckon we're in for some rough weather.'

An emerald glint shafted through a rent in the clouds and the falling pressure brought ants to Emma's skin.

'Time to put out the storm anchor,' Bailey said. 'It never hurts to be sure.'

He lowered the massive bower anchor on its studded chain into the dinghy and rowed away from the sloop, letting the chain out behind him. When he was a hundred yards away he backed his oars and tipped the anchor over the side. It sank in a froth of bubbles and he returned to the sloop.

'That should hold us,' he said. 'But there'll be no going ashore today.'

The sky darkened. Lightning flared. The wind was steady now from the east and strengthening. Beyond the shelter of the hill the bay was flecked with white.

'I'm thinking we'd best get the dinghy out of the water as well,' Bailey said to Ephraim. 'We don't want it blowing away on us.'

They brought the light craft inboard and lashed it securely atop the main hatch. They stripped the mainsail from the yard and stowed it and the jib in the sail locker. They checked that all hatches were secure.

The children were grizzly, Richard in particular put out at missing the chance to go ashore.

'But you promised…'

'And so you will, dear. As soon as it's safe.'

Which it was a long way from being at the moment, with the sky as dark as night and the wind blowing in increasingly heavy gusts.

'Perhaps tomorrow,' Emma hoped.

They drank tea and ate some of the damper she had cooked the previous day. They listened to the wind while the hull shook around them.

'I am going on deck,' Emma said.

Ephraim looked at her. 'Are you mad?'

'I need the air.'

'Make sure you hang on tight.'

A light mist of rain was blowing in from the sea. Legs set sturdily apart, Emma faced it, feeling it wetting her hair, running down her face, soaking into her clothes. A dribble of moisture found its way under the neck of her dress and ran down between her breasts.

The touch of the rain was liberation after the hours she had spent cooped up below deck. *Are you mad?* Ephraim had asked. Well, perhaps she was. And perhaps she didn't care either.

'If I get wet I can always change,' she said.

The rain would have washed the salt out of her clothes which meant they would soon dry.

She had not explained to the men in case Ephraim really did think she was mad, but she was playing out a ceremony to express the lightness that filled her spirit at journey's end. Returning from the mainland the previous day Ephraim had spoken of the land's rich potential; she was therefore also praying he was right and that it would provide them with both a home and the wealth that had eluded them so painfully in Van Diemen's Land. Success was important for them all, especially for Ephraim whose dreams had been so sadly devastated.

She was determined they would triumph. If God so willed.

A crackle of lightning savaged the darkness and the thunder, following close behind, echoed roaring around the peaks of the island behind which they were sheltering.

As Emma went below the rain came with sudden fury, hammering on the deck. The wind rose in a screeching crescendo that drove nails into their ears. Through the portholes they saw the sea lashed to frenzy by the wind. William screamed and fought in Emma's arms, Richard sat mute and round-eyed with terror. The adults stared at each other in the lantern's lurching light and waited for the storm to pass.

They had to wait several hours but by mid-afternoon the worst was over. The rain stopped and the wind eased. The sun came out. Soon they would not have known there had been a storm at all but along the mainland's littoral it was a different story, with broken driftwood littering the shore and sandy beaches washed away. The destruction extended inland with many trees down.

Emma thought the storm signalled the death of their plans, on this coast at least. Ephraim too was wearing a dubious face but Bailey had a different view of things.

He pointed across the water at the debris-strewn shore. 'What are we seeing there?'

'Wreckage,' Emma said. 'The whole area's devastated.'

'But what about us?'

'I don't understand,' Emma said.

Bailey threw up his arms. 'That's the trouble with people. They don't use their eyes or their brains. A storm like that and we're safe. No damage at all. What does that tell you?'

Confused, Emma stared at him.

'It means this harbour is safe,' he said. 'Ships can anchor here and know that even the strongest storm won't damage them. You think the masters of cargo vessels won't understand that? Even the bankers will get the message. We want to ship cattle south, or timber, the boats will be queuing up to take them. And this harbour's big enough to take a dozen vessels at a time. Which means finance won't be a problem either. It will be the making of us!'

The next morning the sea was calm, the sky blue, and they decided to explore the country. They crossed to the mainland, adults and children together, and picked their way across what two days before had been a beach of golden sand. Now there was bare rock, splintered tree trunks, stranded fish and debris of every kind.

Hundreds of jellyfish had been washed up and were drying in the tropical sun but Emma saw no snakes or other dangerous creatures. She kept Richard close all the same, William cradled in a shawl around her neck. This was not a place where it was wise to be too trusting.

Mosquitoes plagued them as they went up through the trees. Everywhere pools of water swarmed with larvae. They followed the same route through the timber that Ephraim and Bailey had taken two days before. When they reached the creek they found it in flood, its racing waters thick with yellow foam and crested by gnashing waves. At this point the stream was a hundred yards wide.

'No way we can cross here,' said Bailey, shouting to be heard over the torrent's roar.

'Maybe we should try upriver,' Ephraim said. 'There may be a crossing up there.'

From this point the ground rose steeply to the ridge. Along the creek bank the mud was thick and Emma knew Richard would not be able to manage it.

'You go,' she said. 'We'll stay here. We'll be all right.'

The men looked doubtful.

'I have the pistol you gave me at Derwent,' she said.

Although whether she would be capable of using it in an emergency she wasn't sure.

More doubtful looks but eventually the men agreed.

'We'll be back within the hour,' Ephraim said.

She watched them clambering over massive boulders as they made their way up the slope. At one point they stopped, Bailey pointing at the ground in front of them. They spent a minute or two clearly discussing what they had seen, looking about them with pistols drawn, but eventually they carried on. Nerves on edge, Emma watched them crest the slope and disappear.

Are you saying the fire was deliberately lit?

Shadows watched. Once again she was alone.

Richard was exploring the creek bank.

'Stay close,' she told him. 'Don't wander off.'

Half an hour after the men had left Emma heard the sound of pistol fire. Her heart lurched. Looking up, she saw the two men reappear at the top of the ridge and come, leaping and bounding down the rocky slope.

1982

Tamara had walked with Grant all over his land.

'It's like a pocket handkerchief compared with Derwent,' Grant said.

He was right but it still covered a good area and his crossbred merinos looked in fine shape.

'She'll be right as long as the wool price holds up,' Grant said.

His feet seemed well anchored in this land. He had told her he had only leasehold title but since it was for twenty-five years Ringarooma was for practical purposes his own. Tamara told herself she was pleased for him, but the truth was she wanted him with her at Derwent, not here, and would prise him away from this place if she could. Always assuming he wanted her for the long term. But did he? How could she be sure?

Confusion everywhere she looked.

They parked at a high point and drank coffee from a flask Grant had brought with him. They looked out over the ridges, peaks and forests of the high country spread below them and she asked herself why anyone should think of leaving this place.

'I hear you've been making some changes at Derwent,' Grant said.

'The computers help paddock management.'

'Place as big as yours, you need something like that.'

'Not everyone would agree with you,' she said, thinking of Bec.

'None so conservative as a high-country grazier,' Grant said.

'You got that right.'

She shifted in her seat, feeling a residual tingle from the renewed lovemaking with which they had started the day. She knew she had to tell him about Dad and Raine and Jaeger yet was dreading it.

He was watching her and she knew he was sensing the conflict in her mind.

'Problems?'

'You could say so. Dad's back.'

'What about it?'

'You know what he's like.'

This time he did not help but watched her, saying nothing.

'He's always believed a woman shouldn't run Derwent. I guess he doesn't think I'm up to it.'

It was like stripping away the skin and the flesh beneath.

'You run it now.'

She shook her head, staring out of the ute's windscreen, tears not far away: tears she was scared Grant might think proved her father right. The tension was unbearable, her universe poised uneasily between triumph and catastrophe.

'I do. But I'm afraid he has someone else in mind.' She turned to him and clutched his fingers tightly in her own. 'He's brought a woman with him. She has a son by a former marriage and Jaeger's told me he expects to be a beneficiary of the trust with his mother a trustee. They're planning a takeover – I can feel it.'

'How can that be? They're not family.'

'I think Jaeger's mother may have ideas about that.'

'You mean, if your dad wants the mother that's her price? He has to make room for her son?'

'Something like that.'

'And if you were married?'

'I'm not sure it would make any difference. I suppose it might, depending how much of a hold she has on him.'

'But you're willing to give it a try, aren't you?' He released his hands from hers. 'Is that why you're here?' he said. 'To stop this woman and her son from cutting you out?'

1834

Paralysed by shock, Emma was unable to move. Her mind was blank. She could barely breathe.

The two men were halfway down the slope when the figures of other men came swarming over the crest. They were naked, black-skinned, with spears in their hands. One spear was hurled after the two white men, clattering on the boulders behind them.

Off to one side other men were running through the trees. They too were brandishing spears and Emma saw they were covering the ground much more quickly than Ephraim and Bailey.

Sight of these new men filled Emma with terror. She must not let them catch her or the boys. She had to get away. But where?

Richard was clinging to her skirts, seeking the only refuge he knew but which she knew with sickening certainty she could not provide. *Ocean Rider* was as far away as the moon; there was not the remotest possibility of her being able to reach it before being caught.

What would the black men do to her? She thought that death was the best she could hope for. They might not choose to kill her at all, or not at first.

The treetops were a swirl of green as she turned this way and that in an agony of indecision, knowing that whatever she did would be useless, useless...

Ephraim and Bailey were close now, still alive, still unwounded. They were her only hope but what could they do against so many?

She had the pistol Ephraim had given her but it was no use; however scared she might be she knew she would never have the courage – or, with only one bullet in the gun, the capacity – to kill the children or herself.

The two men reached the bottom of the slope and came panting through the mud towards her.

'Run!' Ephraim said, gasping for air. 'If we can reach the top of the slope we may be able to hold them off. They know we've got guns.'

He scooped up Richard with his left arm, his right hand still clutching his pistol.

Their pursuers were no more than thirty yards away and coming fast. Again a spear hurtled through the air; again it fell short.

Emma, clutching a screaming William to her chest, ran with the two men on either side of her. Ran as she had never run before.

It was amazing what terror could do. Even Ephraim's limp did not seem to be slowing him down.

Her lungs were on fire by the time they reached the top of the slope and flung themselves down behind a screen of trees. She was trembling so much she doubted she could have held her pistol, never mind use it. For the moment she could do nothing but suck air into her lungs and wait, vision blurred, sweat running into her eyes.

Bailey was cursing as he reloaded and fired, reloaded and fired again. Ephraim was also firing, but more deliberately, aiming each shot. What they were shooting at she couldn't see; she didn't know where the black men had gone.

William had exhausted himself into silence; Richard was whimpering with terror. Poor boy, Emma thought.

They lay still. No sound or movement came from down the slope.

Had the natives abandoned the chase? Or – horrible idea – were they working their way around behind them so they could attack them from the rear?

That thought made Emma's hair stand up.

The two men had reloaded their guns. Again they waited. Time passed.

'I reckon they've given up,' Bailey said in a low voice.

She hoped he was right but how could they be sure?

Inch by inch they edged backwards down the slope behind them. When they were far enough below the crest they scrambled to their feet, eyes everywhere, and made their way, stumbling and running, towards the beach.

The mosquitoes were especially bad, forming a singing, stinging cloud about their heads. Emma was covered with itchy red bumps while the wretched creatures continued to feast on her. She barely noticed them: there were more important things to worry about than mosquitoes.

They emerged into hot sunlight. The men began to haul the dinghy across the broken ground and into the water. As soon as it was afloat Emma lifted Richard in, raised her skirts and climbed in after him. Bailey started to push the dinghy into deeper water.

There was a chorus of yells as a group of black men came charging down the beach towards them. Ephraim had fought the natives before and suffered the consequences; he turned to face them, pistol raised.

A spear flew and took him in the side. He staggered, half turning towards the boat, and fell to his knees as the natives screamed in triumph and flung themselves towards him.

Bailey abandoned his grip on the dinghy and raced back up the beach. He fired into the advancing men. One fell; the others hesitated. He snatched up Ephraim's pistol, drew back the hammer and fired again. Another of the attackers screamed and fell.

Bailey turned to Ephraim. The spear had been dislodged as he fell but he was lying helpless in a pool of blood on a ridge of jagged rock. Moving as fast as he could, Bailey half dragged, half carried him down to the water's edge.

Emma threw him the end of the dinghy's painter. He hauled it in, shoved Ephraim aboard and scrambled in after him. Renewed yells came from the savages as they saw their enemies escaping.

Again they rushed towards them but Bailey snatched an oar and used it to push them into deeper water. He was barely in time; a volley of spears fell into the water, barely missing them. He seized the oars. None of the black men tried to follow and in half a dozen strokes he had put them out of range.

Ephraim's head was cradled in Emma's lap.

'How is he?'

'Still breathing.'

But Ephraim's blood was everywhere, his face as white as clay.

'Get him aboard, he'll be right,' Bailey said. 'Let's hope.'

'Of course he will,' Emma said, her every breath praying it would be so.

It was a struggle to lift Ephraim on to the sloop's deck but they managed it eventually. Now they were all covered in blood.

William was oblivious but Richard watched his motionless father with apprehensive eyes.

'Help me get him below,' Emma said.

Another tricky operation but somehow they managed it.

Emma eased Ephraim out of his clothes and inspected the wound. 'It is very deep,' she said.

And still bleeding; it was hard to imagine one body could hold so much. She used cloths to staunch the wound but knew patching up the outside of his body might not be sufficient; what damage had been done to the inside she had no way to know.

'You will not die,' she told him fiercely. 'We need you. All of us. You will not die.'

Words alone would cure nothing but words were all she had to offer.

Bailey was watching the shore. 'If we don't move *Ocean Rider* we could all die. That mob may have some of them bark canoes they make. Even dugouts, maybe. I reckon we'd best get on up the coast.'

Kneeling at Ephraim's side Emma spared Bailey a glance. 'Ephraim needs proper medical attention. We must go back down the coast, not further north.'

Ephraim was conscious, then unconscious again. Inflammation flared along the edges of his wound, then died down. Fever raved in his blood.

'Twice,' he whispered with what might have been a smile. 'Those spears seem to have a liking for me.'

'You beat them the first time,' Emma said. 'You'll beat them again.'

It was true that he did seem a little stronger. He ate some food, drank volumes of water, began to talk in a faint voice of the future, how when he had recovered they would go back and somehow persuade the natives that they came in peace and presented no danger to them.

'It will be as you say,' said Emma who given the choice would have sent in a troop of marines to dispose of the savages once and for all.

The next day they were hit by another storm that drove them far out into the ocean. They saw no one. After the storm there came days of calm, drifting without enough wind to fill the sails, then the breeze came back and they headed on down the coast.

'We shall put into Sydney,' Emma said. 'The doctors there will help him get better.'

But Ephraim's teeth had grown too large for his sunken face while the skin around his eyes formed twin pools of darkness. The fever returned, worse than before. A crust had formed on the wound but threads of infection ran beneath the skin. He talked; he raved. Emma sat beside him day and night, willing him to fight, be strong.

Often he did not know who she was.

It was a sombre time, with Richard frightened and hiding himself away, but Emma refused to give up hope. 'Mr Bailey says we should be in Sydney tomorrow or the day after,' she told Ephraim. 'Then we'll get you sorted out.'

Did he hear? Did he understand? She did not know nor in the end did it matter.

Sydney was just over the horizon when Emma woke from a doze and sensed that something had changed. She got up and went to Ephraim, dread in her heart.

'Ephraim?'

Silence. Ephraim was gone from her. She stared at him, tears welling, and her heart was full of grief.

'My dear love, we found each other once,' she said. 'How will I find you now?'

'What shall we do?' Bailey asked.

'We shall bury him,' said Emma.

'Where? In Sydney? We can be there in under a day.'

'Not in Sydney. We shall bury him here, in the sea.'

In the cool clean sea.

'Do that and they may think we did away with him deliberately.'

'It is what he would have wished,' Emma said. 'But leave me with him for a minute.'

She was afraid to put her hands on his lovely face for, despite all that had happened to his poor body to make him ugly, his face was still lovely to her. As was all his savaged flesh. She was afraid to touch him for fear that she might disturb the spirit that perhaps still lingered, that the eyelids were closed only to keep hidden the radiance of Ephraim Dark, who had made much out of little and might have made much more had he not been betrayed by Emma's uncle. He had made Richard, and William, and had loved her with a steadfast faith that might have brought tears had she not been determined to prevent them, because what she was doing in these last moments of privacy was celebrating the man he had been and to her still was. A man with weaknesses, like all men, but who had helped her in the beginning when she had already loved him and helped her also down the years. Not as many years as she would have wished but holy all the same.

She thought of him at her side, helping her escape the purgatory of Arthur Naismith and his aunt. She remembered the flame that had leapt between them in Barnsley Tregellas's office when after three years she had seen again the face she had thought lost forever. She thought how his visions of what might be had buoyed them both when their world had collapsed around them.

She heard what must surely be a miracle: the sound of his voice, trumpet clear, saying they were one being and would be so for ever, and she felt joy and sorrow in the emotion that united them.

She cleaned the body and shrouded it decently in a sheet and with Bailey's help let the weighted corpse of her love slip into the waves.

They arrived in Hobart Town two weeks after their escape from the north.

Emma's head and limbs were aching as she disembarked with the two boys. After the stress of Ephraim's death it was not surprising and she said nothing to Bailey about it. She took his hand.

'Thank you for all you've done.'

He nodded briefly. 'Sorry things didn't work out better. What you want done with the boat?'

'She's yours. I've no money to give you but maybe you'll accept the sloop in payment for all your work.'

'That's too much,' Bailey said.

'You might as well have her,' she said. 'If you don't my uncle will take her anyway.'

'We can't have that,' he said. 'All right, then. I will take her with many thanks. What will you do?'

'Go to my uncle's house and hope he'll take us in.'

'You reckon he will?'

'I believe so. He won't be happy about it but I believe he will have little choice. He will be too afraid of bad publicity to do anything else.'

'You want me to come with you?'

'Better not,' she said. 'If I were you I'd get *Ocean Rider* away while you can. My uncle will seize her if he knows she's in port.'

'I might try the South Pacific,' he said. 'Good trading opportunities there, I hear. Beautiful women too, they say.' He was joking, which was good, but then looked embarrassed at having said such a thing so soon after Ephraim's death. 'Begging your pardon.'

Emma touched his hand. 'Don't apologise. I wish you every good fortune,' she said. 'With the trade and the women.'

'You'll be all right? You're not looking yourself.'

'I am perfectly all right,' she said.

But she wasn't and she knew it. She set out with the two children to walk to her uncle's house. It wasn't far but seemed so, each step an effort. She got there but only just. She was swaying on her feet when she pulled the massive doorbell and was in a state of near collapse by the time a maid opened the door.

The maid was new and did not know Emma. She thought the strange woman was drunk and would have slammed the door in her face had not by good fortune the housekeeper been passing.

'Why, Miss Emma…' Mrs Alsop ran to assist her. 'My goodness, what a state you are in! What has happened to you?'

Emma mumbled but was falling, falling. Darkness filled up her eyes.

When she came to she was in bed but felt frail and old.

'I must get up,' she said. 'I have the boys to see to.'

But when she tried found she could not.

'Why am I so helpless?' she cried.

Summoned by the maid, Mrs Alsop put her hand on Emma's forehead. 'Hush now. The doctor's been and says you are suffering from exhaustion. Your uncle has said you must stay here until you are fully recovered.'

'I daresay he'll put it on the bill,' Emma said.

'Hush, now.'

Heat was rising, a growing furnace threatening to devour her.

'The boys?'

Somehow she managed the words.

'They are fine. Rest now. You'll feel better after a good sleep.'

Emma's body was insisting that the fire engulfing her was something altogether different from simple fatigue but speech had become impossible.

She huddled in her bed, drifting in and out of a troubled sleep. Her mind churned with incomprehensible thoughts. She believed they had been in Hobart Town for several days. For some reason it was important to work out precisely how many days but she could not, or work out how long they had been on their journey south. Perhaps they had not yet arrived?

Ephraim's voice was calling her.

'I am here.'

Did she say it or imagine it?

If she could get on her feet and shake off this foolish indisposition all would be well.

'I must get up,' she told the bedroom's empty vault.

She could not.

Her mind renewed its crazy, endless calculations. Fifteen days? A month? How could it possibly matter?

How long had Mr Bailey and the children been gone? It seemed like minutes; it seemed like days. The meaningless thoughts raved on: what year was it? How old was she?

She hid in the reeds while the under-keeper searched.

Ephraim, frowning. You could not be troubled even to bury me in the welcoming earth? Dust to dust?

We was all gone on Ensign Dark, miss.

You could not be troubled –

A scream of anguish in the darkness.

The night descended, with ice. She was shivering. Never had she known such cold. She had ice in her veins, her head, yet when Mrs Alsop brought the children to see her she was once again consumed by heat. She flung herself to and fro, gabbling meaningless words. Someone was trying to hold her, piling more and more blankets on the bed. The sweat poured off her while she wept, pleading for release.

A hand was sponging her with cool water, but the fever remained.

Then, suddenly, the fire in her blood died; the ice withdrew; lucidity returned.

'I feel so good,' she murmured. Her voice was thin but she was smiling. 'I shall sleep now.'

And later, when she woke: 'Am I better?'

A man was looking down at her, his face concerned.

'Let us hope so,' he said. 'For the moment, anyway.'

She heard him talking to Mrs Alsop.

'I have seen this illness before. It is caused by bad air, a sickness for which there is no cure. There is a Latin name for it: *mal aria*. Bad air. It causes recurrent bouts of fever that come and go, progressively weakening the patient.'

'But she will recover?'

'We can only hope,' the doctor said.

I am feeling much better, Emma thought. Such talk is nonsense.

Yet she could feel something waiting in the shadows. Waiting patiently. Watching. She knew it would take over her body again if it had the chance, pour the fire and ice into her veins, her blood. I must fight it while I can, she thought. I shall not let it conquer me.

But return it did: heat and a form of madness, so that she no longer knew who or where she was. She hung on to a woman's hands, gripping them tight.

Where is Ephraim? Where is my husband? Why is he not here?

She could not understand the answer. If there was an answer. If she had asked the question.

Again reality returned. She knew herself to be weaker but her mind was clear.

'Mrs Alsop, I need to see my uncle.'

She waited. Eventually Barnsley came. Mrs Alsop came over to the bed but Barnsley stood by the door and Emma saw he was frightened by her illness.

'You are better?' he said.

'For the moment.'

It was no more than a whisper but she was feeling so tired that speaking at all was a triumph.

'You wanted to say something to me?'

She saw he could not wait to be gone.

'There is gold,' she said. 'Nuggets of pure gold, lying on the ground. Enough to pay off what you claim we owe you.'

The words were a hook, snaring his interest. 'Gold? Where?'

'In the north.'

'Mrs Alsop, you may leave us,' Barnsley said.

'I want her to stay.'

His expression showed his vexation but he said nothing and Mrs Alsop stayed.

'Where in the north?'

'Before I tell you that I want you to promise me that if anything happens to me you will look after the boys.'

'You will be on your feet in no time,' he said. 'There is no need for promises.'

'Promise me,' she said.

'William is your son. Of course I shall look after him.'

'Richard also,' she said.

'He is not your blood.'

'He is my son nonetheless. My son by adoption.'

Emma saw Barnsley was embarrassed by Mrs Alsop's presence. He said nothing.

'I want your word,' Emma said.

A pause. Now it was Emma's turn to wait.

Barnsley sighed. 'You have it,' he said.

'Your solemn oath?'

'My solemn oath. Tell me about the gold. You have seen it?'

'I know a man who has. There are tropical islands far to the north. They call them the Whitsunday Islands...'

Perhaps the gold was there, as Bailey had said, perhaps not. But Barnsley had promised, in front of a witness. The boys' future was secure. That was her greatest triumph of all.

The fever returned, the heat and ice. Emma went down into darkness, deeper and deeper. The darkness stifled her so she could not breathe. Briefly she fought it then, at last, came a blessed release.

At three o'clock in the morning after she had extracted Barnsley's promise before Mrs Alsop as witness, Emma Dark, nee Tregellas, the twenty-five-year-old widow of Ephraim and mother of William, with everything to live for, died.

Barnsley Tregellas believed in showing respect for the dead but in his heart he wished his niece had never been born.

It was as though a curse had accompanied her; all his dealings with the strong-willed, foolish girl had proved disastrous. Coming to the colony at all had been an imposition; even her friendship with Lady Arthur had failed to produce any dividends as far as Barnsley was concerned.

She had turned up her nose at the succession of excellent matches he had tried to arrange for her and had then insisted on marrying a man little better than a brigand who had made off with a fortune. A fortune that by rights and indeed by law belonged to Barnsley himself. Admittedly he had been compensated to some extent by the acquisition of the estate in the midlands that his niece had fancifully called Derwent, but the rank injustice of the loss was a festering wound.

Two hundred thousand pounds when he doubted the estate was worth one fifth of that, to say nothing of the problems and cost of stocking and administering the property... Even with the sheep he was having brought from New South Wales it was obvious that Derwent was a nightmare in waiting. He supposed he might make something out of the forestry, in time, and the trading schooners would be worth something, but the ridiculous half-completed port would never be worth anything, for all the money Emma's foolish husband had thrown at it.

And now she had foisted on him these two children in return for a story of gold far away that might, or might not, be there. His hands were tied; within days the word would be all around the colony that the two brats had been delivered into his care and, rich and powerful though he was, his reputation would be ruined if he failed to accept them.

Yet only one of them was of his blood. Very well; as far as the world knew he would take them both but in private would treat only the baby William as his nephew and heir. He would pay for Richard's upbringing because he had no choice but the son of the man who had cheated him would get nothing more, neither affection nor interest nor inheritance. He would arrange for William's surname to be changed to Tregellas but Richard Dark would have to find his own way.

1913

Conan Hampton had always had a way with horses. He had worked in the stables at Derwent, which itself had been an adventure, with certain things happening that he had not expected and on one occasion something not happening when he had thought it would.

Well, that was life, he thought.

It was years since he'd left Derwent but as the local blacksmith he still dealt with horses on a daily basis. These days they were mostly working animals and not fine-boned thoroughbreds, and he put shoes on them rather than saddles, but they were still horses. He also mended the ironware on carts and made farm implements but some said he'd come down in the world and there were times when he thought the same, pounding the red-hot metal in an explosion of resentful sparks.

The rhythm of his violence echoed the pounding of the cannon at South Africa's Blyde River crossing on the one occasion in his life he had reached out to touch the heights of heroism, when he had dismounted to rescue Daddo Penrose after the Mauser had blown Daddo out of his saddle.

He had carried him bleeding to safety in defiance of the ambush set by the crack-shot Boers and why they hadn't dropped him too he never knew. The colonel had congratulated him for his courage and presented him with a cheap watch as a token of regimental approval because Daddo Penrose, heir to the vast Derwent estate, was an important man in the Tasmanian high country.

For an hour or two Conan had been everybody's friend; there'd even been talk of a medal, but the moment had passed and the clatter of the hammer, the uneasy shifting of the placid animals, echoed the long descent his life had followed since that day when he had dared hope that all things might be possible.

'Ruined me, that business,' he told any drinking companion who cared to listen, because drink had become his friend. 'Never knew I had it in me nor ever did again.'

He had been known to weep in his beer after the memories grew too much.

So he became resentful of the man whose life he had saved and who later had given him back the Derwent job that Bessie Penrose had sworn he would never have. During Daddo's lifetime he had stuck, just to spite her, but after his death he did a runner to stop her giving him the flick.

Now he had reached the point where he was able to deny there had ever been a moment when he had sensed the might-have-beens that had plagued him ever since.

It was not to be expected that Conan, boozy eyes and bitter heart, would approve of his daughter's friendship with Jonathan Penrose but when Jonathan turned up unexpectedly he was away from the forge, which was a blessing.

Bec's heart was pounding but at least she knew how to hide it; Mum, on the other hand, started to run this way and that like a dozen scalded cats, but Mum had always been scared of shadows and what people might say. What in particular Dad might say.

Bec was fond of her mother, as one might be fond of a pet chook, but from the time she had been capable of thinking she had known she was a separate being who would find her own path in life so, when Jonathan asked she said yes, she would be delighted to go for a walk with him.

In the end Dad's absence made no difference for when he got home and found the strange horse tethered nearby and his daughter missing, the ferocity of the forge fire was at once rekindled in his heart. After questioning his quivering wife and giving her a tap for letting it happen and another to remind her that it was his place to decide these things and not hers, he returned to the forge where he stoked his anger beside the red-hot iron of the horseshoes. From which, after hearing the fading clop of hooves as Jonathan rode away, he later emerged.

His face was red with alcohol and the fire's heat.

'What you bin doing, girl?'

She eyed him warily; Bec had always found it easier to relate to her father's belligerence than the curds and whey with which her mother sought to appease the world but now his ferocity looked as though it might spill over into actual violence.

'Nothing, Dad.'

'The way I heard it, you went for a walk with that Jonathan Penrose.'

'That's right.'

'Call that nothing? Where'd you go on this walk?'

'Through the woods.'

'You go into the woods with Jonathan Penrose and you call it nothing? People know you done that, what they gunna say, eh?'

'We didn't do anything!'

'Blokes like Jonathan Penrose ain't for people like us,' he said.

Suddenly she was willing to challenge him. She was sixteen and willing to challenge him. 'A walk! That's all it was! I said we didn't do anything and we didn't!'

They stared at each other.

He was big-chested, big-bellied, his temper stoked by flame, but Bec saw domination in a leather apron scarred by fire, in the slant of the man's unshaven jaw.

And so she flung her resentment at him.

She hadn't expected it; nor, she saw, had he. But she saw too that she could not back off. Do that and her rebellion would be over.

Perhaps he saw it, too, and believed violence was the only way to restore the authority he would lose if he did nothing. Perhaps he did not know what else to do.

He lifted his hand to her; she stood firm. And he hit her. Not to damage but to spell out his status as her father. It was meant to be only a tap but he hit her higher than he'd intended, across her right eye. It made the eye swell up at once and instead of restoring his authority it marked the end of it.

She did not cry; she did not speak. She stared at him, chin up, then turned and walked away.

The next day, when the blacksmith had gone to Ross, she walked to Waldren's Corner and spoke to Mrs Painter who, observing Bec's swollen eye, offered her a bed.

'Only temporary,' she told her husband Oswald. 'She can give me a hand with the baby until things settle down.'

Although when that might be no one knew.

Bec went back to the forge and packed.

'Don't do it,' Mum said. 'Don't break the family.'

'He's already done it.'

'But –'

'You've got to put up with him. I don't.'

Wearing her straw hat and buttoned boots she turned her back on the past and walked away down the road.

A kookaburra squawked.

'You tell 'em,' Bec said.

Mr Painter was uncertain of the wisdom of getting involved, warning there might be difficulties, but since Oswald Painter was the constable Conan Hampton kept away.

'What was it all about anyway?' Oswald asked his wife.

'Something to do with Bec being matey with Jonathan Penrose. Her dad doesn't like it.'

'I don't wonder he doesn't like it.' The constable believed in the natural order of things, which was why he was a constable. 'Not that it will make any odds, in the end.'

'Why d'you say that?'

'You see old Mrs Penrose putting up with it? Bec Hampton and her grandson? She'll eat young Bec for breakfast, if I'm any
judge.'

Although another and far more likely possibility had occurred to
them both: that Jonathan Penrose was interested more in getting
into Bec than in Bec herself and would drop her like a stone once
he'd managed it.

It would have been unseemly to put such thoughts into words,
so they didn't.

Bec knew the risks as well as the Painters. You'd have to be a dummy
not to be aware of them but she liked Jonathan, had always liked
him, had for years had a crush on him.

That was what they called it, wasn't it? *Having a crush on someone.*

It meant wanting to be with someone yet being scared of them
too. It meant wanting them to admire you while being scared
they'd think you a fool. It meant wanting to show them how clever
you were but when you dredged up the courage to say something
finding that every word came out like a ball of wool.

Oh yes, she knew all about having a crush on someone. At least
on Jonathan Penrose; she'd never felt like that about anyone else.

It was no good, of course. As her dad had said, his sort wasn't
for people like her. She'd hated him for saying it but it was true.
Jonathan Penrose and Bec Hampton? It was more than stupid; it
was impossible.

She sat on her bed in the Painters' cottage and thought about it.
Since their meeting at the Campbell Town show she had thought
of little else.

What of it? she thought. She liked him; it seemed he liked her.
That was enough to be going on with.

They'd done nothing – just the one walk – but even that was
more than she would have expected. She hadn't expected to see
him at all, except maybe at a distance. When he got married, for
instance. Or out riding.

What she would do was take it step by step and see how things played out. She already knew there were things she was prepared to let him do, things she was not.

So far he had not laid a finger on her. She wondered how she'd feel about it if he did. When he did.

So Bec Hampton came to live at the Painters' place at Waldren's Corner, the spot where two tracks emerged from the scrubby hills and joined to become the road that climbed the flank of the range and connected with the highway just south of the Derwent boundary, where a sheer cliff called Blackman's Head dominated the landscape.

Bec gave a hand with the baby, as Mrs Painter had intended, and in time helped in so many other ways that one night three months after her arrival Mrs Painter confided to her husband that she didn't know how she'd managed in the days before Miss Hampton had come to join them.

The two women had become friendly but first names were out. Status was important, and the social levels that maintained society.

For Oswald Painter this created a problem. He shared his wife's views about class and the proper order of things and the regular visits of young Master Jonathan to see Miss Hampton challenged those views. He was a nice lad and he had no complaints about Miss Hampton, either, but the relationship between them was a worry.

'It's none of our business,' his wife said.

Oswald Painter wasn't too sure about that. His wife was starry-eyed in the presence of what she had begun to hope might be True Love, so he felt her opinions might be discounted. Also the girl was staying under his roof and responsibility could not be avoided.

'I wonder if I shouldn't have a word with Mrs Penrose,' he said.

It was Mrs Penrose senior he meant – no one in their right mind would ask Mrs Rose Penrose for an opinion about anything more challenging than the weather – but Mrs Bessie Penrose presented a problem too, and a formidable one.

One thing the whole district knew was that Mrs Bessie did not tolerate people poking their noses into Penrose family business, and to speak about her grandson's regular visits to see Miss Hampton certainly fell into that category.

'I'd keep well away from it, if I was you,' said Mrs Painter, who would no more risk crossing Bessie Penrose than jump off Blackman's Head. 'You want to say anything, have a word with young Jonathan. If you're really determined to stick your beak in.'

So her husband, who had no such intention, kept out of the way when Jonathan Penrose came a-calling.

'We keep seeing each other like this, people will start talking,' Bec said.

'Let them talk,' Jonathan said.

'All right for you.'

'You want us to stop seeing each other?'

'You know I don't want that.'

'Then?'

'Just saying, that's all. If your grandma finds out –'

'What do you want me to do about it?'

Bec, whose bones dissolved whenever she saw him, knew exactly what she wanted Jonathan to do but did not see how she could put it into words. 'Not for me to say.'

They were sitting side by side on a level patch of ground shaded by gum trees. Blackman's Head rose sheer behind them, its outline dominating the landscape. From there they could see for miles, to a point well beyond Waldren's Corner where the eucalyptus bush blurred into a continuous blue-grey line.

It was their special place. Times without number Bec had seen Blackman's Head flush rose-red in the light of a thunderous dawn but never before had she associated it with love.

Now she did. This patch of shaded ground below the Head was the place they visited more regularly than anywhere else. There was nothing up there, not even sheep, so there was no reason for anyone else to visit. They were alone, they were together, and to Bec it was like heaven.

Something else too.

It gave her an extraordinary sense of owning not only herself and the circle of air and stillness that surrounded her but the land she could see stretching away into the distance.

The land called Derwent, to which the man beside her was heir.

Her feelings for Jonathan gave her feelings also for the land that would one day be his, yet that idea was so huge she could not get her head around it.

What was Derwent to her?

She told herself it was nothing yet that was not true. It was a promise, although of what she could not have said. Only that it was there, that she and Jonathan were there, that somehow they were all bound together. They were prisoners of fate.

'You know we're related?' Jonathan said.

'Ever so long ago though,' Bec said. 'Cousins about a million times removed.'

Of course she knew it but the relationship meant nothing. Both sides of the family could trace their origins back to Ephraim Dark but it was the Penrose branch that had the money; the Hamptons had nothing. That was what mattered.

Whenever Bec went to see her Grandma Jane the old lady was always sounding off about it. You couldn't blame her; why wouldn't she be narked when she might have inherited a fortune? If things had worked out differently she'd have married some wealthy bloke, had a good life. As it was she'd ended up with her parents' small farm and Jake Hampton, a decent enough cove in his own way but not one who'd ever make a fortune.

'I blame William,' Grandma Jane had said. 'Any justice, he'd have died on the gallows, I reckon.'

As it was he had died in bed, leaving a fortune that his daughter Bessie, Jonathan's monstrous grandmother, had almost doubled by marrying a sook called Phelan Penrose, whose idea of work was to lie under a shady tree, getting fat and checking out his toenails.

People said it was a wonder Bessie Penrose hadn't booted him off the property years before he did it for her, trying to roger a parlour maid and going off pop when he was still in his fifties.

'It's too long ago to matter, us being related,' Bec said.

'I don't take your meaning,' he said.

But he did, and she knew he did.

They were friends. At the beginning, in the first weeks after their meeting at the Campbell Town show, she would have been happy to settle for that, already more than she would ever have imagined possible, but now she knew friendship was not enough.

It was a dangerous time. She was pushing against barriers society had rigged to separate people like them. Bec Hampton and Jonathan Penrose might be descended from the same ancestral tree yet it made no odds; the barriers of wealth, custom and education existed. Somehow she must find a way to break them down without frightening him off. She could not bear the thought of losing him yet if they did nothing the relationship would go nowhere, and she couldn't bear to think of that, either.

She was pretty sure he felt the same.

Do something, she implored him silently. Anything.

She wanted it so much yet was scared too. She sat and waited, hands folded in her lap, her face grave and still. They'd had a dry spell and she could taste the dust that rose from the parched ground.

She could not tell whether his feelings for her were skin deep or came from his heart. She told herself that when the time came she would know.

It seemed the time of miracles had not passed because after sitting silently for a long time he sighed and turned to her and she knew even before he touched her that this was right and all would be well.

He kissed her and she felt him trembling, as she was trembling.

'Bec,' he said. 'Oh Bec.'

She could have swallowed him whole or in her turn been swallowed. He had become the brightness of sunlight, the soft shadows of dusk. He was everything.

Dear God, she thought. She would never have believed she could love another human being as much as she loved him. Again and again he ran his hands over her, his big hands touching her with such delicacy that they set her nerves on fire. She gloried in his touch. She was a reed shaking in the wind. She clutched him to her, hard against him, hips stirring, while he continued to caress her, slowly, steadily.

'You are driving me mad,' she said.

It was hard to speak at all, tongue tangled in her quickening breath. There were imperfections in their bodies, as in all bodies, but they were beautiful. They were alive and together and life was beauty.

'Please...' she said.

She looked up at him, gathering him to her, surrendering to the sensations flowing through her. She sensed his power but was not intimidated. It was glorious. Growing, mounting, the moment not far off now...

'Oh,' she said. 'Oh yes. Oh.'

Later she heard herself cry out, the sound forced between her parted lips, and finally, and finally...

A splendour of sunlight on the hillside, with the shadows slipping away below her, and there was joy and peace and a sense that at last she had reached the place that had been her destiny from the moment of her birth.

Afterwards there were gentle tears, a sense of gratitude and peace, a bottomless pool drawing her down.

1834–1850

There were times when Richard thought he had always been frightened. He could not remember his mother but had always been aware of an emptiness in his life where she should have been. She had died when he was born. Father had said it was not Richard's fault but he had known that it was; if it hadn't been for him his mother would still be alive so of course it was his fault.

Things had been all right as long as he'd had Father and Mama but now Father was dead. Richard had seen it happen, seen the horrible spear sticking in him, and knew it was a sight he would not forget.

Worst of all, Mama had died too, not from a spear but from some terrible illness. She had been like a real mother. She had been kind and made him feel safe but she was not there any longer.

Now there was only the man who never smiled. Who told him never to call him Uncle. Who had mean eyes and a mean mouth and was always nasty to him. Who had said more than once that Richard was not a real member of the family but someone taken in out of charity and that he would find himself out on the street if he didn't do what he was told.

The people who worked in the house were nasty to him too. Only Mrs McIntyre the cook was kind. Mrs McIntyre and her daughter Alice. Alice was the same age as he was; she was his friend. They did things together. They had adventures.

They grew older, which was another adventure.

Time passed.

Alice hated Barnsley Tregellas because of the way he treated Richard.

It was unfair; worse, it was cruel.

He and William were half-brothers but William went to the best private school in Hobart Town while at the age of twelve Richard was packed off to sea aboard one of Barnsley's whale ships.

'Told me it was time I started earning my keep,' Richard said.

It wasn't right but neither of them could do anything about it so to sea Richard went.

Alice wanted to go to the harbour to see him off. She could see that Richard was scared but not too scared to tell her to keep away.

'Don't you want me to say goodbye to you?'

'Of course I do. Only I heard him telling the captain that I was a mother's boy. That I had to be toughened up. If they see you down there saying goodbye it'll be like telling them he was right.'

'I hate him,' Alice said. 'Hate him! Hate him!'

He. Him.

They could not bring themselves to say Barnsley Tregellas's name.

She understood what he was telling her. If they thought he was soft the crew would bully him worse than ever. So she said goodbye to him at the house as he left in his sea-going gear: pea jacket, heavy shirt and pants, boots that looked several sizes too big for him, a round hard hat clamped to his head.

She could barely recognise him, face white, expression tight, hands like ice. Overnight he had become a stranger. She tried to say something, to wish him well, but found she could not utter a word.

Under the brim of his hat his eyes said how frightened he was.

Then he was gone and the next morning when she looked she saw that the whale ship had gone too.

Alice missed him more than she would have thought possible. She walked around the house, aware of the spaces where Richard should have been and was not.

She tried to imagine him in the depths of the Southern Ocean doing brave deeds, earning the respect and admiration of his ship-mates, but knew it would never be like that. Richard was as he was, a hero in the way he faced things that he knew were impossible for him, but that was not the sort of heroism that the men aboard a whale ship were likely to understand. She knew she would have handled the challenge of whale ship and ocean better than Richard could. It was nonsense to think of any woman in such a situation yet in a world that honoured physical courage but took no account of the inner resolution that was the hallmark of the truly brave, she knew she would have survived better than he could.

When he came back from the sea six months later he was a stranger.

Physically he was the same, stronger in his body but otherwise unchanged, but he had become hard-edged, with an emptiness behind his eyes that frightened her; he had learnt to hate the world. She would have hated it with him had he allowed her to, but he shut her out. They were not one being any more; the Southern Ocean had divided them.

To some extent that would have been inevitable even if he'd never gone away at all. They had both had their thirteenth birth-days; in his case through experience, in hers through physical inevi-tability, they were children no longer.

Nevertheless she was determined to win him back.

It wasn't easy. They talked but not as they had in the old days. He seemed to have forgotten the life they had shared. She asked him what his life had been like on the whale ship.

'We killed whales,' he said.

'But I mean what was it like for you?'

He looked at her with his stranger's eyes. 'I told you. We killed whales. That was all we did.'

Of course it wasn't. He'd lived too: it was that she wanted him to tell her but he would not. She wanted things to be as they had been; they were not. She wanted her feelings and his to unite as they once had but he prevented that. She watched him do everything he could to keep himself apart.

There were days when she found herself wishing he had never come back, knowing she did not mean it.

Alice discovered in herself something she had never thought to find. It was love – not the love she had for her mother or for life; she'd always had that. Her feelings now were entirely different, both more intense and more painful, the love she felt for a man. Richard was scarcely a man, as she was scarcely a woman, but she knew with surprise but also certainty that she loved him, had always loved him without realising it.

It was a feeling entirely separate from the pity and indignation that she felt at the unfairness of his uncle's treatment of him. Her mind touched her love wonderingly, as her fingers might have touched a jewel of fabulous worth. Whatever Richard had become, wherever he might be hiding behind the protective shell he had acquired during his time on the whale ship *Ariadne*, she would find him. She would bring him home.

She discovered that love and silence were enemies. She found him mooching, head down, in the garden. They had met there often in the old days when he had made a deliberate effort to keep out of his uncle's way. Now there was a different feeling, a defiance that she knew was directed not at his uncle but at her.

She was no longer prepared to keep out. She went up to him, standing in the path so he could not get by.

'Where are you?' she said.

'I am here,' he said.

Now or never. She launched herself at him. Her clenched fists hammered his chest.

'You are not! You are somewhere else.'

His cold eyes inspected her. 'You're talking nonsense.'

'We used to be friends! What did they do to you?'

She stared at him defiantly. Pleading. For a moment nothing, then his mouth began to work and she saw something happening to him that was horrible yet offering the possibility of relief. His features blurred as the barriers he had erected against the world dissolved. His eyes…

Tears?

She was hugging him, soothing him, knowing that the next moments would be crucial. If he thought for a moment she was patronising him…

She too was in tears and she sensed that this might save the situation, save them both.

'Look at me!'

Weeping, they stared at each other. And the barriers – at last – were down.

They found a corner of the grounds behind the potting sheds. They sat on the grass and Richard talked. After being dammed up so long, the words poured out.

Her fury grew as she listened but she was determined to say nothing until he was finished. He described being stripped naked. Being covered in tar. Being hoisted on a halyard to the mizzen top and left there for hours while the southerly wind drove shards of ice into his skin. He told her about scraping his food off the deck after his tin plate had been upended accidentally on purpose by the cook.

'Did the officers do nothing?'

'They were the worst,' he said. 'They put the men up to it.'

'But why?'

'Because he had told them to toughen me up.'

He.

'That was their way of doing it, I suppose.'

'Didn't you feel like killing them?'

'All the time.'

She took his hand in hers. 'I think you are the bravest man I know.'

'I'm a coward. If I'd been brave I would have done it.'

'No. Because that way they'd have won. You defied them by *not* killing them.'

'It makes no difference. I could never have managed it anyway.'

'I am glad you didn't try.'

Alice's heart was overflowing. With love; with relief that they were finally together again. She was tempted to say something about that but did not, sensing that the moment was not right to talk to him about her feelings.

'Remember this,' her mother had told her. 'Men, especially young uns, are easily scared where us women is concerned.'

She decided it was a wise saying. She therefore did not allow her feelings to show. She let him think they were friends, no more than that. There was no reason for him to be frightened of a friend. Occasionally, when she was alone, she took out her love and polished it in wonder that she felt as she did, knowing she always would.

Twice more Richard went back to sea. He never talked about it again but she got the feeling that the terrible traumas of that first voyage were not repeated. He was a man now and other boys took his place. He was never willing to talk about them either or the way their treatment might have mirrored his own and Alice decided it might be safer not to press him on such matters.

Once again, the years passed.

1982

Tamara stared back at Grant. She felt a shortening of her breath, a tightening of the muscles around her heart.

Is that why you're here? he had said. *To stop this woman and her son from cutting you out?*

Now everything was in play: the future, Derwent, her love for this man, all dependent on the next few minutes.

She drew her breath deeply into her lungs. She made no attempt to touch him or give any hint of the anguish that hovered so close to her heart.

'I am here because I love you.' She spoke simply, her heart in every word for him to see, if he were willing. 'When you went away after your father died I understood why you had to do it, how wounded you'd been by the things that happened to you in Vietnam. I understood yet my heart was breaking. Seeing you at Agfest was like having a light switch on again; I knew then I had never stopped loving you, that nothing else in my life came close to the feelings I had for you. Everything that has happened between us since – everything – has only strengthened that feeling. I love you more than I have ever loved anyone and will go on loving you, I believe, forever.'

They sat side by side in the ute and stared at each other. So close; so far apart. Now only Grant could bridge the gap.

She could not tell from his expression what he was feeling.

'Tell me about Derwent,' he said. 'Tell me what it means to you.'

'It's been in my family for a hundred and fifty years,' she said. 'It represents all the generations of my ancestors in this country. All the things that have happened to us and to other people.'

'A story of Australia,' he said.

'One of the stories, anyway.'

'And you want it to be yours but without a man in your life there's a good chance it won't be.'

'I feel for Derwent,' she said. 'Of course I do. And I feel for you. I have told you that. Not very ladylike of me, but I've said it anyway, and it's the truth. But you mustn't tie one thing to the other. They are quite separate.'

Grant did not answer but opened the ute door and got out. She watched through the window as he walked to the point where the land fell steeply into the lower country hundreds of feet below. He stood with his back to her, staring out.

She wondered whether or not to join him – even such a simple action might make a difference.

She was conscious of her heart as she got out of the ute and went and stood beside him. She too stared out at the expanse of trees and hills fading into the blue distance.

'I love this island,' Grant said. 'I never felt right when I was away from it.'

'It's something worth loving,' she said.

Without taking her eyes off the view she sensed that he had turned his head to look at her.

'If I were to suggest we should maybe get married, do you reckon your dad might change his mind about Derwent?'

'Oh no,' she said. 'You don't catch me like that.'

But she was fighting a smile as she said it, because now she felt a quiver of what might be hope.

'What d'you mean?'

'Too hypothetical. You want to ask me, ask, and I'll give you my answer. But let's have no more of these maybes and might bes. A girl's got her pride.'

'That right?'

'Take it to the bank,' she said.

'Doesn't look like I got much choice then, does it?'

He turned to face her. He placed his hands on her shoulders and turned her towards him.

'You're not asking me to kneel, I hope?'

'We can skip the kneeling,' she said.

'Tamara Penrose,' Grant said. 'I love you with all my heart. Will you marry me?'

You can bet your life on it. Or: *What took you so long?*

All the smart and clever answers. But Tamara said none of them. She looked up at him, her face wet with tears, her heart naked in her eyes.

'Yes,' she said. 'Yes and yes and yes.'

Yet later practical considerations raised their head.

'What about Ringarooma?' Tamara said.

'I'll get a manager in,' Grant said.

'Maybe I can give you a hand?'

There was love in Grant's smile. 'I'll think about it.'

1913

Jonathan might have dropped off the planet. A week had passed without her seeing him. She was tempted to go to Derwent and seek him out but told herself not to be stupid. Instead she went for a walk and met him, he on horseback, she standing at the roadside.

What had happened had not diminished her but made her more stalwart in her self-respect. They had shared something precious – both giving, both receiving – and she spoke to Jonathan as an equal.

'I wondered if you were dead. Or maybe dying. You want me to send for the undertaker? Or will the doctor do?'

'After what happened I wondered whether you would want to see me again,' he said.

Heaven help us.

'I thought I'd died and gone to heaven. It was the most wonderful moment of my life.'

Not the way a lady would talk but Bec had never pretended to be one of those.

He dismounted and took her hands in his. 'You mean it?'

'Every word.'

Bec marvelled at the plain way she had spoken to him. Well, she had said it. Now it was up to him.

Jonathan knew that Grandma would be livid when she discovered he had no plans to marry Judith Hargreaves. When she discovered he had chosen Bec Hampton over the daughter of a senior official. *Bec Hampton*, the daughter of the disreputable Conan Hampton, a former servant without a bean to his name? She would not let that happen without a fight.

Well, let the game play out as it would.

He took his horse and rode to Blackman's Head, to the patch of ground where they had made love. He wanted to relive every moment of that wonderful afternoon, to revisit the emotion that had so meaningfully enriched and changed his life.

He sat quietly in the shade and was one with all that had happened here. One of the moments he remembered best was not the actual lovemaking but afterwards, when Bec had unwound herself from his arms and, getting up, had picked some wild flowers before coming back and sitting with legs crossed at his feet. She had sat and arranged the flowers in neat piles of yellow and white blossom on the warm ground, her neck bent to watch the quiet movement of her hands, and he had known that in this way, without a word being spoken, she had been laying claim to him and to the future.

It was lunchtime the following day. From her position at the head of the table Grandma Bessie twinkled at Jonathan.

'Have you made any arrangements about your next visit to the Hargreaves?'

Jonathan was tucking into soup, with a rack of lamb waiting. 'No.'

'Don't leave it too long, will you?' Her smile would have frightened a regiment of heroes. 'It is impolite to keep a lady waiting too long.'

Now we come to it, he thought. 'I shall keep her waiting indefinitely, Grandma. Judith has no place in my plans.'

Grandma's lips tightened. 'I wish you could see how unattractive it is to carry such resentment. I have told you, you must ignore Judith's earlier behaviour. I don't condone it but it means nothing, nothing! She will settle down when she has a ring on her finger.'

A plate of lamb, pink and delicious, was put in front of him. He helped himself to carrots and potatoes.

'Maybe she will,' he said. 'But it won't be my ring.'

Now Grandma's smile was quite extinguished. 'Surely you can see the advantages –'

Jonathan chewed on the tender lamb and swallowed. 'I shall not marry her. I don't trust her. I am not even sure I like her.'

Confrontation.

'I should warn you,' Grandma said. 'If you are thinking of forming another attachment –'

'I have already done so. Someone I am fond of. But I am over twenty-one, Grandma. My private life is my business, nobody else's.'

'It is not only your business where Derwent is concerned,' Grandma said.

A moment's icy silence.

'Who is the girl?'

'A friend.'

'Does this friend have a name?'

'She does.'

'And what is it?'

'You will be the first to know. When I am ready to tell you.'

'This is not a game,' Grandma said. 'Derwent is your heritage.'

'Nothing I am planning to do will have any impact on Derwent,' Jonathan said.

'But you refuse to tell me who she is?'

'For the moment, yes.'

'Then let me say this. You have rejected Judith Hargreaves. Very well. I regret it, I think it is a foolish and wrong-headed decision, but if you have made up your mind –'

'I have.'

'Then I must accept it. But if you intend to become entangled with someone whose name you are ashamed to tell me –'

'Shame has nothing to do with it.'

Grandma's voice overrode him. '– someone clearly unsuitable, I have to warn you there will be consequences.'

'And who is to decide whether this person is unsuitable or not?'

'I control the trust and its assets. I will decide what happens to them on my death.'

'Are you saying that if I choose someone you disapprove of you will disinherit me?'

'I have faith in your intelligence so do not believe it will come to that. But you have a clear choice. You can make an unsuitable alliance, Jonathan, or you can have Derwent. I will not permit you to have both.'

Jonathan put down his knife and fork. Deliberately he wiped his mouth with his napkin. He stood. He said, 'What sort of man do you think I am?'

Shoulders squared, he left the room. He left behind his grandmother ready to hurl plates in her fury. She sat rock hard and unmoving in her chair. Later she heard the clatter of hooves as Jonathan rode out and down the hill.

The blacksmith's forge was built low to the ground, its walls strong and hunched, like the shoulders of its owner. Who emerged from the fiery interior, hearing the arrival of what might be business.

Conan's scowl deepened when he saw who the horseman was.

'My daughter don't live here no more.'

'It was you I wanted to see.'

Conan folded brawny arms across his chest. 'Just so long as you know. What is it you're wanting?'

Truculence came with the territory where Conan Hampton was concerned.

'I want your permission to marry her.'

A derisive grin. 'Marry my Bec? What's your gran gunna say about that, eh?'

'Never mind that. She's only sixteen. I need your permission.'

'You think I don't know me own daughter's age?'

Jonathan waited. Conan's glare darkened. 'Do what you want. She walked out on me. I reckon that means I don't have no say what she does. Nor want to, neither.'

He went back into the gusting heat and slammed the door.

Jonathan thought, At least I tried.

He mounted and pointed the bay to Waldren's Corner.

When Mrs Painter saw her visitor she was turmoil on legs.

'She's out the back somewhere. Collecting eggs, I think. Come in. I'll see if I can find her.'

Jonathan waited and presently the constable arrived. He nodded, man to man, but had nothing to say and later, hair in a tangle, cheeks flushed, Bec Hampton came also.

'Step outside with me,' said Jonathan, his fingers touching hers. 'I want to ask you something.'

Starlight; bird song; the bright flames of dawn. Disbelief followed by joy filled Bec to the brim.

'You mean it?'

'I would never say such a thing unless I meant it.'

'But won't your grandmother be angry?'

'Probably.'

'What about Derwent?'

'She's already told me she'll disinherit me if I don't marry the woman she wants.'

'But you can't give up Derwent.'

'She's left me no choice. I'm not going to let her run my life.'

'Is that why you asked me to marry you? To defy your grandmother?'

'I asked you because I love you. Because I want you to be my wife. Because I am yours. Derwent has nothing to do with it.'

Bec knew Derwent had everything to do with it. If he lost Derwent because of her he would end up hating her. She couldn't let him do it. But it would break her heart to turn him down.

'If you give me up to keep Derwent your grandma will have won,' she said. 'But if you give up Derwent for me won't she still have won?'

'How do you work that out?'

'Because you *should* inherit it, Jonathan! She's no right to stop you.'

'Of course she has. It's hers; she can do what she likes with it.'

'You told me she's always saying how important the family is. You're family. She'll be punishing you for not letting her get her own way. That's putting her first, not the family. What is she, your gaoler?'

'Of course not.'

'Then we mustn't let her do it.'

Not *you* mustn't. *We.*

She remembered sitting in the shadow of Blackman's Head, looking across the rolling land that was Derwent and thinking how her feelings for Jonathan gave her feelings also for the land that would one day be his.

At the time that idea had been so huge that she had been unable to get her head around it. Now she could.

Jonathan was hers. He had said so. Did that not mean Derwent was hers also?

She would fight to make it so.

The genius that had lain dormant in Bec Hampton stirred into life, filling every vein with heat. She took his hands in hers. Unrehearsed, the words flowed from her heart and her heart, suddenly, was larger than herself or Jonathan, larger even than Derwent itself.

'You are so strong. I've known you and loved you all my life and I know you won't let anyone beat you. Not me or my dad or your grandma. No one. Because that is the man you are.'

She believed what she was saying absolutely and in that certainty discovered a power she never knew she had, making her conscious as never before of her strength and beauty.

She tightened her hands on his. 'Did you mean it? You really want to marry me?'

'I did mean it and I do.'

'Then I will tell you what you must do.'

1851

By July 1851 Richard was twenty-three and working as an overseer on one of the Derwent farms when his half-brother William arrived home from school for the winter holidays.

As far as Alice was concerned William's arrival was not good news. Even as a child they had not got on. William was smart but in a bad way. He had been up to every trick in the book yet somehow had always managed to pass the blame on to Richard. Or sometimes to her. On his last visit home, six months earlier, he had looked at her in a way that had left her feeling she had been smeared with dirt.

This time she suspected he would come looking for her and the day after his arrival he did.

'Come and walk with me,' he said.

'I'm too busy.'

'Uncle Barnsley is getting a bit long in the tooth and I hear that new Dr Morgan's been visiting. I suspect one of these days soon I'll be inheriting this property,' he said. 'The rest too, I suppose.'

'Perhaps,' Alice said.

'I doubt you'll be telling me you're too busy then.'

'Who can say?' Alice said.

'*I* can say. And if there's any sense in that pretty head of yours you'll agree with me.'

He might have been ten years older than he was, the way he spoke to her. That was what being rich did to you, Alice thought.

'You don't inherit me with the rest of the estate,' she said.

'That's true.' His smile was pure malice. 'And your mother?'

She looked at him.

'She's getting on a bit too, isn't she? Might find it hard, getting another job at her age.'

He would do it; it was all over his face.

'Come and walk with me,' he said. 'We can have a chat. Maybe see a few birds. Uncle says there are lots around here. Do you like birds?'

Barnsley Tregellas always liked to boast that his property stood between wood and water, one side of the ten-acre block with its face to the Derwent River at the bottom of the hill, the other side bordering the woodland that extended up the slope to the mountain.

It was towards the woodland that William led her now. Alice was in a quandary. What William had said was true; if her mother lost her job she would find it hard to get another one. That was the only reason she had agreed to go for a walk with him but she wasn't a fool. She knew that walking was not all William had in mind but walking with him did not mean she was willing to let him do anything else. Even if she did – and she would not! – there was no guarantee that Mother would keep her job anyway.

We can have a chat. Maybe see a few birds. Uncle says there are lots around here. Do you like birds?

What a question! She doubted he would know one from the other.

Yet still she walked at his side. Her mind was in turmoil but still she walked.

The Tregellas property was separated from the woodland by a stone wall but there was a gate which William now opened.

'Come,' he said.

The metal hinges creaked as he shut the gate behind them. Ahead of them the close-knit trees cast a green darkness.

Into which they walked side by side.

Aloysius Murphy, the main agent for the Derwent farms, had an office in a building near the stables at the rear of the big house. He was a great one for meetings and held one every week so his overseers could keep him up to date on the state of the properties under their control.

Richard Dark had no problem with the meetings; it made sense that Murphy should want to know what was going on since he was answerable to Barnsley Tregellas and he, beginning to fail as age and sickness tightened their grip, was still a harsh taskmaster.

Richard needed no one to remind him of that because Barnsley had never forgiven him for the loss of the money he claimed Richard's father had stolen from him, a resentment that had become even more potent when two expeditions to the Whitsunday Islands had failed to find any gold.

'Debts you've got, by rights you should work for nothing.'

Barnsley was king of grudge-holders; if he'd said it once he'd said it fifty times. He would probably still be saying it on his deathbed and William, taking his cue from his uncle, apparently thought the same.

Too bad; the benefit of being accused so unfairly and so often was that eventually you ceased to hear it at all. Richard had a job, he was good at it and resenting the past served no purpose.

There was another reason he was happy about the meetings; they gave him the chance to visit the house and, if he was lucky, spend a few minutes alone with Alice McIntyre.

His feelings for her had deepened since his return from the sea. Perhaps even before that; as children they had been close, then had come that catastrophic first voyage and its aftermath, when he had felt the world had turned against him, but since that bad time they had grown close once again.

He had made up his mind he would marry Alice McIntyre when the time was right. He had never spoken to her about it but from everything that had passed between them over the years he took it for granted there would be no problem.

The meeting was over. Richard had looked for Alice but missed her. He was riding down the drive towards the estate gates when he saw her walking with William near the stone wall on the far side of the grounds.

He had never expected to see Alice McIntyre and William Tregellas walking together.

He drew his horse to a stop and watched, the blood flushing into his brain as he saw them go through the side gate and disappear into the woodland.

Not speaking of something he had thought inevitable was far distant from not caring. For the first time he realised that one of the reasons he had never spoken to her was his doubt that he possessed whatever quality was needed to hold a woman. He saw too that a woman was not a creature to be taken for granted, that it was his ignorance and stupidity that had created the present situation. It was as though he had pushed her into William's arms.

They would see about that.

He put heels to his horse. Soon he was flying, hair loose, hat taut at the end of the string that held it to his throat. He entered the woods and quickly found a track he remembered. He rode more gently now, ears alert, hearing only silence. He dismounted and tethered the horse. He settled his hat on his head and walked deeper into the trees. His heart was pounding, he had a sickness in his throat, but somewhere not far away he would find her. That he knew. He would not think of what might happen then.

There were ferns and silence broken only by the thin whisper of streams flowing from the mountain.

Alice knew what William wanted, knew that he was never going to get it. Yet she sensed that William, years younger than she, was older and more experienced in certain areas into which they now entered.

William was big but soft. She would not have expected that in a man of his age. Because he *was* a man, she saw that now, and his hands were knowing. First his right hand took her left. She would have pulled away but did not, looking at him in the deserted wood while her mind seethed with uncertainty. He ran his fingers lightly up her arm. She did not shiver but knew they were moving towards something and was unsure whether she had the ability to prevent happening what she knew was already happening. The guileful hand momentarily cupped her breast beneath her dress, moving away before she could protest. She did nothing but the blood was drumming in her head.

'I like to come here,' he said. 'Alone with the birds and the trees.'

His eyes were bright and knowledgeable as he looked down at her. As again he touched her breast, watching her, and this time did not move it away but caressed her thoughtfully. Her blood was raging now as he kissed her.

His fingers touched the buttons of the dress.

Alice might have yielded her heart as her flesh had already declared its willingness to yield but at the last instant she saw herself, teeth shameful against his teeth, and was revolted.

She gathered herself to fight him but he was too strong, despite his softness, and things had gone too far. Nevertheless she fought anyway, would fight to the last. She was as angry with herself for her temporary weakness as with William, resisting, twisting as he tried to subdue her.

'Stop it!' And when he showed no sign of doing so she screamed as loudly as she could. 'I said stop it! Leave me alone!'

He did not and she saw her unexpected resistance had made him as angry as she. She began to panic, flinging herself to and fro in the arms that continued to crush themselves about her.

Suddenly all changed. She felt rather than saw it, a wind scything the air that dragged them apart, she stumbling, falling, opening her eyes to see William being smashed repeatedly, flung bleeding to the ground to be dragged limply to his feet and hit again, his face a mask of blood.

Who? What? For an instant she could grasp nothing of what was happening then saw that it was Richard, a Richard she had never known, an avenging creature with muscles hardened by years of physical work, whose fury stained the air as red as William's blood. So that Alice cried out again, in fear and protest.

'Stop! You're killing him!'

He was deaf until she snatched at his arm, crying in terror now as she implored him over and over again, and at last saw the madness leave his face. He stopped, letting William drop, and stood with head thrown back, his contorted features imploring the sky that was hidden behind the breeze-shimmered leaves.

Richard and Alice looked at each other. *Now what do we do?*

'We must help him,' Alice said.

Together they eased William to his feet. He swayed but could stand. Just.

'You'd better wash your face,' Alice said.

He nodded.

Alice went to help him but he flinched away from her touch. With William moving like an old man, they made their way to a nearby rivulet. He crouched and gingerly washed his face. Slowly he stood.

Richard's frenzied rage had created an emptiness in the air which made speaking hard but there were things that had to be said and Alice knew she was the one to say them.

'We went for a stroll in the woods,' she told William. 'That's all: just a stroll. You decided to climb a tree and fell. You understand? Unfortunately you knocked yourself about a bit but luckily Richard and I were able to help you.'

William stared at her, saying nothing.

'I got bruises where you grabbed me. You know where. I shan't say nothing about them unless I have to but if you make trouble for either of us I shall tell Mrs Hickmot the truth, that you tried to rape me and Richard saved me.'

'No one would believe you,' William whispered. But would not look at her.

'Dr Morgan would. People say he's an honest man. I'd show him and he'd know. Maybe you'd go to gaol, maybe not, but think how people would talk. Your uncle wouldn't like that much, would he?'

Richard went to speak but her raised hand hushed him. Her eyes were intent on William's damaged face.

'Look at me,' she said.

Reluctantly he did so.

'We got a deal?'

For a moment nothing; then, slowly, he nodded.

'Say it.'

'I won't tell anybody,' he said.

'Then we can all be friends,' she said. 'That's best, isn't it?'

They headed back towards the house, William walking a little easier now, but his face was like a shipwreck. At the edge of the woodland they stopped and Alice turned to Richard.

'I don't think you should come to the house,' she said.

'Why not?'

'Look at your hands.'

Richard looked at his skinned and bloody knuckles.

'People might wonder,' Alice said.

She was obviously right but he led her to one side.

'Watch out for him. He's tricky.'

'You think I don't know that?'

'I need to talk to you. Tonight.'

Alice thought. 'Six o'clock. I'll have time before dinner. I'll be walking down the lane.'

Richard mounted and rode away. Alice watched him go then returned to William.

'Let's get you home. And remember what we agreed.'

His puffed eyes looked sideways at her. 'And if I don't?'

'Next time he'll kill you.'

'Not if I have him arrested first.'

'Then I'll do it,' Alice said.

William laughed, painfully and unconvincingly. 'Just joking,' he said.

'Best not make jokes like that,' Alice said.

They went back to the house. Alice stayed with him while he explained his state to the housekeeper.

'Fell out of a tree?' Mrs Hickmot said. 'At your age? Whatever next?'

'He was ever so brave,' Alice said.

Mrs Hickmot sniffed. 'Play the fool like that, he needs to be brave. Lucky your uncle's away from home.'

'Where's he gone?

'To Melbourne. Along with about a million others, from what I hear.'

'Why? What's happened?'

'Haven't you heard? They've opened up another goldfield at a place called Ballarat.'

At six o'clock that dark evening, cold with the breath of coming frost, Alice McIntyre met Richard Dark along the lane bordering the Tregellas estate.

She had been undecided about meeting him at all; she felt bad about having gone into the woods with William, worse about how her feelings had jumped about when he'd first touched her. She thought how things might have worked out badly had Richard not turned up in time. Now she was scared he might ask what she'd been doing in the woods with William Tregellas.

She decided to go anyway – avoiding him would only matters trickier still later on – and it turned out he did not want to talk about that at all.

He dismounted and she watched him, all arms and legs and his tongue in knots as she waited for him to say what he had brought her here to say. Eventually he managed it.

'I reckon we should get married. If you're willing.'

Her heart leapt over the mountain. 'Why's that, then?'

She did not say it to tease him or because she had any doubts but because he had not said what had to be said.

'Please...'

By his expression she might have knifed him but she persisted. 'Why do you want to marry me?'

Richard found the words at last.

'Because I love you. I've loved you since we were kids and I want us to be together always. I want you to be my wife. If you're willing.'

Alice felt the tears flowing in her heart and beginning to prick behind her eyes. 'Of course I'll marry you. I'd marry you this minute if I could.'

'You don't think your parents…?'

Her smile engulfed the world. 'You think I'd let them stop me?'

'When?'

'With the banns and all that… Say two months?'

'Two months it is.' He made a long face. 'Seems like forever.'

'Don't be silly,' she said and laughed joyously. 'Aren't you going to kiss me, then?'

A kiss, she thought. And all the rest of it. It was funny to think about that and wonder how it would feel. I'll find out soon enough, she thought.

She felt so tender towards him. He had said nothing about the business with William. She wondered whether that was why he had proposed but she too said nothing. William had never really been the present and was certainly not the future. It was easy now to consign him to the past.

They said goodbye and she went back to the house, breaking into a skip and hop every few yards as excitement took possession of her.

Two months… The days would soon pass.

Charles Mason was sixty-nine years old. He lived in a large and strongly built house that stood on the high ground above Salamanca Place. It had unparalleled views of the Derwent River and was one of the grandest houses in Hobart Town. In this it suited its owner admirably because Charles Mason was by way of being grand too, being a banker with substantial interests in land and property across the whole of Van Diemen's Land.

Charles and his ineffectual wife had one child, born in their middle years long after they had given up hope of having any children at all. Cynthia was nineteen years old and recently widowed after Archie Styles, her reckless husband, had overturned the carriage in which they had been racing along an icy road. The accident had left Archie dead and the five months pregnant Cynthia with a miscarriage. Nor was that all.

Dr Campion had attended Cynthia after the accident. Later he and Cynthia's father had held a session behind closed doors and it was not a pleasant experience.

'Surely something can be done? A physician of your standing...'

Dr Campion had treated the highest and mightiest on the island and needed no one to remind him of his standing.

'There is nothing I or anyone can do. The injuries your daughter suffered mean she will be unable to have children. I am aware this is unwelcome news. If I could give you reason to hope I would. The simple fact is I cannot.'

And dusted his fingers; facts were facts.

Charles Mason frowned. This was serious news. He felt for his daughter, of course, but there were financial implications too, because the daughter of a wealthy banker had a commercial value. Cynthia's inability to have children, if it became known, would reduce that value considerably. In the worst case he might not be able to marry her off at all, leaving him with the unedifying prospect of maintaining her for the rest of his life.

As a banker Charles Mason was a confident man. He prided himself on giving sound advice to his customers. It gave him a sense of self-importance that he relished but now, ironically, he found himself in something of a predicament himself. The making of certain investments had coincided with the discovery that his late son-in-law had left significant debts. While he had no legal obligation to settle these debts the simple fact was that a banker rose or fell by his good name and to renege on the sums owing by the dissolute wretch who had unhappily married his daughter would do him no good at all. The result of this coincidence was that Charles

Mason found himself stretched, a situation as unfamiliar as it was unwelcome.

Therefore when on the first Monday in August his clerk announced the arrival of an unexpected visitor, Charles Mason was more than usually interested.

'Mr Barnsley Tregellas, you say? Show him in, Mr Murtle, show him in at once. If you please.'

At sixty-two Barnsley Tregellas had become a personage in the town, as feared as he was well known. He dressed up to his reputation: a black woollen topcoat over clothing of a London cut and a snow-white stock. His hair was grey but plentiful. His sturdy body was hard as was his expression but Barnsley's expression was always hard, his eyes chips of glass in a granite face. Charles Mason knew that in different circumstances this man might have made a formidable rival but fortunately the banking world of Hobart Town was big enough to accommodate them both without friction.

'Mr Tregellas, an unexpected pleasure. I had heard you were away.'

'But am now back,' Barnsley said.

'Such excitement in Victoria... They say the gold will be the making of the colony.'

'I have come about your daughter,' Barnsley said.

'What of her?'

'A sad business. I trust she is recovered?'

'Thank you, yes. She is very well.'

'Although no doubt mourning the loss of the child.'

News of the miscarriage had been well guarded but Barnsley Tregellas had a way of worming out everybody's secrets; Charles wished his own spy system were as efficient.

'It is to be expected,' he said. 'But she is young. She will get over it.'

The cold eyes inspected the room before refocusing on Charles Mason. 'You say she is young. How young, precisely?'

Charles had to think. 'She is nineteen,' he said.

'And already a widow. But young enough to remarry.'

'In time. And to the right man. One hopes so.'

Behind the granite features Barnsley's mind absorbed the information. 'I have a business proposition to put to you,' he said.

Barnsley sat pensively in his carriage as he was driven back to his house.

His informants had told him Charles Mason was stretched financially: no doubt only a temporary setback, but embarrassing to someone of Mason's status in the community. The thought pleased Barnsley; anything that disadvantaged a rival – and who in the commercial world of Hobart Town was not? – was to be treasured and used when the opportunity arose. As he believed it now had.

Yet he was uneasy. His discussion with Charles Mason had gone smoothly; he had pointed out that a marriage between Mason's daughter and his nephew William would offer advantages to both families. In the normal way of things he would have expected a period of haggling, with talk of trusts and guarantees and each man trying to squeeze what benefit he could from the other, but there had been nothing of that; Mason had gulped down his suggestion with an eagerness that had set warning bells ringing in Barnsley's head. In the business world they inhabited it wasn't how things were done.

Something wasn't right.

As soon as he got home he made enquiries and found what he had expected, that Charles Mason's shortage of funds was temporary only and would have no long-term significance. So it wasn't lack of cash that was the problem.

He sent a messenger to fetch Dr Campion, who arrived shortly afterwards with a speed that was gratifying but not unexpected.

'I have a question to put to you,' Barnsley said after he had got the doctor settled in an easy chair, a glass of sack in his hand.

Campion inclined his head. 'I am at your service. As always, Mr Tregellas.'

'Just so. The question concerns Mrs Cynthia Styles, formerly Miss Cynthia Mason. I believe Mrs Styles is a patient of yours?'

'That is correct. I have acted for the Mason family –'

'You attended her after her accident?'

'That is so.' The good doctor was a picture of complacency. 'I believe I may claim to have been instrumental in restoring her to her present excellent health. I have found that judicious bleeding of the patient –'

'Excellent health, you say. In every respect?'

Dr Campion pricked up his ears. Much of his local information came from gossip but it was a fact that Barnsley Tregellas had an unmarried nephew and a man would have to be a fool not to appreciate the significance of such a question.

'She may be a little troubled in her mind but that is a purely temporary condition, natural in someone bereaved at so young an age.'

'But physically?'

Campion was a man who believed in sticking to his guns. 'Undoubtedly.'

'You are certain of that?'

Campion was not a man given to self-doubt but was uneasy at the direction of the conversation. 'Mr Tregellas, you will not object if I speak plainly?'

'Speak.'

'Then permit me to remind you that as physician to the Mason family in general and Mrs Styles in particular I am bound by the ethics of my profession to the confidence inherent in those duties.'

Public opinion might have called his manner of speech pompous. The doctor cared little for public opinion but wealthy patients of standing in the community, and even more potential wealthy patients, needed a different approach.

'I trust you will excuse my bluntness,' he said.

Barnsley inspected his fingertips before replying. 'You are saying Cynthia Styles has something wrong with her?' he said.

Campion bridled. 'I said nothing of the sort –'

'Earlier, Doctor, you claimed her general health was excellent. If that were so I see no reason why you would now have to rest on the ethics of your profession.'

'Her general physical health is excellent.'

'Then what is the problem?'

Campion studied the sack swirling in his half-empty glass. 'This is very difficult for me.'

'Then permit me to assist you. Mr Mason is a colleague, a man I greatly respect. However, the Masons are a dying breed. Charles Mason is several years older than I and has told me himself he is in uncertain health.' Mason had said no such thing but Barnsley told the lie easily; he had long experience in telling lies. 'Moreover, he has only one female child who, in the nature of things, is likely to remarry. The Masons will soon be extinct. I, on the other hand, am in excellent health with a young nephew who in years to come will no doubt have descendants of his own. In other words, Dr Campion, we are a dynasty in the making. It is for you, Dr Campion, to decide where you see your future.'

'Mr Mason told you of his health problems?'

'Not two days ago.' Barnsley drained his glass. He got to his feet and walked to the window, where he stood with his back to the room, the warm room and crackling fire in marked contrast with the wintry scene outside. 'I am receiving good reports of this new Dr Morgan,' he said.

Campion stiffened. 'A former medical superintendent aboard a transport? No doubt his fees are low.' He sniggered. 'I suspect they will have to be if he hopes to attract patients.'

Barnsley turned and walked back to his chair. 'Cynthia Styles?' he said.

'I am not prepared to discuss my patient's medical history. To do so would be quite wrong.' Barnsley opened his mouth but Campion beat him to it. 'However...'

'However?'

'You spoke of creating a dynasty. In your position I would not build my hopes of achieving such an outcome on Mrs Styles.'

'And why should that be?'

'My dear Mr Tregellas, I regret I can say no more. As I mentioned, ethical considerations –'

'But you are sure of the situation?'

'Absolutely sure.' Dr Campion's head was down, his eyes staring at his feet, but he had said it. *Absolutely sure.*

'Let me refresh your glass,' Barnsley said.

At ten o'clock the next morning Barnsley Tregellas walked briskly down the hill to Charles Mason's bank.

Charles's eyes lit up when Barnsley was announced but his enthusiasm was soon quenched.

'Tell me about Cynthia's health,' Barnsley said as soon as the two men were alone.

'What about it? As I told you she has made a complete recovery from the accident –'

'I am advised differently,' said Barnsley.

'What nonsense have you been told?' Mason put on his most ferocious expression but he had been caught out in a lie – by omission, but still a lie – and his anger lacked conviction.

'I have it on reliable authority that in consequence of the injuries she suffered when the carriage overturned your daughter is no longer capable of having children.'

'Who told you that?'

'Who told me is unimportant. What matters now is a simple answer to a simple question. Is your daughter, Cynthia Styles, able to have children or is she not? Yes or no, Charles? Yes or no?'

More and more Charles Mason was looking like a rat with its tail in a trap. 'The doctors are unsure…'

'And you never thought to tell me. When we were talking three days ago. About a possible marriage between your daughter and my nephew.'

Crack. Crack. Crack. Barnsley broke his sentence into three parts, each as brutal as a musket shot.

'Until I was sure…'

For the first time Barnsley smiled: genial yet with a hint of teeth. He sat down on the visitor's side of Charles's desk and leant forwards, elbows on the polished mahogany surface. 'Don't worry,

Charles, the game isn't over. It will mean changing the details a little but the game isn't over. Not by any means. I believe we'll be able to come to an amicable agreement despite your attempt at a cover-up. Hmm?' To a stranger his laugh might have sounded genuine. 'This is what I propose. For the moment there will be no transfer of assets.'

Mason blinked; he had not been expecting that. The basic rule in business was if you wanted something you had to give something in return, yet now Barnsley was saying no assets transfer? There had to be a snag.

There was.

'No transfer *now*,' Barnsley said. 'I like to keep things simple. No asset transfers, no family trusts, no secret agreements. Everything clear and above board.' He gave a wolf smile, this man who acquaintances said couldn't lie straight in bed.

'What do you have in mind?' Charles Mason said.

'A simple agreement. To be entered into the day your daughter marries my nephew.'

'Saying what?'

'That on your death your bank's assets will merge with the Tregellas Bank. After making suitable provision for your widow – shall we say one hundred thousand pounds? – your other assets will go to your daughter.'

'Which means to your nephew.'

'With the law as it stands, that is true. But consider, sir, your daughter will be well off, a member of a highly esteemed family. She will be properly looked after and well regarded. In the mean time she will be off your hands, with no one needing to know about the unfortunate consequences of her accident.'

Was it an implied threat? Charles could not be sure.

'I may outlive you,' he said.

'You may. But the agreement will stand,' Barnsley said.

Barnsley kept his parting shot until he was about to leave, having shared a glass with his outmanoeuvred host. 'To think I had a dozen of my ex-cons on stand-by to start a run on your bank…' He chuckled whimsically. 'Well, well, it seems they won't be needed after all. Not for the moment, anyway.'

When Cynthia Styles was expecting her first child she had been grateful for all her blessings. She knew that apart from praying on her knees at the side of her bed every night she had done nothing to deserve her good fortune, being timid by nature and, as her father had told her more than once, not very bright.

She had never thought she was much of a catch and hadn't been able to believe her luck when Archie Styles had proposed to her, especially when it appeared Papa had given his approval. Archie was everything she thought she wanted in a man. He claimed to have aristocratic connections: with the family of a duke, no less. He was also both handsome and dashing and he excited her when he drove their carriage as though he were one of the charioteers she had read about in the annals of ancient Rome.

When she found she was expecting a child she believed there was no woman on earth happier and more fortunate than she.

Then had come the accident.

She spent weeks wishing she could die, as her husband and baby had died. She did not pray for death since that would be a sin but would have welcomed it nonetheless.

She knew she had been foolish to expect the happiness she had not deserved so became more timid than before, as though that would compensate for her presumption. Nevertheless, when her tyrannical father came up with the name of the man whom he had nominated as her second husband she was distressed to learn that, wealthy or not, he was of no family to speak of. It was a bitter comedown after her previous marriage. Cynthia was prepared to resent her husband-to-be even before she had met him but her father made it clear that she had no choice in the matter.

'The Tregellas family is one of the wealthiest on the island, with interests not only in land but in the Victorian goldfields,' Mr Mason said. 'You will be the mistress of a magnificent house and estate and will enjoy a status enjoyed by few other women. So we'll have no more of your nonsense. You are marrying William Tregellas and there's an end of it.'

The dictatorial reputations of her fiancé and his uncle were well known even in the closeted world of Cynthia Styles; she would be exchanging her father's tyranny for her new husband's but there was no help for it. She would be dutiful, as would be expected of a wife, and make the best of things.

From childhood she had been taught that a woman's life was fulfilled and glorified by service to her husband.

Alice McIntyre married Richard Dark on 14 August 1851 in the lopsided church of St Madern, the Cornish saint name chosen by Emma in the days of the Dark prosperity but otherwise unknown. The church, erected by convict hands, stood in the high country on a piece of land allocated to it from the original Derwent grant.

It wasn't Alice's first choice – it was a long way to go and she'd have been happy marrying in the local pub had that been permitted – but Richard was determined.

'It was my father's originally,' he said. 'I was there while it was being built.'

Not that he remembered much about it but setting up another generation in the place where things had begun had a significance he would have found hard to put into words.

For once Uncle Barnsley came good, or reasonably so. He arranged the transport and the overnight accommodation (bride and bridegroom decorously apart on the journey north) with a reception of sorts at the big house that Barnsley was considering renaming Tregellas.

'Your uncle is a great one for changing names,' said Alice, thinking how William had been a Dark too until Barnsley had intervened.

Not that she cared about William's name or his feeble fiancée, who combined a simpering expression with an arrogance that showed how little she cared for her soon-to-be new family.

'Looks like a woman who's lost a tanner and found a ha'penny,' Alice's mother said.

For the last twenty-five years Enid McIntyre had been cook at the Tregellas house outside Hobart Town, a position of some status given Barnsley Tregellas's wealth. She had been born a Stott which was another way of spelling nobody and made a habit of large floral hats that she thought or hoped might make up for it. She also enjoyed a nice glass of port from time to time in nice company. As for Richard, she thought he was a nice lad, a poor motherless orphan badly treated by life, a feeling which, along with the hat, gave her the warmth of a shared experience. Alice's dad wasn't into company of any sort but his solitary disposition did not prevent his swigging a surreptitious beer in a corner of the vast living room and staring out at the view.

William was there too because his uncle had insisted; he shepherded the slow-witted fiancée who had been foisted on him by an uncle who in all his life had never taken no for an answer. He whiled away the time staring at Alice in her wedding gown while his fancy drew pictures of how she would have looked without it.

The one who got away, he thought. But maybe not forever, in the light of what his uncle had told him.

'You're telling me Cynthia can't have kids?' His outrage had been close to genuine. 'What's the point of marrying her if she can't produce an heir? I don't even *like* her, for God's sake.'

Barnsley had smiled his iron-plated smile. 'I am told that lots of men dislike their wives. And the material benefits, let me assure you, are huge. I am sure a man of your initiative will have no difficulty in finding a woman to give you a son.'

'But —'

Barnsley's smile became harder still. 'The process of adopting a child is not difficult if you possess money. Why,' he said jovially, 'I could even adopt one myself. If my fortune is no longer of interest to you.'

In the nature of things they could not have expected many guests at the church or afterwards at the house. It was too far away from

Hobart Town for those who might otherwise have had an interest but Barnsley had ensured the presence of some of the Derwent workers, suitably scrubbed, since it would have looked bad if only half a dozen had been present. The bride and groom could not expect much in the way of gifts from people who did not know them but most were happy to give Alice and Richard their good wishes, if little else.

Barnsley gave Richard twenty-five guineas in a genuine leather purse. This might have seemed mean to those who thought of Richard as more or less a member of the family but he was only an overseer, after all, and with the promise of an ongoing job too, which was worth a lot. So Barnsley thought his gift generous and Alice, who had dreamt the impossible dream of being presented with a small farm of their own, wisely kept her mouth shut.

Her bits and pieces were already loaded in the back of the cart that Richard had borrowed from the farm the previous day. Now Alice loaded herself aboard as well, smiling and waving as custom demanded but easing off the shoes that had been pinching her poor toes. Underneath the smiles she was calm but resolute. Before her was her life and her husband's life and she was determined to make something of them, although what that might be she could not at that moment have said.

There were other rituals to be performed before she could consider their future but before she could even think of the unknown territory of the marriage bed she had to come to terms with this married woman who, surprisingly, was herself.

The married woman looked at the countryside through which the cart was slowly progressing. She had never before seen it as she saw it now – the greens and greys and browns of the verdant valley with the line of purple hills beyond – and identified this strangely unfamiliar land as the gateway through which she must travel in order to enter her new state.

She was content and even hummed a little, listening to the steady hooves of the old horse as it drew them forwards into the place where she would find herself anew with the man sitting at her side, his strong hands holding the leather reins.

She remembered things: her mother laughing and teasing her taciturn father; a game called pegotty top that she had played as a child with other girls; a cat called Ginger. Yet it seemed to Alice in the creaking cart that those memories had nothing to do with the woman she now was, even less with the woman she was about to become.

I am a married woman now, Alice thought.

She had wanted this with all her heart but the finality of the change bit deep as she sat in the rocking cart and looked ahead at the mild brown ribbon of track finding its way downhill into a massive green bowl with trees at the bottom and the sparkle and flash of water flowing over a stony bed.

'Do you get devils in these parts?' she said.

'Some. You hear them sometimes screeching in the dark.'

Something else that was strange.

'I heard of someone who had a devil as a pet but we never had none around us in Hobart Town, did we?' said Alice.

'We get eagles here,' Richard said. 'Got to watch out for the young lambs when eagles are about.'

Her husband eased the horse to a stand. That too was something new, the brown corded arms that she looked at in the motionless cart, the arms that she had seen ten thousand times over the years yet now had a different look about them. *Husband.* The word was strange in her mouth; the idea of it created a measure of apprehension in her heart. *Husband.*

'We'd better walk here,' he said. 'It gets steep further on. We wouldn't want this old cart to run away with us.'

Alice Dark, who felt she had been run away with once already that day, agreed. *Alice Dark.* That was strange too but she would not permit herself to doubt. She would love him, she thought, and the strangeness would disappear.

They walked beside the trundling cart as the patient horse drew it steadily down the hill. Which was indeed steep and rutted with gullies where past rains had eaten the brown soil.

'Where is the house?'

'Round the next bend,' Richard said.

Soon it came into view: stone walls and a shingle roof.

'That won't blow away in a gale,' Alice said.

It was bigger than she'd expected. She looked appreciatively around the green bowl of the valley, the slopes thick with sheep.

A good place for children. I shall be happy here.

Already she was making plans. The house was solid but plain. It needed prettying up.

I shall plant a rosebush by the door. A yellow one, if I can find a cutting. Maybe hollyhocks, if the winds aren't too strong. And a vegetable patch at the back.

So she took possession of the house, which, for the moment, was the future.

They cooked in a shack separate from the main building, for fear of fire.

'There's some mutton,' Richard said. 'And flour.'

'I shall make damper,' Alice said. 'To go with the mutton.'

They ate their evening meal. Now their eyes were bumping into each other, their movements more hurried. Alice felt her breath tremulous in her throat.

Their souls were intermingling now.

They rinsed their plates and looked at each other and the time had come. Together they went to the bed against the wall and later under the thin blanket found each other and themselves. The moon shone through the window and Alice lay awake thinking and feeling, sensing her changed flesh and the sleeping body of the man. For the moment she was content but her first urgency of possession had passed at some time during the night and now she compared what they had with what she knew would in time belong to her husband's half-brother, the man who had tried to ruin her, and to the stupid woman he planned to marry, and thought how unfair it was and how it was up to Richard and herself to do whatever it took to improve their future. They were as good as William and his fiancée and in time would prove it. So between the time of their arrival at the house and the morning's first grey light Alice's plans had changed.

She waited three months. Richard had been her friend nearly all her life but a husband was different from a friend and she needed time to adjust her thinking to her new state, and to sort out her plans for the future. In the interim she did what she had all along assumed she would do: she did the washing and cleaned the house and tended the cabbages behind the house and cooked the meals and made love to and with her husband in the narrow bed in the darkness. She had discovered that Richard was a shy man or perhaps one of those who found something shameful in the sexual act so that he wished to consummate their relationship only at night and with the lantern quenched.

Alice would have made love in the open, naked before the eyes of the indifferent sheep. She thought it might be exciting to do this provided no one else was about but she did not wish to frighten Richard so did not suggest it. It was also exciting to bathe naked in the creek flowing below the house so she did this instead. It left Richard at a loss and she knew she embarrassed him but he said nothing and her love for him grew stronger because he did not try to impose his disapproval on her.

When she was ready she told him her thoughts.

He sat on a felled log, face troubled, as he considered what she'd said. 'Are you sorry about us? The marriage, I mean? All of it?'

She took his hand. 'I'm that happy I can't begin to tell you. Really happy. But I want more for us than we've got. It's not right William should have everything and you nothing. It's not fair but your uncle obviously doesn't plan to do anything about it. So I reckon if we want to get ahead – for us and any kids we might have – it's up to us to do something.'

'Like what?'

'Like Ballarat.'

His eyebrows vanished into his hair. 'Go to the goldfields?'

'Why not? There's fortunes being made, from what the papers are saying.'

'You think we could be that lucky?'

'I think we can do whatever we want.'

'What do we use for money to get there?'

'I've got a bit put by. And you're an overseer; you must have something.'

He had: that was true. He hesitated for a moment – did he really want to risk everything he had on what might prove to be a foolish venture? – but even as he did so he knew he would do it. For her sake and hopefully his own.

She was overflowing with love and purpose and laughter because she saw that he would do it, now she had put the idea into his head.

'I've got too much on at this time of year,' he said. 'It wouldn't be right to walk away from it. When do you want to go?'

'Soon as you can get away,' she said.

At their next meeting Jonathan spoke to Murphy about getting someone to take his place as overseer.

'Might take a while,' Murphy said. 'Good blokes don't grow on trees, you know.'

'When?' Richard said.

'Maybe in the new year? I'll have to clear it with Mr Tregellas but I doubt he'll stand in your way. He's got interests over there himself, I understand.'

'In the gold?' Richard was surprised; it didn't seem Barnsley's style.

'In the land. William's over there now, keeping sweet with the people running the show.'

'He's just got married,' Richard said.

'So he has,' said Murphy. 'Seems like he couldn't wait to get away from that new wife of his. In his shoes I'd do the same.'

Murphy was from Cork via the convict ships and was willing to speak his mind, so long as his employer could not hear him.

'I doubt we'll be meeting up with him,' Richard said. 'He'll be staying at some posh hotel.'

'And you?'

'We'll be in with the mob.'

1913

It was the last week of April and autumn was well on the way. The welcome swallows were long gone and now the goldfinches had followed. Along the creeks the poplars burnt like yellow candles in the sunlight and when the wind blew the air was a torrent of falling leaves.

Now, unexpectedly, there was mystery in the air as well as leaves. Everyone at Derwent knew something was on the go but what it might be was the question.

Two days before the old lady had received a letter that had given her enormous satisfaction. Gladys, one of the maids, had reported meeting Mrs Penrose in the long gallery and hearing her humming a tune. Nobody had heard of such a thing before.

Now, suitcases and hatbox packed, Grandma had taken off in her carriage, saying only that she would be back the following day.

'Or possibly the day after,' she told Mrs Harris, the housekeeper.

Bec and Jonathan were up by Blackman's Head. They hadn't made love yet because today was a special occasion: Jonathan had decreed they would have a picnic.

'I'll get Mrs Gadd to knock us up something,' he had said.

Now they unpacked the picnic basket. Mrs Gadd's something consisted of potted meats, slices of ham and beef, a cold fillet of salmon, a loaf of crusty fresh-baked bread with farm butter and what Bec thought of as a righteous pork pie.

She said as much to Jonathan, who laughed.

'Delectable, I'll give you. Even ambrosial. But righteous? What's righteous about a pie?'

'Don't you go teasing me with your smart words,' she said. 'All food's righteous, when it's like this.'

That was a measure of the gulf between them, she thought, that he should take such things for granted while she didn't.

He kissed her. 'I stand corrected. Righteous it is.'

There was also a bottle of wine, still moderately cold, with a corkscrew and two glasses.

Jonathan drew the cork and poured; Bec examined the contents of her glass, pale yellow in the sunlight.

'I never drank anything like this before,' she said. 'What do you call it?'

'It's called Riesling. It comes from Watervale in South Australia. The family has an interest.'

Again the casual assumption of normality. One or other of us has a lot of learning to do, Bec thought, if we're ever to be comfortable together.

She sipped cautiously and made a face.

'It's sour!' Then tried again. 'But I think it could become quite pleasing. With practice.'

'It does, I assure you.'

'It makes my head feel funny,' she said.

'I know the treatment for that,' he said.

He kissed her so long and so hard that soon her head was spinning for reasons other than the wine.

'You'll spill it,' she said.

'Tip it down,' he said. 'Then it won't be a problem.'

She thought that sounded like good advice, so she took it. And later had no more thoughts about the Riesling wine at all.

Later Bec lay at Jonathan's side on the ragged blanket she had begged from Mrs Painter, who had been wise enough not to ask what she wanted it for. The breeze was cool on her skin; the autumn gales would soon be here and making love in the open would be out of the question.

'Make my titties wrinkle like lemons,' Bec said.

Jonathan had been half asleep. 'What?'

'I was thinking what it would be like to do this in the snow.'

'Heaven forbid.'

'Might be all right with a few rugs,' she said.

For the moment, though, Bec was content to lie there and listen to the voices of the bush about her.

The teacher at her local school had sensed Bec's potential and lent her lots of books. She'd read how trees lived for many years, which had made her think about all the things they must have seen in their time. In her imagination she had identified with the movement of the black bands through the high country, sunlight shining on the quartz tips of their long spears.

'What happened to them?' she asked Mrs Roberts.

'Mostly they died.'

'But how?'

'Disease for the most part. But also fighting each other and the settlers.'

'Are there any left?'

'Some, not many.'

'That is sad,' Bec said.

'Yes, but it's how the world is,' Mrs Roberts said.

Lying on the threadbare earth, Bec sensed shadows parting to reveal the shy movement of wallaby and quoll, the menace of snakes, the wide-awake eyes of possums.

All these things were part of the land.

We have our place too, Bec thought. We are as much part of the rhythm of things as those others. It was more feeling than thought but it made her proud and humble at the same time. In the voice of the wind she could hear the distant resonance of didgeridoo, of

vanished voices singing the dawn. Everything that had ever happened was there in the trees and the dusty scrub, the orange sweep
of Blackman's Head soaring into the sky above them, every day
turning blood-red in the morning sun. The kookaburra greeting
the dawn.

We are part of it, she thought, part of the footprints criss-crossing the land.

She would have shared her feelings with the man, had it been
possible, but she did not have the words. Instead she lay silently,
eyes wide and senses alert, knowing herself to be a part of the whole.

Later, when for the second time that day they made love, it was
for Bec not merely a celebration of the flesh but an offering to the
spirits of the land.

Just before lunch the next day Mrs Harris looked out of Derwent's
drawing room window and saw what looked like a black beetle
crawling slowly up the track that connected the big house with the
north–south road, trailing smoke as it came.

'What on earth is it?'

Walter, the assistant gardener and a bit of a know-all, provided
the answer.

'It's a motor car, Mrs Harris.'

Mrs Harris's hand was on her palpitating breast. 'Why's it coming here?'

'I reckon you'll find Mrs Penrose has gone and bought it,' Walter
said.

Most of the staff were staring now.

'I've seen pictures,' Gladys said, 'But that's the first real one I've
seen.'

'I wonder what type of motor it is?' Walter said.

'You're saying there is more than one type?' said Mrs Harris.

'There are lots of different types,' Walter said. 'It's the coming
thing, Mrs Harris.'

Mrs Harris was not happy with coming things. 'Oh dear.'

They watched the motor creeping up the hill.

'It's going very slowly,' Mrs Harris said. 'You think it'll manage to get up here?'

'Won't the old lady be mad if it doesn't?' Walter said.

'Best get on,' Mrs Harris said. 'Don't want her to catch us idling.'

When she arrived Bessie was more the lady of the manor than ever: an achievement that most would have thought impossible. She sailed into the house like a liner entering harbour, berthed herself in her favourite chair and sent for Mrs Harris. Whom she favoured with her best chatelaine smile.

'Any excitements while I've been away?'

'Nothing, Mrs Penrose.'

'No births, marriages or deaths?'

'None that I'm aware of.'

'I saw the staff all agog as I came up the hill.'

'Many of them have never seen a motor car before, Mrs Penrose.'

'They'd better get used to them. There'll be plenty about before long. I understand they are quite the rage in England. I believe the king has one.'

'Is that so, Mrs Penrose?' Mrs Harris knew better than get into technicalities. 'Did it come from England?' Because surely it could not have been manufactured locally.

'From America. It was made by a man called Ford. I ordered it some time ago. It is called a Model T Ford and as far as I know is the first one in the country.'

'That is very impressive, Mrs Penrose.'

Mrs Harris's success in her career had been aided by her ability to say the right thing when the right thing needed to be said.

'I daresay my grandson will be interested,' Bessie said. 'These days young people seem to like mechanical things. Is he somewhere about?'

'I believe he is out, Mrs Penrose.'

'Do we know where he is?'

Mrs Harris, who knew almost to the inch where Jonathan was, shook her head. 'He didn't say, Mrs Penrose.'

It took Jonathan two hours to get back to Derwent House.

After dropping Bec at the Painters' place his emotions were in such a state that he decided to go back to Blackman's Head. He went there because it had become important to him and because he had things to work out.

He sat listening to the peaceful sounds of the horse grazing and thinking of everything that had happened there. Bec's sighs of fulfilment as they made love echoed in the silently watching trees and he knew it had been then, lying in each other's arms beneath the towering mass of the Head, the wind-rustled leaves of the overarching trees, that the bond between them had been forged.

This was the place.

He spoke aloud to the scrubby bush. 'I shall not let her down.'

Easily said, but the challenge facing them was immense. Grandma Bessie had never tolerated opposition. He knew she would do whatever she could to make sure her legacy remained true to the image she was determined it should have. And one thing was sure: no way did Bec Hampton fit into that image. Money, power and prestige were what Grandma Bessie valued and Bec had none of them. Jonathan doubted there was a woman in Tasmania who in Grandma Bessie's opinion would be less suitable to becoming the wife of Derwent's owner than Bec Hampton, the blacksmith's daughter.

Would she really disown him if the marriage went ahead?

He supposed she might. He would just have to talk her round.

God knew how.

He mounted Hector and set off for home.

Mrs Painter gave Bec a questioning look when she came into the house. 'Gone, has he?'

Bec gave her a nod and a quick smile but did not speak. Her heart was in turmoil and she was afraid if she said anything it would show. She went into her room and closed the door behind her. She lay on the bed, staring up at the ceiling.

This new Bec.

She thought: You've done it now.

Love was a foreign country, lying somewhere between the marsh and the twin hillocks where passion lived, but it was not alone; there was also fear. Bessie Penrose had always been a tyrant; if she felt herself or her plans threatened she would be merciless.

Bec had read of people who had sacrificed everything for love; she had the uneasy feeling she might be close to doing exactly that.

Then she thought, No. She was strong; she was determined; she was in love. She would not let an old woman ruin her life. She would fight. God knew how, but she would fight.

1854

In the end Barnsley Tregellas had proved more difficult than they'd expected, saying too many workers had left already and he was sick of it.

'Leave me now and there'll be no job for you when you come back.'

'If we find gold who cares?' Richard said to Alice.

But Alice was more practical. 'And if we don't?'

So it was 1854 by the time they got away and now they were there it was obvious the mining operations were much more extensive than they'd expected.

They'd heard Ballarat long before they saw it for the noise of the diggings was indescribable. First off there was the barking of thousands of dogs, used to guard claims from thieves who without the dogs might have stripped the diggers to the bone. Later they made out the inane cackling of kookaburras, bellowing of bullocks and profane cursing of the drovers that provided highlights to a continuous and muffled roar of voices: the thousands of miners above and below the ground digging in a frenzy that defied belief.

They had teamed up with a bloke they'd met on the track. Rascal Jones, which he insisted was his real name, had been at Mount Alexander. He had drawn a blank there and had now decided to chance his luck in Ballarat. He was lean and hard and about thirty years old. His face looked like it had felt a fist or two in its time and they thought he might be a useful companion in an increasingly rough world.

The three of them stood on the high ground and looked down at the confused bedlam of the tent city that was the mining camp.

'At least we won't be lonely,' Richard said.

A termite mound wasn't in it, with what looked like a million tiny figures swarming everywhere they looked.

'We've been a week on the road from Melbourne,' said Alice. 'Let's be thankful we've made it in one piece.'

'Damn right,' said Rascal Jones.

'Let's go and get rich,' Alice said.

They shouldered their packs, squared their shoulders and went on down the hill into what they had been warned was the gateway to hell.

It was all of that, a boiling pot of noise and activity.

'You have to shout even to hear yourself think,' Alice said.

On all sides men – and a handful of women – were digging, sifting and washing soil. Mounds of worked earth were everywhere and the air was foul with the stench of smoke and sewage.

'We gotta find the gold commissioner's tent,' Rascal said. 'He'll tell us where there's vacant claims.' He made a sour face. 'And charge us for them.'

'Charge?' Richard said.

'Licence fees,' Rascal said. 'They knows how to sock it to us, believe me.'

'And if we don't pay?'

'The goldfield police will chuck us off if we don't have a licence. You got to produce it when they ask so make sure you always keep yours with you.'

They found the tent and paid the fee for two adjoining claims.

'You got to give it a name. For our records, see?' the commissioner's clerk said.

'I tell you what,' Richard said. 'I remember Mama telling me about a Cornish word meaning a mine or place of work. Wheal, the word was. We'll call it Wheal Alice. How about that?'

'Fancy you remembering that. You were so small,' Alice said.

'Small maybe. But I remember good. Wheal Alice it is,' he said.

The clerk entered the name in the register, came and pegged the sites and they were ready to start.

'Each one is only eight feet square,' Richard said, looking at the licence in his grubby paw. 'Doesn't seem much for thirty bob a month.'

'That's the way it is,' Rascal told him. 'Now we'd better go buy ourselves some shovels to dig with. And a screen for sifting what we dig out.'

They bought shovels and pickaxes from the blacksmith and a tent, windlass and fifty fathoms of rope from the general store. The prices made their eyes water but there was no choice: articles like these would have been far too heavy and awkward to bring with them, but they couldn't survive without the tent or get at the gold without the tools.

If there was gold in their claims to find.

They rigged the tent, ate the little food they had with them and slept the sleep of the exhausted. There were sly grog sellers everywhere so there was plenty of drunken yelling but even that, coupled with a cacophony of screams, howling dogs and gunshots, failed to disturb them.

First thing the next morning, heads down, hopes up, they set to work. They worked in shifts, Alice taking her turn.

'Full marks for effort,' Rascal Jones said. 'Not your fault you ain't got the muscles.'

By evening they were three feet down and had found nothing, with Rascal shaking his head.

'Don't like the look of it.'

'Still early days,' said Richard.

'At Mount Alexander it was the top layer where they found the nuggets.'

'Maybe Ballarat is different,' Alice said.

'Maybe.'

He sounded doubtful but Alice said she'd overheard blokes talking when she went to the shop for food.

'If you can call a tent a shop,' she said. 'If you can call it food.'

'What did you hear?'

'They're saying the real wealth is further down.'

'How much further down?'

'I heard hundred, two hundred feet.'

Rascal whistled. 'That's deep, sure enough.'

'It would take months to get down so far,' Richard said.

'And we'd need to shore up the shaft,' Rascal said. 'Or we'd likely have it come down on top of us.'

'How do they know what's down there, anyway?' Richard said.

'Seems some have gone down and struck rich ground,' Alice said. 'That's what they called it: rich ground. The beds of what used to be underground rivers.'

'Which brought down the gold? When was that?'

'Thousands of years ago. Leastways, that's what they were saying.'

'Rivers of gold,' Rascal said. 'I likes the sound of that.'

'How do we know there'll be any under our claims?' Alice asked.

'We don't.'

'And if there's not?'

'Then we're broke.'

'So what do we do?'

They looked at each other. Alice lifted her chin and ignored her pounding heart. 'We're miners, ain't we? That means taking risks. If we lose, we lose. I say we go down.'

They laughed, excited by the challenge and the risk they were embracing. They all spoke together.

'We go down.'

Alice knew she would never forget that time.

It took them the best part of three months to reach the gutter where in the distant past the underground rivers had flowed. Thank

God for Rascal, she thought. Without him they would never have managed it. Richard was strong and willing but one man alone could never have done it. Even working shifts both men were utterly spent when they crawled out of the steadily deepening shaft. There was no point Alice offering to help; they all knew that physically she was not up to it. What she did was use the windlass to haul up the buckets of clay twenty feet, forty feet, sixty feet as they were filled. That was an exhausting business too but something she could just manage.

Each night all three of them died a deep death as sleep overwhelmed them.

Outside the shaft trouble was brewing. Everybody knew it. As their neighbour Karl Leipzig said, it had been coming for months.

'There will be deaths before it is through,' he said.

Of course Karl was not the most optimistic of men.

'That's his blood speaking,' said Willy McNab, another neighbour. 'That's a German for you.'

Willy was biased, having been in Stuttgart at the time of the 1848 uprising, but people wanted to believe him so most, Richard among them, did.

Richard's horizons were limited to the shaft that was sucking up their hopes and energy and the little money they had in a seemingly endless war against the recalcitrant earth. 'We've too much on our plate to worry about what's going on anywhere else,' he said. 'I doubt it'll come to anything, anyway.'

Alice wasn't so sure. She had always liked to keep herself informed and what she was hearing did not make for a quiet mind.

The first intimation of trouble had been back in June when the newly appointed lieutenant governor, Sir Charles Hotham, had infuriated the diggers by introducing weekly licence hunts.

'So tyranny starts,' Karl Leipzig had said. 'First they harass us by checking the licences once each week. Next – you vill see – they vill increase the number of hunts. Twice weekly, maybe more.'

'Nonsense,' said Willy McNab.

On 13 September Sir Charles Hotham ordered the licence hunts to be carried out twice weekly, while the goldfields police grew more and more aggressive.

'It's almost like they're looking for trouble,' Richard said.

Maybe they were; in mid-October the disabled servant of a Catholic priest, a non-miner, was beaten up for not having a mining licence. Later the policeman who attacked him charged the servant with assault.

'You can feel it,' Alice said.

'Feel what?'

'Trouble. It's like milk rising in a pan. At this rate it'll be boiling over pretty soon.'

'Who says so?' said Richard.

'I say so. I can smell it.'

'You and your nose,' Richard said.

'Me, I'm gunna steer well clear of it,' Rascal Jones said. 'I never bin much for boiled milk.'

'It'll quieten down soon enough,' said Richard, determined to be optimistic.

In the meantime digging went on as the shaft, with excruciating slowness, drove deeper and deeper into the earth.

Water was a problem. It started to seep into the mine when they'd gone down twenty feet. After that it got steadily worse. They bought a share in a pump that helped keep the flood under control. They were running out of money but had no choice. No pump, no chance of reaching the gold they went on telling each other would be waiting for them when they reached the gutter.

Shoring up the sides of the shaft took almost as long as the digging but again they had no choice. Being buried alive, as had happened to some miners, was not an option that appealed to them.

Finally, finally, when the pain of endless digging had come close to overwhelming them, at eight o'clock in the morning in the last week of November, Richard hoisted the final load of mud on his shovel and found he had reached the rock gutter marking the bed of the ancient river where they had told each other for so long the gold would be waiting for them.

He sat in the enclosed space with the dank smell of wet earth in his nostrils, the darkness barely pierced by the guttering candle flame, and caught his breath as he looked at...

Nothing.

The gutter that had claimed all their hopes and energy was empty. When Richard fought his way to the sunlight his face said it all.

'You're saying there's nothing down there?'

It was hard to believe, *impossible* to believe, but that was the way it was.

'Nothing.' Richard's voice was as heavy as the gold they'd hoped to find.

'I'm gunna have a look,' Rascal said.

'Be my guest.'

But the gutter, as Richard had said, was empty.

'We're still in with a chance,' Rascal said when he regained the surface. 'We need to clear the gutter to the limits of our claims. Then we'll know for sure. There has to be a ridge across the gutter to trap the gold when it was brought down by the river. Just one ridge and we'll be in business.' He gave Richard a keen look. 'I'll go down if you've no heart for it.'

'Don't even think about it,' Richard said.

The work went on.

It was close to impossible to breathe at the bottom of the shaft so they rigged a canvas sail over the shaft mouth to deflect the breeze downwards. It helped a little.

Slowly the chamber at the bottom of the shaft grew bigger while, on the surface, the storm clouds grew darker by the day. There was murder and arson at the Eureka Hotel. Protest meetings were attended by thousands. Forked lightning flamed along the horizon as the governor rejected pleas for reform. Day by day, hour by hour, the storm drew closer.

Another meeting. Men were carrying arms openly now: pistols mostly, although old Karl Leipzig found a blunderbuss from somewhere that he stuffed with old nails and sawn-up horseshoes.

'Got any powder for that thing?' Richard asked.

'Not hard to find powder in a mining camp,' Karl told him.

'As long as you don't point it at me.'

Karl did not say whether the gun was loaded or not.

'Maybe the look of the thing will be enough,' Richard said.

But in the Ballarat goldfields the look of things was no longer enough.

Two days after reaching the gutter Richard sent up a bucket full of gravel and small pebbles. He followed the swaying bucket to the light. They stood and looked at what he'd found.

'What do you reckon?'

'It's heavy.'

Heavy as gold?

No one dared say it but hysteria was not far away.

'One way to find out,' Rascal said.

They took their findings to the crushing stamps at the end of the valley. The next day they had their answer.

'Fifteen hundred quid? From one bucket?'

It was hard to get their heads around it.

'We're rich,' Alice said.

They stared at one another. Close to broke one day and now...

'There's heaps more where that came from,' Richard said. 'All piled up against a rock ridge, like Rascal said it would be.'

His words formed a hollow echo in Alice's head. Now nothing would serve but shinning down the shaft to see their discovery for herself.

Richard said that even the idea made his blood curdle. 'I won't allow it.'

She raised her chin. 'We called it Wheal Alice, didn't we? *My* mine. Of course I must have a look.'

'That shaft is almost a hundred and fifty feet deep. If you slip...'

'Why should I slip?' She gave him a merry grin. 'I'm as nifty as you are and you've been doing it for weeks.'

Down into the darkness, then. Down into the heat and an almost paralysing humidity. Despite her brave words it was a scary business, the candle flame leaping and gulping and throwing its light on both sides of the shaft, the constant seeping of water shining and the square of daylight soon far above her head as she eased her way down the slippery steps they had made in the shuttering.

It must be a hundred and twenty degrees, she thought. More. How had the two men managed it day after day, shifting all the muck to get so far down?

I've married a champion, Alice thought.

After all her effort there wasn't much to see when she reached the bottom: the wet floor of the shaft, the piled-up mass of gold-bearing pebbles. Heat; silence; the oppressive weight of countless tons of earth leaning inwards to cut off the light, cut off *her* light...

Terror seized her. It was all she could do not to scream. Slowly she began the upwards climb.

Somewhere far overhead, the shuttering that held the shaft walls in place gave a protesting creak. A splatter of damp soil fell past her into darkness.

1913

Jonathan walked into the Derwent living room to find his grand-mother enthroned in the massive easy chair she had called her own for as long as he could remember.

She gave him the pleasant smile that kills. 'May we hope you have recovered from your ill temper?'

He decided he might as well stand up to her now as later. 'I don't accept that I was in an ill temper.'

'I see. Is it too much to ask where you have been for the last –' she checked the long case clock in the corner of the room '– two and a half hours?'

'No, it is not too much to ask. I have been with Bec Hampton.'

Grandma, eyes black as boot polish, was swelling in her chair. 'With whom?'

'Bec. The blacksmith's daughter. You remember Conan?'

'You spent two hours with the blacksmith's daughter?' She spoke each word carefully, as though fearing it might break. 'May one ask why?'

'I asked her to marry me. And she said yes.'

It was extraordinary how the colours came and went in Grand-ma's face: red to white and back to red again. With her hand pressed to her heart. 'The blacksmith's daughter. You cannot be serious.'

There was no point answering her so Jonathan didn't but sat, looking at her silently.

'Rebecca Hampton as mistress of Derwent? You want us to be the laughing stock of the district? I will not permit it.'

'I love her,' Jonathan said.

'Love...' Bessie Penrose spat the word like filth. 'I think you mean lust, don't you?'

'Have it your way,' Jonathan said. 'But I intend to marry her.'

'No,' she said. 'You will not. I shall make sure of that.'

The number of times Bec had heard her dad say Grandma Jane Hampton was a loony she might have believed it, had she not known otherwise.

Certainly Grandma had her ways and some of them were strange. Also she was given to telling tales about the old days, although whether the tales were true or made up few people knew or cared.

Bec cared. Bec believed that knowing the past made it easier to work out who she was. That was an ongoing problem for Bec because there seemed to be two of her. On the one hand there was the woman who was in love with Jonathan, heir to the vast Derwent run, the biggest and richest property in the midlands, and a man who had actually proposed marriage to her; on the other she was Miss Nobody the blacksmith's daughter.

Bec went to see her grandmother.

To work out which of the two women she really was? Or to ask for her help in what she suspected would be a fight to the death with Bessie Penrose? Because Jonathan she would have, one way or another: that was the one certainty in her life.

Lots of times Bec had listened to Grandma Jane Hampton rattling on about the people she'd known in the old days, the things she'd heard and the people she'd heard them about; what she wanted to know now was whether the old lady knew anything that might help her knock Bessie Penrose on her bottom.

Grandma Jane lived in a small dank cottage at the end of a small dank lane where a rivulet flowed beneath matted vegetation. When the clouds broke over the hills the rivulet grew ten times bigger overnight, flooding the path and more often than not spilling under the door and into the cottage. A less stubborn woman would have moved but Grandma Jane made a donkey seem sweet and swore she'd die where she'd lived ever since her husband had carked it back in ninety-two.

She had a vegie patch behind the cottage and was sitting beside the creek shelling peas into a bowl when Bec turned up.

'Just in time to help,' she said. She grinned; she was fifty-seven years old, looked twenty years older and was as toothless as a turnip.

No help for it; Bec sat on the grass at her side, smoothed her dress and got stuck into the peas.

'Haven't seen you around for a while,' said Grandma.

'Yeah, well...'

'Been busy, I hear.' Grandma's eyes, bright as buttons, glinted out of the nest of wrinkles that was her tanned-leather face. 'I hear things, even in this rat hole.'

'What sort of things?'

'Got yourself a sweetheart, they tell me.'

'That right?'

'All the district's talking.'

'Can't believe all you hear,' Bec said.

She cracked a pod open, discovered a nest of maggots inside. She flicked them into the creek.

'You still got trout here?'

'Plenty. We'll have a couple directly, if you're planning to hang around a while.' Fingers still busy with the peas, the eyes watched.

Bec concentrated on what she was doing.

'What's the old lady gunna say?' Grandma asked.

No point trying to deny it. 'Do her block, most likely.'

'You're not wrong.' Grandma had finished the peas; she eased her back, grabbed a knife and started peeling the spuds. 'I reckon a nice fresh trout will just about hit the spot,' she said. She flashed Bec a warning glance. 'You wanna watch out for that old bitch. Cross her, she'll be lookin' for blood.'

'What can I do about it?'

'Walk away, you got any sense.'

'I love him.'

Grandma nodded, morose over the half-peeled spud. 'I guessed.' She sighed. It might have been Bessie Penrose's throat, the way she slammed the knife through the potato. 'Love's a bastard, innit?'

'Is that why you married Grandpa?'

'I always fancied him so when he asked me after Dad died I jumped at him. A farm needs a man, so there was that too. But I loved him, no error.'

'You've known Bessie Penrose a long time?' Bec said.

'We were supposed to have been born the same year: 1856. I was, certainly, but I'm not so sure about her.'

Bec heard something Grandma had not said. 'What you mean?'

'Some thought she might've been a year older.'

'So what?'

Grandma sighed again and stood up. 'You're right. So what? It's a long time ago now. Let's go and fry them trout.'

Later, over the fish: 'What did you mean, there was talk?'

'We're cousins, her and me. You knew that?'

Of course Bec knew it. She'd heard Grandma bellyaching about it since she was little.

'I heard,' she said.

'Bessie Tregellas and Jane Dark. Although mind you her dad was a Dark too, when he started off. Him and my dad was half-brothers.' She cackled. 'And look at us now. Lady Muck on top of the hill and me down here. Funny how things work out. But I'll bet these trout are fresher than any she has,' she said fiercely. And forked a slice of the white flesh into her mouth to prove it.

Bec refused to be sidetracked. 'This business about her age... What's the story there?'

'You don' wanna go down that road,' Grandma Jane said. 'My advice to you is give it away. Find yourself another bloke.'

'I don't want another bloke. It's Jonathan I want. I told you already: I love him. Can't you understand that?'

'Of course I understand it. But what about him? Does he feel the same?'

'Yes,' Bec said.

'You know that or hope it?'

'I know it.'

'Pray God you're right. Because that old witch will fillet you like this trout if you're wrong.'

For a minute or two they carried on eating in silence, then Bec put down her knife and fork. 'You're hiding something. Something about Bessie Penrose's birth.'

Grandma chewed for a while, eyes fixed on distance. Then she too put down her knife and fork. 'It's only rumour, mind. No proof.'

'Jonathan has asked me to marry him,' Bec said. 'You said it right: she'll stop us if she can. If you can help me...'

A Berkshire sow would have been proud of Grandma's snort. 'Does Bessie know about you and her grandson?' she asked.

'I don't know. What I do know is she's threatened to disinherit him if he marries someone she doesn't approve of.'

'Meaning you.'

'Meaning me. I dunno if she means it.'

'She means it, all right. But what does Jonathan say?'

'He says he'll give up Derwent if he has to. But I'm afraid if he does that he'll come to hate me for it.'

'He could, at that. I was lucky but most men are fickle creatures.' Jane Hampton studied her granddaughter. 'So you're looking for a way to stop her doing that?'

'That's right.'

'So you've come to the only woman in Tasmania who can maybe help you?'

'Because I know you'll help me if you can,' Bec said.

'I don't *know* anything but I'll tell you what I heard. What I believe is true. Like I said, there's no proof; what you choose to do about it is up to you.'

1854–71

Alice was bathed in sweat, terror threatening to freeze her limbs.

Below her was eighty feet of darkness. If she fell, death was certain. Above her the shaft seemed on the edge of collapse. That too would mean certain death.

At that moment the thought of making a fortune from the gold they had found seemed unimportant. Life was the only thing that mattered.

She forced her hands away from their death grip and reached for the next rung. And the rung after that. She was weeping in terror, eyes blind, an insect burrowing in the dark. She could hear her own plaintive cries.

Another rung. Another.

Limbs shaking, sweat flooding.

Another step. Her foot slipped off the greasy rung. She hung, weeping. *Save me, God!*

She regained her footing and took a series of deep breaths. Her hand ventured, closing on the next rung. She dragged herself higher. And higher.

She dared not look up but knew she must be nearing the top because now she could see the shuttering that was still holding the sides of the shaft in place. Where the fall of earth had come from she did not know but was reasonably sure she was above it now.

Below her feet the darkness opened its jaws, determined to drag her back, but Alice was more determined still. She reached up and climbed. Reached up and climbed. The light and waiting faces welcomed her.

She stepped away from the shaft, breath shuddering, body shaking. She collapsed on the ground and lay full length. The smell of the sun-warmed earth, the noise of voices, of machines, of dogs… She was safe now.

How beautiful was life!

That night was celebration time. The Eureka Hotel had been burnt down back in October so instead they went to the John o' Groats, a wooden building across the road from the Gold Office among a scattering of the first permanent buildings in Ballarat.

The old Eureka had had a bad name, being home – or so it was said – to Vandemonians.

'What are Vandemonians?' Rascal Jones had wondered.

'People like us,' Alice had said. 'People from Van Diemen's Land.'

'What's the problem with them?'

'Most of the ones here are ex-cons,' Alice said.

'Like me, you mean?'

'Who'd want to eat in the same hotel as people like us?' said Richard. He was ebullient at the thought of the gold they'd found. 'Fifteen hundred quid,' he marvelled.

'And plenty more where that came from,' Alice said.

Although it would be a cold day in hell before she ventured down that shaft again.

Fifteen hundred quid. It was a figure to conjure dreams. Why stop there? Why not fifty thousand? A hundred? The world was wide and they, incredibly, were rich.

Never mind the riots, the looming threat of trouble, the fact that soldiers of the 12th Regiment had been stoned passing the Eureka

Lead, that diggers were rumoured to be burning their licences –
now they would celebrate.

The John o' Groats seemed if anything rougher than the old
Eureka but they didn't care; they could look after themselves.

Chops and steak and tumblers of a drink called Blow Your Skull
Off. They'd asked the waitress about it before ordering.

'What's in it?'

'Rum, opium, spirits of wine and cayenne pepper.'

'Kill many, does it?' Richard said.

The waitress, well endowed around the chest but with not too
much between the ears, gaped. 'Eh?'

'Never mind. I'll give it a go.'

'Me too,' said Rascal.

Alice decided she'd had enough danger for one day.

'I'll stick to water.'

'The water's horrible,' Richard said.

Even so...

They were halfway through the meal when Alice saw a face she
recognised on the far side of the crowded room. She put her hand
on Richard's arm.

'Look over there. It's William.'

'What's he doing here? I wouldn't have thought it was his sort of
place at all. I'd have said silk sheets and a silver service were more
his style.'

'I doubt there's one silver service in the whole of Ballarat,' Alice
said.

Richard studied William with a mixture of contempt and
dislike – having money in his pocket made that easier – but he
wasn't really interested and soon went back to sawing at his saddle-
tough steak.

Alice continued to watch and wonder. Richard was right; the
John o' Groats wasn't William's style. Neither was the whole goldfields scene. But there he was, large as life and twice as ugly, as
her mum would have said. And there was something else that was
interesting: William was not alone.

They'd heard that William had married Cynthia Mason shortly after their own wedding – needless to say, they hadn't been invited – yet there he was in Ballarat with a woman who clearly was not his wife. Paying her a fair bit of attention too.

Alice continued to watch. The woman was about the same age as she was, with black eyes and black hair, thick black brows in a face as white as bone. She had a strong rather than lush figure but was still showing most of what she had above the deep cut of her dress, and there was an air about her that said *watch out.*

A whore? Alice doubted that; she had more the tight mouth of someone who'd cut a man's throat before she'd sleep with him, and not think twice about it.

A chance acquaintance? Not likely, Alice thought, the way she was clinging to William's arm.

It was no business of hers but what had happened between her and William in the woodland at the back of Barnsley's house – never mind what *might* have happened – seemed somehow to make it so. It gave her the strangest fellow-feeling with the sabre-sharp woman, which was nonsense, of course.

So she continued to watch. She couldn't hear what they were saying over the hubbub, but everything William did made his feelings for the strange woman clear. He can hardly keep his hands off her, Alice thought. And the way she was lapping it up showed she had no problem with that, either. Brother Willy had best look out for himself, Alice thought.

At that moment William looked her way. She held her gaze and saw shock smooth his face as he recognised her. Then his expression cleared. He said something to the woman. She turned and stared at Alice across the rowdy, smoke-hazed room, a stiletto stab of the black eyes and Alice saw that this woman would regard the whole world as competition.

William got to his feet and strolled across the room towards them.

'He's coming over,' Alice said to Richard.

'We are honoured,' Richard said.

He leant back in his chair. He took a few sovereigns out of his pocket and turned them casually but obviously as William reached their table. He took note of what Richard was doing.

'You must be doing all right. Well done.' Smiling, patronising.

'Not bad. And you?' Smiling between equals.

William laughed lightly. 'I'm not here to dig holes in the ground. I leave that to tough men like you, people used to manual labour. The family owns a lot of the land. Uncle bought it when he was over in fifty-one. Pays to keep an eye on it, don't you know? And to keep in with the powers that be.'

'How's your wife?' Alice said.

William smiled easily. 'Very well, the last I heard.'

'Aren't you going to introduce us to your friend?' Alice asked.

'I'm afraid Maria's over-particular of the company she keeps,' William said.

'What's she doing with you, then?' Rascal Jones said.

William turned with exaggerated slowness. 'And you are?'

'Rascal Jones.'

'Appropriate, I'm sure.'

'You'd better believe it,' Rascal said.

'Your friend's coming over,' Alice said.

Close up Maria looked even more dangerous than she had at a distance. She had a scar on her left cheek and her voice was harsh enough to break glass. She stared at Alice and the two men as though taking possession of them.

'Richard and Alice are old friends of mine,' William said. 'The gentleman with them tells me his name is Jones.'

'I heard of you lot,' Maria said. 'Struck it rich, people are sayin'.'

'People say all sorts of things,' Alice said.

Maria smiled. Her teeth were sharp and Alice knew she had seen the coins in Richard's hand.

'Sometimes they're right, an' all.' She flicked a glance at Alice but spoke to Richard. 'You with this one?'

'Alice is my wife,' Richard said.

While Alice's eyes would have killed the dangerous woman where she stood.

'Just askin',' Maria said. She turned to William. 'We gunna eat or what?'

Friday 1 December 1854 was notable for two things: a marked increase in the aggression of the goldfields police and a visit to Wheal Alice by William Tregellas and Maria Hack.

Very picky with her boots was Maria Hack as she winced her way through the mud left by the late spring rain yet Alice would have been prepared to bet she'd waded through a lot worse, her looks saying she'd packed more into her years than most people did in a dozen lifetimes. Not much of it good, either.

Maria wore a magenta and orange dress – enough to poke your eyes out, Alice thought – but expensively styled, discreetly bustled and more modest about the throat than she'd been in the John o' Groats. She carried a silk parasol. She was the epitome of smart although Alice thought how putting a gold collar on a viper did nothing to milk its venom.

Maria gave a delicate shudder as she eyed the gaping mouth of the shaft.

'Is it very deep?'

'Hundred and eighty feet, give or take,' Alice said.

'Blimey...'

Alice saw Maria was trying to play the part of Lady Muck on a visit to the peasantry but making a hard job of it. She suspected Maria's voice would smash rock if she ever decided to raise it.

'And your two mates go down there?'

'I been down myself.'

'To the bottom?'

Alice nodded. 'Nothing to it.' Not for quids would she admit how terrified she'd been.

'So you've seen the gold?'

'More or less. It doesn't look like much. It's not just lying there; it's in rocks. You got to crush the rocks to get it out.'

'And now you're rich?'

'We're getting by.'

Maria flashed an avaricious gleam. 'People I've spoken to say you've made one of the best strikes in Ballarat.'

'Better than some, I suppose.'

'By luck.'

'Luck and hard work,' Alice said.

'What you do with it?'

'With the gold? Stick it in the bank,' Alice said.

She was lying. She'd banked some but not most of it. It was a bone of contention between her and Richard, but Richard didn't trust banks and said they'd be better off looking after it themselves. The unbanked portion was locked away in a steel box under the bed they'd bought now they could afford some of the comforts they'd had to do without for so long. Alice had been all in favour of the bed, which was a lot kinder to her back than the hard ground had been whenever Richard had felt in a loving mood, but she was certainly not going to tell Maria Hack there was the best part of three thousand quid hidden not ten feet from where they were standing.

'You gotta keep some of it back, though? For living expenses, that sort of thing?'

'Some.'

'Ain't you afraid someone will steal it?'

'We keep our eyes on it,' Alice said.

'Just as well, I'd say.'

Maria walked away, her knowing smile like a trophy.

Alice watched her back and did not think she had much to smile about because she had seen something in the other woman she had not expected.

'Has William been here long?' she asked Richard.

'He said about two weeks. But he told me he's been coming over regularly for about six months. Not just here. Bendigo too, seems like. Uncle Barnsley has been buying land all over.'

'Why would he do that?'

'Because he's smart. Everywhere gold's been discovered the price of land has gone through the roof. Five times, ten times the price they paid. Sometimes more.'

'And without having to work for it,' Alice said.

'That's right. William was saying Uncle sends him over every few weeks to keep an eye on things.'

'Not all he's been doing, either,' Alice said.

Richard looked questioningly at her. 'What's that supposed to mean?'

'That woman's pregnant,' Alice said.

'Are you saying…?'

'Who else?'

Not that it was Alice's problem; there were more important things to worry about than Maria Hack.

Everyone knew the district was on the edge of trouble. Tempers were raw since the commissioner had raised the licence fees yet again – and the authorities seemed to think the situation serious enough to order more troops into the area. The word was that General Nickle was on his way from Melbourne with eight hundred men.

Talk, more talk and black looks by the bushel.

After the business of the stoning, the soldiers kept out of the way but everyone knew they were there and their presence, seen or unseen, ripped holes in what little remained of the diggers' patience. Everywhere there was talk of resistance, even of rebellion, and the nagging presence of the bully-boy police did nothing to cool people down.

'The police haf always behaved like the bastards they are,' said Karl Leipzig, 'but recently they've become even worse. As I said they would. Now it's every day or two, sometime more than once a day. Is it any wonder diggers are burning their licences? These are free men; they vill not be treated like slaves.'

For once Willy McNab had nothing to say.

'You know Father Smyth is telling us to lay down our weapons and pray for peace?' Karl said. 'I ask you: pray for peace? Vith the authorities trying to take avay our freedom?'

Later that day Wheal Alice had a visitor.

Alice had been washing clothes and her arms were suds to the elbow when she saw Police Corporal Jenkins with a couple of troopers and the load of trouble that always seemed to travel with them.

Jenkins had greased-back hair and blue eyes so pale they were almost white. He had a bad reputation: a bully who people said enjoyed causing as much trouble as he could. He was carrying a pistol holstered on his belt, an iron-bound baton in his fist, and his heels bruised the ground.

'Jenkins,' the man said. 'Goldfields police.'

'Again,' Alice said.

'Again,' he agreed. 'So you know what I want, ducky.'

Alice couldn't abide being called ducky. 'What's that then?'

Tap, tap went the baton.

'Looker like you, you shouldn't be askin' a red-blooded man that sorta question. Might take it as an invite: know what I mean? Now, show me your licence. An' quick about it, *ducky*, if you don't want me to run you in.'

'Pardon me for breathing,' said Alice, but knew she had no choice. She showed him her licence.

'There you go! That wasn't so hard, was it? Now: where's the rest of your mob?'

'My husband's sleeping.'

'Then you better wake him up.'

'He's been working all hours,' Alice said. 'He needs his sleep.'

'You do it or I will,' Jenkins said. 'Your choice.'

Alice went into the tent and shook Richard's shoulder. 'Those police bastards want to see your licence.'

'Easy with the language, missus.' Jenkins had followed her into the tent. 'Wouldn't want me to run you in for non-cooperation, would we now?'

'In my pants pocket,' Richard said.

Alice turned to pick them up from where an exhausted Richard had dropped them but Jenkins beat her to it. He picked up the pants, held them upside down and shook them. The licence fell and a couple of coins.

'Doin' well, are we?' he said. He looked around him. 'Ain't there supposed to be another bloke with you?'

'He's down the shaft,' Alice said.

'Tell him to get up here,' Jenkins said.

'No way of getting hold of him down there,' Alice said. 'You want a squint at his licence, best you climb down and ask him yourself.'

'Sassy little bitch, ain't you?' Jenkins said. 'No worries; we'll be back later. You can bet the farm on that.'

'You're worse than the plague, you lot,' Alice said.

'Best you don' forget it, neither,' Jenkins said.

He went out of the tent with Alice following him.

'You planning on keeping that coin?' she said.

'Coin?'

'The one you took from my husband's pants.'

'Dunno what you're on about,' Jenkins said.

A well-dressed man was walking towards the tent. Jenkins straightened at once and threw a smart salute.

'Morning, sir!'

William flipped a finger to his hat brim. 'Morning, Corporal.'

Jenkins mounted his horse and rode away, the two troopers clattering behind, all three of them figures of upright and honourable men.

'How come that bastard treats me like dirt but hands you a salute?' Alice said.

'Friends in high places,' William said. 'You should try it sometime.'

'Since when are people in high places gunna take a spit of notice of me?'

'Introductions, that's what you need.' He gave her his best remember-what-good-times-we-might-have-had-together smile. 'I can arrange it, if you'd like.'

Another sassy article, Alice thought. Not one who would ever learn, either. She looked at him scornfully. 'Wearin' clothes like I got and stinking of sweat? You're dreaming.'

'Never hurts to dream. But I'm sorry to disappoint you, dear, I came to have a word with your husband.'

'He's sleeping.'

'We'd best not disturb him, then.' He gave her a warm smile and Alice didn't trust him an inch. 'As you know, there are strong feelings all over the goldfields,' he said. 'People are getting really worked up. And now there's talk of another increase in the licence fee.'

'A lot of the miners are battling to survive as it is,' Alice said.

'I know.' William shook his head, Mr Sympathy himself. 'There'll be trouble any day now. Serious trouble.'

'When?'

'Today? Tomorrow? Nobody knows. All it needs is a spark. The only thing we know for sure is that when it comes it'll be ugly. You won't want to get involved in that.'

'We can't do anything about it.'

'I think perhaps you can. You know they've been building a stockade to keep the troops out? I hear they're even making their own flag. Might be best if you went there. It'd be safer.'

'Why should you care?' Alice said. 'You're not a miner. It doesn't affect you.'

William opened his eyes wide. 'Of course I care. You're family, aren't you? I came to warn you.'

'Warn us of what?'

'The dangers of staying put. Can you see the soldiers firing on their own people? I can't. But the police are a different story. You know what they did to that priest's assistant? There's been talk of rape too. You're so vulnerable here. You want to get out while you can.'

'And go where?'

'The stockade. Where else? There will be a lot of people there and you know what they say about safety in numbers. Besides, the more people we have there, the more likely the authorities will be to listen to what we're telling them. Think about it: licence fees cut, that'd be a start. And maybe – who knows? – we might even be able to get the police off our backs. But I am sure of one thing: when the shooting starts you'll be a lot safer there than you are here.'

'You told us you didn't have no interest in the miners or the gold. It was the land that interested you. That's what you said.'

William waved a vague hand. 'Somehow one gets sucked in.'

Alice looked at him uncertainly. He was a nasty bit of work – she knew that better than anybody – but he was nobody's fool and she thought his words made sense.

'Mind you, there'll be some rough characters there too. If you do decide to go it might be wise to take a weapon with you, so you can protect yourself if you need to.'

'We don't know nothing about weapons,' Alice said.

'I brought a gun for you,' William said. He spoke softly, glancing this way and that, and took a pistol from under his coat. 'Here. Take it.'

She looked at it as though it might bite her. 'Will you be there? In the stockade?'

The warm smile returned. 'In the front line. You can count on it. It'll be good if you're there to support me. Darks and Tregellases shoulder to shoulder? That'll be something to tell your grandchildren! And if you need to find shelter – not that you will! – the John o' Groats will be the place.'

Still she didn't trust him but where else could they turn for help? Police violence was an established fact and if there was trouble there was no way to know what people like Corporal Jenkins might do. And even William – surely? –couldn't control what went on in the stockade.

'He said it's called a Navy Colt revolver,' Alice said. 'Fires six shots, he told me.'

'Why would we want it?'

'He said if there's trouble we'll be safer if we have a gun.'

She'd told William that guns and the Darks were strangers and she'd prefer to keep it that way. But things were coming to a boil fast and she no longer knew what to do for the best.

'We've known him since we were children,' Richard said. 'In his whole life he's never lifted a finger to help anyone but himself. Why should he want to help us now? I don't trust him.'

Neither did Alice but it made no difference. The stench of trouble was everywhere. She was scared what the police might do and knew that having a gun would make her feel safer than she did now.

Richard looked at her. 'Do you really think you'll feel more comfortable inside the stockade if there's trouble?'

'Rather than stuck here? I reckon I would,' Alice said. 'I'm like you – I'd sooner stay out of it altogether but what if we can't? You know what these goldfield wallopers are like. I've a nasty feeling the soldiers might be even worse.'

'Then we'll go the first sign of trouble,' Richard said.

That night the rumours came flocking like crows.

The soldiers were coming; the soldiers weren't coming. There'd been fighting with people dead; there'd been no fighting and all was calm.

It was impossible to know what to believe. From the day they arrived in Ballarat there'd been gunfire every night and they'd grown used to it. Not now.

The next day, Saturday 2 December 1854, they told Karl Leipzig they were going to move into the stockade.

'Don't be fools,' Karl said. 'That is the first place the verdammt Soldaten will attack.'

They did not believe him.

'I'm staying put,' Rascal Jones said. 'If things get too hot I'll hide down the shaft. I'll be safe there.'

'Can we trust you?' Alice said.

'I reckon you've seen enough of me to know the answer to that.'

He'd always seemed a decent cove so she thought he was right. 'Then if you do go down make sure you take the money with you. And mind,' she said, 'we'll want our share when we come back.'

'Don't worry,' Rascal said. 'It'll be there.'

They went to the stockade, where they were made welcome.

'Where is William Tregellas?'

Who knew?

The night was still, the tension thick enough to cut. Across the goldfields there was the usual nightly hullaballoo. Sleep was out of the question.

The hours passed.

Whispers. Rumours.

'Syd says he saw soldiers formin' up by the Eureka Lead.'

'They say the governor's comin' to talk to us. Comin' himself...'

The hours passed.

Dawn came like a thunderbolt. Alice would have said sleep was impossible yet she must have dozed because she woke to screams and yells and bullets, a world gone mad.

The first thing she saw as she sprang to her feet was the dim light of morning shining coldly on a forest of bayonets as a skirmish line of red-coated soldiers came surging through the wall of the stockade, too fragile to prevent the attack.

Bayonets and screams, yells of defiance, outrage and despair, and the bellow of guns as Alice stood trying to gather her wits, still her racing heart and decide what they must do, must do *now*, in the few seconds of grace while decision remained possible.

We must get out of here.

No doubt about that. But where? And how?

She turned to Richard. Like her, he had confusion written all over his face but she needed a decision and when he snatched her hand and began to turn away from the advancing mayhem of the soldiers' attack she went with him.

Her whole body was urging her to run when Richard staggered, cried out and fell.

Terror seized Alice's heart. She saw him on the ground, his face contorted with pain. She fell to her knees beside him, her helplessness a wound.

'Where did they get you?'

'My leg...' Speaking through gritted teeth.

At least it wasn't his head or – heaven forbid! – his heart. She looked. There was some blood; not much. She looked over her shoulder. A melee was holding up most of the soldiers but it was obvious that resistance wouldn't last long. Already some of the soldiers had broken through and were advancing across the level ground towards them. She saw bodies, some moaning, some still.

Alice's head cleared, her panicked heart slowed. What she had to do was plain. She would save Richard and herself or die in the attempt.

'How bad is it?'

'Hurting like hell,' Richard said. 'But I'll live.'

She thought the bullet might have clipped his thigh. A flesh wound, she told herself, willing it to be so.

'Can you stand?'

Because my love my dear love we need to get out of here. Get out of here now. If you can stand. If you can walk.

'I can try.'

Richard was halfway to his feet when Alice saw a soldier swerve towards them. His expression was maniacal, his rifle extended, the bayonet gleaming in the morning light.

Richard had dropped the revolver when he fell. She snatched it up. Holding it with both hands she pointed it at the soldier.

'Keep away from us!'

Her voice was full of terror and determination.

The soldier came on.

'Keep away!'

The soldier came on.

Now only a few yards separated them and he was not stopping. Was not stopping…

There was sickness in her throat. Alice shut her eyes and pulled the trigger. She staggered as the recoil flung her back.

She opened her eyes and saw the soldier on his back, coughing, blood running from a massive chest wound.

The redness of his blood… Horror engulfed her. If they caught her with the gun they would hang her. She flung it away. Her face was wet with tears but there was no time for sorrow. With Richard's arm draped around her shoulders, hers around his waist, they hobbled away.

'Where are we going?'

'As far away from here as we can get.'

It wasn't easy with chaos everywhere. The troops had gone rushing on while the bayonets continued their bloody work and now outside the stockade shots were being fired repeatedly through tents where dozens of people were cowering.

'Most of the people out there had nothing to do with the protest,' Alice said.

'The soldiers don't care,' Richard said.

A covered wagon, mule-drawn, was heading into town, moving fast to beat the roadblocks that were bound to be set up once the killing was over. It gave them a lift.

'Where you wanna go?' the driver asked.

She remembered William's advice. 'Drop us off at the John o' Groats. I was told they'd look after us there and my husband needs a doctor.'

'Not dyin', is he?'

'No!'

Although he was close to fainting with loss of blood.

'I killed a soldier.' She felt a pressing need to confess what – surely? – must be a sin.

'Good on yer. Time them bastards got a taste of their own medicine. I wouldn't be boastin' about it though. Never know who might be listening.'

Boast? It was the last thing she felt like doing.

Simon Cohen moaned but it was his wife Thora who was in charge at the John o' Groats and she said they could stay.

'Such trouble we are having!' she said. 'How can you think of refusing them? Of course they must stay.'

Still bellyaching, Simon hid them in a tiny loft under the thatch. It had a boarded floor but there was no room to stand. It was accessed by a rickety ladder.

The doctor came. He told Richard he would live – luckier than some, he said – sluiced iodine over the wound and warned he might have a permanent limp.

The first evening it rained and they discovered the thatch leaked: *tap! tap! tap!* Alice lay on the blanket in the dark and listened to small creatures rustling and scampering in the straw two feet above her head. It was hot and airless but she was too busy counting her blessings to worry about that. They were there; they were safe; the doctor had said Richard's wound wasn't too serious. For the moment the future could take care of itself. Hopefully, after all the drama had simmered down, they would be able to get on with their lives.

Two days later, between one minute and the next, things changed.

'Utterly shameful,' William Tregellas said.

'You can say that again, sir,' the major said. 'One of my own men was gunned down in the performance of his duty. Reports say by a woman with a pistol. A woman, sir! Outrageous!'

'What kind of people are they?' William said.

'I'll tell you what they are, sir. They're savages. Absolute savages.'

'I fear you are right, major. One fears for the future of the colony. One really does. I heard some of them are trying to hide in town. The John o' Groats was mentioned. A Jewish couple owns it, I understand.'

'Jewish, eh? Hmm. Thanks for the tip. I'll have it checked out.'

Shortly before dark Simon Cohen hauled his flab up the ladder to tell them that search parties were coming down the street.

Alice's heart lurched. 'What do we do?'

Simon was breathing like a furnace and it took him a minute to answer her. 'Blow out that candle for a start. Then sit tight and keep your lip buttoned. Not a squeak, you hear me? They hear a squeak, we're all done for.' Apprehension made him angry.

'Won't they come up here?'

'You better pray they don't.'

He closed the trapdoor and they heard him cursing beneath his breath and a scraping sound as he dragged the awkward ladder away. Alice blew out the candle, as instructed. They waited. Seconds seemed like minutes, minutes like hours.

A hammering on the street door. Harsh voices in a suddenly profound silence. The sound of heavy footsteps on the hotel's boarded floors. A crash as something fell. The footsteps came closer. A pause, then closer still. Another pause, then voices: clearly audible now.

'Nothing here. We're wasting our time.'

'That bloke tole the officer they was 'ere. At the John o' Groats. I heard 'im say it. An' watch out, he said. They got a gun.'

They were in the room immediately below the loft. Strips of light showed through the cracks in the floorboards. Alice held her breath. In the errant light she saw Richard's eyes shining. Neither moved. She was conscious only of the pounding of her heart, drum-loud in the silence.

'Can't believe a word those bastards say. They hate us –'

Any minute they might look up. Any minute they might wonder what there was in the roof space above them.

Alice's skin crawled.

'Simkins died.' The first voice spoke savagely. 'Shot down in cold blood. Twenty-two years old.'

'We dunno which one done it –'

'I don' care which one done it. Have my way we'd 'ang the lot of 'em.'

'Well, there's nothing 'ere.'

'I'd like to burn the whole place down. That would flush 'em out.'

'There's sheds out the back. Maybe we should look there.'

Footsteps retreating. Silence flowed back.

Alice dared breathe. Softly, softly… Her heart was still racing, the sweat cold under her clothes. She didn't dare hope the searchers were gone yet the silence grew stronger as the minutes passed. The walls of the hotel breathed.

It was a long time before sounds from the room below told them the ladder was being replaced. The trapdoor creaked open.

'They've gone,' Simon Cohen said.

Thank God.

William Tregellas was lying in bed with Maria Hack at his side. They were naked. They had made love earlier and now he was play-ing idly with one of her breasts.

She slapped his hand away. 'If you want to do me again, get on with it, but don't mess me about.'

'You are how many months gone?'

'Comin' up to six.'

'Then I think it might be a good time for us to make a move,' William said.

'Make a move where?'

'My uncle has a property in Sydney. We can stay there until the kid's born.'

'Suits me,' Maria said. 'Sooner this business is over the better I'll like it.'

'Such touching affection,' William said.

'Don't you get sarky with me. What happened about them two we met before the stockade business: that Richard Dark and his missus?'

'Nothing. I told them to go to the John o' Groats if there was trouble but the soldiers searched it and found nothing. It looks as though they must have got away.'

'Takin' their gold with them, more's the pity. People said they had a fortune but when I checked there was nothing in that tent of theirs.'

'Perhaps they came back for it.'

'Or maybe you got there first. Bastard like you, I wouldn't put it past you.'

William smiled and again took hold of her breast. 'You'll never know, will you?'

'Just so long as you pay me what we agreed when this blessed baby's born.'

'Easy money I call it but that's what we agreed so that's what you'll get.'

'Easy for you. You're not the one 'avin' it. When you plannin' to give that wife of yours the good news?'

'When we're in Sydney.'

'She better not make no fuss. Not with me. She try anythin' like that I'll cut her, so 'elp me.'

'She won't.'

'You wanna play or doncher?' Maria said. 'Make up your mind.'

It was like picking over the ruins of a lost war.

The bodies had been taken away but many tents had been destroyed and the people they saw had the lost and wandering look of the dispossessed.

People they spoke to said there had been wholesale looting, in many cases by the soldiers.

Alice and Richard looked at each other, dread in their hearts, and set off as fast as they could to find their own tent.

They couldn't find it, or old Karl Leipzig's tent next door. Both had vanished, with everything that had been inside them, and a passer-by they knew as a face in the mob told them that old Karl had thrown in his hand and gone away.

Of Rascal Jones there was no sign either. So much had happened while they'd been hiding in the roof space of the John o' Groats that it was hard to know where they were or what they should do.

The windlass rope was hanging slack. Richard went down but found nothing.

'All of it?' Alice said.

Every last penny, with the steel box in which it had been kept.

'Who could have taken it?'

'Anybody.'

There was no way to know; despair had become a feature of the landscape.

'We're back where we started,' Richard said.

By his expression he could have wept.

'Not quite,' Alice said. 'I know you aren't keen on banks but I put some in anyway, just in case.'

'How much?'

'A thousand quid.'

Thank God for Alice.

A woman they knew saw them and stopped to jaw a minute.

'Good to see you back. I thought they'd taken you in.'

'Why should you have thought that?' Alice said.

'They've taken in plenty,' the woman said. 'And your names was on the list they stuck up. You're wanted, you are.'

'How could they have known our names?' Alice said.

'Search me,' said the woman. 'But I wouldn't hang around here or they'll have you for sure. I was you I'd clear off altogether.'

'There's gold down there,' Richard said.

'Gold ain't much use if they top you.'

'Why should they hang us?' Richard said.

But Alice remembered shooting the soldier. Maybe he had been the one the searchers had mentioned, the man called Simkins who had died. She knew he would have killed them if he'd had the chance but that didn't stop her feeling like a murderess. Not that feeling bad about it would stop them stringing her up if they caught her now.

'I think she's right. I think we should get out while we can.'

'Not without the money in the bank,' Richard said.

They knew they were taking a risk but they managed it without any problem, and three weeks later they were back on the island.

It rained all the way to Melbourne where they would stay a day or two before heading on to Sydney. William stared out of the coach window as it lurched its tedious way through the puddles of the rutted track.

'Will it ever stop?'

Maria Hack was inclined to be more philosophical. 'At least it should keep them bloody bushrangers to 'ome.'

'You'd think the governor would want to do something to improve communications,' William said. 'Ballarat, after all, is a major source of revenue to the government. But I suppose we are foolish to expect efficiency from these people.'

Maria glanced sideways at him. 'Someone got up the wrong side of the bed this morning. I'd'a thought you'd be glad to get outta that dump. I know I am.'

'I am sorry those two slipped through the net,' he said. 'But I suppose there's no help for it.'

He had certainly done all he could to get his own back for the way Alice and Richard had treated him, with Alice first encouraging him then turning against him, and Richard attacking him the way he had.

He had sworn to punish them for that. It was frustrating that somehow they had got away. It just showed what Uncle Barnsley had always told him: if you wanted a job done properly you did it yourself. At least he'd got their gold money, but he had hoped to see them hang as well. Well, maybe there'd be another opportunity in the future.

William turned his mind to other matters. 'I'll have to go down to see my uncle once I've got you to Sydney. But there are servants there who'll look after you.'

'And make sure I don't nick nuthun,' Maria said.

'Something like that,' William said.

Cynthia Tregellas stared at her husband.

'You've done what?'

'I need an heir,' William said. 'You're not able to give me one so it has been necessary for me to make other arrangements. The woman in question is waiting for us in Sydney and we shall journey there together.'

'Do you know how humiliated that makes me feel?' she said.

His cold eyes, so like his uncle's, stared her down. 'About as humiliated as I felt when I discovered you were incapable of giving me the heir every man requires.' He sipped from the glass he was holding. 'Look at you. Useless, utterly useless.'

For once in her life Cynthia's outrage overcame her timidity. 'This child... You expect me to pretend to the world that it is mine. That *is* your plan, I take it? Well, I won't do it. I won't!'

William crossed the room in two swift steps.

She flinched as his strong fingers seized her chin and forced her eyes up to meet his.

'You will do as you are told,' William said.

'I curse the day my father forced me to become a member of your vile family,' she said.

He let her go. 'Curse it as much as you like. You are a member and that's the end of it. You will do as I say.'

She did not have the will to defy him any longer but at least she did not cry. It was poor comfort but better than nothing.

With the money they'd brought with them Richard and Alice bought a small farm.

'Sheep and maybe a cow. Vegies. We'll get by,' said Alice. 'I thought to plant a rosebush at the last place. This time I'll do it.'

'We won't ever be millionaires,' Richard said.

'I don't care,' Alice said.

Two years later, on 20 June 1856, Alice gave birth to a daughter.

'She's got a voice on her,' Richard said.

So she had but was fit too, which was what mattered. They called her Jane. Jane Eyre Dark, after the title of a book Alice had read.

Cynthia remembered her time in Sydney as the most humiliating episode in her life.

It had not entered her head she would be living under the same roof as the woman but that was how it worked out. Worse; not only was the Hack creature there, showing off her jutting belly, but William made it plain how much he preferred her to his wife.

From the moment of their arrival Cynthia saw she was there only so she could play her role in the deception upon which her husband planned to base his dynasty. A dynasty that – most appropriately – would be built on a fraud.

Alone in her room at night she stared at her reflection in the mirror. 'I will have vengeance,' she whispered.

How or when she did not know – she was only too well aware she was physically incapable of doing anything against either her husband or his vile paramour – but the day would come when she would be avenged; she was determined about that.

She had no idea what the arrangement was between her husband and Maria Hack but one day, three months after the baby's birth, she was gone and Cynthia saw her no more.

Twelve months after arriving in Sydney Cynthia Tregellas returned to Van Diemen's Land holding in her arms the child, large for its age, that the world was told was hers.

She had nothing but hatred and contempt for her husband, feelings enhanced by the displeasure he showed that the child was a girl and not the wanted son, but foresaw no problem in bringing up Bessie as though she really had given birth to her – the circumstances surrounding the birth were not the child's fault, after all, and it was not unheard of for a married couple to adopt a child – but she discovered in herself something she had not expected: a deep and abiding resentment that she, who had lost her own child, was being forced to present to the world a baby who was not only not hers but who she discovered she did not like. She might have come to terms with the arrangement had William let her tell people the child had been adopted, but he had made it plain that was something he would never do. Bessie was not only another woman's child but an imposter.

How was it possible to resent an innocent baby? But she did and could not help it; by her existence Bessie had deprived her of the little self-respect she had left.

She did her best; she was not cruel to Bessie, but love was out of the question.

Alice and Richard spent peaceful years on the farm they named Proud Acres. He had wanted to call it Wheal Alice after the mine but Alice had said once was enough.

Nothing happened. Everything happened. There were excitements in the world, an ongoing war with the Russkies in a place called Crimea where some woman called Florence Nightingale had made a name for herself, but it had nothing to do with their lives and made no impact.

The things that mattered were ordinary things but special in their ordinariness.

The child Jane grew, as healthy children do. They hoped for more and tried often enough. Things didn't work out that way for all their efforts and in time they became reconciled to the situation. A cow calved. There was drought and once they were almost washed out.

They stood at the window of the house, staring at the swirling floodwaters, and asked God or themselves whether the rain would ever stop. It did, of course. It was just weather.

They saw nothing of Richard's half-brother but couldn't avoid hearing about him. William had become a big name in the district and probably beyond. From what they heard, he was cordially hated too, for his harsh ways. And perhaps because everything he did seemed to turn to gold, which made blokes envious, but the people who mattered would have forgiven him the bad things he did, had they even noticed them.

'They're rich too,' Richard said. 'They're all the same, that mob.'

Richard had become cynical in a mild way. Not that he knew much about being rich, having experienced wealth only once in his life and then losing it. Almost before he'd had it, you could say.

He might have regretted that but didn't, not really. Those days spent burrowing like moles in the dank earth were no longer real to him. At least they had escaped from Ballarat and its troubles with a whole skin, which was more than you could say for some.

'I wondered what happened to old Karl,' he said once. 'That German bloke at the diggings? You remember him? What was his surname?'

'Leipzig,' Alice said. 'His name was Leipzig.'

'So it was. I wonder what happened to him.'

But they would never know, except perhaps by chance, and it didn't matter.

'That kid of William's,' Alice said. 'That one landed on her hoofs all right.'

Richard had been reading stock sale figures. 'What you on about?'

'You know what they used to say about that wife of his? How after that accident the doctors told her she couldn't have kids?'

'The doctors got it wrong, then, didn't they?'

'I'm not so sure,' Alice said. 'I reckon Bessie isn't hers at all.'

'Why do you say that?' He wasn't particularly interested but said it to humour his wife, who had always tended to be the curious one.

'You remember that woman who was with William in Ballarat? That Maria Hack?'

'What about her?'

He wouldn't admit to knowing her because Maria Hack might have been a bad lot but was one of those women who had the knack of pricking lust in any man.

'She was pregnant. They skipped Ballarat together, didn't they? Her and William? I reckon Bessie is Maria Hack's kid, nothing to do with silly Cynthia.'

Which was the unkind nickname she'd been given by the locals.

Richard couldn't see it mattered.

'I'm sure of it,' Alice said. And nodded, assembling in her mind all the inside information she didn't have.

A man came by once, when Richard was away at the market with a load of spuds. Said he was looking for some place Alice had never heard of.

She gave him a cup of tea. He admired her rosebush, which had come on well.

Alice was happy; better than that, fulfilled, and had no plans but to live with her husband until she died, but the sneaky desire for adventure and challenge that had impelled her to the goldfields still flickered from time to time.

It flickered now and she knew that with the right words or even the right look something could come of it. She was tempted, no doubt about it – he was a personable man, with the type of luxuriant moustache she had always admired in a man – and her thighs yearned just for a minute for something new, but she did nothing about it and the moment passed.

Afterwards she looked up at the bone-bleak hill behind the farm (it was a dry year) and told herself she was glad, yet for weeks afterwards, under lamplight, she would touch her thighs and wonder.

Time passed.

Bessie Tregellas grew up aware that her father, although distant, loved her but that her mother did not. She did not know why that was so, only that it was.

Since her father was away a lot and busy even when he was at home, Bessie did not see much of him. On the rare occasions she did he was friendly in a preoccupied way, as though he didn't know quite what to do with her. He talked to her awkwardly, with intervals between his words, while her mother, Mrs Tregellas, tended to smile at her without warmth and say nothing at all. So that Bessie, without knowing what the word meant, grew up lonely.

Home was a big house in the middle of the city and Mrs Briggs, the severe nanny, said she should be grateful.

'You do not know how lucky you are,' said Mrs Briggs, as though somehow it was all Bessie's fault.

While Moxie, one of the maids, who was mean to her when no one else was about, told her she'd been found in a paper bag outside the kitchen door and had only been taken in out of kindness.

'Mighta bin me instead of you,' Moxie said. 'Some folks has all the luck.'

Mama had told her that Moxie's mother had been a convict and therefore allowances must be made but Bessie had heard her saying nasty things to Moxie, and Mrs Briggs said that Mrs Tregellas had a down on all convicts and the children of convicts.

Bessie was confused. 'Was you a convict, Mrs Briggs?'

Mrs Briggs bristled like a hairbrush. 'Certainly not!'

Bessie found a stray kitten and made friends with it but not for long. Mrs Briggs said it might have fleas and took it away. Bessie never saw it again.

When she was four she met an old man who she was told was her grandmother's uncle. Mama told her she must be on her best behaviour because Grand-Uncle Barnsley was very rich and expected people to be polite to him.

Grand-Uncle Barnsley did not look rich. He didn't look happy, either. He wore shabby clothes, walked supported on sticks and had a mean mouth. His hands shook and he made a hissing sound when he breathed. Bessie was scared of him. He stared at her with hooded eyes but never said a word, which made Bessie more scared than ever.

A month later Mrs Briggs dressed Bessie in a black dress. Mama's dress was black too while Papa wore a tall hat and a stern face. They all went out of the front door of the house and down the steps and got into a closed carriage drawn by horses wearing black plumes on their heads. There was another carriage drawn by more horses also with black plumes. On the carriage was a kind of long box covered in flowers with huge heads and Mama said that Grand-Uncle Barnsley had gone to heaven.

They went to a place which Mama said was the cemetery. There were lots of people there whom Bessie didn't know and a man Mama said was a clergyman who had a lot to say. There was a hole in the ground and men took the box off the carriage and used long ropes to lower it into the hole. Afterwards Bessie was given a flower which Mrs Briggs said she must throw into the hole which seemed a pity but she did what she was told and watched as people threw earth on top of the box.

'Is my grand-uncle in that box?'

'Be quiet,' Mrs Briggs said.

Later Moxie told her yes, that her uncle had been in the box and they had covered him with earth so that no one need see his nasty face any more.

'But how will he breathe?'

'He can't breathe, silly. He's dead.'

That was when Bessie learnt that to go to heaven you first had to be buried in the earth although she still did not understand the business of not needing to breathe.

She was very small when she first saw Derwent. Afterwards she did not remember much about the visit except that it took a long time to get there and when at last they reached the house on top of the hill she was not allowed to go out.

'Why can't I go out?'

'Because the Abos might steal you.'
'What are Abos?'
'Never mind.'

Left to her own devices for so much of her life, Bessie grew up with
the idea that doing things was important. In order to protect herself
from the Mrs Briggs and Moxies of the world she taught herself to
let no one tell her what she had to do. She had been bullied when
she was tiny; as she grew older she learnt to bully others and discovered she was good at it.

She had grown no closer to Mama over the years – she thought of
her more as an acquaintance than a friend – but had discovered she
was a twitterer, scared of Papa, scared of life and increasingly scared of
her daughter. Bessie was untroubled; where there had never been any
real affection it was hard to feel respect for someone so ineffectual.

By contrast Papa was a strong man, hard and determined. By the
time she was old enough to see these things Bessie understood most
people were scared of Papa, who was even more of a bully than
she was. A worthy heir to his uncle, he had expanded the Tregellas
Bank and acquired businesses across the state and on the mainland.
He was still a young man or at least not old. He had put on a lot
of weight and grown more florid with the years but had been successful in everything he did. Bessie didn't care about his weight but
admired his strength and business skills; she made up her mind to
do everything she could to model herself on him.

Mama was unhappy with a daughter who seemed determined
to be a man. From Bessie's earliest days she had told her again and
again that it was a woman's duty to defer to her husband. It was an
opinion Bessie did not share; in her world respect had to be earned
and there was no way she would defer to a man simply because he
was a man or because she was married to him. A man like Papa
would be different, of course, but how many men were like Papa?

Rather than engage in painting watercolours or embroidery, Bessie became interested in the family businesses. The bank was a key
pillar of the family's wealth yet banking struck no sparks in Bessie's

breast. Her interest lay in Derwent, the reality of Derwent, the power and influence that Derwent bestowed on its owner. Power and land, she thought. They were what mattered in this world. And the family, of course.

By the time she was sixteen she knew the estate as well as she knew herself. It was then that her world changed, when Papa took her into the room in Derwent that he called his study and told her there were people coming to dinner.

'A Mr and Mrs Penrose and their son Phelan. They will be staying overnight. They are important people who own a lot of property in the district.'

'How much?' Bessie asked, very much man to man.

'Twenty thousand acres.'

Father and daughter looked at each other.

'Good land?'

'I believe so,' William said. 'Depending how things work out, I suspect we may be seeing a lot more of them. I shall be discussing business with Mr Penrose and Mama will look after Mrs Penrose, so I thought it would be nice if you could take care of Phelan for me.'

'What's he like?'

'A few years older than you – around twenty, I believe – but he's just back from Europe so should have interesting stories to tell about his time there.'

'What was he doing in Europe?'

'He went to school but afterwards he spent a year or two travelling around before coming home.'

'What's he going to do now he's back?'

'Perhaps he'll tell you, if you ask him.'

Phelan was amiable; you could say that for him. He had pretty eyes and was also handsome in a loose-jawed way. He smiled at her encouragingly.

Daywear had become more modest than in the past – a change that Bessie, secretly proud of her bosom, regretted – but somehow

Phelan conveyed his awareness of her as a woman without stepping beyond the line of propriety. Bessie enjoyed that and the warmth it created beneath her high-necked gown.

Phelan showed no sign of being over-assertive: he wasn't assertive at all. If there was a word to describe him Bessie thought it would be languid: a quality as unlike any she possessed as it was possible to be. On the other hand she had discovered in a book she was not supposed to have read that a languid man might also be passionate in his private life.

Phelan's inviting eyes suggested that might be true.

She was fascinated by the thought that it might be possible to be dominant in daily life but accommodating in private. It would be a challenge but challenge, after all, was an important part of life. And to be *willingly* accommodating was itself another form of domination, was it not?

The idea excited her. There was also the question of the twenty thousand acres.

She thought he might do.

Her mind made up, Bessie saw no point wasting time. Most improperly she enticed Phelan to accompany her on an unchaperoned walk beside the river. Demurely, she permitted him to kiss her. The deed was done.

They made the announcement on their return to the house and were congratulated.

In the privacy of his study Papa told Bessie he was proud of her. Mama twittered. Mr and Mrs Penrose were agreeable and did not comment on the hasty nature of the courtship. Champagne was drunk while William's later discussions with Albert Penrose took on an increased urgency.

Later William called in his lawyers. A prenuptial agreement was drawn up and a trust deed prepared.

Afterwards William told his daughter what he had decided.

'I cannot leave the estate to you or any part of it.'

Bessie was indignant. 'Why not?'

'Because as a married woman any assets you possess automatically belong to your husband.'

'That is outrageous!'

'It is the law,' William said. 'But you needn't worry. On my death everything I own will be transferred into a family trust.'

'What does that mean? And how does it help me?'

'The trustees become the legal owner of the property. In practice it won't affect you at all. As beneficiary you will still receive all the income but it stops the estate being transferred into your husband's name.'

'He can't touch it?'

'Not a penny.'

'But who would run things if anything were to happen to you?'

'The trustees would appoint someone.'

Bessie gave him a sharp look. 'Someone?'

'That someone being you. And anyone you wanted to give you a hand: in running the bank, for example.'

'And no one else could interfere?'

'Absolutely not. The trustees will act on your instructions. The trust is simply a device to keep the estate in the family.' William laughed. 'In any case I am not dead yet.'

'And hopefully not for many years,' Bessie said.

'That is my intention,' William said.

Two days later William Tregellas collapsed during an afternoon stroll. He was carried to the house where he lay, semi-conscious and raving about shadow walkers watching him from the foot of his bed.

'What is he talking about?' Bessie said.

'I fear it is the devil,' Mama said. She had become notably religious over the past twelve months and spoke of God having struck her husband down. 'For his misdeeds,' she said.

'What misdeeds?'

'Our lives have been a lie,' Cynthia Tregellas said. 'It is not my fault, not at all. Your father is to blame.'

She was unwilling to be more specific so Bessie began to suspect Mama might also be afflicted.

The Penrose family arrived: father, mother and son. They looked grave as was appropriate but Bessie suspected there was more to Mr Penrose's stern expression than concern for William's health and prospects of recovery.

There was land involved and several businesses; inevitably questions had to be asked about who would be the right person to run them. Should William, unhappily, be taken from them.

'Not that we are thinking of anything like that,' Albert Penrose said.

That was nonsense, Bessie thought. Of course he was thinking about it; he'd be a fool not to. With Papa so ill and she so inexperienced, Albert Penrose would be pondering how he could get in his own people to run things. She had no worries on that score – the terms of the trust deed would prevent it – but there was another problem. If Albert found he couldn't run the show himself he might decide to walk away from the relationship altogether: there were other heiresses, after all.

She had to make sure that didn't happen; if it did she could kiss goodbye any prospect of getting hold of the Penroses' twenty thousand acres.

Papa came back to the world. No more talk of shadow walkers; no more haunted nightmares that had reduced the hardest man Bessie knew to screaming tears.

His voice was there but only in whispers. His lips were loose in his head, as though they might drift away. It was hard to make out what he was trying to say. He beckoned urgently; she bent her ear to his mouth.

'You must marry him. Don't wait. Don't give his father an excuse to break the agreement.'

'I won't,' Bessie said.

William, not a smiling man, managed one now. 'I'll be watching. Not sure where from but I'll be watching.'

There was no point pretending there was any prospect of Papa's recovery: death was painted on his features and would not be long denied. Even the effort of those few words had exhausted him. He panted for a while.

'Better send your mother in,' he said.

'I'll make sure of everything,' Bessie said.

'Erridge is a good man,' William said. 'You can trust him. He'll help you.'

Erridge was the family lawyer, he and one of his junior partners the trustees of the family trust.

'I shall be glad of his advice,' Bessie said. 'But we'll manage. Do not worry.'

William's head sank back on the pillow, yet an echo of his buccaneering past returned one more time. 'I have watched your fiancé these last weeks. I have no doubt you will be able to handle him without too much difficulty.'

'You may be certain of that,' Bessie said.

'Get your mother in here,' he said. 'And remember: marry Phelan as quickly as you can. Next week if you can manage it. Don't let that slippery Albert Penrose sneak away. He probably doesn't think you're capable of running things without me so he might try it if he thinks he can get away with it.'

Later that night, after Papa had died, Bessie liked to think how their last words had been of Derwent, Albert Penrose and how to prevent him reneging on the deal they had made.

She had expected she would be distraught at Papa's death but was not. She was William's daughter and had businesses to run; she had no time for grief. Any tears she would shed in private; the public display of grief she would leave to Mama, so much more experienced in weeping than Bessie.

'I'll do what you wanted,' she promised his memory, wondering whether he could hear her. 'You rest easy. I'll take care of everything.'

She would do it for him and for herself. She would keep the faith.

After the funeral they all went back to the house. Bessie made sure the staff had an abundant tea. Albert Penrose thought it was a waste of money bordering on disrespect for the departed, and said so. Bessie did not, and said so.

'Continuity is important,' she said. 'They need to know their future is assured.' She gave Mr Penrose a smile so sweet it almost cramped her lips. 'Of course a man understands these things so much better than a woman. Why,' she said, 'I feel quite helpless. I am so thankful that Phelan will be there to support me. And you, of course. How grateful I am that I can rely on your assistance, dear Mr Penrose. I declare I would be quite lost without the pair of you.'

Albert was gratified. He had feared this pushy girl might present a problem but now was willing to believe he had misjudged her. Trust or no trust, it was obvious she would need mature advice in running her inheritance. It seemed to him there was every prospect of her being amenable to his suggestions. One of which would be to make him a trustee of the Tregellas trust, giving him effective control of all the Tregellas assets. He therefore favoured immediate action.

'I know it is customary to wait in these circumstances,' he said. 'But I really wonder whether a delay is necessary. No disrespect to your late father would be intended and in my experience it is better that arrangements of this nature be implemented as soon as possible.'

'It was my father's dying wish,' Bessie said. 'The sooner the better: they were his last words.'

Mama was the only person to protest. 'What will our friends say about it? My dear, they'll think you're pregnant.'

'I hope I soon am,' Bessie said. 'And who cares what they think?'

Fortunately Mama's protests could safely be ignored.

A special licence was obtained. Two and a half weeks after William Tregellas's funeral Bessie and Phelan Penrose were married in the little church Emma had had built when Ephraim Dark first obtained title to the land. Mama might have thought it inappropriate to have the wedding so soon but at least, Bessie thought, it gave her the excuse to shed more tears.

She hadn't known what to expect. Friends who claimed experience sang its praises behind their fans, raving about sensations beyond belief or description. On the other hand she had overheard a maid discussing her latest boyfriend, calling him a Johnny Come Quickly.

At the time Bessie had not known what she'd meant. Now she did.

She wondered whether it was Phelan's fault or her own. She wondered whether it was a question of fault at all. She thought it was a disappointment that might come right in time even though there had so far been no sign of it.

Later still she decided it was a good thing. Sensations beyond belief were dangerous, hinting at enslavement. The way things were, Bessie was free.

Alice and Richard were astonished when they heard the news of William's unexpected death.

'Still in his thirties,' Richard said. 'Makes you think. I wonder what happened to him?'

'Probably somebody shot him,' said Alice, who might have a curious nature but was not the forgiving kind, and had not forgotten the Eureka Stockade and how she would always believe William had set them up.

'Should we go to the funeral?' Richard said.

'If you go you'll go alone,' Alice said.

'He was my half-brother.'

'So he was. And never lifted a finger to help us, did he?'

'We wouldn't have taken it if he'd offered.'

'That's not the point.'

So they gave the funeral a miss. The next thing they knew, Bessie had married Phelan Penrose. The way the papers went on about it, the Tregellas and Penrose clans might have been royalty. Which by local standards Alice supposed they were.

'William hardly cold in his grave and Bessie already married?' Alice said. 'What kind of people are they?'

'Rich people,' Richard said.

'I'll bet she's pregnant too,' Alice said.

But in that, to her private disappointment, she was wrong.

Mama's reaction to Papa's death tried Bessie severely. She had always been limp but now, after Papa's death, she became more so than ever, as though without William's ruthless strength she was a rudderless boat drifting on seas without horizon.

She spent more time in her room, sometimes not appearing for days at a time. Bessie was busy but made it her business to go and see her when she could. Most days she managed a few minutes with her, sometimes as much as half an hour.

'You should get out more.'

'I don't feel like it, Bessie.'

'I'll get Wilkins to take you out in the carriage.'

'I don't feel like it, Bessie.'

'I'll get...'

But what was the use? Mama had put down anchors and was not to be moved.

Weeks passed. Bessie employed a woman to keep an eye on Mama. One morning the woman came to see Bessie in the room she used as an office.

'I think you'd better come, madam.'

Mama looked as though her life were draining into a bottomless void. Her fingers clutched the sheet; her lips were drawn back. Yet the look she now directed at Bessie was something Bessie had never expected to see on her face: an expression not of apology but malice.

'I am sorry I have not been a better mother to you. There was a reason but I should have tried harder.'

'Don't let it trouble you,' Bessie said.

'It troubles me very much. I agreed, you see. It was never your fault.'

Bessie had no idea what Mama was talking about.

'I promised your father I would never tell you but I believe you have the right to know.'

'To know what?'

Mama's eyes closed, then opened again. She drew a deep breath. 'To know you are not my child.' She smiled as though the words gave her the greatest possible pleasure. 'I had to tell you, you see. I hope he knows what I have done. I hope he does. It is the only chance I shall ever have to punish him for what he did to me.'

1982

Bec press-ganged four maids, who scrubbed and cleaned St Madern church until, as cheeky Doris put it, the bride and groom could have scoffed the wedding breakfast off the aisle floor and the sun, shining through the solitary stained-glass window, threw multi-coloured puddles of light on the chancel steps.

Bec had also suggested press-ganging the bishop from his Hobart hidey-hole, but Tamara had had a run-in with him once and said over her dead body, so they gave that one a miss. A run-of-the-mill vicar would do although Bec was inclined to mourn the purple robes.

'Getting quite the snob in your old age,' Tamara said.

'Nothing of the sort,' Bec said. 'I'm a bit light on granddaughters so I thought I'd put on a show for the one I've got, but I'm sure we can find a whisky priest hiding in some ditch, if that's what you would prefer.'

Although the man they got did not live in a ditch and seemed to prefer tea to scotch, which Bec thought a severe failing on his part. At least Giles was there to give his daughter away. Bec wouldn't have been surprised if he'd tried to dodge what he called the show – after all, he'd done blow-all for Tamara for most of her life – but he assured everyone who would listen he wouldn't have missed it for the world.

'Long life and happiness to the pair of them, that's what I say.'

He even came up with a half-decent cheque, which was a surprise but welcome nonetheless.

The downside was that Raine and Jaeger would be there too, which was a pity but couldn't be helped. Nor, with Mr Elphinstone digging into Raine's background, did Bec think it would matter, in the end.

Tamara came to her wedding in an open carriage. She sat with Megan, an old school friend, who was acting as bridesmaid.

'The road ought to be lined with serfs to cheer me on,' Tamara said, but coming down the steep road from the house there was a severe absence of watchers of any kind.

'Where's a good serf when you need one?' Megan said.

'I'll have my own bloke,' Tamara said. Even in joke it was hard to believe. 'Provided he turns up.'

'I was thinking of me, not you,' Megan said. 'All this is making me randy.'

Bec had arranged flags and bunting on the trees lining the narrow roadway that wound its way uphill from the main road to the church. The sun was out now but it had rained in the night and underfoot the ground was damp.

'Here's where I fall flat on my face,' Tamara told Megan as she prepared to step down from the carriage, but in the event she managed it as nimbly as a ballet dancer.

There were people waiting on either side of the path and outside the church's open door. Some were talking, others laughing, while one or two by the look of them had anticipated the festivities by getting in a belt or two first. The tree branches overhead splintered the sun's rays into arrows of brilliant light.

Tamara looked at the people waiting. 'A better turn out than I'd expected.'

She walked quietly and slowly up the path. When she had woken that morning she remembered asking herself whether she was the right person to marry Grant or anyone, but now she found she had no doubts at all. This is today, she thought, and after today we shall have tomorrow and all the tomorrows after that.

She entered the church; the sense of being one with an age-old tradition engulfed her. The church, its stones sombre with age, greeted her. She saw Bec in the poshest of hats but did not smile or acknowledge her. Now she was one with past and future and time, as she paced arm in arm with her father down the short aisle, had no meaning. As she placed her hand in Grant's hand a thousand generations of women accompanied her in what had for centuries been the ritual of the woman's surrender to the man.

They had come a long way from the days when a woman came to the ceremony with the halter of subservience about her neck; now it was more a question of sharing equally, the ceremony not degraded by the past. Tamara listened to the words flowing like honey in the tiny church and, as she uttered her responses, felt the warmth and fulfilment of one who had finally come home.

The reception was held back at Derwent House.

As at Bec's birthday party there were lots of guests. Bride and groom were congratulated. There were gifts, some generous, others less so. Raine was particularly cordial but her eyes said what her words did not, that she and Tamara were at daggers drawn over Derwent and that she regarded the marriage as no more than a gambit in the battle they were waging on the chessboard of the future. She was no fool either, and, marriage or not, Tamara knew the battle was a long way from being won.

Jaeger, by contrast, was inclined to sulk, which brought a barely concealed joy to Tamara's heart.

After sea trout, oysters and roast lamb, champagne and wedding cake, both bride and groom were well-wished half to death and Megan found a friend of the groom who she thought might do in the absence of a suitable serf.

The shadows were long across the grass as Grant and Tamara stepped into the car that would take them to the hotel outside Hobart where they would spend the night before flying out to Malaysia and a week at an up-market Penang resort, a choice Bec thought particularly appropriate when she remembered how the Chans of Penang had saved the family's bacon back in the 1930s.

Now the lamps were turned low. They could hear the wind's soft voice, see through the bedroom window the river's polished shield gleaming silver beneath the moon as it followed its course to the sea, the waiting sea. Now, at last, they were alone.

'Love me,' Tamara said fiercely.

1913

After her run-in with Jonathan Bessie Penrose sat and thought for a while.

That Hampton clan, she thought. They'll be the death of us if I don't stop this nonsense. The blacksmith's daughter mistress of Derwent? Her father the stable boy lording it in the living room? It was unthinkable.

She had to make sure it never happened. It was tricky; maybe it was no more than a passing whim – a lot of men, her husband included, had been incapable of keeping their hands off the maids – but her instinct said this might be more serious than that. In any case she couldn't afford to take the chance. If her grandson cared so little for the family's good name she would have to take care of it for him; the one thing she knew for certain was that never would she countenance a member of her family marrying the daughter of Conan Hampton.

'I'd kill her first, if it came to it,' she told the empty room.

Or more probably arrange for someone to do it for her.

She got out of her chair. It was a simple enough action yet every day it seemed harder to do. She hated the idea of being decrepit – fifty-eight was hardly old – but had discovered that arthritis could put years on the strongest, more was the pity. Willpower helped fight the pain but there wasn't much it could do about stiffening joints.

Well, she must manage the best she could. The most important thing was that no one should have an inkling of the problem; she was determined the rest of the world should go on seeing her as the warrior she had always been.

She put on her hat and coat and went to look for the chauffeur.

She checked the appearance of the motor. It shone like a mirror in the sunshine and she nodded approvingly before hauling herself painfully into the back seat.

She gave Bennett his instructions and sat back, looking out of the window as the car negotiated the steep hill. She was smiling, determined to enjoy the ride. Besides, she was looking forward to what she was confident would be a satisfactory outcome to the coming confrontation.

Ten minutes later the motor car pulled up in front of the cottage where Constable and Mrs Painter lived.

Mrs Painter came skittering from the house like a storm of chooks.

'Oh my, Mrs Penrose. What a pleasure...'

Bessie gave her most gracious smile. 'Good day, Mrs Painter. I hope you are well? And your husband too, of course?'

'Fine, Mrs Penrose. We are both –'

'I believe you have a young woman staying with you? A Rebecca Hampton?'

'Yes, indeed, Mrs Penrose. She gives me a hand with the chores. I hope there's nothing wrong –'

'A small matter. Nothing to reproach yourself with, I assure you.' Bessie's smile had all the charm of Constable Painter's manacles. 'Might I have a word with her? If she's free?'

1982

Bec was sitting in her favourite spot: the chair on the deck of Derwent House, protected by a collapsible awning from the worst of the fierce summer sun yet with views over the vastness of the land lying to the north.

After so many years it still seemed miraculous that for all her adult life she, the blacksmith's daughter, had been a member of the family that owned the fifty thousand acres that made Derwent the largest property in Tasmania's high country: twenty thousand from the original grant, ten thousand more from Barnsley and finally twenty thousand acres of what had once been Penrose land.

Bec had read an article in a farming magazine that had held up the Derwent operation as a shining example of an iconic property that unlike many, and thanks of course to Tamara, had not been afraid to embrace new techniques.

And now there was the obvious danger that, despite her marriage, Tamara's rightful place might still be usurped by an outsider.

In the noonday shadows she saw them: Emma and Bessie who had made Derwent what it was, Grandma Jane who more than any other being had united her with what had proved to be her destiny. They were the forerunners and she was determined she would be worthy of them and of Tamara, who was the future.

I hold past and future in my hands, Bec thought, and I will not fail.

It was easy to say but not so easily done because Raine Armitage had a tight grip on Giles's affections and it would need clear and incontrovertible evidence to dislodge her. Evidence that for the moment was lacking.

Mr Gardiner of Elphinstone and Partners had been back to her the day before and given her the little information he had been able to obtain from his firm's Zurich correspondents. It wasn't much: certainly not what Bec had been hoping.

Basically the Lardner family and its legal advisers had refused to give any information at all about what they called their private affairs.

In their place Bec would have done the same yet she remained convinced that it was in Raine Armitage's past that the solution to the problem would be found. She was determined on one thing: in no circumstances would she tolerate the prospect of Raine's son Jaeger getting his hands on Derwent.

For the first time she understood how Bessie Penrose must have felt sixty-nine years before when the blacksmith's daughter had appeared on the horizon of her life.

'I am planning something radical,' she had told Tamara after Mr Gardiner had left. 'I am going to Zurich.'

Tamara had looked at her.

'I know what you're thinking. You think it's madness at my age and so it is but I see no alternative. This is something I have to do.'

Now the arrangements had been made, the tickets and hotel booked, her passport updated. At six o'clock the next morning she would be aboard the early flight from Launceston to Melbourne where she would connect with the Swissair flight to Zurich.

What happened after that would be in the lap of the gods. All she knew was that if determination was the criterion she would win.

Bessie must have felt as I do, she thought. Certainly she did everything she could to stop me.

What a battle that had been.

1913

Bec kept Bessie Penrose waiting for several minutes before she came sauntering down the path between the lavender bushes.

'Yes, Mrs Penrose?'

Not much give in her expression, Bessie thought. Well, we'll soon change that.

'Good morning, Rebecca. It is Rebecca, is it not?'

'That's right, Mrs Penrose. People call me Bec but Rebecca is the name on my birth certificate.'

'I thought we could go for a drive and have a little chat. Would you like that, Rebecca?'

'I don't mind.'

'You disappoint me, Rebecca. I thought you'd be excited. Have you been in a motor before?'

'No.'

'Then get in for the ride of your life. Something you can tell your friends about.'

Bec delayed responding just long enough to send Bessie a message, then got into the motor car and closed the door behind her. She sat with her hands in her lap. She looked through the windscreen and did not speak.

Clouded in dust from the car wheels, the road unwound steadily behind them.

'I believe you know my grandson,' Bessie said.

'That's right.'

Bessie waited – for a confession, perhaps? – but Bec said no more. For a few minutes neither spoke. Then Bessie said:

'Poor Jonathan… I fear he will have many heavy responsibilities in his life.'

'Running Derwent, you mean?'

'That is very important, certainly,' Bessie said. 'And of course all the family's other interests. For most people it would be all they could handle.' She permitted herself a light laugh. 'I daresay for many it would be a lot *more* than they could handle. But members of my family have always known that more is expected from them than from most. Jonathan is no exception, I'm afraid.'

The motor car rounded a bend and found itself face to face with a mob of sheep being driven down the road. The dust, noise and smell of the sheep were all around them. Dogs ran and nipped, red tongues lolling. One in its excitement leapt on the back of a panicked ewe.

The back of Bennett's neck showed indignation that the motor car he was driving should be blocked by a mob of sheep but his employer, who liked to get her own way in everything, seemed unconcerned.

'The pleasures and perils of country life,' said Bessie Penrose. She opened the window as the drover came by. 'Good day, Thomas.'

He touched his cap. 'Day, Mrs Penrose.'

Bec saw him take note of her presence in the car. That'll make for even more gossip, she thought.

The road clear, the motor drove on.

'That is an example of what I mean,' Bessie said. 'The owners of Derwent have social responsibilities also. People know who we are. They have an image of how people in our position should behave and it is our responsibility to ensure we live up to it. In all things.'

Silence but for the noise of the engine.

They reached the top of a rise; Bessie leant forwards and spoke to Bennett; the motor drew to a halt. In front of them the land sloped gently into the valley. In the distance were the hills.

'I love the view from here,' Bessie said.

'All Derwent land,' Bec said.

'As you say. It has been in our family for almost a century. Legally we are its owners but in reality it owns us. It is our responsibility to nurture it, expand it, devote our lives to it and eventually pass it on to future generations. There are times when that can be a burden, Rebecca. Times when it requires us to make sacrifices that perhaps we would rather not make,' said Bessie Penrose.

'A big job,' Bec said.

Since it was plain that something had to be said.

'Exactly,' Bessie said. 'So big a job that quite frankly I do not believe any of us could manage it without support. Support from a loving husband. Or a wife capable of accepting the social responsi-bilities of her position. Of being accepted by the community.'

Which you will never be. The words remained unstated yet were as loud as trumpets in the motor's enclosed space.

Someone socially acceptable, Bec thought. Someone, impor-tantly, who was not Conan Hampton's daughter.

Bessie had exposed her hand. Now it was Bec's turn.

Go for it.

'Where does love fit into all this?'

She thrust the word like a mailed fist into what until now had been more or less a monologue. A dull flush spread across Bessie's throat: she was unused to what had sounded dangerously like a challenge.

'Love is essential, of course.'

But might have been the plague, the way she spoke.

'I love him, Mrs Penrose.' There: she had said it – and to the enemy too. 'And he loves me.'

'You *think* you love him,' Bessie corrected her. 'I suspect you are a little young to know the true meaning of that word. What are you now? Fifteen?'

'Sixteen, Mrs Penrose.'

As you know very well.

'You look younger,' Bessie said. 'Less mature.'

'And you feel that only someone from your own social level could be right for Jonathan.'

Bessie thrust out pugnacious lips. 'I do not intend to get into a discussion of the whys and wherefores, Rebecca. I am sure you are a delightful girl in many ways but my grandson is not for you.'

'Why?'

Now the challenge was clear. Bessie's eyes grew mean and small; there were limits to how much impertinence she was prepared to tolerate. 'I have told you –'

But Bec, inexcusably, cut in. 'Are you saying that only people with the right background are suitable to marry into your family?'

'I do not intend to discuss it with you.'

Bec felt something stir in her: the courage to confront this formidable woman who stood between her and happiness. 'Because if that *is* what you're saying, Mrs Penrose, then I have to wonder about that. Given your own background, I mean.'

Bec had heard of people blowing up like toads but had never seen it before.

Bessie, swollen face and body, spoke in little more than a whisper. 'You dare say such a thing to me?'

Bec said: 'Does the name Maria Hack mean anything to you?'

'I have never heard of anyone of that name.'

But Bessie had slumped back in her seat, face suddenly white, and Bec saw that her breath was coming fast in response to a question she had no doubt never expected to hear.

She is lying, Bec thought. So Grandma Jane's story is true.

'Seems strange,' she said. 'Seeing the convict Maria Hack was your mother.'

It was indeed a strange business, because Bec had discovered another person inside her, a being whose existence she had never suspected until now. She would never have believed that she, Bec Hampton, was capable of saying what she had.

By her port-wine complexion it was clear Bessie would never have believed it either. Yet her voice, when she spoke, was so quiet Bec could barely hear her.

'You have been talking to your grandmother. She has been saying these things for years. You must know they're nonsense.'

'I told her that was what you'd say,' Bec said.

'Then what are you talking about?' said Bessie.

'There is a letter,' Bec said.

'There is a letter,' Jane said. 'My mum wrote it. Your great-grandma Alice. She was there, you know, at the goldfields. She was in the Eureka Stockade.'

Bec had heard the story a dozen times but had never known whether to believe it or not. She'd heard lots of tales of Eureka and the way the soldiers had gunned down the miners, but she suspected that those with the most to say had never been near the place.

A letter, if one existed, was a different matter.

'Have you seen it?'

'I got it, girl. Got it safe. Always thought it might come in handy some day. Now I think maybe it has.'

'You never talked about it?'

'Uncle Will Tregellas wasn't the sort to mess with. An' after he died there didn't seem much point. Not until now, anyway. I'll tell you somen else. Maria Hack was supposed to have murdered someone back in London. But they wanted breeding stock for the colonies so they sent her out instead of topping her.'

'You're saying Bessie's mother was a murderess?'

'That's why I'm telling you. You're heading for trouble with that one, I'm any judge, but Bessie wouldn't want people knowing about Maria Hack, would she? And there was another matter too.'

'What was that?'

'Hobart was a small place in them days. Everyone knew everyone else's business. My mum told me a lot of people had heard that William's wife, her that had been Cynthia Mason, couldn't have children after the accident she had. She always reckoned that was how Maria Hack got in on the act.'

'To have William's baby?'

'So he could pass it off as Cynthia's. You got it.'

'And the baby was Bessie?'

Grandma Jane smiled. 'Bessie Tregellas till she married Phelan Penrose. One more thing. Mum's letter says how the people in Hobart who knew about the accident was that surprised when Cynthia come back from Sydney with a baby that looked older than they would have expected but of course no one questioned it. They just thought they must have got it wrong.'

'Why did my great-grandma write the letter in the first place?'

'To get her own back.'

'No doubt it would help if I knew what you were talking about,' Bessie Penrose said.

'I'm talking about a letter written by your Aunt Alice. She knew your mother in Ballarat.'

Bessie laughed merrily. 'I was born in Sydney. I have never been to Ballarat in my life.'

'You were born in Sydney after your dad took Maria Hack there to give birth to you.'

'Supposition,' Bessie said. 'Conjecture. You have no proof.'

'Other than the letter,' Bec said.

She saw that the skin around Bessie's lips was white. With every instant Bec was becoming more confident her fortune had changed and was now carrying her forwards on a cresting wave. For the first time she truly believed she had a real chance of realising her dreams.

'This letter you say exists,' Bessie said. 'Of course the contents of a letter like that prove nothing but, as a matter of interest, have you seen it?'

'Oh yes.'

What was a lie in a good cause?

'And where is it?'

'Safe,' Bec said.

'And you are saying this letter claims your great-grandmother met my father in Ballarat?'

'Him and Maria Hack. People said Maria was a murderess,' she said casually.

'I know nothing about Maria Hack. Maybe she was a murderess, as you say, but that has nothing to do with me,' Bessie said. 'Maybe my father had a child by her, maybe he didn't. There is no way to know the truth of it now. But what I do know is that I was born in Sydney in 1856 and that before her marriage my mother was Cynthia Mason, daughter of one of the richest bankers in the colony.'

'1856? That what it says on your birth certificate, is it? Not 1855?'

'I shall listen to no more of this nonsense,' Bessie Penrose said with a return to her iron-hard voice. She rapped the handle of her stick on the glass partition separating the passengers from the driver.

'Back to the house, Bennett. If you please.' She turned to Bec. 'I shall drop you at the Painters'.'

The car began to return the way it had come. Bessie Penrose, a model of outrage, sat motionless at Bec's side. She said nothing nor would, perhaps, for the rest of the journey but Bec could hear the whistle and sigh of her still-agitated breath.

By contrast Bec was feeling detached from everything that had passed between them. Of the letter's existence she had no doubt. Of the reality of Bessie's birth she had no doubt. Proof was unimportant; this was not a legal business but a question of reputation. Bec need do nothing now but sit and wait for the truth to work its poison in the veins of the woman sitting beside her.

The cresting wave carried her on.

She smiled at the woman at her side.

'You were saying, Mrs Penrose, that my great-grandmother's letter has nothing to do with you?'

'That is exactly what I am saying, Rebecca.'

Silence again, the paddocks flowing back.

'Then you won't mind if we give it to the newspapers?'

Turning to observe Mrs Penrose's face, she was in time to see the shock strike home.

'It could be of great historical importance,' she explained earnestly. 'A letter from the goldfields… It is part of our heritage, isn't it? And to think your father was there! How wonderful! You must be very proud of him.'

Bessie's eyes were shut. Slowly they reopened. Something not entirely human peered out. Something that saw the abyss and did not believe what it contained. But would exact vengeance.

'You shouldn't give it away, Rebecca. That would be foolish. As you say, the letter – if it exists – is of historical interest. And if it relates to my dear father then I think you will agree my family should have the first option to buy it. To have it on display in the Derwent library. What do you say?'

'I think you're right,' Bec said. 'But maybe we should put it up for auction? That might be the best way.' Again the earnest look. 'What do you think, Mrs Penrose?'

Bessie's lips were tight as tight. 'I was thinking perhaps five pounds. If the letter is genuine.'

'That's a lot of money,' Bec said.

'It is indeed. Are we agreed, then?'

'I think maybe I should discuss it first,' Bec said. 'With Jonathan? If you don't mind?'

She knew very well how Bessie Penrose would hate that.

'I do not see how my grandson's opinion can have any relevance.'

'I discuss everything with Jonathan,' Bec said. 'Only right I should. I mean, seeing as how we're going to get married?'

After dropping the Hampton girl at the Painters', Bennett drove Mrs Penrose home. Thunderclouds accompanied her all the way. At the house she struggled out of the motor – those joints again! – and, doing her best not to limp, made her way as briskly as she could into the house.

One look at her face and the maids all made sure they were busy somewhere else. Bessie plonked herself down; even her favoured chair was careful not to squeak. Daddy's portrait mocked her from its place on the wall.

We'd have known how to deal with that little trollop on the goldfields.

Bessie shut her ears. If she never heard the word *goldfields* again it would be too soon. As for the woman who had birthed and then abandoned her…

How could you love and hate someone at the same time?

In the meantime she had to do something about the Hampton girl. Had Rebecca been anyone but Conan's daughter she might have been able to come to terms with it, but the prospect of having Conan's child as a member of the family was intolerable. As was Conan being Jonathan's father-in-law.

At all costs she had to prevent that. But how?

She had threatened to disinherit Jonathan if he didn't cut ties with Rebecca; it hadn't worked. Perhaps he had not believed she would do it? *Would* she do it? It would be easy enough to arrange: as trustee and principal beneficiary all she had to do was to instruct the lawyers to remove Jonathan from the list of the trust's beneficiaries. But could she afford to do that? Did Derwent not need him? There was a ragbag of cousins but all on Phelan's side of the family, and a nephew of her pathetic daughter-in-law Rose somewhere up in Queensland. There was no one in the direct line and they were all gutless wonders in any case. It *had* to be Jonathan, but Jonathan without Rebecca Hampton.

She would have offered Rebecca a bribe if she'd thought it would do any good but why would she be interested in a bribe when Derwent itself was there for the taking?

She could tell the Painters to get rid of her, say there was something suspect about her character, but Rebecca was well known in the neighbourhood and to do anything like that would be a risky business.

The homeless waif, treated so harshly by the wicked grandmother…

Oh yes, she could see her playing that one for all she was worth.

Bessie thought some more, her face sour with resentment. An idea came.

How old had Bec said she was? Sixteen. Jonathan was of age and could do what he liked. Whereas Bec...

Sixteen.

The next morning Bessie had Bennett drive her into town. She had no appointment but was confident Mr Willis the bank manager would see her. She had sold the family's interest in the bank years before, but her name still carried weight. Bessie Penrose of Derwent? He would jump at it! She was right.

They went through the motions: coffee on a silver tray, small talk about the tragedy of Captain Scott's death in the Antarctic. Then: 'There is a confidential matter I wish to discuss with you, Mr Willis.'

The banker inclined his head. 'I am at your service.'

'Of course. I understand that a Mr Conan Hampton is a customer of your bank and is indebted to you.' She'd had the chauffeur make cautious enquiries and knew it was true. Now she raised her hand as the banker tried to interrupt her. 'I quite understand you cannot discuss a customer's affairs but if it happens I am correct – and I am not asking you to confirm that either, Mr Willis – I have a small favour to ask of you. If it is not too much trouble.'

Half an hour later, well satisfied by Mr Willis's response to her suggestion, she instructed Bennett to drive her home.

A week later Grandma Bessie Penrose appeared at the entrance to Conan Hampton's forge.

They had not spoken since Conan had left with Bessie's son Daddo for the South African war. She had wondered how she would feel after all this time and was relieved to find she felt nothing. Certainly she had not come to dredge up the residue of past temptations. She was a mature lady now and mature ladies did not lust after the local blacksmith. Or admit it, especially to themselves, if they did.

She looked at the man who had kindled fires in her eighteen years before and thought: how could I have wanted this man?

Conan, in her memory so strong and hard and lean, had quite a belly under his leather apron and was losing his hair. His cheeks had more than their fair share of broken veins and his eyes were red. He stank of booze and fire, the hard tyranny of hot iron, and had about him an air of dissipation and barely controlled violence. Give him another eighteen years and he would be an old man and by the look of him a bad-tempered one at that.

He stood in the doorway of the forge and she saw the firelight casting quivering red shadows across the walls and ceiling, heard the sigh and chink of a horse waiting to be shod.

'You've put on a few pounds,' Conan said.

Bessie had no intention of permitting liberties.

'Is there anywhere we can talk in private?'

He gestured at the adjoining cottage. 'The missus will give you a cup of tea while you're waiting. I won't be long.'

She heard the violence of a hammer on hot iron as she went to the open cottage door.

Ten minutes later he joined her. He was holding in his hairy fist a teacup big enough to swim in. He sat down and drank with a gusty sigh. 'Blacksmith's work is hot business.'

Bessie smiled.

Conan finished his tea. 'What you want?'

'I hear on the grapevine the bank is pressing you?'

'None of your business if it is. And why should you care, anyway?'

Bessie gave what some might have mistakenly thought was a coy smile. 'The trouble with age is that you tend to remember things you'd sooner forget.'

'You're not that old.'

'Was the grapevine right?'

'How did you hear about it?'

'Never mind that. Is it true?'

'True enough, I reckon.'

'How much do you owe them?'

'More'n I can pay, that's for sure.'

'How much?'

'Best part of three hundred quid.'

'Do you have it?'

In the open air Conan would have spat. 'Nuthun like it.'

'What are you going to do?'

'Gawd knows.'

Bessie's handbag was just so in her lap. Now she moved it a fraction of an inch. 'I have a suggestion that might interest you.'

Conan checked the emptiness of his cup to give him time to think. 'What you on about?'

'I could lend you the money,' she said. 'Get the bank off your back.'

'Why would you do that?'

'Because I need your help.'

At least that was honest, he thought. 'Got some 'orses you want shoeing?'

Because a man had his pride.

'Your daughter thinks she's in love with my grandson.'

'That right?'

'I've no objections in principle,' Bessie said, 'but it is important that young people should know their own minds. It is a lifetime commitment, after all.'

'You don' think my Bec's good enough for your grandson. That what you're saying?'

'Nothing of the sort,' Bessie said. 'I simply believe she is too young to know her own mind. I think you would be doing her a favour if you refused permission for her to marry until she's of age.'

'Five years,' Conan said.

'No time at all if she truly loves him.'

'And for that you'd get the bank off my back?'

'I shall lend you three hundred pounds. Nothing formal, nothing in writing. No set date for repayment. I know very well,' Mrs Penrose said, 'how hard it is to make a living nowadays.'

'You'd trust me with three hundred quid?'

She smiled. 'We have always been friends, you and I.'

Which was untrue, as they both knew, but three hundred pounds was not to be sneezed at.

'All right, then. You lend me what I need to fix up the bank, I'll tell Bec she can't marry until she's twenty-one.'

'I was sure we'd think of a way to help you out of your troubles,' said Mrs Penrose.

'Yours too, sounds like.' He lifted his bath-sized cup. 'More tea?'

But Bessie was already standing up. A polite but formal smile, now she had got what she came for. 'I only wish I had the time.'

Driving home in the back of the motor Bessie was gratified by the outcome of her chat with Rebecca's father. His appearance had come as quite a shock, all the same, so different from her memory of him in his youth.

It was not often she indulged herself by journeying back into the past but she did so now.

1875

In 1875, when Richard and Alice were coming forty-seven and Jane nineteen, Richard had a nasty accident with a scythe. Afterwards he couldn't have said how it happened, knew only that the blade had gone down to the bone and his leg wouldn't be healing any time soon.

'Gunna be a cripple, that's what,' Richard said. 'A right bugger.'

Enough to make a bloke mad. The trouble was, he was right, which meant they would have to get help.

There was a man called Jake Hampton, not young but strong, who knew his way around a farm. He turned a tough face to the world but Alice suspected that underneath he was a lot softer than he made out. They took him on and things worked out well.

Time passed and Alice began to notice that Jake's eyes lingered more and more frequently on her daughter. She had the idea Jane fancied him too: not that Jane, powerfully inclined to secrecy, would ever say anything about it. Alice said nothing, either; in that department things would work out or they wouldn't. In the meantime Jake was a good worker, which was just as well, because as the months went by Richard's leg didn't mend.

'Feels like it's on fire,' he told Alice.

Alice could feel it when she put her hand on the leg, which was swollen and throbbing and a red colour she didn't like.

They got the doctor in and he looked grave and talked about deep-seated infection and in the end did no good at all.

'I'll bet he charged, though,' Richard said.

'He's got to live too,' Alice said.

'You got to wonder why,' Richard said.

He was sinking. They both knew it, with the deep-seated infection, as the doctor had called it, spreading. The swelling was up into his groin now, and he was feverish and in constant pain.

Alice did what she could which was more or less nothing.

'Face it, girl,' Richard said. 'I'm a goner.'

A week after his forty-seventh birthday he proved himself right.

Alice's world was a desert, a desolate place of screaming birds, swirling in black flocks against a lurid sun.

What happens now? she thought. She had never expected she would be the one left behind; she had planned things differently, even to the point of asking herself how he would manage afterwards. But there it was.

She thought to appeal to God, Jane, the empty and merciless hills, but what was the use? Richard was dead.

She sat alone. If she wept she was unaware of it. Jane came and sat with her. She looked at her daughter. Jane too was lost. Jane too needed to find her road into the future. Alice drew a deep breath. She remembered fighting the terrors of the mineshaft as she forced herself to climb up from the blackness. She remembered the hours in the loft at the John o' Groats, barely daring to breathe while the soldiers searched the room below. She had been strong then. She would be strong now. She knew that from this day loneliness would be her destiny but she would not let it get the better of her, or her daughter.

She would survive; Jane would survive; the farm, such as it was, would survive. She considered what she must do. Two weeks after the funeral she spoke to her daughter.

'Jake Hampton,' she said.

'What about him?'

'You fancy him.' It was not a question.

Rose-pink Jane would not look at her mother. 'He's all right,' she said.

'How does he feel about you?'

Rose pink had turned to crimson. 'He's never said.'

'But you must have an idea.'

'I think maybe he likes me.'

'Does he know how you feel?'

'How could he?'

'There are ways. He's not a bad bloke. You could do a lot worse.'

'What can I do? I can't say anything. It wouldn't be proper.'

Jane had had a bit of schooling from Mrs Worsley, down the lane, and Mrs Worsley had been hot for what was proper in a young lady and what was not. Alice had never had time for that: being proper wouldn't have got her far in Ballarat.

'Let him see how you feel. You don' have to say anything. A smile would be a start.'

Jane looked doubtful. 'It seems so cold-blooded, somehow.'

'You like each other. That's a good beginning. If you're lucky and work at it, love may come. No reason it shouldn't. But in the meantime you need someone to help you run the farm; I won't be here for ever.'

Alice gave it another week, then spoke to Jake. It was hot summer, the air hay-scented and heavy with flies.

'You got any plans?'

'About what?'

'About staying? Going?'

'I hadn't thought of going anywhere,' he said. 'If that's all right with you.'

'I'm glad to hear it. Jane will be glad too. She's very fond of you, you know.'

He looked startled. 'You reckon?'

'I'm sure of it.'

'A bit old for her,' he said.

'Shouldn't she be the one to decide that?' Alice said. 'Don't tell me you haven't thought about it.'

'It would be my dearest wish,' Jake said.

'Then speak to her, Jake. Why don't you? You may find she's more willing than you think.'

It would be the best thing for her, Alice thought. She misses her dad. Jake is fond of her, young enough to work the farm and keep her safe, but also able to be the father figure she needs. I think it's the right thing. For her; for all of us.

1876–1900

Jane Hampton had her baby on her twentieth birthday, 20 June 1876, which was nice, making a special occasion out of what would otherwise have been only a birthday.

They called him Conan because it was an Irish name. Years before Jake's dad had told him they were descended from someone who'd been a king in Ireland in the old days. Jake didn't care one way or the other but giving the baby an Irish name did no harm.

Jane knew how lucky she'd been in her marriage. Back-breaking work and a perennial lack of money were the realities of her life, but Jake treasured her and that, and Conan, compensated for most things. Not for everything; she felt like spitting every time she saw Bessie Penrose drive past in her gilded carriage. By rights she should have inherited a fortune from her father too, just as Bessie had, and it made her mad things hadn't worked out like that: not just for herself but for Conan as well.

In Jane's world Bessie was the daughter of a murderess who had no right to her place in society or her wealth. But resentment was one thing; doing anything about it was something else.

She told herself Conan would sort things out, make something of the name of Hampton. Her love for her son became edged with flame, hard and shining, an ambition for him that would thrust him through dangers and difficulties into certain triumph.

'You will be our honourable knight,' she told him after she had read a library book about King Arthur and his Round Table. 'You will restore the grail that we somehow lost.'

It became an article of faith in Jane's hard-scrabble world.

As soon as Conan was old enough Jake got after him to give a hand around the farm. Jake's health was bad so Conan didn't argue but his real interest was not in farming but in horses. They became his obsession.

'He might have *been* a horse, the way he is with them,' Jane told her friend Mrs Agnew.

She was right; Conan would happily have spent every minute of every day with them, had it been possible. What he really wanted was to work at Derwent where there were plenty of horses and jobs for stable hands, but with Jake's health the way it was and the farm to run he could do nothing about it. In 1895, when Conan was nineteen, that changed.

It was mid-winter when Jake got caught in a storm. Soaked to the skin he did nothing to dry himself off or change his clothes. The wind was cold enough to cut and in no time he came down with pneumonia. A week later he was dead.

Jane told Conan to get a job at Derwent since that was where his heart was.

'What about the farm?'

'Forget the farm,' Jane said. 'I plan to sell it anyway. I know a cottage I can rent for more or less nothing. I'll move in there and live off whatever I get from the sale of the farm. I'll be fine.'

Conan took her at her word, walked up the drive to Derwent and got taken on as a stablehand.

Jane moved into the cottage on the banks of a creek with trout and platypus for company.

Horses became the main thing in Conan's life but they were by no means the only thing. He was nineteen years old and his way of life meant that he'd known few girls and had played with none of them.

He decided he should do something about that.

The first time he played was with one of the maids, an older woman called Adelaide who sneaked him into the hayloft and showed him what he had to do.

'You're quite a stallion yourself,' she told him.

When they got down to business the whole thing was over almost before it had started but it didn't matter; when it came to the point he felt he'd been hit by a thunderbolt.

'Oh my God,' he said when it happened. He was still thinking it hours later, couldn't wait to try it out a second time.

It wasn't long before he got more picky. Adelaide had been a good teacher but she was too old, must be getting on for thirty, for God's sake, and her tits were a bit daggy, like the rats had been at them, so he did her now and then to keep her sweet but mostly concentrated on instructing the younger ones. Some of whom needed instruction, some of whom did not.

He discovered something that surprised him: that where the best-looking young maids were concerned he had competition in the form of Phelan Penrose. Conan had heard that lawyer Erridge was something called a trustee, which he assumed meant he was the legal owner of Derwent, but everyone knew Phelan's wife Bessie really ran the show and her husband with it. Bessie Penrose was known to be a hard woman; everyone quivered when she walked past and people wondered why she let her husband get away with rutting the way he did because he made no secret of it.

He was always after one girl or another. Conan received differing reports. Some of them said Phelan was no match for him; one or two said the opposite. Conan didn't care one way or the other. In fact it was a comfort; Phelan Penrose could hardly fire him for getting up to the same games he did.

One of the girls fell pregnant. From things she'd said Conan was pretty sure the kid was his but he had no money so she went crying to Phelan Penrose instead. Conan reckoned Phelan must have sorted her out because he heard no more about it. Soon the maid went away and Derwent saw her no more.

Conan hadn't been at Derwent long before he met David, Mrs Penrose's son. To kick-off he wasn't sure about him. The family called him Daddo and Conan wondered whether he might be a sook but he soon showed himself otherwise. He was in his mid-twenties and rode like a dream.

A bloke who rode like that deserved all the hero worship he could get and they became good mates. Conan's job was in the stables and Derwent, under Bessie Penrose's management, expected you to work for your wages, but they managed to ride out together once or twice a week.

Conan was twenty-one when he and Daddo returned from one of their rides to find Rufus Binchy, the head groom, waiting to tell him that Mrs Penrose wanted to see him as soon as he got back.

'What have I done?'

'Get over to the house and I daresay you'll find out. But if I was you I'd have a scrub up before you go. Particular about that sort of thing, Mrs Penrose. And make sure you're polite or you'll find yourself out the door before you can turn round.'

'It'll be that Mary Smith,' Conan told himself as he sloshed his face under the pump. 'She's gone crying to the old lady, that's what she's done.'

And cursed himself for being such a fool. Mary Smith was twenty-three and fresh out from Home. Thing was, with her Pommy accent and pink and white complexion she'd turned him on as soon as he'd set eyes on her, and Conan had never been the sort to let sleeping maids lie.

She had been shy and squeaky to start with, her pale skin flushing like a rose as soon as he touched her, but he'd soon taught her what was what.

They'd done it three times when she told him she loved him.

Bloody hell!

To make matters worse Mrs Bessie had taken a fancy to her too and given her a job as her personal maid.

He'd been trying to think out a way to tell the stupid girl that what they'd been doing was a game, nothing more serious than that, but now crossing the stable yard to the house his guts were in uproar because it looked very much as though he was about to lose his job. And where would he get another one that suited him anywhere near as well?

He presented himself at the kitchen door. He was let in by Bronwen, a kitchen maid with a well-filled blouse who smiled knowingly at him – for the best of reasons – and passed him on to the housekeeper, Mrs Toop, the one they called Mrs Boops behind her back.

Mrs Toop looked him over, a hangman's look if he'd ever seen one. 'What have you been up to, I wonder?' But looking as though she knew all about it. 'Show me your fingernails.'

She examined his hands for a minute but it seemed they passed muster.

'I'll take you to Mrs Penrose now,' Mrs Toop said. 'And take your hat off, for heaven's sake.'

Luckily he'd remembered to comb his hair.

Bessie had been thinking about it ever since she had first caught sight of the new man working with the horses. She had made enquiries. Conan Hampton, they said. Son of a local farmer. She had kept her eye on him ever since and had finally come to a decision. Now she sat waiting. Waiting and thinking.

There were days when she thought she had been at war with convention all her life.

Convention decreed that only a man had the mental and physical resources to operate a successful business. That was rubbish; Bessie had been running Derwent and the rest of the Penrose empire for years.

Convention also tolerated a man distributing his sexual favours far and wide but gave no such freedom to a woman. Bessie thought that was rubbish too. A woman had physical needs just as a man did.

On the first night of her marriage she had discovered that she and her husband didn't hit it off in bed, so from that day onwards her sexual life had played second fiddle to running the family and its businesses. Phelan had given her the son she wanted but they had slept apart ever since.

She knew their acquaintances wondered how she could tolerate a husband who pursued every maid who stepped under Derwent's roof but in truth she welcomed it. It freed her from obligations she would otherwise have found tiresome.

It did not mean she had no feelings; desire remained but the opportunities to satisfy it were few; it was five years since she'd had a man in her bed.

It irritated her that a woman was denied the freedom men had in such matters yet she was well aware how dangerous it would be to challenge public opinion too blatantly. She was rich, she was powerful and people were scared of her. If they caught her out behaving in a way convention said was unacceptable they would –

She rang the bell with an imperious hand.

A maid came. She ordered coffee.

'And quickly, girl!'

What would they do? They could do nothing.

The coffee came in a silver pot and a scurry of rapid feet. The maid poured.

'Thank you.'

Bessie took the cup and sipped, walking to the window. Below the house the long valley was hazed with summer heat. Derwent land. The family's land. Her land.

If she broke with convention – if, for instance, she took a lover – they would talk, of course, but she was sure they did that already. How well Bessie knew the temptation to do something outrageous because she could. To spit in the eye of those who would condemn her. Yet to take a lover, or lovers, would be like stepping into another room. Do that and there would be no way back, no more invitations from the governor's house.

How she resented the way the world looked down on women! Society women were the worst; when it came to their own sex they were more judgemental than men.

Why should she not satisfy her body's needs? It did no harm to anyone yet it was not something you could talk about, even to a friend; no respectable woman would discuss such matters. Think about them perhaps, but *talk* about them? Never!

But she was not a respectable woman, Bessie thought. She was the daughter of a murdering slut, a convict. Even she, the lowest of the low, had abandoned her. *Paid for her trouble, Papa's wife had said.*

The day Cynthia had told her that Bessie was not her child would be branded in her memory forever.

'Not your child? But Papa –'

'Was your true father. Oh yes. Your mother was someone he got to know in Ballarat. I could never have a child, you see, and like most men he wanted an heir. So there was this… arrangement.'

'You agreed to it?'

'I did not know about it until you were already expected but I agreed to the deception, yes. I thought it would do no harm. I never expected to feel as I did.'

'What did you feel?'

'Resentment. I had wanted a child of my own, you see. Wanted one very much. I had been expecting one but there was an accident and the doctor said I could never have another. When I agreed to your father's plan I thought I would come to love you as my own. But I never did. Instead I resented you. I saw in you everything I had missed in my own life. It was wrong of me but there was nothing I could do about it.'

Being able to do nothing had been the story of Cynthia's life.

'What happened to my real mother? What was her name? What do you know about her?'

Questions to fill the void that had opened in Bessie's life.

'Her name was Maria Hack. I understand she had been a convict.'

'Was Papa fond of her?'

It was a cruel question to ask Papa's widow but Bessie felt violated by what this woman had told her and cared nothing for being cruel in return.

'I believe he may have been. A little.'

'I suppose that's something. Where is she now?'

'I don't know. My understanding is that Papa paid her for her trouble and she left.'

'Her trouble? Is that how you saw me? Her *trouble*?' Bessie's bitterness overflowed. 'Why did you have to tell me?'

She stormed out of the room but knew she would never outpace the revelation Mama had thrown at her. She was convinced it was true but at another level of her mind found it too painful to accept or even comprehend. She found herself walking, going nowhere, with each step grinding her heel into the face of the woman who had deceived her all these years; into her own face for no longer being the person she had thought herself to be; most of all into the face of the mother who had abandoned her.

Papa paid her for her trouble...

Dear God! How she despised her. It was ridiculous to seek advice from such a woman, someone whom she could not even remember, yet in her spirit she knew her. In their shared blood they were one.

What would Maria Hack have done?

She knew the answer without needing to think about it. Her birth mother would have ignored convention, followed her own road and damned the eyes of those who said no.

She had more freedom than I, Bessie thought. So what use was money? Freedom existed in the heart, if it existed at all.

She could feel the hunger, the ungratified heat.

I am Bessie, harlot's daughter. I shall do as she would. I shall follow my own road.

She settled in her chair, set like a throne at one end of the withdrawing room. She sent for her maid Mary.

Mary Smith was twenty-three years old and frightened of Bessie, eager to please. She was a pretty girl too. Bessie had allowed Mary to believe she had made friends with her, encouraging her to confide.

The maid was pink and white, newly out from England, and shy in a dun-coloured land that hid its beauty from strangers, where all was new. Her parents were dead and she and her sister were alone. In her loneliness she was happy to share her secrets with her kind employer.

Yes, she had a boyfriend. He was wonderful, a strong man, with a good job, well regarded by the people he worked for. A man she loved; who she dared hope loved her.

'Will you marry him?'

Smiling kindly, seeing the hunger in Mary's eyes.

Perhaps she would. In time. If asked.

Mary did not mention her friend's name. Bessie did not pursue it but later spoke to Mrs Toop, who told her the boy's name was Conan.

'Conan? Isn't he the stablehand who is friendly with Master David?'

He was the one.

'What's he like?'

Mrs Toop was unwilling to commit. He was outside staff and she barely knew him but had heard no ill of him. If Mrs Toop wondered why Mrs Penrose should have asked she kept it to herself.

The next day Bessie sent for Mary Smith.

'I want you to do something for me. Get hold of a member of the outside staff and ask him to take a message to the stables. There is a stable boy whose name I understand is Conan. Say I wish to see him at the house. Now.'

She saw that Mary was alarmed, staring at Bessie with frightened eyes.

'Well, girl, what are you waiting for?'

Young and pleasant looking, no wonder she had a lover. Such a foolish girl, to risk a good job at Derwent. Yet when Bessie said run, she ran.

It was a thought to brighten the day.

When Conan arrived she examined him.

He had a look about him. Also a smell of horse but that troubled her less than she had expected.

She thought: if I do this I shall be stupid. It would also be dangerous. But danger meant excitement. And oh, how she needed excitement in her life.

She did not know she had made her decision but it seemed, somehow, to have taken command of her.

'I don't want to see you now,' she said. 'You have work to do.' The words took shape before she would allow herself to think too much about them. 'When do you finish work?'

'At eight, Mrs Penrose.'

At eight it would be dark.

'I have something I wish to discuss with you. Come back then.'

'Very well, madam.'

She saw him thinking and her mind shouted caution. But her mind was not the motivating factor.

'Conan will be coming back this evening,' she told Mary. 'At eight of the clock. Please bring him up to my private sitting room.'

The two women looked at each other. Bessie saw the shadow in Mary's eyes and lifted her chin a little. Mary could not be sure but could always wonder.

'That will be all, Mary.'

She watched the retreating maid's back. Lust and cruelty, she thought. Is that really the woman I am?

No, she thought. She was neither her father nor her mother; nor was she her wretched husband. She would not cheapen herself. She would not make herself a target for those who would be glad to damage her.

At eight o'clock that evening, as directed, Mary brought Conan to Bessie's private sitting room.

'Thank you, Mary. That will be all.'

And waited until the door closed behind the maid.

She turned her head and looked at Conan who looked back at her. Yes, she thought, she had been right. He was an oaf with a conceited look. Bessie knew what he was thinking as surely as though he'd spoken his thoughts aloud.

He thinks I want him in my bed.

A stable boy reeking of horse. The lover of her maid. And no doubt other maids.

How dare he?

Never mind her fleeting fantasies. She was not Catherine the Great, ordering guardsmen into her bed. Even the idea of it now seemed absurd. Yet he was here because she had ordered him to be here. She had to think of a reason for having summoned him; if she simply packed him off again who could say what lies he might tell?

'I asked you here tonight because I have a proposal I wish to discuss with you.'

He blinked; that wasn't what he had been expecting.

'I am informed you have an understanding with my maid Mary Smith.'

'I know her.'

'I am very fond of Mary.' Such a warm smile Bessie gave him then. 'I am sure you intend to do the right thing by her.'

He looked as though she had lighted a fuse under him.

'You have a good situation here,' Bessie said. 'So does Mary. I would be willing to keep you both on in your present positions after the wedding. If that was what you wished.'

Conan was drowning in deep waters. 'Well, I –'

'Good. That's settled then. I would be happy for you to have the reception here. At my expense, of course. Perhaps you'll discuss it with Mary and let me know how you feel.'

Sitting in her empty sitting room Bessie smiled at the expensive ornaments it contained: the picture in an ornate frame of her with Papa when she was small; a cloisonné vase; an ostrich feather someone had brought from Africa; a candle in a gilt candlestick; a watercolour of cherubs. Managing people was the key to success and she was pleased with the way she had handled Conan and herself.

To think she had almost been tempted... No, she thought, that was nonsense. She had been playing a private game, no more than that. On that subject her mind was resolute.

Conan couldn't believe it. He'd been in no doubt what he could expect when he'd turned up at the house. Handle things well and he could be looking at a rosy future with this wealthy, older woman whom he would bind to him, eager for his kisses.

Now this.

He'd had no intention of getting himself tied down at this stage of his life but could see no way out of it. He would have to marry Mary – that was all there was to it. Of course it wouldn't stop him taking advantage of any other opportunities that might present themselves from time to time but it was a bit of a let down, all the same.

Very well. He would talk to Mary, as Bessie had instructed. The stupid cow would be over the moon; even the thought of her delight was enough to drive a bloke to drink. It was certainly enough to stop him telling her tonight. Fifteen-year-old Katie had been sending him signals; he thought he might visit her first.

Time enough to pay his respects to his fiancée in the morning.

Conan had been married three months when Daddo Penrose came to him, said he was off to fight in the South African war with the Tasmanian Mounted Rifles and asked if he'd like to go with him.

Conan couldn't wait.

1913

'What d'you mean, I can't?'

Bec Hampton was distraught. Confronted by unfairness in the form of a stubborn-mouthed dad, she had nowhere to turn.

'We had it all planned,' she said. She was close to tears, and Bec was not the weepy type. 'You said you didn't care what I did,' she accused. 'Washed your hands of me: that's what you said.'

'A father's got responsibilities,' Dad said.

'But we love each other.'

Bec saw she was wasting her breath, as she was when later she ran to her mother.

Mrs Hampton, who had come out with her sister from Home in the days when that mattered and had never got used to the idea of colonial living or her brawling, brawny husband, blinked short-sightedly and was no help. She said nothing of the visit they'd had from Mrs Penrose, which she suspected might have had something to do with her husband's change of heart, but the man was head of the household, was he not, and she would no more have thought of querying his decision than of doubting the vicar, whose spiritual guidance gave such comfort.

'Your father thinks it's best you should wait,' she said.

'Wait for what?' Bec said.

'When you're of age you can make your own decisions.'

No consolation there. Five years was an eternity to sixteen-year-old Bec; besides, there was always the fear that if they had to delay so long Jonathan might change his mind.

Jonathan, when she pleaded with him, was no help either. He would have done something had it been possible but it was not.

'It is the law,' he said.

'I hate the stupid law,' Bec said.

How she wished something would happen to change her situation. Wishing was useless; she knew that. Therefore she prayed to God, if he was there and willing to help. She was prepared to believe God had created the world and everything in it, fire and storm, but they were the big things; she doubted he would have the time to sort out what to him must surely be an insignificant matter.

'Not so insignificant to me,' she told him.

She might have promised to live a holy life if he helped her now but decided against it, fearing that might be interpreted as an attempt to bribe. She prayed anyway, doggedly but with little hope.

The rain, at first welcome after a prolonged period of drought, began three weeks later. Tin roofs rang with the percussion of the rain. Gullies that had been dry for months dribbled, spouted and overflowed, spilling water across the thirsty paddocks which became inundated in time. Creeks rose.

All across the high country the land was submerged. Water seeped relentlessly or erupted in thunderbursts of spray and roaring flood. Windblown trees streamed. Placid rivers became torrents yet their sound failed to drown the hammer blows of the rain, which continued to fall. Roads became impassable.

Livestock drowned, their carcasses swept away. Hilltop homesteads became islands. Grandma Jane Hampton's cottage was inundated but miraculously stood firm. Not everyone was so lucky; of many low-lying properties nothing but the roofs could be seen, with many destroyed altogether.

Some families, seeking foolishly to escape in carts piled high with possessions, were swept away by the unrelenting floods. Some escaped; some drowned.

People rallied round, as people do. Teams of women in canvas shelters handed mugs of tea and mutton sandwiches to refugees from inundated houses. Men in shiny slickers set out in boats, bringing back people and dogs and chooks and reporting others trapped in trees. Unpredictable currents swirled the boats this way and that, sometimes tipping the occupants into the mud-brown froth, to be hauled to safety, swearing and spitting, by the men in other boats.

One boat, seized by a vicious undertow, plunged over a freshly formed waterfall below which the stream swirled in sucking eddies. The boat, upside down, vanished downstream, eventually coming to rest in a nest of willow branches. Two of those in the boat, one the blacksmith from Waldren's Corner, drowned.

A decent interval was necessary if scandal were to be avoided but a month after the funeral Jonathan came and talked to Bec's mother.

'A terrible tragedy, of course, but you must be so proud.'

His words were chosen for the occasion but as he uttered them Jonathan watched Mary Hampton apprehensively. Bec's mother had always been timid and Bec had warned that the loss of her husband, bully though he had been, might have put her over the edge. But no. The shock had been undeniable, that a man who every day had triumphed over flame and iron should have been destroyed by water, but the effect on his widow was different from Bec's expectations.

Dominated by others all her life, Mary Hampton's willpower had lain dormant. Now, of necessity, she coaxed it into being and for the first time discovered she was capable of making decisions for herself.

'I was sorry to hear about your loss,' Jonathan said. 'A true hero, died helping others.'

'At least I won't be gettin' no more black eyes,' Mary said. 'There's that, I s'pose.'

That almost threw Jonathan but he battled on.

'He saved my father's life, you know.'

'Worst day's work he ever done,' Mary said.

'Why do you say that?'

'Showed him what he was capable of. Spent the rest of his life trying to live up to the idea that he really was a hero but never managed it. That business in South Africa: I reckon that was just a fluke. Then to get drowned the way he did... Didn't make no sense but he would go. Never mind me. Had to prove what a brave bloke he was. Fat lot of good it did him.'

'What are you planning to do?'

'Go to my sister in Hobart. We always got on; I reckon she'll have me. But that's not why you're here, is it? You want to know what I'm gunna do about my Bec.'

Her attitude was far from what he'd expected. Bec had said talking her round would be a formality; now he was not so sure.

'Mr Hampton thought she was too young to know her own mind,' he said. 'I don't think that's right.'

'She's not seventeen yet. That's young.'

'Not too young to know what she wants.'

The ghost of a smile. 'She's always known that. Don't mean she's always been right, though.'

'If you speak to her –'

'I will. Don't you worry about that.' Mary's eyes, bird-bright, scoured him. 'You done good, coming to see me.'

'Not such a monster,' Jonathan said.

'Never thought you were. But with you she'd have a different life from what's she's used to. Bein' rich is all very well but I ask myself whether that'll make her happy.'

'That won't,' he said. 'But loving me and being loved by me will.'

'And you don't want to wait five years.'

'Would you?'

'Maybe I'd have done better for myself if I had,' Mary said. 'And what does your grandma say?'

'She wants me to marry a government official's daughter.'

'Got her head screwed on, that one. Can't go far wrong marryin' a government official's daughter.'

'Except that I want to marry a blacksmith's daughter.'

'You willin' to go against your grandma in this?'

'If I have to.'

'She's a tough one.'

'I'm tougher.'

'We'll see.'

'Very soon, I hope.'

'You want to marry my underage daughter, you got to wait on my say-so, don't you?'

'How long?'

'Long as it takes.'

'Well?' said Bec.

'She says she'll think about it.'

'What's there to think about?'

'You tell me.'

'I'll go and see her,' Bec said. 'I'll sort her out.'

'Be careful. She's discovered she can make up her own mind about things and I think she's enjoying it.'

'Just so long as her decision's the right one.'

Prim hat and button boots, Bec Hampton marched purposefully down the road to the old forge. The floods had subsided but the signs were everywhere – scoured earth, wrecked trees, the smell of death where some animal had been swallowed by the mud – but Bec was determined to be cheerful. The sun was shining, the creeks and dams were full and the lush countryside was already recovering.

'This year and next,' Bec said to the bright air. '1913 and 1914. They'll be good years. They'll be the best.'

'So you're planning on changing your name,' Mum said.

'Soon as I can,' Bec said.

Mercifully the cottage and forge had escaped the floods although the forge fire, for the first time Bec could remember, was out.

The cottage already had the forlorn look of a house about to be abandoned.

'What will you do now Dad's gone?' Bec asked.

'Sing Alleluia,' Mary said. 'I'm beginning to realise what I've been missing all these years.'

'And afterwards?'

'Go and stay with your Auntie Mavis, I reckon.'

'You're still young,' Bec said. 'You might want to marry again.'

'Not me,' Mary said. 'Once bitten twice shy.'

Bec sipped her tea, strong enough to melt the cup.

'What about me?' she said.

'What about you?'

'Me and Jonathan?'

'I dunno.'

Bec squeezed up her face. 'Please, Mum...'

'What you want to get married for? Enjoy your freedom while you got it, my girl. That's my advice to you.'

Bec with her pleading look, saying nothing. Mary sighed.

'Such a different way of life. You sure you're up to it?'

'Never know till I try, will I?'

'Bein' rich is nice but it's not everything. Happiness is what matters.'

'Happiness and love.'

'The old girl won't like it, you know that? She'll make your life a misery.'

'She'll try. I won't let her.'

'Easily said.'

'I won't,' Bec said. 'I really won't.'

They watched each other: the daughter pleading yet certain, the mother doubtful. But doubt yielded in the end.

'All right then. I won't stop you. But don't blame me if the wheels come off.'

The next day Mrs Bessie Penrose turned up in her posh motor. When Mary Hampton went out of the cottage to see her, the chauffeur gave her a haughty look but said nothing – that Bennett had been a snooty bugger from the day he arrived. The air was vibrating around Mrs Penrose's head in the back seat but she leant forwards with a smile that would have pole-axed a bull.

'I came to ask how you were coping.'

'Good. Thank you for asking.' Mary spoke politely but as between equals; the frightened Mrs Hampton of old had been buried alongside her husband. 'And you? Did you lose much stock in the floods?'

If Bessie was surprised by Mary's temerity in asking such a thing – and in such a way – she concealed it well. 'We were fortunate,' she said. She spoke to Mr Bennett, who came and opened the car door for her. She stepped out. 'I wonder if I might have a word with you?'

And led the way up the path to the cottage.

'Please yourself, I'm sure,' said the new Mary Hampton to the silk-clad back. Which showed no sign of having heard.

Inside the cottage Mrs Penrose looked about her, seeming to fill the room. 'Did your late husband mention the money he owed me?'

Perhaps she had thought the direct approach might frighten Mrs Hampton; if that was so, she was disappointed.

'First I heard of it,' Mary said.

'Three hundred pounds.'

'First I heard of it,' Mary repeated. 'Got a piece of paper, have you?'

In the old days she would never have dared ask such a question.

'It was an understanding between friends.'

'Between friends? I see.' Calm face; calm voice.

'I understand you have given your daughter permission to marry my grandson.'

'That's right.'

'Even though she is under age.'

'That's right.'

'As to the money you owe me, I was hoping we could come to an amicable arrangement. I would not be ungenerous.'

'Like I said, I don't know nothin' about it.'

'The last thing I want is to get lawyers involved.'

The old Mary Hampton might have trembled; not the new one. 'Without no piece of paper, I don't see what anyone can do,' she said. 'Lawyers or no lawyers.'

'I see you are determined to marry your daughter off to a rich man. I had thought better of you.'

'You must think what you want,' said Mary Hampton.

Later, after Bessie Penrose had swept out, outrage in every curve, Mary Hampton thought about the husband who had imprisoned her and in dying set her free. Now the daughter too would be gone to what the world would call a good marriage. Well, time would tell.

In the meantime, for the first time she could remember, she would have a life.

After leaving the blacksmith's cottage Bessie instructed Bennett to drive her to Campbell Town, where the family's legal adviser had his rooms.

Fortunately Mr Miller was able to see her at once. Defying arthritis, Bessie marched into the lawyer's office and plonked herself down in the chair facing him.

'Mr Miller, I wish you to explain to me my rights under the Derwent family trust.'

It was not Bessie's way to indulge in small talk, nor did she believe in wasting time. Twenty minutes after entering Mr Miller's office she was on her way back to Derwent, grimly delighted by what the lawyer had told her.

Seated in the Ford she reviewed the situation. The three hundred pounds was lost. That was obvious but of little consequence. However, if Rebecca Hampton believed she had got the better of Bessie Penrose she could think again.

She revisited her conversation with Mr Miller.

'Am I right in believing that the estate's assets are all tied up in the trust that was set up by my dear father?'

'That is so, Mrs Penrose. Every yard of land and every business.'

'And that, as trustee and principal beneficiary, I have total and unfettered control over all the trust's assets and activities, including how the income is distributed among the beneficiaries at year's end?'

Mr Miller touched judicious fingertips together. 'That is correct.'

He opened his mouth to say more but Bessie was already on her feet.

'Thank you, Mr Miller. That is what I wished to know. I will detain you no longer.'

Now, her mind and resolution clear, she considered her options.

She had her finger in every pie in the family and knew Jonathan had virtually no assets of his own, his only income coming from the trust. If he went ahead with this ridiculous marriage a significant reduction in his annual income could therefore be easily arranged. She would do it, too, to bring home to him what should have been obvious from the first: that defying his grandmother came at a cost. Coupled with Rebecca's evident unsuitability Bessie thought it would not be long before he realised how foolish he had been. She was convinced that shortage of money would drive such a wedge between them that within a year the ill-omened marriage would be over.

The car turned off the highway and began the steep climb to Derwent House.

And if she were wrong? If, despite everything, the marriage survived?

Bessie's jaw was always set hard; now it was set harder than ever. All her adult life she had believed that Derwent's future mattered more to her than anything else; now she discovered that was not so. Rather than risk the blacksmith's daughter getting her hands on the estate after Bessie's death she would wind up the trust and sell the assets for what they would get. One way or another, she was utterly determined that Rebecca Hampton would never win.

Daffodils that had somehow survived the flood were in flower around the church, and there were more in the lawn at the back of Derwent House, a spring display to welcome the bride.

Escorted down the aisle by Constable Painter, whose wife had pushed him into lending the proceedings not merely a hand but a complete arm, Bec looked out of the corner of her eye at the handful of people making up the congregation and felt disbelief, apprehension, but above all an overwhelming joy that she was about to realise the dream that had been hers for as long as she could remember.

During the big flood, water had covered the church floor; the smell of damp still lingered but Bec didn't care about that.

Her mother was there, almost buried in a hat that looked like a giant cream cake, and Auntie Mavis and Grandma Jane Hampton with her crooked grin; so was Jonathan's mother, who had spent most of the years since Daddo's death hiding in her house in the Whitsundays but had come back especially for her son's wedding; so too – surprisingly – was Bessie Penrose. Bessie had sworn she would never attend the humiliation of her grandson's marriage to a child better suited to the scullery than the drawing room, but in the end had obviously decided that image was all and that family solidarity mattered even more than her personal likes and dislikes. Unless something had happened to make her change her mind.

While Bessie, once again confident that she could prevent Rebecca from ever getting her hands on any of the Derwent assets, saw no reason why she should not attend her grandson's wedding. Vengeance, after all, was a private matter.

1982

The Swissair flight put down at Zurich's Kloten Airport at ten-fifteen in the morning local time beneath a grey and rain-spitting sky that exactly matched Bec's mood. The flight had seemed forever.

'You've borne up pretty well for such a decrepit old fossil,' she told herself briskly. 'So stop your fussing.' She was no more inclined to put up with nonsense from herself than from anyone else. She had even managed an hour or two's sleep during the flight but age was an undeniable burden and she couldn't wait to get to her hotel.

She trundled her case through the arrivals hall and grabbed the first taxi off the rank.

'Hotel Storchen,' she said.

The driver, suitably impressed, loaded her case into the taxi boot.

'The Storchen is a hotel of the first class,' he said.

What he meant was that it was expensive: that always went down well in Zurich, a city Bec had visited several times over the years. Clean, efficient and unlovable, Zurich was a city of a thousand bankers and a million secrets but the driver was right: the Hotel Storchen was indeed first class; she had stayed there before.

It did not disappoint her this time, either.

She stood in the middle of her suite, the one with the terrace overlooking the river, and felt the room swirling around her, jet lag a painful reality. She could have dropped where she stood but at shortly before noon that was a luxury she would not permit herself; the only way to beat jet lag was to fight it and go to bed as close to her normal time as she could manage. She therefore had a long hot shower in the million-dollar bathroom, slopped smelly stuff all over her and stared with disgust at the reflection of her nude body in the full-length mirror.

Now there was a sight for sore eyes, she thought. If you didn't have them before you looked you would certainly have them afterwards. Eighty-five: there were times she thought age should be a criminal offence.

No matter: being sorry for herself wouldn't help, nor would it get her to first base with Ilse Lardner, if what she'd heard about the lady were even halfway correct.

Discipline! she told herself.

She dressed slowly and deliberately in the clothes she had packed in her case. Of uncrushable material, they had survived the flight better than she had. She took meticulous care with her make-up. She ordered a light lunch and afterwards phoned Herr Füssli, the senior partner of Elphinstone's correspondent firm, who told her in excellent English that he had managed to arrange a meeting with Frau Ilse Lardner at her office for ten-thirty the following morning.

'It was fortunate that I was able to do this,' Herr Füssli said. 'Frau Lardner has many commitments and is not always available but has agreed to set aside fifteen minutes to see you.'

Bec listened, translating to herself as she did so.

I have done an outstanding job in arranging the meeting but she is a formidable lady so watch out.

'Light blue touch paper and stand clear,' Bec said. 'I understand.'

'Blue touch paper?' She had the impression that Herr Füssli was not comfortable with jokes, especially Australian jokes.

'Not important,' she said. 'And thank you for your trouble.'

'Nothing,' Herr Füssli said.

'You will of course send me your account.'

'Of course.'

The traffic was formidable but Bec had given herself plenty of time and was ten minutes early for her meeting.

On the tick of ten-thirty she was ushered into Frau Lardner's office: a large room beautifully furnished with alpine pictures on the walls. There was a crucifix mounted on an ebony base on the wall behind Frau Lardner's desk.

Frau Lardner was a substantial presence, both in build and personality; Bec thought that no one entering this room would have any doubt who was the boss. Her doughy face was not that of a woman who wasted much time smiling.

'Welcome to Zurich. I trust you had a good flight. How can I help you?'

'I am making enquiries about a mutual acquaintance.'

'Raine Armitage,' Ilse Lardner said. 'Herr Füssli mentioned that it was in connection with Raine Armitage that you wished to see me.' And waited, face expressionless.

'I should explain that my son is a widower who controls substantial properties in Australia –'

'I am aware of your circumstances,' Frau Lardner said.

Of course, Bec thought. It was to be expected she would have made enquiries.

'Then you may be aware that Ms Armitage has struck up an acquaintance with my son.'

'Raine Armitage is no longer this family's responsibility. She has chosen her own life and we have had no communication with her for many years.'

'So I understand. But –'

'Therefore I see no way in which I can help you.'

A long way to come for a brush-off like this, Bec thought. But she wasn't beaten yet.

'There have been a number of questions about Ms Armitage's background,' she said. 'Unanswered for the most part since she has been unwilling to talk about her past. It was only through a chance remark that we even found out she had spent time in Switzerland.'

'Certainly she did,' Ilse Lardner said. 'I can confirm that, if that is what you wish to know. Her son Jaeger was born here.'

'It is a matter of some concern to me, you see,' Bec said. 'Since it seems possible that my son and Raine Armitage are planning to get married.'

Bec walked into the passenger concourse at Hobart airport and knew from the expression of Tamara's face – grey and twenty years older than her years – they had a problem.

'What's happened?'

'Too late,' Tamara said.

'What do you mean?'

'They announced their engagement last night.'

'We'll see about that,' Bec said.

Giles was in what Bec had always called the little parlour. He was reading the newspaper but stood up when she came in. Raine and Jaeger were nowhere to be seen, which made Bec's task simpler.

'Have you come to congratulate me?' Giles said.

He said nothing about her having been away; perhaps he had not noticed her absence.

'I have indeed,' Bec said.

She wasn't as tired as when she'd arrived in Zurich; she was empowered, energy bubbling.

'I'm glad. To be honest,' said Giles who had never been honest in his life, 'I was afraid you might think I was a bit long in the tooth to embark on a new adventure.'

'Sit down,' Bec said.

He looked at her uncertainly but obeyed.

'I do congratulate you. Not on what you had planned to do but on the fact that you have had the good fortune to escape from what would have been an embarrassing situation.'

'I have no idea what you are talking about,' Giles said.

'You cannot marry Raine. She is already married.'

'That is nonsense. She's divorced.'

'I have just returned from Zurich, where I had a lengthy discussion with Raine's mother-in-law, a Mrs Lardner, who has informed me that, as Raine is well aware, she and her family are devoutly Catholic and that there has therefore never been any question of a divorce or even an annulment. Raine and Mrs Lardner's son are still married. Mrs Lardner also told me that Raine had herself suggested that Jaeger was not her husband's child.'

Giles, gaping, tried to bluster. 'I don't believe a word of it.'

Bec handed him an official-looking piece of paper. 'It is written in German but it's an affidavit prepared by an attorney and bearing the stamp of the district court in Zurich. It confirms that Raine and her husband Felix Lardner are still married. Check the date. The affidavit was issued two days ago.'

'There's been some mistake.'

Giles's mouth was set in the stubborn line she knew so well. That had always been his way; when things didn't work out his first response was to deny: half-truths, self-evident lies, everything.

'What were you doing in Zurich, anyway?'

'I was talking to Raine's mother-in-law.'

'You were trying to break me up with the woman I love,' said Giles.

'Be thankful I did. You could have found yourself in a messy bigamy situation if I hadn't.'

Raine found her an hour later. 'Where d'you get off, spying on me?'

'You know the ins and outs of the law. You wanted my son to make you a trustee of the Derwent Trust and Jaeger a beneficiary. You did this, pretending you were divorced when you knew you weren't, in order to gain control of the estate and deprive my granddaughter of her legal rights as a member of this family. I call that fraud, Raine. What do you call it?'

'I don't believe I'm hearing this. I always thought we were divorced. That Zurich bitch *told* me we were divorced.'

'I don't believe you. Divorce is never on the cards for Catholics as strict as the Lardners, and you knew that when you left Zurich.'

Later that day Bec took her little red sports car – the one that had
come so close to flying ten years before at Nitwit Corner – and
drove down the four-lane highway howling with traffic, then on
a side road signposted to Gimbaloo, finally across country along a
barely discernible gravel track until, half an hour after leaving the
house, she came to a deep valley that aeons before a glacier had
carved between towering basalt cliffs.

The valley was a geological freak – the only other place she knew
where there were cliffs like that was miles away down the Tasman
Peninsula. Jonathan had first brought her here in the final week
before he went off to war. When she wanted to be near him without
having to drive all the way to the place on the coast where he had
been lost, it was to this spot she came. Perhaps that was why there
was always a ritual to her visits.

She drew to a stop at the mouth of the valley and sat in a
silence broken only by the wind and the ticking of the cooling engine and stared at what lay in front of her: the vegetation
watered by a permanent creek where trout hugged the shadows,
the forested slopes rising to the base of the black cliffs where
shy creatures – wallaby, echidna, the wide-eyed brush-tailed possums, sinuous and menacing tiger snakes – watched the intruder
with wary eyes.

To Bec this valley was the one place in a frenetic world where the
ancient environment remained unsullied; since it was not possible
to lie at Jonathan's side she had often felt she would like to leave
her bones in this place, which seemed to her to retain echoes of the
world's first days.

In the towering black cliffs, the lushness of tree fern and ancient
forest, she unfailingly found peace when she most needed it.

She needed it now.

She had taken a huge risk in speaking to Giles as she had. During the return flight from Zurich her choices had challenged her: to
confront him with the truth or do nothing, pretend ignorance and
let the cards fall as they would.

The fact was she had never had a true choice – it was not in her nature to close her eyes to reality – but she had not underestimated the danger.

There was also nothing to prevent him ignoring Raine's married status and shacking up with her anyway.

Bec thought his instinct would probably favour that course – a gesture of defiance to damage the mother who had interfered in his affairs, along with his daughter whom he no doubt saw as Bec's co-conspirator – but she had gambled on Giles's vanity, that he would be so affronted by Raine's deceit in concealing the truth from him that he would dump her.

She sat for a while then got out of the MG and walked down the gritty track into the valley. Solitude embraced her. In the stillness the sound of the creek was loud. She watched the shadows of trout feeding on a hatch of small flies whose name she did not know. She had never attempted to catch the trout; to Bec this was a holy place and to take life wilfully would have been a desecration.

She walked deeper into the valley, observing a wedge-tailed eagle soaring, wings outstretched. She reached the place where the cliffs swung inwards, squeezing the valley so that the only way a walker could continue was to rock-hop down the creek itself. She'd done that a lot at one time, following the rushing water downstream until it reached the falls and jetted out into the forest far below, but those days were gone.

She thought it would make an interesting end, to follow the water in its vertical flight into oblivion. But that time was not yet, and who could read the future?

She sat for a while on a rock at the valley's end before walking back to the car. She drove home and the blessed peace of the valley went with her.

Tamara met her.

'They've gone.'

'All of them?'

'All three.'

So had Giles abandoned Raine or not? It seemed not; at least for the moment.

'Did they say anything?'

'Not a word. But if looks could kill I wouldn't be standing here now.'

What would be the outcome? Impossible to say.

'What do we do?' Tamara said.

'What we always do. We carry on.'

1913–17

Bec had expected war from Grandma Bessie and got it. From the first day of the marriage pistols were not only at dawn but at every minute of every day. What nobody including Bec had expected was that nine months into her marriage there would be a war of another and even more lethal kind.

As expected, Grandma Bessie was vocal about that too. 'Of course you aren't going,' she told Jonathan. 'Who will run Derwent while you're chasing around Europe? What's this nonsense with Germany got to do with us?'

Bec said the same, only more quietly and in private. 'Why do you feel you must?'

'It's my duty,' Jonathan said.

'Don't you think you have a duty here as well? To Derwent? To us?'

She was careful not to say *to me*.

'Of course, but I have to do my bit. It won't be for long; they say it'll be over by Christmas.'

Bec wondered whether Jonathan might be right, in which case there seemed no point in going so far for so short a time, but her instinct told her this was likely to be a longer trial than her husband supposed.

J.H. FLETCHER

'What's the war about?' she asked Jonathan.

If she were to lose the comfort of her husband even for the few months he expected it seemed reasonable to know why but it soon became clear that Jonathan did not know either. In any case war was a man's thing so it would have made little sense to her anyway.

Jonathan signed up and two weeks later received his orders. In the morning he would be leaving with a lieutenant's badges of rank on his sleeve.

They made love passionately that night, clinging as though each had abandoned the other, and only their shared passion showed it was not so.

In the morning, after the tears and loving and despair, Bec was calm. 'Make sure you write to me, Johnny.'

Rose Penrose was up at her place in the Whitsundays and did not come to say goodbye to her son, which might have been a blessing, for Rose would have wept and daylight was not the time for tears. While Bessie Penrose, stalwart and hard as Blackman's Head, ordered her grandson to be courageous for the sake of king and country and the family's good name.

Although why the family's name should be affected by a war on the other side of the world Bec did not understand.

She did not underestimate the problems she would face, alone in Derwent with her grandmother-in-law. She had hoped they might be brought closer by Jonathan's departure but it became obvious even before he left that there was no chance of that.

'I will be accompanying Jonathan to Launceston,' Bessie said. 'I have business there that can't wait.' Her smile was drenched in acid. 'Such a pity, Rebecca, that you won't be able to travel with us, but I'm afraid the motor won't take three passengers.'

Bec had no intention of being separated from her husband until he boarded the troopship. Observing the size of the Ford and anticipating there might be a problem, she had therefore made a plan.

'Don't worry,' she said. 'You take the motor. We'll go by train.'

Bessie's mouth snapped tight. 'That is completely unacceptable —'

'Jonathan and I have talked about it. We agree it's the only way.' It was Bec's turn to smile. 'Such a pity but, like you say, that motor of yours is very small.'

Now Bessie's glare might have melted glass. It confirmed what Bec supposed she had always known: when Bessie Penrose hated you, you stayed hated.

'I shall speak to my grandson,' Bessie said.

And did so, to no avail.

She would not give in over the motor so set off in solitary state, her scowl blighting the sunlight, and was waiting at the railway station when the train pulled in. Here her fury was compounded on discovering that Jonathan and Rebecca were taking the ferry to Melbourne together.

'In that case I am afraid you will have to find your own way home,' she told Rebecca. 'I take it you will be returning to Derwent?'

'Oh yes,' Bec said. 'Us'll wait for Jonathan together, ain't that right? A bit of company for each other.'

Us'll? Ain't? And this creature would be the chatelaine of Derwent? The prospect put Bessie's teeth on edge. What made it worse was her suspicion that Bec had put on the accent for Bessie's benefit.

A bad beginning, nor did things improve as time went by. Bec was barely back at Derwent when she found she was in the family way. She had mixed feelings about it; in other circumstances she'd have been over the moon but as things were it was a worry. People said men were dying like flies over there. What if Jonathan never came back? What would the baby's future be then?

Giles was born in a scowling storm, black and thunderous, and a gale of wind that Bec, lying on the stripped bed and fighting a storm of her own, thought might have ripped a lesser house from its foundations. As it was, in the tremulous intervals between the contractions that more and more denied her control over her body, she felt the building shudder in the gusts.

It was around the middle of the day but beyond the window the sky was dark and Minnie Thwaites, who had come with

Dr Farmer from Campbell Town to provide her with what assistance they could, told her trees were down in the forested area below the house and the air was full of flying leaves.

It seemed like a prediction that the storm should die as the child was born.

'A regular little peacemaker he'll be,' said Minnie. 'Your hubby will be that proud of his son when he gets back from the war.'

Bec had hoped the baby might change Bessie's attitude; once again she was disappointed. Shortly after Giles's birth she overheard her talking to the housekeeper about him.

'We can't even be sure it's my grandson's child, Mrs Harris.'

Bec was not the sort to ignore a comment like that. She collared the old bitch when she was alone.

'I'd be a bit careful, Gran, I was you. You start makin' remarks like that, there's no way of knowin' when they might come back and bite you. Ain't that so?'

Bessie's port-wine face showed what she thought of that. And in her own drawing room? Even the silk-lined curtains were aghast.

'I've not breathed a word,' Bec said. 'Not so far. And I won't, neither. Not so long as we understand each other.'

Never in a million years would she have imagined having the nerve to speak to Bessie Penrose like that, but she had done it and the world had not come to an end. It gave her the oddest feeling, like it must feel to be drunk, and she saw something she had never thought to see: that Bessie Penrose, terror of the high country, was frightened. Frightened of her. She saw too that Bessie would never forgive her for that and that she had been fooling herself to imagine the old lady would ever accept the blacksmith's daughter as a fitting wife for her grandson. They would be enemies for life. Well, so be it: she no longer cared. It was not what she would have chosen but if that was the way it was going to be they would have to live with it.

'Somen else I wanted to tell you,' she said.

Bessie's expression was pure hatred. 'What is it now?'

'I've invited me mum to come and stay for a few days. She used to work here, you remember. Mary Smith as was? She'll be wanting to see her grandchild.'

'You've invited her to stay here?'

'No need for you to worry: I'll sort something out with Mrs Harris.'

And left her, Bessie close to apoplexy. True to her word, Bec tracked the housekeeper to her lair adjoining the kitchen.

'My mother will be coming to stay for a few days. I thought perhaps the Flinders room?'

Named for the famous navigator, the Flinders room was the grandest visitor's room in the house. Mrs Harris's expression was like a locked safe.

'Very well, Mrs Penrose.'

Inside, Bec was smiling.

Mary Hampton arrived and made much of the baby. Bessie, carefully polite, was as welcoming as an ice floe in winter, but inside her head Bec's smile was broader than ever.

There were other fights, more than Bec could count. Enmity simmered through the months and years, because Jonathan's prognosis had proved wrong. The boys were not home for Christmas or the one following. The war dragged on with tales from those returning – many maimed in body or in mind – of horrors beyond imagining, of friends buried alive in mud or blown into rags by the endless shells – but somehow Jonathan survived, his letters as regular as moonrise and sunset, and it was only their lack of emotion that betrayed the horrors that lay behind the formal words.

I am well. The weather has been fine. Charlie Forsyth is dead.

The newspapers were full of it. There had been a huge battle at a place called Pozières, which no one had ever heard of. It must have been important even though apparently it didn't exist any more; thousands of Aussies had died in capturing a piece of shell-cratered land that by the sound of it hadn't been worth having in the first place.

'I shall never understand this terrible war,' Bec said, and thought of the mothers whose sons would never come home. 'It's not right. It can't be right.'

She'd known one German, an outback trader, who'd had his donkey shod at the forge in the old days, and as far as she could remember he'd been all right. But now it seemed he was a Hun and therefore a devil and must be killed.

Bec and Grandma Bessie saw little of each other and said less, sensing that only through a shared silence could the form of civility be preserved.

More and more Bessie kept to her room. One day Mrs Johns, Bessie's personal maid, came to Bec and said she was concerned for Bessie's health. 'She seems to be worried about something. Keeps saying she has to change the trust, or something like that. Wants me to get her lawyer. Poor old lady, I think she's losing it.'

'Hardly old, Mrs Johns. She's not even sixty. I expect it's just a dose of the wartime blues. We all get them from time to time. I'll come and talk to her, find out what she's on about.'

But when she went Bec was taken aback to see how Bessie had gone downhill in the week since she had last visited her. Even her scowl lacked the venom of the past.

'What's this about wanting to see your lawyer?' Bec asked.

It was tricky because Mr Miller was off at the war like so many others. In any case Bessie did not seem to hear her.

'My turn now,' she said, her head restless on the pillow. 'When he was dying my father said shadow walkers were watching him from the foot of his bed. Now it's my turn.'

'You'll be good for years yet,' Bec said. 'But I can get the doctor to give you a look, if that's what you want.'

Bessie was off in another world and did not answer. 'I did what I could to stop you,' she said. 'I was determined you would never set foot in this house. But you beat me in the end.'

'Time to put all that behind us,' Bec said.

'I'd have done it if you hadn't found out about my mother. I hate her and I hate you. I'll hate you till I die.'

'That's a pity,' Bec said. What else was there to say?

But rage, no longer confined, had Bessie by the throat. 'I'd have buried you, if I could. Buried you alive. Conan Hampton's daughter lording it over Derwent? It's intolerable. I hate you, you hear? Hate –'

And stopped. And gasped, breath dragging through open mouth.

Bec ran to the door.

'Mrs Johns, send Bennett for the doctor. Quick as he can. Looks like Mrs Penrose has had a seizure.'

Mrs Johns ran. Bec went back into Bessie's room. She crossed to the bed. One look told her all she needed to know. Bessie Penrose was beyond the help of doctors now.

Two doctors arrived with a policeman, their purpose not only to confirm that Bessie Penrose was dead but that her death had been caused by natural causes and could not be pinned on her grandson's wife who after all had a lot to gain. Bec suspected the cop was disappointed that handcuffs would not be required but she gave him a cup of tea and he was mollified.

On their heels came a lawyer, from Melbourne Town no less. Self-importance in a tail coat, Mr Dominic Trueblood talked at her and did not try to conceal the contempt he felt for a woman endeavouring to interest herself in matters of business and law that were clearly beyond her understanding. He would not have tried such tricks with Grandma Bessie but she, admittedly a woman, had been one of a kind.

Bec did not try to hide her ignorance. 'It is because I don't understand that I would like you to explain things to me,' she said.

It did little good.

'It was Mrs Penrose's wish that I should become involved in the affairs of the family trust.'

'In what way involved?'

'Mrs Penrose's instructions were not clear. I was hoping she might have left a letter.'

'I've seen no letter. In any case there is a trust already. My husband is one of the trustees, together with Mr Miller, a Campbell Town lawyer. You may have heard of him.'

Mr Trueblood's manner made it plain that he had little regard for Campbell Town lawyers. 'No doubt. But that is an entirely separate matter, you see. Mrs Bessie Penrose expressed the wish that I should oversee the running of the estate in her grandson's absence,' said Mr Trueblood, even by lawyers' standards more opinionated than most.

'She never said that to me,' Bec said.

'No doubt she thought it best not to trouble you with such matters,' he said.

Bec might be ignorant of the law but was the woman who had rescued a child from a menacing bull at the Campbell Town show; she was not to be intimidated by a lofty lawyer in a black tail coat.

'When did she tell you this?'

'Some time ago. But I have no reason to believe she had changed her mind.'

'Got a letter?'

'Mrs Penrose did not believe in letters,' said Dominic Trueblood. 'She believed in trust.'

'I have a copy of Mrs Penrose's will appointing my husband Jonathan Penrose to administer Derwent's affairs after her death,' Bec said. 'I believe in that.' She smiled at the lawyer, secretly astonished how the words flowed so easily from her lips. 'You say Mrs Penrose didn't believe in letters. I do. I have a letter from my husband authorising me to act for him in his absence fighting for king and country. I believe in that. Nowhere have I found any reference to you, Mr Trueblood. Nor any reference to the family trust.'

Mr Trueblood was affronted. 'My dear madam, you are surely not suggesting –'

'I am suggesting nothing,' Bec said. 'I am stating facts.'

'But Mrs Penrose, consider… You are young and inexperienced. How can you possibly hope to administer a property as complex as Derwent?'

'It won't be easy,' Bec said. 'That was why I was hoping you might help me by explaining all the things that I have to do, but I see that would be asking too much of you.'

Not so lofty now and anxious for his vanishing fees, Mr Trueblood did what he could to retrieve the position but it was too late. Bec thanked him for his assistance to the late Mrs Penrose but made it clear she would have no need for his services in the days ahead.

'But madam, I assure you –'

'Thank you, Mr Trueblood.'

There was a funeral to arrange which no doubt would be attended by the high and the haughty, who would stare at her and say how sorry they were for her loss and privately think she should be sent round to the kitchens where she would be more comfortable with the rest of the servants. There would need to be suitable refreshments for after the funeral, even accommodation for those who had come from far away.

She found herself wishing it was she who had died and not Bessie Penrose. At least Bessie would have known what to do. How was she ever going to cope?

She had to reply to the hundreds of condolence letters that came from everywhere. Even the prime minister wrote and you'd have thought Mr Hughes had enough on his plate with the war. She had been sending a weekly letter to Jonathan ever since he'd gone overseas; now she must write again once she had worked out what to say to him. In many ways Bessie had been an absolute monster but as ruler of Derwent she would be hard to replace.

All these things, scary though they were, were good in one way because Bec relished a challenge and knew this would be a hard one. It had never entered her head that she would have a say in running the estate but now, with Jonathan away and Bessie dead, she saw she would have to learn. And quickly too.

The offices of the Australian Farms and Produce Company were scrunched up and insignificant in a down-market Collingwood back street, with no money wasted on such fripperies as a coat of paint or smart furniture. The clerks were down at heel too, which was not surprising considering the level of their wages.

Lemaire Forrest, owner of the building, the company and, some said, everyone who worked for him, set his staff a fine example, being the most down at heel of them all; the jacket he wore might have been made back in 1874, the year of his birth.

Lemaire Forrest dressed poor but was one of the richest men in Victoria, hard-featured and merciless. Untouched by the tales of horror and courage at the front, he thought the war a blessing, giving the astute businessman opportunities to grab significant profits by supplying the military with wool for uniforms, with boots and winter underwear, not to mention providing a hungry home market with butter, mutton and cheese. It also provided him with the opportunity to pick up some choice properties in Victoria and Tasmania, the owners having been mowed down in Flanders or lost their sons in the same way.

'Happy times,' he told Hedley Crabbe, the solicitor who had tipped him off about Derwent.

'The finest estate in the Tasmanian high country. One of the top merino producers in the Commonwealth.'

'What about it?'

'The owner died recently, her son is dead and her grandson, the heir, is fighting overseas.'

'Who's running it now? A manager?'

'Better than that. The old lady's granddaughter-in-law is having a go.'

'Does she know what she's doing?'

'I doubt it. She's nineteen years old with a baby and has never run a business or property like Derwent in her life.'

'Check it out,' Lemaire Forrest said. 'See how the granddaughter gets on. If she makes a muck of it there could be an opportunity for us down the track. Particularly, heaven forbid, if the husband is killed.'

'We can only hope,' Crabbe said.

After she'd chucked Mr Trueblood out the door one of the first things Bec did was teach herself to drive Grandma Bessie's Ford.

A motor car was still unusual enough to attract attention when she drove into Campbell Town or Ross and often she would come out of a shop and find it the centre of a crowd of urchins to whom she liked to introduce the motor as though it were a living person.

'This is Buster,' she would say to the children. And to the motor: 'Say g'day to them, Buster,' and would blow the horn and set them laughing before driving gaily away, one hand on the steering wheel, the other waving goodbye.

As Jonathan's wife most people knew her, at least by sight, although not everyone approved of her or her antics. She overheard one lady, a member of the haughty brigade, talking to a friend.

'One wonders what Bessie Penrose might have had to say about her behaviour.'

Bec didn't care. 'At heart I'm an urchin too.'

She liked to grab fun where she could find it because there wasn't a lot about; the news from France was dire and she also had Derwent to run. To begin with that had been a nightmare.

After Bessie's death she had been appalled to discover the extent of the Derwent operation. It was not simply the estate; in the years before the war Bessie had acquired an interest in a number of businesses: among them a cheese-making factory, a clothing manufacturer and an ironmonger in Launceston.

She found herself confronted by endless paper: returns, crop figures, sale futures of the merino clip, shipping contracts and sets of accounts. To begin with they were mostly incomprehensible to her. And she, Bec Hampton the blacksmith's daughter, had the cheek to think she could run such an operation? It was insanity; she told herself she could not hope to get the hang of it. Her courage ran away like water. There was no help for it; she would have to eat her pride and ask Mr Trueblood for help.

She thought about that. She slept on it. In the morning she told herself she was not Bec Hampton. She was Rebecca Penrose; she wasn't Jill in the nursery rhyme either; no matter what, she would not come tumbling down the hill. The thought of Mr Trueblood's smug expression was all the incentive she needed.

'At least you know you don't know,' she told herself. 'That's a start. So find people who can help you. When you don't know, ask.' She heard sniggers of derision from the part of her that doubted but she became more and more resolute as the weeks passed and stamped the sniggers down. Each night before sleep she looked at her reflection in the bedroom mirror and told herself she was not afraid. It wasn't true but the lie helped.

She gathered a team. It was expensive but the only way. She told the managers of the various farms making up the Derwent property to keep her up to date. Some of them were a bit toey about reporting to a woman but Bec made it plain they had no choice.

'I think of us as a team,' she said. 'Until Mr Penrose comes home we all have to pull together. For his sake as well as ours.'

Lawyer Maurice Miller had been discharged from the army after taking a bullet through the arm in the trenches. Mort Meredith was a wool classer who knew the markets and the world. He had no problem reporting to a woman; far from it, his warm eyes sending signals.

I shall have to watch him, Bec thought.

Jed James was the manager of the factory in Ross that made woollen garments. It was a small operation and she wondered whether perhaps it might be made bigger.

'Sell things overseas when the war's over,' she said. 'Why not?'

Andrew Rippon, an accountant who had recently opened a practice in Campbell Town, was a man who knew figures like a second language but also, thank the Lord, had a sense of humour and never pretended to be the smartest man in the room.

Finally there was the most important team player of all: Mrs Harrington, the kindly new housekeeper at Derwent House, whose job – a secret discussed between them over tea and crumpets one winter's day – was to make Bec into a lady.

'Or as close to it as you can get,' Bec said. 'Like it or not, I got to run this estate until Mr Penrose comes home from the war and that will mean mixing with all sorts. The prestige of Derwent is at stake,' she said, making a joke of it but meaning it all the same.

The housekeeper assured her there was nothing to it but there were cursing and swearing days when Bec thought Mrs Harrington had the hardest job of all.

Six months later Crabbe got back to Forrest.

'Disappointing news,' he said. 'The granddaughter seems to be handling things well. We've asked around but everyone says she's doing a good job.'

'And the grandson?'

'Still breathing, the last I heard.'

Lemaire Forrest stroked his chin. 'Does she know we've been sniffing around?'

'Bound to have heard something. You can't keep these things secret.'

'No matter. There may be another opportunity, one of these days.'

1918–32

When Jonathan came back from the war Bec discovered that the man she had married had not survived after all, that part of the old familiar Jonathan had drifted off somewhere and never come home.

For the first time she realised she was really still a bride. Not so surprising; she'd had little chance to be anything else. They hadn't been married that long before he left and you couldn't count the years he'd been away. They'd written regularly but letters weren't the same and she saw that as a married woman she had it all to learn. That might have scared her but she knew she'd made a fair job of running Derwent in his absence and that gave her confidence she'd be able to handle this problem too, given time.

Jonathan made much of the boy, which she took as a hopeful sign. Giles was three years old. The two men, as Bec called them, were strangers to each other but Bec sensed a kind of groping affection in the way Jonathan tried to get on terms with his son.

He didn't get much encouragement. Giles was a wilful child; growing up in a house full of women he had learnt he could get away with a lot and resented this stranger who had moved into spaces he thought of as his own.

Bec believed, or at least hoped, that Giles would get used to this strange dad, in time. She hoped she would get used to him too.

There were good days when he was as she remembered, friendly and loving and kind, but there were terrible days too. One day she found him in tears and did not know whether to comfort him or pretend she had seen nothing. Instinct led her to put her arms around him, he weeping and shaking as she held him. And held him, keeping him safe from the chasm into which she was afraid he might plunge. If that happened, she thought, he would be lost forever.

'I will save you,' she told him. 'I will make you whole.'

If she could.

There were other days when it was like having a stranger in the house. He was given to moods when he went off somewhere into the bush. He said he needed the silence after all the violent years but Bec thought he was trying to find the world he had known before the war. She wanted to tell him it couldn't be done. The land hadn't changed – the grass still blew in the wind, the rains still came and the sun, the ewes dropped their lambs on schedule – but the man had. The pre-war Jonathan wasn't there any more. The war had changed him.

Bec never said this. She never told him about how hard it had been for her, having to deal with Bessie, then learning to run Derwent and handle the men and all the other problems she'd had. He never talked about the war but she'd read things in the papers and heard from the wives of other diggers who'd come back and wondered how any of them had remained sane, the things they'd been through.

One day he gave her two wild orchids he'd found in moist ground by a creek.

'Why, they're lovely,' she said.

Holding them she could have wept for the shy beauty of the flowers and for the man who expressed his love so tenderly.

Jonathan still went walkabout from time to time but his eyes were clearer and Bec dared hope he had learnt to accept the skin of the man he had become. When he came home she had taken it for granted that he would be running the estate but at first it hadn't worked out like that. It wasn't that he didn't want to but that he did not seem to know what he had to do. He drifted through the days, aimless and disconnected, while Bec got on with things.

The farm managers, one called Isaac Slack in particular, didn't like it. They had put up with her while the war was on but hadn't bargained on doing so when it was over. It unsettled them and she was scared their commitment to their work and even to Derwent might suffer accordingly.

She spoke to them about it. 'It's going to take time for him to get over the war but he'll come right eventually. In the meantime we'll just have to hold the fort for him. As soon as he's fit he'll be taking over.' She laughed, trying to win them. 'You can bet your socks on that. I'm for the easy life, me.'

They laughed with her, Isaac half-heartedly, and for the time all was well.

She was right too. The months stretched out and little by little things became easier. At long last, after Jonathan had been back a little over twelve months, he began to pick up the reins again.

The years passed. Australia sold a hundred million quids' worth of wool to Britain (those darn futures again) which was great for the industry and for Derwent. In Brisbane, returning diggers started a war of their own, belting the daylights out of a parade of Bolsheviks. The Prince of Wales skipped in, visited lots of places and six months later skipped out again. In Western Australia, a woman called Cowan became the first woman MP. Women's dresses climbed higher in the skirt and lower in the neck, causing pleasure to some and outrage to others. Tasmania declared itself broke.

'How is that possible when Britain bought all that wool from us?' Bec asked.

'God knows.'

In 1927, two weeks after Giles's twelfth birthday, Bec had a miscarriage.

She had never thought she could feel so bad.

She had been visiting friends in Hobart when things started to go wrong, so they'd rushed her to the hospital. The way it worked out, it was just as well.

The physical pain was bad enough although not as bad as when Giles had been born. She always remembered that as a terrible time: out of her depth, the big house like a gaol with Grandma Bessie the gaoler in chief, her own mother nowhere to be seen and her husband fighting overseas in the terrible war that seemed none of his business.

It had been very bad yet in one way the present situation was worse. There was still pain but she found the damage to the spirit harder to bear; it lasted longer and left her feeling diminished.

'I feel so guilty,' she told the nurse but the nurse was brisk by nature and had heard this sort of nonsense from patients before.

'You shouldn't,' the nurse said. 'These things happen.'

Which might have been meant to provide consolation but did not.

While Bec was in the city Jonathan had a visitor. He was a big bloke, well dressed. In a chauffeur-driven motor car, all very grand, he drove up the hill to Derwent's massive front door and asked to see Jonathan.

'May I know what this is in connection with?' said Mrs Harrington.

She spoke severely; this was a sad house for news of the miscarriage had just arrived, phoned through from the Hobart hospital.

'Tell him his old mate Basil Merton is here and wants to give him the best deal he'll ever get in this world or the next.' His words, like his voice and body, seemed too big even for a house the size of Derwent.

'We were in the war together. You can say Jumbo Webley sends his regards too.'

Mrs Harrington conveyed the message to Jonathan. In the depths of gloom over the baby, he couldn't remember either Basil Merton

or Jumbo Webley but there were many blanks in his memories of
those days, of the people he'd known who'd lived or died.

'I suppose I'd better see him.'

He knew him when he saw him, two men who by a series of
miracles had somehow survived the slaughter of Pozières.

Basil started chucking names about: people they had known,
men who'd walked away and others who had not.

'We've seen some terrible things, you and me,' Basil said.

Jonathan nodded. No one doubted the terror but he had never
wanted to revisit the blood and steel of those days, the ghosts of
landscapes people said had been so delightful in the lost days before
the war.

'We reckoned the world owed us,' said Basil Merton, 'after all
we'd been through. You remember how we said we were going to
make ourselves rich when the war was over?'

'Vaguely.'

Jonathan couldn't remember discussing it with Merton but it
was the way a lot of men had talked at that time, words as bold
as brass providing an antidote for fear, so perhaps he had. At the
moment he was too sad to care what he'd said on that blood-soaked
field. 'So how can I help you now?'

'More a question of how I can help you,' Merton said. 'Of how I
am going to make you even richer than you are already.'

When Bec, sore of heart, sore in body, brought her empty arms
home from the hospital Jonathan told her about his new friend.

'You say you don't remember him?'

'Not very well. Conditions like they were, lots of men couldn't
remember their own names.'

'You're saying he's a stockbroker, got you to invest in some of the
shares he recommended?'

'Just a taster, no more. See if he knows what he's talking about.'

'Hmm...'

She didn't like it but supposed a bit of a flutter, if that was all
it was, would do no harm. It would be nice if he won; if not, it

wouldn't be too serious and she knew better than anyone how Jonathan, even so long after the war, still needed to boost his self-esteem.

'It's as if he blames himself for having survived the war,' she told her friend Mrs Roberts.

'Seven years after it ended,' Mrs Roberts said. 'But I've read somewhere thoughts like that can last as long as life itself.'

The thought seemed to gratify her; everyone had their problems and Mrs Roberts clearly doubted whether Jonathan Penrose, one of the richest men in Tasmania, could be more afflicted than the thousands who were less well off.

Of the five shares Basil Merton had recommended, two rose slightly but the other three went roaring up. Within the month their prices had doubled, then trebled.

Jonathan couldn't wait to get to the papers every morning; every morning he was rendered breathless by his sagacity in buying the shares he had.

Two months later Merton phoned. 'I think we should get out now.'

'But –'

'They've peaked.'

Those shares had become like old friends and Jonathan was sad to sell. He was even tempted to ignore Basil's advice and hang on but did not and a week later he was over the moon; the price of all three runaway stocks had come crashing down as quickly as they had gone up.

Once again Jonathan congratulated himself.

'I think this fellow is a genius,' he told Bec. 'And I suppose you could say I'm not such a fool myself.'

Bec, preoccupied with Derwent's affairs, gave him little attention.

'Yes, dear,' she said.

On Basil's advice Jonathan invested again, a little more this time, and made again. Slowly the sums he put into his share portfolio grew. So did the profits. Admittedly they were only paper profits because now Basil was counselling him to hang on, but they were there, weren't they? Any time he chose to sell he could.

Months passed.

The profits were good, then remarkable, then mind-boggling, because it was June 1929 and the market was surging like a tidal wave and he was riding it, exultation in every heartbeat.

Basil was as excited as he was. 'We're heading for the big time. Give it everything you've got.'

Jonathan obeyed. Better: he gave it more than he'd got, much more. But who cared? It was a mad world, offering unlimited rewards to the brave.

Bec was concerned, then uneasy, then alarmed. 'Get out now! Get out while you can!'

Jonathan took no notice. For the first time since the war, he felt as he had as a young man: free, alive, one with his destiny. Once again where a man should be, in charge.

Up and up went his shares. Up and up. Now the whole world was in on the act. Up and up. A hiccup in September but optimism soon shook that off. Up again. Up.

He pledged his personal assets to the bank – he had plenty of those now, not like it had been in the years before the war – and would have pledged Derwent itself had the trust deed permitted it. He tried to get his co-trustee's approval but Maurice Miller was having none of it. Undeterred, he raised an overdraft on the strength of his being the trust's major beneficiary, bought more shares with the money.

At the end of October Wall Street crashed. Panic swept the markets of the world.

Face grey, sickness cramping his stomach, Jonathan found himself looking at catastrophe. Careless of pride, close to weeping, he pleaded with Basil Merton.

'Sell! Sell everything!'

Basil laughed, if you could call it a laugh. 'Chance would be a fine thing.' He was in as bad a state as Jonathan, possibly worse. 'A lot of our stocks, we'll be lucky to get back twenty per cent what we paid for them.'

'And the rest?'

'For the rest there are no buyers at all.'

'It'll go up again soon, won't it?'

Silence gave the answer.

'But what do we do?'

Like a small child crying for its mother.

'Pray, if you've got the mind,' Basil said. 'Or you could always try blowing your brains out.'

In the meantime Jonathan had Bec to face and the reproachful shades of all those who had held Derwent before him.

To say nothing of the bank.

'An unhappy business altogether,' said Hamish Archer, rubbing his hands.

Not so long ago the bank manager, king of grovellers, would have come close to kneeling whenever Mrs Rebecca Penrose deigned to enter the premises of the Tasmanian Bank. No longer. Now it was all business with not a grovel in sight.

'I must tell you,' Hamish Archer said, 'I did everything in my power to dissuade Mr Penrose from making further investment with the market so high. A correction, I told him, was bound to come. But he was not to be dissuaded. Regrettable, Mrs Penrose. Most regrettable.'

His Hibernian Rs might have cracked walnuts.

'I have no doubt you did what you could,' said Bec. 'That is not the issue. What I need is your advice; how do we extricate ourselves from this hole?'

The crash had given Hamish Archer a power he had never expected and he relished every minute of it. 'The market is in a verra sorry state, Mrs Penrose. My directors have nae expectation that stocks will rise any time soon. On the contrary, they foresee further falls, probably extending over several months. Even longer, perhaps.' Mr Archer shook his head sadly. 'I fear those who willna be guided have to face the consequences.'

He might have been John Knox letting rip about the monstrous regiment of women.

Bec could have slapped the manager's self-righteous face but restrained herself. 'And your advice, Mr Archer?'

'To pay back what you owe.' He took up a piece of paper. 'One hundred and three thousand, nine hundred and three pounds, Mrs Penrose. With interest accumulating every day.'

'You hold the share scrip relating to my husband's investments –'

'Worthless, I regret to say. At this time.'

'But you cannot touch Derwent itself because of the trust.'

'That is true.'

'So what is the position, legally speaking?'

'I think we may safely leave that to the lawyers. Hmm?' He gave a bank manager's laugh, dust-dry and uncompromising. 'Not our field of expertise, hmm? My advice is the same as I am giving others in your situation. Your husband should repay what he owes, Mrs Penrose. As quickly as he can. Lest worse befalls, hmm?'

The implied threat of bankruptcy could hardly have been clearer. What that would do to Jonathan's fragile psyche Bec dared not imagine.

Dear God, she thought as her car trundled down Macquarie Street. What do I do now?

She phoned Maurice Miller and gave him the bad news.

'I see no help for it,' she said. 'I daren't risk damaging my husband more than he's damaged already. I think the trust will have to sell off some assets.'

'The way the stock market is, it won't be easy,' Maurice said.

'I was thinking more of land. Specifically, the land we own along the Murrumbidgee.'

'I'll make enquiries,' Maurice said. 'Get back to you as soon as I can.'

Lemaire Forrest had found the market crash and developing depression a gift from the god in whom he did not believe. He had sold out before the crash so hadn't lost a penny, while the business opportunities arising from those with less foresight were vast.

Hedley Crabbe came to see him. He flicked dust off a fastidious cuff and looked around him with distaste. 'Why don't you get this place tidied up a little? And a coat of paint wouldn't hurt.'

'Because I choose not to,' Forrest said. 'You said you had some information for me?'

'Some years ago we talked about an estate in Tasmania called Derwent.'

Lemaire Forrest was not a man who forgot things. 'In 1916 when the owner died. What about it?'

'They've put some irrigated land on the market.'

'Irrigated land is always worth having. Check it out. Perhaps we can put in a bid.'

It had been a day of almost continuous rain. Rivulets of water created gullies in the rocky soil as they tumbled down the hill. Bec stood at the living room window and watched Maurice Miller's motor car negotiating the steep track up to the house.

Five minutes later the maid came to announce Mr Miller's arrival.

'Thank you, Ivy.'

Bec went to greet him, hand outstretched.

'Come in, Maurice. Ivy. I think we'd like some coffee. Unless you'd prefer whisky?'

Times might be hard but hospitality still had a claim.

'Coffee will be fine.' He stretched his hands to the fire. 'Midsummer? It feels more like the winter.'

She watched him. 'What brings you here in this foul weather?'

'I tried to phone but the lines are down. We've had an offer for the Murrumbidgee land,' he said.

'A good one?'

'Not good at all, I'm afraid. I tried to push up the price but they weren't interested. You could hang on and hope for a better offer but with the world as it is… At least it's cash.'

'How much?'

'Enough to put us in funds for a while. The best we can hope for, the times as they are. Did you see in the paper how many people are out of work?'

'And factories and businesses closing every day,' Bec said. 'It makes you wonder what the world is coming to.'

'Perhaps the wool price will recover,' Maurice said.

'Do you think it will?'

'Not for a while.'

'That land is worth twice what they're offering.'

'It's a buyer's market. It's worth what we can get for it.'

The coffee arrived. Ivy poured. They waited until she'd left the room, the pause as miserable as the weather.

'Who is the buyer?' Bec said.

'Lemaire Forrest.'

'That man,' Bec said. 'He was snooping around after Bessie died. Thought I wouldn't make a go of it, I suppose.'

A burst of rain crashed against the window.

'The right weather for a wretched business,' said Bec. 'But there's no point weeping about it.'

'You want me to tell Forrest we accept his offer?'

'I think we must. But I'll tell you one thing, Maurice,' Bec said. 'God knows how we'll manage it but I am determined that Derwent will survive.' She managed a defiant smile. 'And who knows? Perhaps the wool price will surprise us all. As you just said.'

Although she too doubted it.

1933–36

The market was eighty per cent below its peak in early October 1929; neither had the wool price lifted significantly. They had practised every economy they could think of. They'd sold off most of their horses. They'd put off replacing the roof slates that had been damaged in a winter storm. They ate only the plainest food. They spent their evenings in the half-dark to save electricity. Much against Bec's will they had laid off many of the estate staff.

'I worry how they'll manage,' Bec said. 'If only Derwent was cropping country...'

Or if the companies were making a profit... But it wasn't, and they weren't. It was the depths of the depression with one in four Australians out of work and there were no profits anywhere.

The farm managers had been obliged to forego their annual bonuses for the first time Bec could remember. They'd considered getting rid of one or other of their two cars but had eventually decided against it; they both needed transport. Also they needed to maintain a delicate balance between appearance and reality; they might *be close to ruin* but it was important not to appear so to the rest of the world. Pride was part of it but it also made sense. Even a sniff of bankruptcy would bring the vultures circling.

All these steps only delayed the inevitable. Steadily and inexorably they were going broke. And the bank manager, once again, was on the warpath.

'My directors are verra concairned, Mrs Penrose.'

She could have strangled him.

Jonathan was often alone.

He preferred it that way: when he was by himself he could pretend the shame did not exist. He could walk tall and breathe the air and tell himself he was still a man. In company he could not do that.

It was four years since the crash, when all the bright castles of his dreams had come tumbling down, but the pain remained. He was frightened too. Bec had always been so good to him yet even the best of women must come finally to accept the need to punish him for the vanity that had damaged them so much. At least he hadn't committed suicide, as Basil Merton had, leaving a wife and four children to fend for themselves in a penniless world. At least he hadn't done that yet, but it was fear that drove him to the fishing shack they had on the coast. They'd had it for years. Bec never went there; it was understood that it was his place. They would have sold it after the crash but there were no buyers. The shack had remained, a monument and refuge for the foolish man and his guilt.

It stood amid marram grass dunes a hundred metres above the high-water mark. There was peace there and the solitude Jonathan craved; there was wind and salt air and the constant crying of gulls. There were gannets far out and there were days when he stood for hours with his binoculars, watching them as they carried out their dagger-swift bombing raids on the shoals of fish that moved up and down the coast.

At night the sand gleamed white in the moonlight.

To one side of the shack a padlocked hut sheltered a rubber dinghy, an inflator and oars. There was also a runabout with an outboard motor and fishing gear that Jonathan used when he felt inclined. The fishing was good and often he fired up the barbecue to grill his catch. He didn't drink much but sat and listened to the waves along the shore.

At high tide during on-shore gales the spray from the breaking seas blew high above the shack.

Jonathan would stay there for a week or sometimes two. When he was cleansed he would return to Bec and the world his vanity had destroyed. Even when he was at Derwent he often needed the solitude of the valley called Gimbaloo or the open slopes below Blackman's Head where he and Bec had first made love in the days before the war when they and their world had been young. He sat on the warm earth while the guns of Pozières rained down their shells in his head; he had come to believe he would never be free of them.

Lemaire Forrest was in his sixties but his avarice was as powerful as ever. His many enemies said that dragging wealth from the carcasses of his victims was as necessary to him as breathing.

He sat at his mean desk in his mean office and flashed his mean eyes at Hedley Crabbe, whom he had summoned into his presence. 'You told me on the phone you've heard more rumours about that estate called Derwent. Tell me what you know.'

Hedley was well aware that his client was not only avaricious but unforgiving. So far the schemes he had constructed had all come off but that meant nothing; if anything went wrong he would be blamed for it and, with Lemaire Forrest's appetite for increasingly audacious operations, going wrong was always on the cards. It was enough to make the coolest man sweat because this time there was heavy money involved.

'I've spoken to the minister,' he said. 'He's keen.'

'Of course he's keen,' Forrest said. 'You say they've found underwater aquifers?'

'The diviner we sent in says there is a very strong water flow. The permeable substratum —'

'Never mind that.' Lemaire Forrest had no interest in technical details. 'Will it support irrigation?'

'He says yes.'

'So cropping is possible?'

'Maybe not on the higher ground. But in the valley bottoms he says he's sure of it.'

'How did they manage to carry out the exploratory work without the owners finding out?'

'They slipped one of the managers an early Christmas present to look the other way. Bloke called Isaac Slack.'

'That's a man we'll fire when we take over. I'll not have a traitor work for me. If we give them the go ahead how much of Derwent will be affected?'

'About half. Don't worry, there'll still be plenty of land to run your cattle.'

'I don't worry,' Forrest said. 'I pay you to do that.'

From somewhere Hedley quarried a smile. 'Why should either of us be worrying? If the water's there you'll make a killing.'

'And if it isn't?'

'You'll have the finest property in the Tasmanian high country.'

'Either way, that scoundrel of a minister will make a fortune,' Forrest said, scowling. He hated it when anyone else made money.

'We couldn't mess about with the underground water system without government backing,' Hedley said. 'And he might be useful later. We'll have him in our pocket, won't we?'

'So we should. He'll cost us enough, I have no doubt.' Forrest thought. 'And you say the owners are bankrupt?'

'Heading that way. Or that's what our people are saying.'

'Then we'd better make a move before someone else does,' Forrest said.

Maurice Miller had turned up unexpectedly.

Bec was pleased to see him. Maurice was a good friend and she needed someone to cheer her up. The sun was shining but in Bec's heart it was as dark as night.

They were drinking coffee; at least they could still afford that, though for how much longer?

'It doesn't matter which way I turn,' she told him. 'I can't see my way out of it. Without a miracle the next two months will see the end of us.' She gave him a broken smile. 'Better send me your bill before we are forced to put Derwent on the market.'

'Will you really do that?'

'If the alternative is Jonathan filing for bankruptcy? He'd be likely to blow his brains out. I worry about him,' Bec said. 'He's always going off to the shack, often for weeks at a time. Even when he's here he's out most days. He likes to pretend he's keeping an eye on things but he's not really.'

'Perhaps the wool price will take off,' Maurice said.

'You are always saying that but it never does. It'll have to go sky high to save us now. Anyway, what brings you here this sunny day?'

Maurice drained his cup and gave her a lopsided grin. 'I've had an enquiry about Derwent.'

Bec had been about to lift the coffee pot. Now her hand was still. 'Somebody wants to make an offer? What did you say?'

'I said we'd get back to them.'

She stared at him and at the countryside beyond the window, the paddocks heavy with slowly moving flocks.

'Derwent has been in this family a hundred years... I cannot believe I am having this conversation.' She closed her eyes and pressed her fingertips to her forehead. 'Leave it with me. Let me think about it.'

It was not a case of simply selling Derwent; they would be selling the past, everything the family had achieved and failed to achieve. The future too. All would be gone.

It was impossible, a waking nightmare, a century of history wiped out at the stroke of a pen...

The faces of the dead watched.

She tried to talk to Jonathan about it. It did no good. It was fifteen years since the war ended but the traumas of that time still lingered. They, and his sense of guilt, had paralysed his will.

'You must do what you think best,' he said.

Two days before she had intercepted a bank letter addressed to her husband. Pay, the letter had said, or face the consequences.

No need to spell out what the consequences would be.

Bec lay in her tormented bed. Jonathan was more precious to her than a dozen Derwents. And yet…

She told herself it was impossible even to think of selling. She mustn't do it, would never forgive herself…

Jonathan's life might depend on her decision.

She would have wept, had she the tears.

In the morning, sleepless, she sat and studied the phone. Picked it up. Put it down again.

Oh God. Face it. Deal with it. Accept it.

The phone rang.

She snatched it up, bitterness like vomit in her throat.

'Yes?'

'Maurice,' the lawyer said.

Bec's nerves ripped her patience. 'Are the vultures in such a rush they won't give us twenty-four hours to think about it?'

'Something's cropped up,' Maurice said. 'I'm coming to see you right away.'

It was an electric shock crashing through her. 'What's happened?'

'I'll explain when I see you.'

Bec was left staring at the dead phone.

Within the hour Maurice was driving up the approach road in his bright red Alpha P3. Nerves ragged, fingernails chewed to her elbows, Bec watched with envious eyes; she'd have had one herself if she could have afforded it.

You are a lunatic, she told herself. One foot through the door of bankruptcy and you are lusting after a *sports* car?

The word *irresponsible* came to mind but she'd developed an eye for sleek fast cars. And who could say what news Maurice might be bringing? When you were in the depths of despair, she thought, the only way out was up, and Maurice had sounded brighter than she'd heard him for a long time.

By the time he came through the door the coffee was steaming in the pot.

Of course he started off by telling her about his smart new car, how he'd had the steering adapted to suit the arm wounded in the war, how it ate the miles, how the roar of its engine set the pulses racing...

Somehow Bec managed not to scream.

Finally Maurice said, 'I've been contacted by an old friend of mine in Malaya, a man called Robert Thompson...'

Bec was giving serious thought to murder.

'His family owns rubber estates in north Malaya. One of their acquaintances is a Chinese planter called Chan. Very wealthy, he tells me. Mr Chan lives in Penang but has family in Shanghai. You may not be aware of it but two years ago the Japanese army took over Manchuria. Ever since they've been pushing southwards. Mr Chan's family is concerned about the situation and is looking to invest some of its wealth outside the country while they still can.'

Bec was listening intently now.

'It seems they had intended to send it to England but with the Nazis in charge in Germany they have hesitated. Mr Chan has advised them they should look at sending money to Australia.'

'How much money are we talking about?'

'Robert Thompson believes it could be a significant sum. Two hundred thousand pounds, maybe more.'

Two hundred thousand pounds, maybe more.

The words had magic but clearly there was a major hurdle.

'Are you suggesting we sell Derwent to a Chinese family? How does that fit in with the White Australia policy?'

Maurice smiled indulgently. 'There are always ways around these problems. In any case, I do not believe we are necessarily talking of selling Derwent at all.'

What?

'If that's the case, what are we talking about?'

'It is not in my nature to be overly optimistic –' he drained his cup with a flourish '– but it is my belief that the word we are look-ing for is salvation.'

Bec's hands were clenched in her lap. Hope, recently so unfamil-iar, was bad for the nerves. 'You wouldn't mess me about, would you, Maurice?'

'No, my dear, I would not.' He smiled. 'You don't by any chance have any more of that excellent coffee?'

Her nervous fingers rattled the pot against his cup rim. 'Where do we go from here?'

'I believe the next step is to talk to Mr Chan.'

'You want me to go to *Malaya*?'

'There will be no need for that. At this moment Mr Chan is sit-ting in my car outside your door.'

Bec's jaw dropped. 'What?'

'I explained to him it might be best if I had a word with you first.'

The mixture of fear and joy – of something going wrong and the prospect of what Maurice had termed salvation – was hard to bear. She ordered her nerves to be still. She stood up and sat down again, her thoughts in turmoil. Could it be? Was it possible?

'Be quiet,' she told herself. This was the time to be cold, col-lected, calm. Mr Chan would want a deal. She must think what she was willing to give, unwilling to give.

To keep Derwent in the family she would give anything.

The door opened. An elderly man with oriental features came in. He was a generation older than Bec had expected. He looked frail but was probably tougher than the oldest rope in the Derwent stables. Maurice Miller came in behind him and closed the door. Bec drew a deep breath and stood up.

'Welcome to Derwent,' she said.

'This,' Maurice said to her, 'is Mr Chan Seng Kee. He hopes with our assistance to get some of his family's wealth out of China. Wealth which might otherwise be lost to the Japanese.'

'It is a pleasure to meet you,' Bec said. 'I have ordered coffee. Perhaps you would like to sit down?'

They drank coffee. They chatted amiably about the weather and the beauty of the rolling countryside. The tension in Bec's stomach was almost beyond bearing when Mr Chan at last got down to business.

'Conditions in China very bad,' he said, his English fluent but idiosyncratic and strongly accented.

'So I understand.'

'Japanese seeking take over all country,' he said.

'China will surely not allow that to happen,' Bec said.

'Not if they can help it, I agree. But can they? That is the question. There is much fighting already in China between the government soldiers and a guerrilla army led by a man whose name may be unfamiliar to you, a peasant called Mao Zedong. While they fight each other the Japanese army takes more and more of China. Aiyoh!'

'A difficult situation,' Bec said.

'All things pass,' Mr Chan said. 'China will recover but for the present those with wealth do not wish to be impoverished.'

'They look to protect their money,' Bec said. 'That is wise. So how can I help you, Mr Chan?'

'My family has many business interests. In China, Malaya, Singapore... In the way of business we hear many things.'

Bec drank her coffee.

'Hear Derwent has troubles.'

Bec smiled. 'Is that so?'

'Chan family looking for favours. One good turn deserves another, no? In return may be able to help Derwent.'

'What do you have in mind?'

'Chan family wishes to make investment in land in Tasmania.'

'Australian government policy prohibits this,' Bec said. 'What they call the White Australia policy.'

'That we understand. But solution simple, no? Chan family needs a trustworthy Australian person to own land on its behalf. Also to operate land, earn good profit.'

'Not easy. It could be dangerous to go against government policy,' Bec said. 'Could cause huge trouble.'

'Therefore huge favour must be offered in return. This only fair, yes? Big favours each way.'

Bec's throat was dry. 'What favour does the Chan family offer?'

'Family provide two hundred thousand pounds, Mrs Penrose buy good property in Tasmanian high country. Can?'

'Of course.'

'Further one hundred thousand pounds, stock with best quality sheep, best equipment, proper shearing sheds. Can?'

'Yes.'

'Run property on behalf of Chan family. Can?'

'It would mean employing extra staff, new managers…'

'Can?' Mr Chan said again.

'Can. Certainly. There would be great risk but it could be done. If a suitable agreement were reached.'

'Of course. But Mrs Penrose could arrange these things for the family?'

'Yes. But why would you trust me?'

'Family makes enquiries, receives favourable report. So willing to trust.'

And would no doubt keep an eye on things too, Bec thought. As was only sensible.

'And in return?'

'Family lend further one hundred thousand pound. Interest free, no fixed date of repayment. Lend to you personally, not to family. Use to rescue Penrose family.'

Ohmygod.

The taste of salvation was almost too sweet to bear.

'One further favour required,' said Mr Chan. He smiled benignly but his eyes were implacable.

Oh God, let it be something I can do. Let the taste not turn bitter on me now.

Bec dragged a smile from somewhere. 'What favour is that?'

'Derwent wool clip.'

'What about it?'

'Sell to Chan family interests, next ten years, twenty per cent discount on market price at date of sale. Can?'

'Ten per cent, five years,' Bec said.

Mr Chan smiled. 'Fifteen per cent, seven years.'

'Twelve per cent, six years.' Her eyes challenged his. 'My last word, Mr Chan. You agree?'

Mr Chan smiled. 'Can,' he said.

Weakness overwhelmed her. She was afraid she would wake up and find it all a dream. But no, it was real, it was Christmas Day, Alleluia Day, it was the salvation Maurice Miller had promised.

Tears burnt her eyes but – mercifully! – did not fall.

'I shall get my lawyer on to it immediately –' But stopped as Mr Chan shook his head.

'Nothing in writing. Verbal agreement much better, no?'

'You will trust me with all that money on my word alone?'

'No trust, no deal. With trust, no need for written agreement. Less chance of trouble from government that way.'

'Then how –?'

'One week, all money with your lawyer. Yes?'

Bec was breathless. She stood outside Derwent House and waved goodbye to Mr Chan and Maurice Miller as they drove away down the hill. She turned to look at the house, its massive front door standing open behind her.

'We are safe,' she said.

Hard to believe; harder still to stem the tears that now began to fall. She went looking for Jonathan to give him the good news – how long was it since she'd been able to do that? – but could not find him.

'Have you seen Mr Penrose?' she asked Ivy.

'He went out. While you was with the foreign gentleman.'

'Did he say when he'd be back?'

'No, miss. He was in a big rush. He had this phone call and was lookin' real upset. Just grabbed his hat, jumped in the car and took off. Quite startled me, the way he was lookin'.'

'Did you answer the phone? Who was the call from?'

'It was the bank.'

'Did Mr Penrose take a case with him?'

'No, miss.'

A call from that damn bank manager. Then rushing out like that… Not going to the shack then. He wouldn't go to the bank. It would be either Gimbaloo or Blackman's Head. But which? *Think!*

'I'm going out, Ivy. Shouldn't be too long.'

Thank God they still had the two cars.

Bec drove like a monsoon wind and was soon bumping along the gravel track, constructed five years before, that led to the foot of Blackman's Head.

She prayed she had read Jonathan's mind correctly. This had been their special place ever since the days he had first courted her. But even if she had guessed right there was one inescapable fact: people had jumped off the top of Blackman's Head before this.

Bec saw sunlight glinting on the car when she was still five hundred yards away. Relief surged. But where was Jonathan?

She skidded to a stop, threw open the car door and set out up the slope. Up and up, heart pounding, breath tight in her throat.

Relief flowed through her as she saw Jonathan sitting in the place that had always been precious to them. She ran to him.

'You scared me. Why did you rush out like that?'

'I needed air,' he said. 'And I did not know what I could do.'

She sat at his side on the warm and dusty ground. She saw Jonathan had been weeping, his eyes red, cheeks wet.

She put her hand on his arm. 'Oh, my love…'

Jonathan said: 'The bank manager phoned. I told him you were in a meeting but I don't think he believed me. He said that if we didn't take steps within the next two weeks to liquidate the amount I owe the bank would be forced to take action. His exact words.'

'Did he say what action they were planning?'

'No. But it's obvious. They will push me into bankruptcy unless I am prepared, as trustee of the estate, to sell Derwent. Can't blame them, I suppose.' His eyes stared dully over the expanse that had been the family's land for a century. 'I don't think you or anyone can understand how it feels to be the man who lost Derwent. The stupidity and the guilt.'

Bec took his hand in hers. 'You mustn't think like that.'

'It is in my mind every day. If it hadn't been for the money I lost we wouldn't be where we are now.'

'But –' Bec said.

'Do you think I don't know how you've worked to salvage something from my idiocy? How little I've helped you?'

'But –' Bec said.

'There are days when it's more than I can bear.'

'Listen to me!' Bec spoke sharply and clearly. *'Everything is going to be all right.'*

'I knew there was nothing...' He looked at her, startled. 'All right?' he echoed. 'All *right*?'

'Very much all right. My dear love, it seems we aren't to lose Derwent after all.'

Maurice Miller informed Hedley Crabbe that the Penrose family was not interested in selling Derwent at any price.

Bec, financial credibility restored, travelled to Hobart to complain to the bank's general manager about Hamish Archer's bullying ways.

'As I am sure you will understand,' she told him with the pleasantest of smiles, 'Derwent, the Penrose family and all our other companies will be closing their accounts with your bank. With immediate effect, Mr Horrocks. With immediate effect.'

Horror on the GM's face. 'But madam, I assure you –'

Too late; she smiled graciously and swept out.

'I suspect it put him right off his tea,' she told Maurice later.

A month after Mr Chan's visit Bec was driving back from Hobart. She was using the back road and was nearly home when she saw something unexpected. She drew into the verge and stopped, staring at a group of unknown men working in one of the valley bottoms. What made it interesting was that this was Derwent land and she had no idea why the men were there or what they were doing.

She got out of the car, walked across to them and asked to see the man in charge. This was a surly-looking individual with big shoulders and an Akubra hat.

Bec smiled at him. 'May I ask what you are doing?'

'Who wants to know?'

'I do.'

'And you are?'

'My name is Rebecca Penrose and my family owns all this land. So let me ask you again: what are you doing here?'

He tilted his hat. 'We're with the hydro. We're exploring the aquifer. Checking out the irrigation possibilities.'

'On whose authority?'

'The minister's. But it was Mr Slack who contacted us originally.'

Half an hour later Bec was confronting Isaac Slack in his office.

'You called in a government department without consulting me first?'

'I wanted to see whether we could irrigate the area.'

'Why would you do that?'

An awkward pause.

'Who put you up to this, Isaac?'

'Nobody. I promise you. I just thought –'

She could smell the lie on him. 'And who was going to pay for it?'

He hesitated. 'I was.'

Isaac's eyes were everywhere and Bec did not believe a word of it.

'You are lying.'

'No. I swear…' Isaac began to gabble. 'I heard Derwent was on the market –'

'Where did you hear that?'

Isaac said nothing. He would not look at her.

'One person has expressed an interest in buying Derwent,' Bec said. 'Only one. Does the name Lemaire Forrest mean anything to you?'

'Never heard of him.'

'Or Hedley Crabbe?'

Silence.

His guilt was obvious. Bec looked at him.

'You are finished, Isaac. I want you packed and out of here today.'

'No, please…'

'Today, Isaac.'

He had a wife and two children. She felt sad for them but had no choice. She was prepared to forgive much but disloyalty she would not tolerate.

'Did they find any water?' Maurice Miller asked when she told him what had happened.

'Apparently yes. I saw a preliminary report.'

'What do you plan to do about it?'

'Nothing.'

'It could be worth a huge amount of money to the estate.'

'I think we'll leave it where it is,' she said. 'I don't like the idea of messing about with the water supply. Without the Chans it might have been our salvation but now we're doing OK without it.'

1937–45

Over the years Bec had refused to admit to anyone the flaws in Giles's character.

'He will grow out of it.'

She had said it repeatedly – was still saying it during her battle to keep Derwent in the family – but he never had. Giles was a pupil at St James's College in Hobart, a bright, charismatic and untrustworthy boy who on a number of occasions had come closer to being expelled than Bec had been able to believe.

He was eighteen by the time Bec had negotiated the deal with Mr Chan. She had thought he could assist Robert Jervis, the manager she had appointed to run the estate she had bought on the Chans' behalf twenty miles the other side of Campbell Town, but after six months Jervis sent him home, saying he was unreliable and had no interest in or aptitude for the work.

Bec could have wept. After the traumas of recent years Jonathan at last seemed on the road to a partial recovery; Derwent, which she had thought lost, had by a miracle been found again. Things should have been fine for them at last, and now Giles, the son she loved, was injecting his own brand of turmoil into their lives.

It wasn't fair but that was life. What had fairness to do with it?

The day after Bec's fortieth birthday, Giles came home from a trip to Melbourne in the company of a young woman Bec did not know. Giles informed his parents that he and his companion had just got married and that the twenty-one-year-old Kathleen, an artist's model, was the daughter of David Davies, a wealthy businessman and patron of the controversial artist Norman Lindsay whose nude studies had sparked outrage among the more conservative members of the community.

Seven months later Kathleen, with the aggressively thrusting body and flaring hair seen in many of Lindsay's paintings, gave birth to a son they named David, after Kathleen's father.

After the birth Giles and Kathleen announced they would be moving to Melbourne where David Davies had presented them with a house overlooking Port Phillip Bay and where Kathleen, once she had got her figure back, was keen to resume her life-modelling career.

Bec did not like this at all. In terms of the deed Giles would eventually become a trustee of the family trust, yet it seemed he had no interest in Derwent at all. His roots might be there but his spirit was not, and his spirit would always be the guiding factor in Giles's life.

She talked it over with Giles's father.

'He really has no interest in the place.'

'Except what he can get out of it,' Jonathan said.

It seemed disloyal to be discussing their son like this but facts needed to be faced. What would Giles do if he ever took over control of the trust?

'Giles will do what Giles wants,' Jonathan said. 'As always.'

'The terms of the trust are quite clear,' Bec said. 'Giles becomes a trustee on your death. I only hope he's up to the job.'

'Either way,' Jonathan said, 'I'd like to think it won't be for a few years yet.'

Bec looked at him lovingly. 'Since I plan to die before you it won't be my problem.'

They didn't see much of Giles and Kath after they moved although they did visit them on one occasion.

That was a disaster.

The Melbourne house was large and crooked with floors and turrets architect designed and ceilings slanting this way and that.

'Enough to poke your eyes out,' Jonathan said privately, while Bec feared the warped lines might make her dizzy.

They would have got used to that in time, she thought, but there was one thing in the house she knew neither of them would ever learn to accept.

Kathleen's enthusiasm for her modelling work had spilled over into her private life, except that privacy was clearly not a quality she much valued.

On the living room wall, facing anyone coming through the door, was a full frontal portrait of Kathleen standing and staring challengingly at the viewer, with Kathleen as naked as the day she was born.

On a side table was a photograph of Kathleen as revealing as the portrait.

'She's a good-looking girl, you can say that for her,' Bec said hopefully.

But Jonathan muttered something about strip shows and seeing more than he'd ever hoped to see of his daughter-in-law and it wasn't long before they fled home.

The next thing they knew it was the war.

'Again,' Jonathan said.

As if they hadn't put up with enough from his involvement in the previous one, he would have liked to take part in this one too, but at forty-eight he was too old.

'Thank God,' Bec said.

Giles couldn't avoid it but his father-in-law's influence ensured he never moved outside Canberra.

Jonathan had a few things to say about that too, but Bec was glad.

'This family's suffered enough in Europe's wars,' she said.

Except that it was Europe's war no longer, with Jap submarines in Sydney harbour, bombs dropping on Darwin and Aussie soldiers dying by the thousand in the hellholes of the Japanese camps.

Bec heard nothing from the Chan family, which had presumably been consumed in the furnace of the Asian catastrophe, but she still set aside the profits meticulously.

'Why bother?' Giles asked her. He had red tabs on his collar now and was in Hobart for a meeting. 'Write them off. The land is in our name and no one knows any different.'

Bec did not agree. 'We know. Someone in their family will have survived. In the meantime we shall hold it on their behalf.'

1945–80

The war was over at last.

Civilians danced in the streets. The soldiers returned: some to a rapturous welcome, others to broken homes, broken loves, broken futures. The camps discharged their human wreckage. Across the nation the dead were mourned.

The world went on.

A surviving member of the Chan family, a young man who said his name was Bryan, contacted Bec early in 1946. He had spent the war years in India and spoke fluent English.

He visited Tasmania. He insisted on showing Bec his passport to prove his identity. She took him to see the property she had bought on behalf of his family in the years before the war.

She commiserated over his family's losses, which it seemed had been substantial; he expressed delight at the condition of the estate and the extent of the profits she had been able to set aside for his family.

The White Australia policy was still in force so for the moment the estate could not be transferred to its true owners, but at least Bec was able to assign the banked monies to Bryan and repay the loan that had enabled Derwent to survive.

They promised to keep in touch and Bryan Chan returned to Malaya to start work on restoring his family's shattered fortunes.

The years passed.

It seemed no time at all before one war was replaced by another when on 25 June 1950 the communist North Korea invaded the South and conflict broke out on the Korean peninsula. Again Australia was involved and again Bec was thankful that no member of the family took part.

But there was a bright side: in 1951, at the height of the war, the price of wool had risen to 144.2 pence per pound.

It didn't stay at those levels for long but it was still pretty good and they were looking at what had become a highly profitable organisation again. What a pleasure after the agonies and calamities of the past!

There was more good news in 1955 when Kathleen Penrose gave birth to her second child, a daughter the parents named Tamara.

'Let's hope when she grows up she doesn't give us a free viewing like her mother did,' said Jonathan.

'By the time she's grown up enough to be interesting, looking at girls will probably be all you can do to them,' Bec said.

Although that time, fortunately, was not yet.

In the meantime Jonathan had gone back to another interest. The fishing that had supplied him with food during the dark days of his self-banishment now became a hobby. Once or twice a month Jonathan drove down to the shack. These days Bec often went with him. She didn't go out in the boat – 'I'll never make a water baby,' she said – but was happy on sunny days to sit and watch the water and listen to the surf, the green-sloping waves a blaze of gold and silver light.

It was 1960 and she was sixty-three; on his next birthday Jonathan would be seventy.

'You are growing old,' she told herself. 'Better get used to it.'

A poem she'd read questioned the wisdom of eating peaches; she'd liked the poem but certainly did not go along with that idea.

It was early summer and on the way to the coast they would stop at a farm stall and stock up with peaches, apricots and cherries. After Jonathan came back from his fishing expeditions they would scoff the fruit as they walked hand in hand along the beach in the evenings.

It was so lovely: a lifetime of good and bad days, of ecstasy and turmoil, come to this: two old fogies walking barefoot on a sandy beach, their ears filled with the rumble of surf and screaming of gulls.

'Life,' Bec said. 'Life.'

Each moment was more precious to her than diamonds. A smear of smoke from the barbecue; the taste of the fish they'd eaten for supper; a placid stroll along the beach as the evening sky darkened and the first stars appeared: she could think of no better way to end a day, to end their lives.

Except that she felt more vigorous than she had for years. She thought it was the sea air that perked her up; that and the aware-ness, renewed every day, that she loved and was loved. Forty-seven years married; it was hard to believe.

Three wars, one depression, one near bankruptcy, and there they were.

Often, these days, she thought about her son. Giles was a strange one, no getting away from it, but Bec's love for him encompassed even his sometimes difficult ways.

Giles's son David was twenty-two and showing every sign of fulfilling her early hopes for him; she remembered cradling him in her arms as a baby and wondering whether he would be Der-went's future. He was a fast learner and showed intelligent interest in everything that went on – which was more than you could say for his father. Bec's daughter-in-law Kath had grown away from the glamour of her modelling days and was no longer determined to outrage everyone she met. In its place she had taken up riding and was apparently good at it. Bec suspected Giles was unfaithful to his wife but that was none of her business and she had no plans to interfere.

As for the youngest member of the family… Tamara was five years old and a delight.

Things could have been a lot worse, Bec thought. Better still, there seemed no reason why the tranquil days should not continue for years to come, although she never said it aloud and crossed her fingers even when she thought it.

She'd read some writer who had talked about what he'd called the skull within the sunrise; it was a potent image and Bec watched out for it every day.

She was watching for it on a day in March when she helped Jonathan launch the runabout and take off into a sunrise that seemed to her more brass than gold, with a surly stirring to the waves she didn't like.

'Why don't you give it a miss today?' she suggested.

He looked at the sky and the water and shook his head. 'She'll be right.' He loaded up the tinny and climbed aboard. 'Bumper catch today. I feel it in my bones.'

She stood with her feet immersed in the wet sand; the waves ran up the beach and she did not feel happy at all. She watched the silhouette of the boat draw further and further away from her. The noise of the big outboard faded. Only when the boat was too far away for her to distinguish the details did she turn and make her way back up the beach to the shack.

She thought of going for a walk but didn't feel like it. She picked up a book but couldn't settle to reading. Every few minutes she poked her head out of the door but the sky remained clear, the seas tranquil.

'What is the matter with you?' she said.

An hour passed; two hours.

Hand shading her eyes, she stared out to sea but could see no sign of him.

Time passed. Nothing.

Time passed. Nothing.

It was the middle of the afternoon when she made up her mind she had to do something. She had a horror of making a fuss but he had said lunchtime and it was now nearly four.

Tension eating at her heart she got into the car and drove the two miles into town.

Spotter planes searched; police boats ran this way and that. It had been a calm day with little wind; it was impossible to imagine what could have happened.

Nothing was found.

There were theories; the papers loved theories.

Jonathan Penrose had run away; mention was made of a twenty-year-old model who might have been holidaying in the area although no one could say who she was or where she'd been staying. Another theory hinted but, mindful of the libel laws, never specifically stated, that his wife had murdered him. Less sensational suggestions were that Jonathan had fallen overboard, which did not explain the disappearance of the boat; or the tinny, known to be long in the tooth and lacking flotation tanks, had sprung a leak and sunk.

To Bec none of it mattered. It was a month before she could bring herself to face up to it but at the end of that time she came to a bitter acceptance of the reality. Jonathan had gone, no one could say why, and taken a large slice of her life with him.

In the night he comes to me. He is smiling, happy, the young man I remember from the days before the war. He holds my hands, smiling. He touches my ardent flesh. We are one again and will be so forever.

The months passed. Bec's energy inched back, never as it had been but sufficient to provide solace for whatever time remained to her.

Twelve months after Jonathan's disappearance, Kathleen Penrose walked out on her husband, citing serial infidelity. The divorce cost Giles an arm and a leg but, his income from the trust being what it was, that did not affect his lifestyle at all.

In 1966 the White Australia policy came finally to an end. As soon as it was official Bec contacted Bryan Chan and told him she was arranging for the property to be transferred into the name of his company.

He came for a visit, bringing his wife and four children. They all made a big party together.

In 1980 David, Bec's grandson and Tamara's brother, was on a trip to Europe when he was killed in a car accident, run down by a drunken driver in Milan.

The shock and pain were indescribable. Bec thought she might never become a functioning human being again but she did.

1982

After her return from Zurich Bec had told Tamara they would do what they had to do – they would carry on – but Tamara had the idea it wouldn't hurt if she nudged things along a little.

She spoke to Grant about it and early one morning, after her ritual plunge in the pond Bec still insisted on calling She-Devil's Water, Tamara came to see her grandmother in her bedroom. Her hair was still wet, a towel was hung around her neck and she was carrying a tray of coffee and what Bec called Tamara's significant smile.

Bec was still in bed.

'You,' Tamara said, 'are getting lazy in your old age.'

'At least I am still breathing,' said Bec.

'And hopefully will be for many years yet,' Tamara said.

She poured coffee for them both and sat on the edge of the bed while they drank together and Bec gave her a succession of bird-like glances.

'You are up to something,' she said.

'I am?'

'It's written all over your face.'

'I would never win playing poker with you,' Tamara said. 'You're going to have to manage without me for a couple of days. Grant and I are off to Sydney for a spell.'

'You deserve a break.'

'This is business. We're going to see a man about a dog.'

Bec drank, studying her granddaughter over the rim of her cup. 'The man being your father?'

'And the dog being Derwent.'

'Be careful with him. He can be awkward if you drive him into a corner.'

'He's my dad, Grandma. You think I don't know that?'

'No doubt you'll tell me what this is all about when you get back.'

'No doubt we will.'

Giles lived in the penthouse on the top floor of a block overlooking Manly beach.

A maid let them in. 'He says he'll be with you directly.'

Tamara looked around the flat appraisingly.

'Pricey,' she said.

'All very mod, too,' Grant said. 'A bit different from Derwent. Nice view, though. Plenty of bunnies on the beach.'

'That'll please him,' Tamara said.

Giles came into the room and he was not alone.

'This is a pleasant surprise,' Raine said.

Tamara gave an ambiguous smile. 'We want to talk to you about Derwent's future,' she said.

'That subject is very close to our hearts,' Raine said.

'I am sure.'

'We are simple graziers,' Grant said. 'We know nothing of these things.'

'I am sure we can get a lawyer to draw up a suitable agreement,' Giles said.

'Which is why we decided to obtain legal advice before we came here,' Tamara said. She gestured at the dining table, all plate glass and chrome, standing in the window bay. 'Shall we sit down?'

Giles and Raine looked uncertainly at her, then at each other, but did as she had suggested.

'And what earth-shaking discoveries have you made?' Giles said.

His tone made it clear how much he resented being put on the spot by his daughter. But she had never been one who knew her place.

Grant sat facing them across the table. Shoulders squared, he stared at them both in turn, as uncompromising as a front-row rugby forward. 'Before we go into that, maybe you should tell us what your thoughts are,' he said.

'I would have said that was a matter for the family to discuss,' Raine said. 'In private.'

'I can assure you we have no objection to your being present,' Tamara told her. 'And Grant is a most important member of the family.'

Grant gave Raine the full benefit of his slaughterhouse smile. 'Tamara and I are husband and wife, after all.'

'I have told you what I intend to do,' Giles said. 'As trustee and principal beneficiary of the trust I have the right to realise assets as I choose. I can also have the deed amended to include new beneficiaries.'

'Meaning Raine and Jaeger?'

'Meaning whomever I choose.'

'You see,' Tamara said, 'there is a problem about that. You can't.'

'*Can't?*' Both Giles and Raine sat up straight. 'It is my property,' Giles said. 'I can do what I like with it.'

Tamara was shaking her head. 'No. It is not your property, Dad. It belongs to the trust. And Raine and Jaeger aren't family members. So our advice is they can't be beneficiaries.'

'I intend to adopt Jaeger,' Giles said.

'I don't think so. Both Jaeger's parents are living. For the court to approve an adoption, they'd both have to give their consent. Tell me,' she said to Raine, 'how do you fancy your chances of getting your husband to agree to that?'

'It would be embarrassing if the whole affair came out in court,' Grant said.

'Are you threatening us?' said Giles, reaching for the bridle of his high horse.

But it seemed the horse was unwilling to gallop.

'Certainly not,' Grant said. 'But a well-publicised law case involving such a high profile property...'

'And such a high profile family,' said Tamara.

'Difficult to see how the whole sordid mess could be kept out of the papers,' Grant said.

'So embarrassing,' Tamara said. She smiled at Raine. 'And you a married woman.' She turned to Giles. 'We suggest you resign as trustee. You will retain your interest as a beneficiary, your distribution to be ten thousand dollars a month. Naturally, if you want to fight this in court, the offer is withdrawn.'

'And bear in mind we're doing it to protect you,' Grant said.

'How d'you work that out?'

'It lessens the danger of Raine putting poison in your coffee,' Tamara said.

'I shall sell up the entire estate and you will get nothing,' Giles said. 'How do you like that idea, eh?'

'I doubt the courts will go for it,' Tamara said. 'But you can always try.'

Giles glared at Tamara. 'How can you talk to me like this? I am your father!'

'You should have remembered that years ago,' Tamara said.

'How did it go?' Bec said.

'We got him to see our point of view,' Tamara said.

'And so?'

'He will resign as trustee and I shall take his place. He has agreed not to interfere and as a beneficiary he'll get ten grand a month.'

'He was taking almost that anyway,' Bec said.

'Now it's official.'

'And limited to that amount. What happens to Raine?'

'Who cares?'

'It makes me sad to think of your father being lonely in his old age.'

'No danger of that. With ten grand coming in every month, I don't see Raine going far.'

Bec seemed to have lost her appetite. She'd always been handy with the knives and forks but recently food hadn't interested her and she had an uncomfortable, bloated feeling as though she'd been stuffing herself for weeks. On top of it all she was finding it increasingly hard to drag herself out of bed in the mornings.

'You are getting old,' she told herself. 'What else can you expect?'

Yet she'd been getting old for years and had never felt like this before.

She hated the idea of calling in the doctor. She'd known Doc Walker a long time but still resented the idea of being poked and prodded by a man she barely knew outside his surgery. But eventually it got too uncomfortable to ignore.

'Perhaps he can give me a tonic,' she said.

It was August when she phoned. The doctor came and gave her the once-over. He sent her for a succession of tests which she took, making sure Tamara knew nothing of what was going on.

The whole nonsense infuriated her. 'Such a waste of time,' she said.

The doctor did not give her a tonic but sent her for a full examination in Hobart with a Dr Valerie Shinbone.

Bec thought it a remarkably suitable name for a doctor, and said so.

'Not really,' Doctor Walker said. 'She's a gynaecologist.'

'You think there's something wrong with me?'

'I think it would be a good idea to have a look.' He gave Bec a professional smile. 'That way we'll know for sure there's nothing to worry about.'

So to Hobart Bec went and had the examination and listened to what Dr Shinbone had to say about things before heading home.

Well, she thought, getting to be a hundred might prove more of a problem than I'd thought.

Tamara pounced on her as she came through the door. 'Well?'

'Stop fussing, girl. She told me I had the heart of a twenty-five-year-old.'

'I am surprised she had an opinion on your heart at all, seeing she's not a cardiologist.'

Bec might have guessed Tamara would check.

They walked into the drawing room. Through the big windows Bec could see Derwent's lands glowing golden in the evening light. They sat down in easy chairs and looked at each other.

'I looked her up,' Tamara said. 'Dr Shinbone is a gynae-oncologist.'

'Yeah well,' Bec said.

'It's cancer, isn't it?'

Straight questions deserved straight answers but Bec still chewed over it before coming out with the truth. 'Talking about it somehow makes it more real. Foolishness, of course. Very well. Yes, cancer it is. Ovarian cancer, she tells me. But it's really of no consequence,' she said brightly. 'My ovaries are past their use-by date anyway, wouldn't you say?'

Tamara was not deceived. 'Did she give you a prognosis?'

'Three months,' Bec said. 'Six tops.'

Tamara's hand tightened on the arm of her chair. 'Did she talk about an operation?'

'At my age she says my body wouldn't stand it.'

'So what does she suggest?'

Ever since her discussion with Dr Shinbone Bec had been fighting shock. Now she mustered her courage and poured it into her smile, making it radiant. 'Something along the lines of putting my affairs in order and having palliative care available when the need arises.'

'And that's it?' Bec saw that Tamara was willing to go to war with the fortunately absent Dr Shinbone. 'She's saying there's nothing she can do? Nothing?'

'That's about the size of it.'

'You'll get a second opinion, of course.'

'I've had all the tests and there is no doubt about it. And Doc Walker says that in her field Valerie Shinbone is the best in Australia. I don't plan on being messed about more than I've been already so the answer, Tamara, is no. No second opinions.'

Tamara still wanted to fight. 'There must be something you can do.'

'I told you. I shall put my affairs in order –'

'Other than that.'

'Of course there is. Lots of things. I'll do them too, or as many as I can. If I could I would walk every inch of Derwent land and say hurroo to each tree and blade of grass. If I were up to it I'd climb Blackman's Head and say see you later to the eagles. That would be the way I'd do it, given the choice. They've been around a lot longer than I have.'

'I doubt they'd thank you for it.'

'I couldn't manage it anyway, not now. You die by inches and don't even realise it. I did climb it once, you know.'

'You told me.'

'I daresay I did. A dozen times, probably.'

Tamara smiled. 'Something like that.'

'There are one or two other things I'd like to see sorted too. As Derwent's trustee you should be thinking of having a child to continue the line.'

'How old-fashioned of you!'

'Old, I grant you, but there's nothing old-fashioned about wanting to see the future settled. It's the women of this family who've made this place what it is. Women like us. That's how things have been ever since Emma's day. Because of her, Lady Arthur persuaded her husband to issue what may well have been the last free land grant in the colony. Without Emma there would have been no Derwent. Without Alice and Bessie and Jane there would have been no you or me. The women of this family have always been the movers and shakers.'

'Like you,' Tamara said.

'I've kept the flame burning,' Bec said. 'I think I can say that.'

'If you hadn't gone to Switzerland Dad would have married that ghastly woman and her son would be busy turning Derwent into a golf course right now.'

'Let's not forget the wind farm,' Bec said.

'Bye bye, eagles,' Tamara said.

'*Glory be to God for dappled things*. A poet said that. But Jaeger isn't the sort to let a few eagles stand between him and a profit.'

Bec took her granddaughter's hands in hers. 'Now it's time to pass the torch to you. You've been managing the place for a good while anyway but there's a big difference between being a manager and a custodian.

'Derwent is our heritage – yours, mine and the future generations. Of course it needs to be managed but whoever's in charge has to be someone who understands the significance of the past. Because the past *is* the present, and the future.'

'What does the custodian do?'

'Provide an heir whenever you're ready. Cherish the land. Derwent is our burden, perhaps, but also our grail. It is up to each generation to keep it safe and eventually pass it on down the line. That has to be the way of it. Each of us is here for such a little time but the land endures.'

The land endures…

How true that was. You could be sure of the land but it was a different story where humans were concerned.

Bec wondered how things worked out on the other side of the threshold. Would her spirit remain nearby or would it simply evaporate? Would she meet up with the past that had been her present for most of her life? Was there, could there be, a reunion of the dead, or did people become insensate ectoplasm borne on the wind, travelling perhaps into the darkness beyond the stars?

The Venerable Bede had described life as a sparrow that flies into a lighted hall before leaving again, with no one able to say whence it came or where it went.

Was that how things were?

She would like to know, if it was permitted, to learn the answers to all the questions.

In the meantime she would say goodbye to the things that had been important to her. All the dappled things.

Three months, Dr Shinbone had said. Six tops. She would not wait for the inevitable conclusion, drugged and choking for one last breath on a sweat-stained bed. What was the point of that?

She could see them waiting in the shadows. Emma and Alice and Bessie and – yes! – Maria and Jane and her own mother. Even Rose Penrose was there, in the parade of past faces, for without her there would have been no Jonathan. Now, finally, there was Tamara, the latest incarnation of all those who had gone before. In her Bec's hopes and the family's future would be borne: a feather, as Hildegard of Bingen had described herself in the twelfth century, borne upon the breath of God.

The grail, as she had said. And this grail too was holy.

When the day came she would know. She would have chosen to lie at Jonathan's side. Since that was impossible she had always told herself she would drive to the Gimbaloo valley hidden between its basalt cliffs. With the last of her strength she would drag herself down the creek until she reached the lip of the fall. She would look down at the canopy of the trees far below then, with Jonathan waiting, she would launch herself into whatever lay ahead.

That was what she had always intended but now she had a different idea. Something that would not involve her bones cluttering up the forest.

A better way to handle things and bring her closer to Jonathan too.

She sorted her affairs. She checked her will, wrote a number of letters – to the bank and the lawyers, to Tamara and a handful of friends – and left them where they would easily be found. She filled up the petrol tank and drove to the coast.

She left the keys in the ignition. She opened up the shed, dragged out the old rubber dinghy and pumped it up. It wasn't easy and by the time she'd finished she felt she'd run a mile.

'I'll never make a water baby,' she'd told herself once. Well, it was never too late to learn.

She put the oars in the dinghy and pushed it out. It was hard to get in – old age was such a *degrading* business – but she managed it eventually. The oars were also a problem but she managed them too. A hundred yards offshore the current took over and carried her further out. She managed to lose one of the oars but that didn't matter now. Nothing mattered now.

The dinghy rocked as she stood up.

'Time to visit the mermaids,' she said.

Maybe, who knew, she might become one herself?

She stepped over the side.

The empty dinghy bobbed and drifted slowly on.

Tamara stood at the bedroom's open window, staring out at the vastness of the land and feeling the breeze cool on her naked body.

The pre-dawn light shone silver in the eastern sky. Below the house the valley lay in shadow but once the sun rose the hills on either side would be bathed in the glory of the golden wattle. From the stringybark trees lining the access road a kookaburra's strident voice summoned the morning.

'She was so keen on our having a child,' she said. 'A pity she missed the news, but maybe, wherever she is, she knows now.'

'I never believed she'd do it,' Grant said.

'It was exactly what I thought she'd do. She was a woman who lived her own life, made her own decisions. Giving herself to death was her way of giving herself to life. She often told me that she saw our ancestors – that the so-called dead had as much claim on us as the so-called living. I believe that myself.'

'Right or wrong, she knows now,' Grant said. 'So where do we go from here?'

'Onwards and upwards. I want to put up a memorial to her, a granite one to stand up to the weather, and stick it up near the shack. After that we'll be busy enough. We have an estate to run. If we intend to make it the best property in Tasmania as well as the biggest we'd better get on with it.'

'Is that what you think?' said Grant.

She turned and looked at him lying on the bed. He was as naked as she was. God, she thought, how beautiful he was.

'Maybe in a little while,' she said.

She walked towards her husband and the future.

AUTHOR'S NOTES

The immigrant ship *Admiral Cockburn* sailed from London on 29 September 1826 and arrived at Hobart Town in Van Diemen's Land on 14 February 1827.

Trusts are a legal device commonly used to preserve and administer property. They or their equivalent have been in existence for thousands of years. A form of what was effectively a trust is mentioned in the Old Testament. They were also commonly used in Roman days. They remain widely used today.

Contrary to rumour, many people of part Aboriginal heritage still live in Tasmania today.

Whaling was a significant source both of revenue and catastrophe in the early years of the colony. The name of Van Diemen's Land was changed to the present name of Tasmania in 1856. The system of free land settlement was abolished in the early 1830s.

The storming of the Eureka Stockade, one of the best known events in Australian history, and the conditions prevailing in Ballarat at the time, were as described. The intransigence of Sir Charles Hotham, lieutenant governor of Victoria, was a significant factor in causing the insurrection. It is one of history's ironies that Sir Charles died unexpectedly, a year after the storming of the stockade.

The relationship between mosquitoes and malaria was unknown at the time Emma Dark died of the disease.

The First Tasmanian Mounted Rifles served in South Africa from 27 October 1899 until 7 December 1900.

Bessie's acquisition of her Model T Ford preceded by twelve months its appearance on the commercial market.

Frenetic speculation leading to the stock market collapse of 1929 had catastrophic consequences throughout the world. Australia was badly affected.

The demand for woollen uniforms to withstand the bitter cold caused the price of wool to rise significantly during the Korean war.

In the face of ferocious opposition from the unions, the so-called White Australia policy was effectively dismantled by the Holt Liberal Government's Migration Act of 1966. This was later amplified by the Whitlam government in 1973.

Quotations are from Samuel Taylor Coleridge, Gerard Manley Hopkins and Hildegard of Bingen, a Benedictine abbess, poet, mystic and musician.

ACKNOWLEDGEMENTS

To Selwa, as always, precious friend, precious agent. Also to my wonderful editors, Annabel and Kate, and to all the team at Harlequin.

ABOUT THE AUTHOR

J.H. Fletcher is the prize-winning author of eighteen novels, published to both critical and popular acclaim in Australia, Germany and the UK, as well as numerous short stories and plays for radio and television. He was educated in England and France and travelled and worked in Europe, Asia and Africa before emigrating to Australia in 1991. Home is a house on the edge of the Western Tier Mountains in northern Tasmania.

DUST OF THE LAND

J.H. Fletcher

There was only one way she could guarantee her future...and she knew that she would take it.

Bella Tucker has come a long way. Born illegitimate and banished to the London slums by her vindictive stepmother, at six Bella is rescued by her grandfather and brought up as a member of the aristocratic Richmond family. Her future seems assured when she falls passionately in love with Charles Hardy, heir to the wealthy Hardy estate — until her grandfather's death changes everything...

Heartbroken and headstrong, Bella flees to Australia, where she is offered a job by the charismatic Garth Tucker, owner of Miranda Downs, a vast cattle station in the stunning and remote Pilbara region. After several near disasters, she finds herself falling in love with Garth amidst the dust, heat and the endless expanse of bush.

Together, Bella and Garth become major players in the new mining industry, allowing Bella to build her dream home, the sprawling homestead, 'Desire'. But after Garth's unfortunate death, Bella is forced to deal with circumstances that bring the family close to ruin...and the business Bella and Garth have built to the brink of collapse.

Can Bella untangle the lies and save the business and her family home? And will she ever lay eyes again on the man she never ceased to love, Charles Hardy?

Dust of the Land is an epic saga of one woman's strength through her trials in love and betrayal on Australia's red frontier.

THE GOVERNOR'S HOUSE

J.H. Fletcher

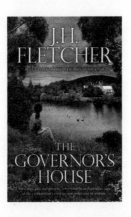

The story of two remarkable women, united by blood but separated by time – from the author of Dust of the Land

Born in poverty, transported for theft, and in love with a charismatic but dangerous man – for Cat Haggard the Tasmanian Governor's House is not merely a beautiful building but a symbol of all she hopes to obtain in life. From convict, bushranger and accused pirate, Cat transforms herself into an entrepreneur and pillar of colonial Tasmanian society. But how is she connected to a missing ship? And could she be involved in the disappearance of a priceless treasure that, one hundred and three years after her death, will be claimed not only by a foreign government but by unscrupulous men determined to use it for their own ends?

Joanne, dean of history at the university and Cat's descendant, is assigned the task of locating the missing artefact. Joanne believes the key may lie in a coded notebook she has inherited along with Cat's other mysteries. But will she be able to decipher the message and put a century-old secret to rest? And will she survive to join her true love in the Governor's House – a house that has come to mean as much to her as it did to her long-dead ancestor?

A WOMAN OF COURAGE

J.H. Fletcher

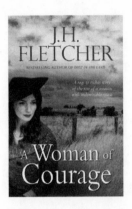

A rags to riches story of a woman of indomitable spirit and of the passionate love that moulds and ultimately changes her life...

Fighting her way from humble beginnings in a foster home to CEO of her own highly respected international company hasn't been easy for Hilary Brand. Even after she seems to have reached the top, troubles abound: her business in China, always fraught with problems, is in peril; and her arch-nemesis Haskins Gould – once her closest business associate, but now her greatest enemy – is gaining traction in his unceasing determination to destroy all she has created.

Hilary's two daughters – unhappy trophy wife Jennifer and brilliant but troubled journalist Sara – also traverse the joys and terrors of love as they try to tread their own paths in the shadow of such a powerful woman.

From the vastness of Western Australia to glittering Sydney and the teeming streets of Hong Kong and Singapore, this is a story of contrasting loves and of a woman of fierce determination... a woman of courage.

talk about it

Let's talk about books.

Join the conversation:

 on facebook.com/harlequinaustralia

 on Twitter @harlequinaus

www.harlequinbooks.com.au

If you love reading and want to know about our
authors and titles, then let's talk about it.